Nicholas Royle was born ~~~~~~~~~~~~~~~, in 1963. He is the author of three novels – *Counterparts, Saxophone Dreams* and *The Matter of the Heart* – in addition to more than a hundred short stories, which have appeared in a variety of anthologies and magazines. He has edited seven anthologies, including *A Book of Two Halves* (Indigo), *The Tiger Garden: A Book of Writers' Dreams* (Serpent's Tail), *The Time Out Book of New York Short Stories* (Penguin) and *The Agony and the Ecstasy* (Sceptre). His book reviews and other journalism have appeared in *Time Out, The Guardian, The Observer, The Independent, The Literary Review, The New Statesman, Esquire* and elsewhere. He lives in west London with his wife and young son.

By the same author

Counterparts
Saxophone Dreams
The Matter of the Heart

as editor

Darklands
Darklands 2
A Book of Two Halves
The Tiger Garden: A Book of Writers' Dreams
The Time Out Book of New York Short Stories
The Agony and the Ecstasy

Edited by
Nicholas Royle

THE EX FILES

NEW STORIES ABOUT OLD FLAMES

Q

Quartet Books

First published by Quartet Books Limited in 1998
A member of the Namara Group
27 Goodge Street
London W1P 2LD

Introduction: *The Ex Ex?* copyright © Nicholas Royle 1998
Copyright details for the stories appears on page 277.

A catalogue record for this book is available from the British Library

ISBN 0 7043 8080 3

Typeset by FSH Ltd, London
Printed and bound in Great Britain by Cox & Wyman, Reading, Berks

For Adèle

Contents

Introduction: The Ex Ex?

Once an ex, always an ex. Or is it possible, I wonder, to cease to be an ex, to cease to be *someone's* ex? I, for example, no longer think of myself as anyone's ex, despite the fact that I am still technically an ex and will always remain one to several people on the planet. They all know who they are, but I'm sure I don't cross any of their minds from one day to the next. Just as most of them don't enter mine in a month of Sundays, these days. Not since this book's dedicatee introduced me to a certain person. And while I hope I remain on my guard against becoming complacent, I no longer dwell on the past quite so much as perhaps I used to.

I have certainly mined it for story material — inevitably and some would say endlessly — but any readers who might be interested to tease fact from my own fiction on the subject of exes will find no opportunity to do so in the present volume. Exes do appear, in a variety of disguises — some thinner than others — in the three novels I have published to date, but mainly, if they have inspired fiction, they've inspired short stories. Since a collection of my short fiction is a book that's yet to be compiled, any interested parties — completists, solicitors, exes on the make — would have to scrabble around to locate various out-of-print anthologies, and magazines that were hard to obtain even when they were published. So, I'm safe. For the time being.

Less safe are the twenty-five contributors lined up to tell their tales in the book you hold in your hands. They are laying themselves open, as they do each time they publish a piece of fiction, to the criticism, appreciation and judgement of the reading public. In the case of this anthology, they are not *actually* making themselves any *more* vulnerable than at any other time, with any other story. This *is* a book of fiction, and some form of the standard disclaimer applies: *The characters and situations in this book are entirely imaginary and bear no relation to any real person or actual happenings.*

Or: *All characters in this publication are fictitious and any resemblance to real persons, living or dead, is purely coincidental.*

Or even: *Any character resemblance to people living or dead is purely coincidental. All the events taking place in this book are imaginary.*

Got that? Imaginary. Coincidental. So, you're not to read anything into any of these stories, right?

Not that you would, of course.

Much.

All it takes is the emergence in the text of a first-person narrator, a single usage of the first-person pronoun, the thinnest of letters and narrowest of characters – I – and the whole shebang, so to speak, is assumed to be no less ingenuous than an entry in the author's diary. I did this, I did that. Me, the author. Don't worry about that fussy little distinction between narrator and author.

No one doubted, when artist Tracey Emin exhibited a tent embroidered with the names of the people she had slept with, that this was in fact a true and accurate catalogue of her past sexual partners. We took her word for it. What, otherwise, would be the point of the exercise?

But fiction, despite the evident playfulness of current British conceptual art, is much more fun. It's a guessing game. Did she or didn't she? Will he or won't he? How true is it? Like all good fiction, the stories written for this book are based in truth and yet they're imaginary; totally made up, they're written from the heart. Purchasing this book gives you the right to make up your own mind. The truth is out there, all right, but it's *in here* as well.

Nicholas Royle, London
March 1998

First
Erica Wagner

Phineas is getting ready for work when the thought occurs to him.
He does not know why it did not occur to him before, why it did
not disturb him last night, a visitor knocking on the doors of his
mind. Last night he simply went to sleep, taking Lucy into his arms
before he drifted off, the crown of her head at his chin, her red hair
drained of its colour by the moonlight that leached in through the
curtains. It smelled waxy, earthy; Lucy's smell, something so familiar
he could barely make himself notice it any more. He kissed her
temple. He loves her. He did not dream.

But this morning the thing he said to her last night stops him
as he steps from the shower, makes him stand in a pool of cooling
water on the floor, the towel in his hand held away from him,
uselessly, like a matador's cape. It seems to him that as he recollects
what it was, precisely, that he said, he feels his ribs shrink a size, as if
they can no longer quite contain his heart and lungs. He tries to
breathe deeply, but finds that it is hard.

He had come through the door just before nine, not late, for
him, set his camera, tripod and lights down on the floor of the hall.
The kitchen light was on and Lucy sat at the table, a half-eaten bowl
of pasta in front of her, the newspapers spread out around.

'Hi there,' she said. She had hardly looked up. She was reading
something in the *Guardian*. She pushed the pasta away from her. 'Do
you want some? I'm finished.'

'Thanks,' he said. He picked up her fork and caught some penne
on the tines, scooped them into his mouth. He wasn't hungry. He ate

two more bites.

'Did you have something already?'

'Enough,' he said.

'How was it?' she asked. 'What was it?' And she looked up, green eyes, scar across the bridge of her nose, curve of her neck into the collar of her flannel shirt. Everything he was was what he looked at, and she was printed on to his sight.

'Some extra studio work,' he said. 'A spread they're doing next week. It was fine.'

'Good,' she said. 'Nice to have you home.' Her smile was a safe harbour.

He kissed her, his hand in her hair. Her mouth tasted of basil and wine. Back in the hall he pushed his gear into the corner so she wouldn't tangle with it in the morning.

He had never lied to her before.

He had first seen Alex – he had first seen Alex again – three weeks ago. He was walking down the length of the office, the tiresome distance between features and news.

'Phineas?' From behind him, he turned and saw her but did not speak. 'Phineas.'

She has a stride, even though she is small. She walks out from the hip like she always knows where she's going. Her head back, chin up: dare me, she says, or seems to, her mouth about to laugh at a joke you haven't quite heard. Dark eyes and straight brows and her hair tight against her skull. She is just the same.

'Hey,' he said at last. 'Alex.'

'Fancy meeting you.'

'What are you doing here?' Blunt in his surprise.

'Features editor. I start today.'

'I had no idea.'

'Neither had I, until a day or so ago. Wish me luck.'

'Well – good luck. Good to see you.'

'You too.' She winked, shuttering one eye against his astonished gaze. 'See you around.' And she walked fast past him, one two three, dark blue silk and black polished shoes, the white of her scalp in the hollow at the top of her spine. He stood still, unable to remember where it was he was meant to be going.

*

It was not that he felt anything for her any more. He had known that. Only it had been ten years since he had seen her, when they last drifted out of touch after some argument about nothing, a play or a film or an exhibition, he really couldn't recall. He had not missed her. Sometimes, he had come to reflect as he grew older, it is simply enough. You move forward into a new life, the new person you gradually become, a process imperceptible until one day you wake up and realize that nothing around you is the same: or that it is just you who is different.

And there is Lucy, the girl he met when he shot a story about a mental home – they called it something else, a facility of one kind or another – that was being closed down by the council in Buckinghamshire. Some of the patients had nowhere to go. It was the same story every time. Lucy Winterson, it said on a tag she wore around her neck on a chain, harried Lucy Winterson with better things to do than talk to Phineas and his embarrassing lens. Yes, she worked for the council. No, she didn't want the home to close. No, there wasn't much she could do about it, yes, she had tried.

Yes, she supposed she would go for a drink with him some time. And that was that. He never thought he would be so lucky. It had been seven years. He remembered thinking once, not long ago – she had gone away, a conference in Hull for a week – that they had knitted together, a fracture repaired, fused bone, something never meant to be broken now mended. He was the one who went off, a moment's notice, first thing in the morning, last thing at night; and when she went life tilted just so much: he could not frame the horizon. After so much time the curve of her thigh resting against his as sleep embraced them was a presence felt only in absence.

But Alex was the first. Alex he met at college, when her dark hair was bleached blank white, when she wore kohl round her eyes and stripy tights that made him laugh the very first time he saw her. What are you laughing at? You, he said. And she put her small hands flat against his chest and pushed as hard as she could, harder than he would have imagined, sent him reeling and walked away. He had to ask someone else who she was. Three nights later she took him to bed. He clenched his jaw to keep his teeth from chattering. She was compact, coiled, white and slippery; her mouth was everywhere, nipping at him, breathing on him, making sounds he had never heard. He only stopped being afraid when he felt himself dissolve into her, sugar into water, his belly full of stars. It was only afterwards she told him it was her first time, too. Seventeen years ago. It hadn't lasted long between them, but then they were friends.

He sees her in the office, the days he is in. She walks through his glance. He notices her, and then becomes accustomed to her. When they pass, she stops and speaks to him, taking up where they left off, it seems, never having to ask what he is up to as it is quite clear the answer would be, just the same. One morning it occurs to him he has something to tell her, something he saw the day before that he thought might amuse her, or interest her, and discovers on this morning that he is looking for her, is disappointed when their paths do not cross. He saves the anecdote in his mind: he will tell her tomorrow, or the next day. He hears her voice in the distance, distinct from other voices, brighter, clearer. She is good at her job, and he is pleased. He is not surprised she has done so well.

He can't for the life of him remember what they argued about, all those years ago. He is sorry that they did.

'Are you all right?' Lucy says, one night. They are in the sitting room, reading, but his eyes are on the ceiling, not on his book. He does not answer because at first he does not hear.

'Phineas?'

His name makes him pull his head around to see her curled on the sofa, legs tucked up under her, her bare feet long and pale, toes pointed like a medieval effigy quickened with pearly life. Looking at her quizzing face he tries, just for a moment, to put himself back to the time when he first saw her, when her face was new to him and its lights and shadows struck him with wonder. He wanted to take her picture. She did not want to be photographed. She laced her fingers in front of her face and taped to the inside of his camera case he carries this image, Lucy revealed to him not through her face but the soft mountain landscape of the backs of her hands, metacarpals prison bars against his gaze, oval nails instead of eyes. The tip of her nose, just visible, her wild hair somehow red even in monochrome.

Earlier that day they sent him to take Alex's picture, to put beside her byline. She leaned against the bookcase in her office and stared straight at him as if she could see through lens, aperture, shutter, film and into the heart of his eye.

'Phineas.' Lucy's voice curious and insistent. He stretches out to her, she puts out her hand and he takes it, holding her, this woman he loves.

All day it sits within him. He tries to put a name to the feeling but cannot. All day it buzzes between his ears, pulling him out of focus, drawing him back one remove from his life as he should be living it. Driving to his first job, he runs through a speed camera, one he knows is there, no reason to miss it; six miles over the limit and the flash pops in his vision. He has eight points on his licence already. It is like indigestion. It is like a tight wad of red thread lodged in his chest, unravelling and unravelling, snaking through his veins until he is woven through with it, the burn of it blocking the flow of his blood, replacing his blood with its own flow, the flow of the lie. It infects him. It makes him someone else.

He has, of course, lied before. I did my homework. I ate the sandwiches you made me. I didn't remember there was an exam this morning. My phone was turned off. I hung around for three hours but no one showed. I love you.

Not for a long time, that last one. He had made himself an honest man. He meant what he said. Sometimes it cost him. But he said it anyway. This was brand new.

He had been standing outside her office near the end of the day, waiting for Helen, the picture researcher, to get back from wherever she had gone to. Out of the corner of his eye he could see the top of Alex's head over her screen. She was sitting forward, concentrating. When she sighed, sat back, stretched her arms over her head, she caught his eye and smiled. He smiled back and moved across her threshold: one step, barely two.

'OK?' she said.

'Guess so. You?'

'Pretty good. Those were great pictures for the Guinness interview. Thanks.'

He shrugged. 'My pleasure. Well. Of a kind. He was a bugger to do.'

'Why?'

'I don't know. Some people are. They wish you weren't there, they don't want to do it, they're in a rush – they think you're a kind of machine.'

'Which was this?'

She pulled one foot up on to her chair, wrapped her arm around her knee. She was sitting on the floor of his college room, those idiotic tights, his ancient jumper – she was sitting in her office, a diamond glittering in the top of her right ear, a silk T-shirt, black jeans. He had thought that women changed. He couldn't tell, with her.

'Bit of everything.'

'Can I buy you a drink for your pains?'

He did not expect her to say it. He blinked. 'OK. Yes. That would be nice.' That would be nice.

She tapped the keyboard in front of her, once, hard, glanced at her watch. 'Now?'

'Well – half an hour? Just some stuff I have to finish up. For tomorrow. Then – yes – ' He was afraid that now meant now and that would be it. He could feel his heart beat.

But she nodded and leaned back in her chair.

'Come and get me when you're ready,' she said.

They went to a wine bar in Hoxton. Leaving the office, he found he had nothing to say, had been silenced, did not know where he was going, where they were going, and as they approached his car was appalled to discover that he was dismayed at the state of it – old, dirty, bits of it ripped off and an oil leak (she couldn't see the oil leak) that he'd never found time to have mended. He unlocked her door.

'This isn't the same thing you had ten years ago?' she queried, frowning a smile, peering round the front to see the letter on the number plate.

'Not quite but almost,' he said.

'Good on you. One of these days you'll have to teach me how to drive.'

'Still?' Maybe you could tell if people changed. Maybe you could be sure of some things. Maybe.

'Still. No longer quite so proud of it.'

'Can't always count on getting a lift, you know.'

'I know. I take the bus a lot.'

'The bus?' He couldn't remember the last time he was on a bus. There was always so much for him to carry around. It seemed fanciful, riding on buses. And she didn't look like she rode buses. She had a taxi look. He was guessing, guessing.

'I like to go on top. You can see where you're going. All of you lot squashed down below. Sit at the front, on top, it's great. Doesn't matter where you go. Just ride.'

'You can't have too much time for that now. Just riding.'

She shrugged. 'I try to make it.'

Rides on buses. He filed it away. A collection of information, stored like slides in the corner of his mind. He could flick through them. There weren't many. He couldn't see a man. He knew once she'd had a girlfriend. Now – a blank slide. Unexposed or un-developed.

Hoxton Square was quiet, away from the light-streaked clatter of Old Street and Hackney Road. He parked the car and then followed as she got out and walked purposefully away. It was nearly seven. Lucy's key in the door, putting her bag down, shaking the day's work from her hair.

Then Alex stopped short and he walked straight into the back of her on the empty street. Her head beneath his chin, warmth, pulling back, his hands in his pockets.

'Sorry,' she said, grinning, and it was dark enough now that her teeth shone in the streetlight. 'Wrong way. No sense of direction. Down here.'

The place she led him to had a wooden floor and brick walls and good beer. She leaned up on the bar, asked for his pint and a brandy, reached into the pocket of her coat.

'Let me,' he said. Put his hand on her arm. Midway between wrist and elbow. Her sleeve pushed up.

'I asked you,' she said. 'That's not fair.'

'No, really.'

'Be gracious about it, Phineas. I want to buy you a drink.'

So he let her. Lucy bought his drinks all the time. What was the matter with him? Later, when he looked back, he could feel the first thread spooling out from his heart right then, at the bar, that moment.

And that is the moment that stands in his mind, his hand on her skin, her money in her hand, the drinks on the bar, the yellowy light and their faces badly reflected in the polish of the wood like something seen through deep water. Not what they talked about, which the next day he will barely recall because it is everything and nothing, the slides he could add to his collection thereafter insignificant – but not so, stored there, waiting.

He adds this to another, as the day draws on, the moment he stood in the kitchen and told Lucy, whom he loves more than anything in the world, something other than the truth. It came out of him. As if he had not wished to say it, as if his will was not his own. But he knows that too is a lie. Tonight he will tell Lucy where he really was – or he will not, and the episode will slip behind them. Or it will not.

Statusphobia
Russell Celyn Jones

A hospital, I tell you, is heaven on the ground. At least, it's the only place where women seem to like me. Women in uniform.

In Guy's, these women give me chemical solicitude – Amitriptyline – a drug so benign it helps me see the comedy in *Hamlet* (I'm reading Shakespeare for the first time in my life in here). But the priest who visits every day leaves me heartbroken and guilty. Thank God for the pharmacy, I say.

And for Nurse O'Brien, who breezed in with that book for me. She took it off the top of a pile in the mobile library; it could have been *Captain Pugwash* for all she knew, instead of Shakespeare's *Hamlet*. That's Providence. Nurse picks this story of the Black Prince, sick of all women, who too might have found a cure in this place.

Nurse O'Brien's small face is active with breathless affection, and seems familiar to me, as if I've known her since childhood. The countenance of a nurse is the more memorable because our desire to be numbered is reflected in their eyes. I number. I matter to Nurse Sheila O'Brien from County Cavan, a dealer in care at an institution that was built out of profits from the slave trade.

As she studies my chart at the foot of my bed, I study one of Hamlet's soliloquies – to demonstrate my gratitude rather than out of any desire to familiarize myself with the text. When I look up again, the freckles on the bridge of her nose are in motion. A sign of irritation, I have come to learn. But not with me. It is my neighbour, the octogenarian Mr Gratan, who disturbs her, demanding his catheter bag be emptied.

She says to the old Polonius in the next bed, 'It's very simple to do it yourself, Mr Gratan, if only you'd try.'

'My wife does it at home.'

'Does she clean your teeth for you too?' she asks.

'Of course not.'

'Changing your catheter bag is about as easy as brushing with Colgate.'

'Not *all* women are as unsympathetic as you, nurse,' he stammers with emotion.

I raise my Longman's Shakespeare. 'Listen to this, nurse . . . "I say, we will have no more marriages!"'

'*Hamlet*, Act 3, Scene 2,' Mr Gratan says without pause.

'Very good,' I applaud, rather surprised. Mr Gratan suddenly acquires a character. He becomes more than just a man with an overflowing urine bag. What *is* he in for anyway?

'I taught *Hamlet* to the lower sixth for twenty years,' he explains. 'Before I retired. Before schools went to the dogs.'

'Why do you think that, Mr Gratan? Why did schools go to the dogs?'

'Discipline broke down,' he retorts simply.

When I think of 'discipline' I think of my headmaster's cane touching the ceiling as he raised his arm, prior to using it, a click of willow on plaster that gave a boy bending over a chair underneath him a second's warning. Mr Gratan's about the same age as he would be now. 'Did you ever use the cane?' I ask.

'Yes, I certainly did.'

'Why?'

'If a child is bad, you administer pain on that part of the anatomy which does the least harm and the most good,' he announces formally.

Nurse O'Brien and I share amazed looks.

'So it follows then,' I say, 'that if a child is good you administer pleasure on that part of the anatomy which does the least harm and the most good?'

'No, no, man!'

'I've got it wrong? Oh dear. Back to the drawing board.'

Nurse O'Brien, taking my blood pressure, gives my arm an affectionate squeeze.

I suffer from a rare medical condition that renders me unstable on my feet. A blow to the head may have caused it, not necessarily a contemporary blow, but one that occurred months, even years, ago. Being a teaching hospital, Guy's has all the experts, but even they don't know how to cure me.

You know you're in trouble when the scientists start sounding like poets.

What the physiotherapist said was, I've lost the melody of walking.

A misplaced inner sense is how the physiatrist described it, and subjected me to electrical tests. This inner sense monitors muscles, tendons and joints, and gives a man his concept of himself. That certainty has been taken away from me.

The clinical term is proprioception. When you lose proprioception, the other senses can compensate to a degree. So standing is possible if I look at my feet the whole time. I blink, therefore I fall.

Statusphobia is another term. The psychiatrist came up with that. I like that one best. It means the fear of standing up.

Or it's hysteria. Hysteria can have the same effects. My ex-wife Alicia concurs with that analysis. She's convinced of it. Odds-on favourite, she says.

It's been a year since she confessed to having a long-standing affair. I'd hardly digested that pill before she announced her intention to live with this other man. I was asked to leave our house (Edwardian end of terrace in Islington) so he could move in. *The funeral baked meats did coldly furnish forth the marriage tables.*

I turned on my heels and walked out of the house, pounding the grief through the soles of my shoes, on what was to be the last of my long strolls, down Canonbury Road and Moorgate, across the River at Blackfriars, into Greenwich via Jamaica Road, collapsing from exhaustion in the Observatory, across the Meridian line.

Alicia has insisted that we need to first agree a financial settlement before my relationship with our eight-year-old daughter, Beatrix, can be resumed. Beatrix is Alicia's bargaining chip. She wants the home and maintenance. In return she will grant me 'reasonable access' every other Saturday, from two to five p.m.

I have spent the long hours here wondering what went wrong. How had I missed the signs, the smells of another man on her skin?

In the years of our marriage I worked for a merchant bank as a foreign exchange trader. I was called a knock-out specialist, buying and selling currency based on where I estimated the rates were going. I'd woo a corporate investor into loaning me twenty mill sterling for six months to buy foreign currency. If the rate I set hit the knock out – the threshold at which the transaction gets closed down – then the investor won a premium on his initial investment. I got a commission for the bank of two basis points. Big salary for me plus a bonus at the end of the year. Gambling on the foreign currency markets was sweaty work. I had to keep a tight ass in the pressure cooker so the rest of the guys in the bank backing me up could keep their noses clean. So sometimes, when I wasn't sure, when the guess seemed less than pure, I'd hedge my bets by entering into a trade with a second investor, that went the opposite direction to the first. So whichever way the exchange rate went I'd be covered, my worst position was to come out even. What a shame I'd not done that on Black Wednesday, the day the whole country lost their shirt.

Now my ex-wife, she runs a gallery. I'd come home and talk about money, she'd talk about paintings. Different languages, parallel lives. She filled the empty space with another man, a penniless artist. I had been neglectful, she claimed, which precipitated her affair. It was really my own fault.

I was an inadequate husband but (and Alicia concedes this much) a good father. Even while she was deceiving me, it was I who changed the baby's bum, read her *Winnie-the-Pooh*. Nevertheless, the father gets crucified on the same cross as the cuckold.

For the first few weeks I mooned around in an hotel. I didn't go into the bank, didn't even call them. My intransigence cost them so many lost deals that, when I finally did turn up, I was fired. I had transferred my anger on to my employers and they counter-transferred it back on to me.

Without a job I could no longer afford to stay indefinitely in an hotel. So I bought a second-hand ambulance, converted it into a camper, with sink, chemical toilet, bunk beds, and spent the winter driving around Britain, alone.

The Lake District, Snowdonia, the Highlands were all petrified by cold weather. Lakes were frozen, the birds mute in the trees. The

Norfolk Broads, Romney Marshes were pitiless.

A converted ambulance gives off confusing emotional messages. One morning in February as I pitched up alongside the River Wye a woman approached me to help her husband get to hospital. He'd broken his ankle while fishing for trout. She wouldn't believe that I wasn't a paramedic.

Then, back from my sojourn in a quiet street in Islington, half a mile from my matrimonial home (where else should I have parked?), I was sawing timbers inside the ambulance, making shelves, when everything dropped to the floor. Then *through* the floor. The doors, cabinets, windows, toilet fell as if into some whirlpool. I looked down at my legs and they were 150 foot in length. Like the twin masts on a schooner, with my torso in the crow's nest. The ambulance pitched and tossed, changed in shape, texture. Lastly I began to list, and fell.

I managed to kick open the back doors. By and by a man walking his bull terrier in the direction of Highbury Fields came along. I shouted to him. 'Excuse me, but could you call for an ambulance?'

'An ambulance?' he smiled.

'Yes. I've lost the sensation in my legs.'

Then he laughed. 'You're already in one, mate.'

'This one is killing me!' I screamed. 'I want the kind that saves lives.'

The physiotherapist has laid down a line of masking tape from my bed on the ward to the bathroom. I keep that in my line of vision while concentrating on my feet as I walk. She's also loaned me a spirit level (her husband's a builder), which I have strapped on to a long cane held parallel to the floor. Even with all these props I can't make it on my own, and she accompanies me there, to catch me if I fall. My movements are clumsy, mechanical, as though I'm riding a bike for the first time. But as I make distance I recover some of my old grace. It's grace I feel too, as anyone who has lost their ability to walk then recovers some of it, a stroke victim say, can testify. The world of the walking wounded is a beautiful world, a utopia.

So long as the physio is by my side, I have confidence. This Swedish Amazonian gives her approval, a constant stream of positive reinforcement, like an act of love. Love in motion. 'Well done,' she says. 'Another yard. Another step to freedom.' These guidelines, such remarks, should be the rules of attraction, of marriage.

I make it to the bathroom navigating from the bridge of my nose.

Back in bed I dip my head, close my eyes to savour the success and hear a starched uniform on the move. When I open my eyes again, the physiotherapist's place at my bedside has been taken by Alicia, my ex. Light from the window glances across her chest. Her face is high up in the shade, above the snow line. Outside the hospital I hear foghorns on the Thames.

'Where's Beatrix?' I ask.

'She's in school.'

'Is she coming to see me?'

'Next time, maybe.'

'Good. Let's celebrate your visit.' I lean over to my cabinet and remove the bottle of malt and two glasses. Alicia frowns at me. 'It's OK,' I explain. 'On prescription. The dietitian said a drink a day is good for me. Dilutes the arteries.'

'But not a whole bottle.'

'Alicia, you are no longer arbiter of what I need.'

'Do I turn you to drink the moment I appear?'

I replace the bottle and glasses. She wins. 'I've been thinking . . . I'd like to take Beatrix on a holiday when I get out of here, in the ambulance. We can go to Cornwall camping. We won't even need a tent.'

'I don't think so.'

'You can come too.'

'Hardly.'

'Bring the boyfriend. He can paint the landscape.'

She doesn't reply and instead looks at Mr Gratan, who is getting a visit too, from his wife. A frail, small woman in her seventies, she is immediately detailed to change his catheter bag. He's been saving the urine all day for her. She does this and other chores, trying to keep up with his string of commands. 'Catheter! Newspaper! Step on it, woman!'

Alicia's face is lit up with moral rectitude. I watch her make a connection, hear her think: I'm just a younger version of that old guy. She could have ended up like Mrs Gratan.

'I walked to the bathroom all on my own today,' I say, only to sound like a child seeking approbation.

I have often been accused by Alicia of possessing a child-like narcissism. Apparently I needed the attention of a parent, not of a wife. But what *is* a wife's solicitude? What's that look like?

She used to say it was difficult to engage with my immaturity in the conjugal side of things and confessed that sometimes she longed to disappear, vanish for ever. 'That's why couples have children,' I countered. 'To prevent you doing just that.'

Beatrix's arrival, I felt, was a great boon to our relationship. Through the act of parenting I lost the need to be parented myself. The experience of fatherhood forced me to shape up. *Stand up.* Now that opportunity is being denied me, how am I to progress into true manhood, whatever that is? What other initiation ceremonies are there apart from love of your children?

This carried no weight with Alicia. When our marriage went on the rocks, the rocks were in our bed. Not only was I an immature lover, but then, as a foreshadowing of my current paralysis, I lost my ability to hold an erection. Alicia's opinion was, I got my rocks off at work, gambling with all that money, and had nothing left at the end of the day for her. She tried rubbing, sucking, carousing, snake-charming, spanking, tickling, but only managed to exhaust herself. I knew her patience was all shot when she started to mock me about it. Driving in the country one afternoon, we passed a white stallion in a field, his dick practically dragging along the ground. 'That's what you need,' she said, pointing to the horse, 'clover and grass in your diet.'

The longer Alicia stays in the ward the more vulnerable I feel, lying on a bed with her towering over me. 'Why don't you get rid of that ambulance anyway?' she suggests. 'It's absurd a man of your age living in a thing like that.'

I tell her that it's easier to get a vote of sympathy in an ambulance than, say, a bedsit. I let the remark drift in, adding, 'And I'm only thirty-five.'

She replies: 'An ambulanceman's appreciated. A casualty commiserated with. In either case, of mistaken identity, you can't lose. But why are you so determined to maintain a victim's position,

Max? Perhaps you should arrange a permanent stay here.'

'I can think of worse places.'

The physiatrist arrives and she asks him for a progress report. As if it's any business of hers, as if she cares. 'Well,' he begins, 'the muscle sense derived from receptors in his leg joints seem to have packed up. It's a medical mystery why this happens.'

'I don't like mysteries,' I manage.

'There's a network of these inner senses. The labyrinthine, the proprioceptive, the visual ... they normally work together to control the body. Like an angel's wings steering you along.'

'That's nice,' Alicia says, flashing him a smile, and the bastard flirts with her. He's coming up with the poetry of the disabled, at my expense, to woo her. I can't believe how opportunist some doctors are. And for a while they forget me altogether, looking at each other across my bed, where I lie defenceless, sexless, unable to fight my way back into the frame.

Several hours after Alicia leaves, Nurse O'Brien returns to guide me into the bathroom. Her shift actually ended five minutes ago, but she's hung around specifically to help me take a bath.

Now how do I interpret that?

The journey, a mere twenty metres, takes all of seven minutes to complete. Inside, behind locked doors, I sit on the edge of the bath. I remove my black silk pyjama shirt as she tackles the trousers. She hooks a strong and practised arm around my waist and guides me into the hot water.

A disabled man having a young and healthy woman sponge his back in a bath has no right to feel so at ease as this. But I do, and I ask if she wouldn't mind washing my hair. My whole body tingles as she sluices shampoo through my hair with the teeth of a comb. A cryptic message gets through to my brain, like a telex, announcing a show between my loins. I apply the same method on that for getting my feet to move...I stare at it. But the command gets lost in translation.

'God, this is good,' I say. 'You're spoiling me.'

'Just don't become like Mr Gratan, will you?'

'No chance. Say, you wouldn't consider a proposal of marriage from me?'

'I already have a husband.'

'Let me know if it doesn't work out.'

She pulls the plug on me. Rather clinically now, she helps me out of the bath. Dripping on to the rug I stand with my arms around her shoulders, staring down her back at her muscular calves. 'Tell me about yourself, nurse. Are you a mountain climber?'

'No,' she says, 'but I have been in the police force.'

That surprises me. 'Your sympathetic nature survived the police, obviously.'

'Am I sympathetic?'

'Yes, you are.' Then I try it on. 'Would you mind powdering my bum?' She steps away from me and I crumble against the wall. 'Oh, Mummy! Why are you so rough?'

'Because you're a naughty little boy, Max.'

Before hospitalization I persuaded Alicia to meet me, to talk things over. It was our thirteenth wedding anniversary, a strategic date on my behalf. I put my faith in sentiment.

I had just moved out of the hotel and picked her up in the ambulance. Driving to an Irish pub in Camden, she laughed all the way: at how a former trader on the foreign exchange could go so downmarket. All things seem possible when you can laugh with each other.

But there was nothing funny about the pub when we got there. A man was lying on the floor near the door. Drunk or dead, we never found out. Everyone had forsaken him to watch the band which had just started up on stage. She wondered where and how we were meant to talk, over all the noise. I watched the men dance cheek to cheek – men, no women – and shrugged.

Alicia squeezed through to the bar, I followed closely behind. I can still see her now, the only woman in, parting the dancers like Moses the Red Sea. When several men asked her to dance she made elegant but firm rejections. That was Alicia. That was my ex-wife. Cool under pressure.

As we reached the bar I realized I'd left my wallet in the ambulance glove compartment. She'd come out without any cash. I was about to turn back, but Alicia protested. She didn't want to be left alone there, so went out with the keys instead.

She reappeared, flushed, shouting over men's heads: 'Max. Come quickly. There's some men fighting over your ambulance.'

'Let them have it,' I said.

'No, I mean they're fighting *on* it.'

'What do you expect me to do?'

'Stop them.'

'There's no point trying to pacify men who enjoy fighting, Alicia. Have a drink.'

'How do you know they're enjoying themselves?'

This was not an issue I thought needed to be discussed, but she was holding out for a reply. 'Well, if they are or not, it won't be you who'll get a glass in the face if we try and stop them.'

Alicia had never been the recipient of a punch in the mouth, otherwise she might have understood the wisdom of this. When I see a fight I cross to the other side of the road.

She accused me of being a coward.

'So? I'm a coward. So what?'

She stormed out of the bar, shouting over her shoulder, 'I'll do it then.'

I followed her outside, into a wall of frightening sound. I saw violently committed couples fighting over the bonnet of my Bedford ambulance. Inching in front of Alicia I placed a hand on one of the four men. He turned around and punched me in the face. I went down, my head ricocheting off the coach panelling, which still has the dent in the shape of my skull.

I think I began to lose my balance, the 'melody of walking', after that night. Alicia has different ideas. 'No, it was Black Wednesday. Black Wednesday was the first time I saw you stagger home like a drunk.'

Night-time in hospital is the worst time, not my time at all. You are in close proximity to strangers whose meandering sleep-talk, rattling cries in the dark, are intimacies you do not want to share. Someone usually dies just a few feet away, followed by the duty sister's feet shuffling across the rubber floor and the sound of screens being drawn around the dead man's bed. Moments later the little red lights glowing at the nurses' station illuminate the duty sister's face as she whispers sex-talk down the telephone to her lover back home. Nurses are very erotic, someone once told me, because their jobs entail a lot of touching, of both the living and the dead.

I have only ever touched money with such sensual consideration.

In the morning Nurse O'Brien finds me in a state of depression as she comes on at the start of her shift. I tell her about Beatrix, how Alicia is blocking my access. Even after a settlement I will only get to see her for three hours every other weekend. That's seventy-eight hours, or three days a year. Over the ten years that remain of her dependency – thirty-one days, tops. A month in the country of childhood. I ask nurse if she would double my dose of Amitriptyline.

Passing down the corridor at the same time, very conveniently from one perspective, is a six-year-old boy wheeling his drip pole to the toilet. Nurse O'Brien informs me that part of his shoulder bone was removed two days ago. He is terminally ill with cancer.

She says, 'You shouldn't be depressed. You're going to live longer than that child. And your own daughter's fit and healthy.'

I can pick up my bed and walk if I want to.

After she leaves me to mull over her advice, I watch Mr Gratan trying to shave himself, looking crestfallen under the shaving foam that is streaked with blood from where he's nicked himself with the razor. A man ruined by his own demands upon his wife.

If this place is heaven then some god, *goddess*, must have placed Gratan in the next bed as a salutary warning. As with any faith, it's my choice whether or not I heed that warning.

Aided by my props I stand on my own two feet. Slowly I begin the long walk to his bed.

And something very fine happens to me, *en route*. I feel a surge as the brain's visual model of my body feeds in to compensate for a loss of proprioception. Like a handshake below the horizon as the sun sets and the moon rises. What I have lost in motor co-ordination, what I have lost in the ego department – I make up for with powers of a different, unchartered form.

'Here,' I say to Mr Gratan, 'let me do that,' and pick his brush out of the bowl of Sandalwood shaving cream. I lather his face, then roll his Wilkinson Sword down each cheek. His grey whiskers jam the razor. I rinse the razor in the plastic bowl of hot water on his table and continue.

Mr Gratan's face expresses no gratitude, but that's OK, the

intrinsic reward is enough for me. For I am on my feet, while my eyes are engaged elsewhere.

So long as I am caring for him, I can stand again, despite all possibilities to fall.

The Myth of the Eternal Return
Edward Fox

Jean-Baptiste is back. He arrived the other night at around midnight, with a bag of duty-free whisky and a carton of French cigarettes. Jean-Baptiste never arrives during the day. He prefers to materialize out of darkness, in a dark cloud of diesel fumes, missed or barely made connections and dramatic time-zone shifts. The night of Jean-Baptiste means whisky, and his arrival amongst us must be viewed through the turbulent medium of the amber spirit. His account of the journey, and of himself, kept us up half the night. The next morning I was bleary with sleeplessness and the black negative of absent alcohol, and the incense of his trademark cigarettes hung in the air. The smell of those cigarettes doesn't leave until Jean-Baptiste does, and I had no idea when that might be. One never does.

He's a friend of my wife, Dawn. I take no responsibility for him. I am almost certain that years ago Dawn was one of his many starry-eyed lovers. She's still sufficiently in thrall to his lugubrious charm to let him stay with us whenever he wants. She fusses over him and makes him breakfast. Jean-Baptiste sits silently at the kitchen table and smokes. He said all he meant to say the night before. You can hear each studious puff as he raises the thick cigarette to his fleshy red lips and ingests the fragrant smoke, a wisp of which climbs up the rugged cliffs of his jagged profile and into his heavy-lidded olive-coloured eyes, making him squint in an attitude of patiently borne pain. Then he contemplatively exhales. Dawn pours his coffee. By eight o'clock in the morning a *film-noir* atmosphere has taken over. Although Jean-Baptiste never initiates a conversation, and gives only cryptic, mumbled replies to my attempts to draw him out, he seems to consider himself my friend, and that it is natural for friends to sit together in silence. Dawn sees him as a model guest. He has a knack of knowing just when to insert himself into the sublunar world to offer to chop a minimum quota of vegetables, without getting inextricably ensnared in the full programme of domestic chores.

He is here to see a woman. Jean-Baptiste always comes to see a woman when he comes, and a different one each time, relations with whom are invariably in a state of acute and perilous crisis. The telephone starts ringing as soon as he arrives, and if I pick it up I find myself dealing with a distraught-sounding female who needs to talk to Jean-Baptiste immediately. Jean-Baptiste's art lies in both causing these crises and seeming to manage and resolve them. A master of the telephone, he is soon on the receiver whispering soothing words, with his purring r's and his mysterious foreign manner, and arranging to meet. Then Jean-Baptiste is gone. If he's not expecting to be back for supper, he's careful to call and say so. But if I pick up the telephone when he calls for this purpose, he always asks for Dawn and tells her. It adds to the air of intrigue that surrounds his activities. Actually, I think he doesn't like talking to men for any reason. He doesn't know what he wants from them.

What amazes me about Jean-Baptiste is that he's able to attract limitless sympathy from every woman he meets. This is because by the time women meet him they have heard about his latest personal crisis, from Dawn or someone else. Jean-Baptiste is seen as some sort of injured creature, in whose necessary recovery everyone wants to get involved. I think it's his air of soldiering on though gravely wounded which attracts women. Before he arrives, Dawn will say, 'Jean-Baptiste has just called. He's in a terrible state. I told him he should come and stay with us for a few days.'

Now he is here to see an Irish girl called Lucy. Two nights after he arrived, when I came home from work, I found this Lucy lying on the sofa wrapped in a blanket, a surprisingly plain-looking girl with thick dark hair. She was sobbing quietly. I took one look at her and then looked for Jean-Baptiste, in the hope that he might vouchsafe an explanation. He was in the kitchen preparing a meal, as if he weren't aware of her existence. It was strange enough that Jean-Baptiste was cooking dinner.

'Did you meet Lucy?' Jean-Baptiste said, with a sly smile.

I said, 'I didn't exactly meet her, no. Is that who that is lying on the sofa, looking like she's dying of consumption?'

Jean-Baptiste assumed a sweetly worried look, but said nothing. I then heard Lucy calling out for Jean-Baptiste, in a pleading, moaning tone that was deeply embarrassing to hear.

'Jean-Baptiste!'

'What's wrong with her?' I said.

'She's not feeling well. I'm looking after her.' So why does he have to do it in my house, I thought.

Jean-Baptiste didn't go to her. He just ignored her and began slicing bread with a bread knife.

'Jean-Baptiste! Please!'

He sawed away violently at the loaf, cutting it into crude, thick, untidy slices. I think he liked the sound of the moaning, and liked the fact that I was hearing it too. It was too much for me, so I sought refuge away from it. But because Jean-Baptiste had taken over two rooms for this personal drama, the kitchen and the living room, I retreated to the bedroom, closed the door and lay down, and waited for Dawn to come back. He was her friend: she could deal with him.

When I emerged, about two hours later, I found that Lucy was asleep on the sofa, that Jean-Baptiste had cooked a reasonably decent dinner, and that Dawn was with him in the kitchen, cleaning carrots at the sink.

'I'm afraid Lucy isn't at all well and won't be joining us,' Jean-Baptiste announced, in a formal tone. The table was set for three.

My dismay at the entire sticky business was suddenly and alarmingly eclipsed when I saw Dawn drawing the cork from a particularly good and precious bottle of red Bordeaux that I had been saving for an occasion when Dawn and I wouldn't have to share it with anybody else, least of all someone like Jean-Baptiste, who at this point I thought of as particularly undeserving of it. I vainly willed the digits of the year of its vintage to turn to something far less historic, but Jean-Baptiste had secured another one of his baffling triumphs.

I wasn't in the mood for a lengthy dinner with Jean-Baptiste, so I left him with Dawn after I had eaten, and retreated again, leaving half the bottle of Bordeaux to the two of them.

Later, when Dawn and I were alone, I said, 'Who's this Lucy and what the hell is wrong with her? What's wrong with Jean-Baptiste, for that matter?' I didn't mean to sound so angry; it came as a surprise to me to realize quite how angry I was.

'Poor Jean-Baptiste. She's an old flame of his, or in this case a reheated soufflé. This has been going on, on and off, for some time. Jean-Baptiste has an ability, or a weakness, whatever you want to call it, to find women when they're at their weakest and most alone, and then pounce. It's usually just after they've split up with or been abandoned by someone else. He talks in that gentle way and women just fall for it. They feel so grateful for his dubious attention that they let him get away with murder. He'll leave her in a few days and go back to Paris. You wait and see. It's what he always does.'

I wondered if she knew this from personal experience.

'I thought you liked him,' I said.

'I guess I do, but – it's hard to explain.' She fell silent for a moment. 'I mean, it's like this.' She then told me about his first affair with Lucy, and how it had ended. 'Jean-Baptiste comes into his own when his affairs are breaking up. He drags it all out to the bitter end, with endless final meetings, and lots of pleading and uncertainty and helplessness.'

'Like guerrilla warfare,' I suggested. 'Wearing the enemy out, winning by attrition.'

'Something like that.'

'He sounds like a sort of last-ditch Lothario.'

'Maybe he is.' She said that Lucy was the sort of person who would occasionally go to church, not because she was particularly pious, but because it was what she was brought up with, and she found the familiar ritual therapeutic at times of need. After one of her scenes with Jean-Baptiste, she fled to a church where a ceremony of the Stations of the Cross was in progress. Jean-Baptiste ran after her, and followed her into the church, and found her kneeling there, weeping on to the back of the pew in front of her. When she looked up (a composition, I imagined, of tearful blue eyes and tumbling, thick black hair, wreathed in the upturned collar of a heavy coat in the church's stony chill), Jean-Baptiste was standing silently beside her. They walked out arm in arm, with Lucy sniffling, and in the entrance she said she recognized one of his cigarette stubs in the holy water font.

'She said people probably mistook them for a serenely married couple at their evening devotions,' Dawn said. 'He left her for good the next day, that is, until now.'

Jean-Baptiste hung around for another two days, and then announced that he would be leaving the next day. That night after we had eaten, and I was alone with him in the kitchen, he produced a bottle of very good champagne cognac which he said he wanted to give me before he left.

'Open it. Let's have a drink,' he said, putting it in front of me on the table, as if to trap me behind it. I rose from the chair and got two glasses, and he sat across from me and we drank. I was, after all, his friend.

'Excuse me,' he said after a minute. 'I have to make a telephone call.' This was irritating, and I put down the glass. He went into the next room and came back fifteen minutes later.

'I was arranging to meet someone,' he said.

He left the next day. After he had gone, we learned that Lucy had insisted on coming with him to the airport, and that there had been a scene of some sort in the departure lounge. Lucy telephoned in tears to ask if we knew Jean-Baptiste's address in Paris. It was my bad luck to answer the phone. 'Didn't he give it to you?' I asked. Apparently he hadn't. Dawn didn't have it, and I certainly didn't. I said that all we knew was that he had gone to Paris, where he had arranged to meet someone. It was a bit tactless to have said this. The heartbroken Lucy eventually hung up. Sometimes I'd rather handle a live ferret than a telephone receiver.

Later, Dawn told me that Lucy had called international directory assistance, asking for every number in Paris belonging to people with Jean-Baptiste's last name. She managed to reach a confused distant cousin who didn't understand what Lucy was saying, but made it clear that Jean-Baptiste wasn't there. Dawn invited her over for supper and she wept the whole time. The table was set for three. Jean-Baptiste had gone.

Black Houses
M. John Harrison

I was introduced to Elaine on the pavement outside Black's club one winter in the early 90s. She was wearing a belted PVC jacket over a Lycra skirt. She had bobbed hair and bright red lipstick, and as I began to say hello she was already turning away to laugh at something someone else had said.

I can't imagine her in Black's. She was less Dean Street than Princelet Street: the ICA was more her line. Originally she had been some kind of performance artist: now, slowed down by years of drugs and touring, she was running for cover, becoming one of those academics who think of themselves as writers. She talked a lot about creative space, which is as much a giveaway as having the words Subsidized Arts tattooed on your forehead. The first time we fucked she called out, 'I can't control this. I can't work out what kind of man you are.' No one had ever said anything like that to me in bed before. Not while they were coming, anyway. I was impressed.

It was a one-night stand that got loose in both our lives and pushed them out of shape. We had nothing in common but each other. She lived near Ely. I was soon commuting to see her at weekends. It was a winter thing from the start. We went for walks. Cold evenings, we would light a fire and lie on a quilt in front of it, or sit in some old pub whose name I forget. We went somewhere on the coast, so she could pore over the map of a drowned town. We visited churches. She loved places, which she called 'sites'. She loved sites and structures. She had a rusty Ford she drove over kerbs with complete abandon. She drove me out into the hard frost and glittering fenland light to look at black houses. Black houses are vernacular; Jonathan Meades probably once said something about them. You find them all over the fens, east into Suffolk, north up to the Norfolk coast. They confront you eerily from the flat, exhausted landscape. Black houses are made of wood. They are either like chicken hutches or big hollow boats, their tarred, closely lapped wooden boards warped with age into the curves of a loaded wherry drifting slowly between reeds against a sky full of thunder. Elaine said that black houses were full of history, death, human stuff. You could imagine it as a sort of smell that filled them, as rich and thick as broccoli and stilton soup. They made her shiver.

Every time we saw a black house she warned me:

'I'll always be alone. I'm the kind of person who always has a bolt-hole ready. I always have a bag packed.'

I mentioned this in my diary, then went on:

'Despite this, all her old lovers still hang around her house. They rent places in the same street, they drop in for cups of tea. An American, a couple of drama-academics like herself – oh, and a piano tuner called Edward, who always gives me a wan, defeated smile. They're kind and good-humoured, with a reassuring fund of intelligence held in reserve.'

While to her I wrote like this –

Dear Elaine:

I wrote you a letter.

Then I ate it, at Burger King, King's Cross station, the dead dog end of a Sunday night.

I wrote you a letter then sent it to myself instead.

I wrote you a letter, took it out into the street and gave it to the first person I saw. They were very surprised.

It wasn't this letter.

I wrote you a letter and tried to transmit it to you by sheer psychic power.

Did you feel anything?

Now I've been with you in your house I can remember your smell.

But only suddenly, without expecting to.

I loved going to sleep with you in the firelight on the floor.

I already miss waking up in the night and feeling your skin on mine, and I love to wake up in my own bed and remember that. Is that wrong? Is it unsuitable? However you answer, I'll miss it. Whatever you say, your skin is so smooth.

I've met people before. But not you. I try to remember most the way you put your head on one side and smile. I try to remember most the things you whisper when I'm fucking you.

I wrote you a letter. I put it in a shoebox and floated it down the Grand Union Canal, past timber yards, gasometers and sleeping swans. It went past Mile End. It went past Islington. It went past Regent's Park Zoo, sinking imperceptibly all the way.

I wrote you a letter, it spoke to the water.

Let's not think.

Let's be happy instead.

Walk my feet off. 'Seal me with a kiss.' Let's not think. Show me your underwear. Draw me into you and I'll fuck you until we know exactly what to do. It's this: I've met people before. But not you.

Not you.

I rarely posted these efforts. I preferred to give them to her in person. I liked to watch her read them, though I can see now how tiring this must have been.

Twelve months on, near the end of the relationship, we were living together in East Dulwich, which Elaine called 'Dull Eastwich'. We had a four-bedroomed house like a great hollow box, and a forsythia, which flowered in the first week of March. Elaine bumped the Ford up and down the kerb, or drove it to part-time creative-writing jobs in Liverpool and Birmingham. I stayed in all day working on my theory that everyone is a vampire; or watched the comings and goings of Lord Arquiss, some Lucanesque family catastrophe of whose had condemned him to live at number 31 across the road.

Lord Arquiss was seventy-seven. He kept a Volvo the colour of a cheap brogue and a fifty-year-old ex-ballerina who claimed to be his wife. From the disaster they had salvaged an amazing Third Reich-style bed, the elongated black wooden posts of which were capped with vast polished eagles like lecterns. Every night you could see the two of them sitting up in this thing like bull terriers in a pram. They never closed the bedroom curtains. People wondered, but I'm certain he was a proper lord. He came complete with Parkinson's disease, a new hip replacement, and an old tendency to booze. All of this caused him to appear in the street naked but for a maroon silk shortie dressing gown and glove-leather slippers. He would root about in the back of the Volvo for something he never found and then drive slowly away, only to reappear less than five minutes later and spend half an hour trying to repark it in a space that would have been small for a Nissan Micra.

In an attempt to go unrecognized, the ballerina wore dark glasses, a white raincoat, and a Hermès headscarf whatever the season. She too left the house each morning. Eleven sharp, she was hurrying away in the direction of East Dulwich Grove, thin, already arthritic, a parcel of anxieties wrapped up in rain. Her tartan shopping trolley clinked with bottles.

Your turn to send something.

Send me a recipe.

Send ricotta & spinach, send tomato & garlic: send seafood risotto. Send ingredients, weights. Send cooking times. Send warnings.

Send Ascii the cat.

Send me the inner door of your studio. Send me the place it leads to once a year (but only if your second name is Rachel). Send the light outside the window, the light inside the supermarket. Send me a picture, pack it in music. Wrap yourself round it.

Wrap it in the touch of you.

Wrap me in the touch of you.

We know everything now. We know nothing until the next time mouth opens on mouth. In the morning it is rain on the roof, a pale diffused light on walls so like the walls of your studio, nothing but to be warm and to have the pleasure of turning towards you naked even as you turn towards me.

'Hello.'

I can remember being so far inside you! I can remember how you bring my mouth down to yours, and how in that moment I notice the air on both our skins, and then my whole perception is withdrawing itself to be there inside, so that my cock feels heavy and languid and filled with me and with the world and I could be this for ever – for ever – or only until I withdraw gently, and gently turn you over and in three or four strokes fuck, fuck, fuck you until you cry out from some feeling I can't imagine. You say, 'We can't live together, this won't work,' but you cry out from that feeling.

I can remember it.

Soon after we moved into the Dulwich house, we were called over to number 31 at one in the morning to help pick Lord Arquiss up.

His wife ran about in the empty street for a while, trying to attract our attention. A light, dry snow was dusting the road, wreathing and twisting along like dust round each quick little step. 'Look at this,' said Elaine, who knew a performance when she saw one. 'Not dancing but waving.' She waved back until the ballerina gave up and rang our bell.

'I wouldn't ask,' the ballerina told us, 'but he's had a little bit much to drink, so we can't really call the ambulance.'

Their front room was full of furniture too big for it, dimly lit by standard lamps with tasselled satin shades. Lord Arquiss lay waiting for us on the carpet at the base of a display cabinet, arranged on the glass shelves of which were hundreds of very small items in a kind of bright blue glass. He was looking up mischievously from the side of his eye. One of his slippers had fallen off. His legs, thick but somehow graceful, poked out of the bottom of the shortie dressing gown, their colour somewhere between white and cream. His skin was very smooth. He had a faint, distinct smell – not unpleasant – which reminded me of babies. We got him up off the floor and back into his chair with difficulty. He was still a heavy man, even in a dressing gown and with naked, biscuit-coloured balls.

He looked unrepentant; the ballerina looked relieved. 'You must have a drink,' they urged; filled two glasses with Famous Grouse; and spent an hour telling us anecdotes of people called Tippy or Ticky – people who were Malcolm Sargent's mistress in some old days even the participants barely now recall – people who had been well used to falling down and being picked up again. They were quite funny stories (the upshot of many of them seemed to be that Ticky had the siffy-wiffy), and the two old bores were as grotesque as you'd like.

But it was all too good to be true, really, so I didn't feel tempted to go back, even though Lord Arquiss knocked on the door a few afternoons later, stood there shaking for a bit, and finally managed to invite us round for a drink that evening. I had a feeling we had cruised the interview and got the job. Luckily, Elaine was in Liverpool, so I could make our excuses.

If you want a black house, we can live in one –

It is a house that belongs to neither of us. From its windows we can see masts, sails, a strip of pebbles at a steep angle to the estuary. At night we can hear rigging tap and flutter against aluminium spars. We can see the moon in the ruffled surface of tidal water. We can hear ourselves crunching back up the shingle after some long rainy afternoon walk.

You say, 'We're too different, we could never live with one another.'

In the black house we already do.

A short flight of bare wooden steps gives access to the small top room with its sloping ceiling and white wainscoting to catch the light. Up there I keep a brass vase, a brass lizard, a perfect brass aeroplane hardly bigger than a button. On one wall of the bigger room on the landing below, a mirror is so placed that, lying on my bed with the door open, I can see up the steps and into the top room.

The door is open now.

It's April, and the light is very strong.

It is like being in a film.

You are naked, standing on an old blue and white towel, washing yourself with warm water from an enamel bowl, sometimes crouched over it, sometimes almost upright, your thigh muscles strongly delineated. You look down at each shoulder as you wash it. You smile. Warm water pours across your breasts. I see all this in the mirror, but at the same time I imagine it, I make it.

I see this too, I understand this:

If I were to enter the mirror, I could be with you in some more acute, more heartbreaking, more real way than if I simply left my room and took the stairs and perhaps clasped you gently from behind and pushed into you standing up so that both our mouths made a surprised O – which in that light and cool air and in that part of the year would be heartbreaking enough in itself. But just as I am preparing to go up into the mirror, you kneel down to wash between your legs. I see the clear water run through your pubic hair, I see the lips of your cunt silhouetted against the light and the water running off them and back into the bowl. Everything in that moment is held in the light, clarified by it; held in the mirror and intensified by it.

So what if you say we can't live together? We can live separately in this house. Almost anything can happen now. Everything hinges on what happens now.

Nothing need happen now.

All the time I lived in Dulwich I knew what was happening. The house smelled of 3-in-1 at night: it was Elaine, oiling the hinges of the bolt-hole door. Her way of reminding me was to say apropos of nothing: 'We've got so much. Why have we got so many problems?' If I started to answer she would go on quickly, 'I really have to think about things. I don't know what to do.' If I didn't, her face would take on an impatient, pitying look, as if she was trying to deal with a teenager. The only way I could vent my anger at this was to jog through the deep sand of the horse-ride in East Dulwich Park. I would do a mile on and then a mile off, for ten miles or so. Sometimes even that wasn't enough. So I would go up to Dulwich Wood and run about in there until all the little hills and fallen logs had worn me down. I would arrive home, lathered in sweat and still feeling murderous, to find Lord Arquiss had finally finished parking his car and was ready for a chat at the kerb in his leather slippers. He pronounced 'fast' as 'fawst'; and talking of other drivers, said things like, 'I mean really some of them are almost menacing you. They're trying to frighten you into driving fawster.'

Then, in the same conversation –

'Novembah! Ha ha yes, Novembah!'

Even in their class nobody says fawster any more. For Lord Arquiss – and Mrs Lord Arquiss – the good days were all in the past. I couldn't imagine what they might have been like. It's hard to visualize what people like them did back then, although I suppose you could put some sort of picture together from the obvious elements. (Somerset Maugham's memoirs. The fawst goings-on in an early Ian Fleming novel.) On the other hand I could easily imagine some of the things they might still feel for one another: a kind of panicky distaste, a dreary alcoholic sense of dependence, a sudden fear of being alone, some mixture of comfort and horror such as you might experience if you slept night after night in sheets you couldn't be bothered to change.

Clearly, they still could feel. They tried to keep up appearances. They tried to keep alive the memory of Squiffy and Jiffy and Phipps. But were they anything much more than a memory of themselves? For each other, I mean? A kind of tired, escaping memory of themselves?

You sometimes heard her shout, at night. Had he fallen down again?

The last time I had anything to do with Lord Arquiss, he needed his shoes fastened. His wife had gone away the day before, for her mother's funeral somewhere in Scotland. So it fell to me. He made his way across the road four inches at a step – I watched him coming, all the way, wondering how I could refuse – and I knelt in my own doorway with the wet light coming in around his big bulky form and put neat bows in his expensive leather laces.

'I can manage the boots,' he told me, 'and the socks. But somehow not the laces. Can't spend the time down there.' Then he said: 'In the seventh year of Parkinson's you get things like that. It's not bad though, is it: seven years?'

'It's not bad at all,' I reassured him, although I really had no way of knowing whether it was bad or not.

Do you like me to say 'cunt'? Do you hate it? It feels dangerous to me, but proper. Male languages are such a threat, even to men. But I love your cunt, and to name it doesn't feel like male language to me.

I can imagine the little room with its sloping ceiling, the bowl of water, the towel, the flicker like a signal between the two poles mirror/world mirror/world mirror/world.

But what we have is to touch. In the end, that's what's so extraordinary. To touch, here and now. To feel the water on your skin on my skin. To have your buttocks fit so perfectly into the hollow of my hips that I think I might faint. To feel you slip so wetly on to me that I don't for an instant feel anything at all. To watch you kneel astride me – still a little damp from the water – to have your cunt licked until you can no longer bear it, and you tangle your hands in my hair and press me to you hard and come.

I can imagine the little room, and the stairs, and the bowl of water, and the towel left forgotten to dry on the floor.

I can imagine the house split in two, and hear you talk and watch you in the summer garden. I've known people feel safe in such houses, shiver with safeness when they hear rain on their skylights, turn luxuriously beneath the delft blue quilt on a cold morning. None of that is so far out of the world. None of that is so hard to have.

So go on then.

Explain to me why yearning is so dangerous and wrong.

Then I can answer:

I know what you mean.

I almost know what you mean.

I think I almost know.

So we live in a house with two houses in it, what's hard about that, perhaps by a tidal river; and are thus enabled to bathe in the same light in different ways; and you come to me; and I come to you; and at the end of it every possible image of both of us is printed imperceptibly on the walls of the house. Whatever else happens, those images are always there, fluorescing; densely imbricated yet always divisible; always lisible. What is so bad about that? What is so bad if only the water, or the light itself, comes to read them?

I know how we could live together now. Make me come into your hand. Use my come to write the alphabet on us in the dark. After that we can start.

We've already started.

A few weeks after the ageing ballerina's mother's funeral, the Arquiss house seemed to close up on itself. The lights were off early, the curtains drawn so that you couldn't see into the upper room with that monstrous black bed and its carved wooden eagles. Mrs Lord Arquiss stopped going out. If you saw Mr Lord Arquiss, he was sheepishly allowing himself to be helped into his car by a competent young woman of his own class. She always made sure he was dressed, but she couldn't park the Volvo any better than him.

Soon, you didn't see him at all. I heard that he had died. I never found out how the ballerina got on without him because by then I had moved on too.

I send you a letter.

I say Elaine to myself.

Pale light flickers away at the edge of vision like some sudden opening-out of the inner landscape. In that exact instant the phone rings.

It's you.

I say 'pale light', I say 'inner landscape', but that isn't what I mean.

You say, 'Everything is wrong between us.'

I say, 'Oh. Hello.'

But what I mean to say is this:

Sit up close to the wall here in this near-darkness with your legs open and drawn up – so you look like a new letter in the alphabet – some character made of residual light or memory or desire itself – and your smile becomes so hard to see it seems progenitive, the first, most elusive, most amiable and indrawn smile there ever was – and whisper to me, 'Can you fuck me like this, do you think you can fuck me like this, do you want to fuck me like this?'

What I mean is, yes, I think I can.

I think I do.

It's you.

Sit up close, here. Open your legs. Or here. Lie down while I kneel above you. Or here. Can I come on you? It's you. Here. I come on you.

I come on you.

You say, 'There's no need to be so gentle.' You say, 'Oh Martin, Martin, Martin, what are you doing to me?'

You say:

'You don't have to be so gentle.'

I come on your skin and feel an extraordinary release.

I write you like this:

Leaning naked against the white wainscoting in the top room of my part of our house – one leg straight, palms of your hands against the wall – looking down at yourself, very relaxed. I don't know what you are thinking. Pale aerial light fills the room, spraying off the walls and across two or three items of furniture – a table, a chair, perhaps a stripped wooden box. I am trying to describe to myself the strange, orangey-gold colour of the hair between your legs. I hear my own voice say:

'Bend your knees a little more. Now slide down a little. No! Not that far! Just an inch or two.

'Yes. That.'

The phone rings two storeys down, far away, unassuming. I kneel in front of you. 'Don't answer, don't answer!' I have found the perfect distance to measure. You raise your head and look away into some distance of your own.

Two white pebbles on the top of the box. A flint with a hole in it. The phone is still ringing. The phone is still travelling imperceptibly further away, like some complex illustration of a point in General Relativity.

'What shall we do this afternoon?'

The afternoon too is slipping away.

If I can avoid it, I don't think of East Dulwich now: but when I do, I think of hailstones – how in March, just before the forsythia flowered, they would begin to fall without warning out of a clear sky, bouncing vigorously off the road like insects. Suddenly, in the abandoned midsection of the day, there would be a movement at the ground-floor window facing me. It was Lord Arquiss's ageing ballerina, shifting uneasily behind the net curtain because she had mistaken the sound of the hail for the sound of an approaching car. Once or twice a week she was allowed to care for her grandchildren. They were girls ten and twelve; their bodies were filled with a kind of brutish energy, their arms with in-line skates. You heard their voices shouting from the house, full of the confidence of their future (or less of their own future, I suspect, than the future of their whole sex). They didn't look as if they had inherited the siffy-wiffy. The ballerina kept them close, surrendering them only to the imperative beep of her daughter's Land-Rover Discovery.

The daughter was one of those women made self-important by an unrelenting consciousness of herself as someone able to cope. She bustled in and out of the street, ignoring anyone else who happened to be there, calling peremptorily to children and grandmother alike, in and out in a moment on her way to the next appointment, the next problem, the next solution. She favoured Sloaney tailored jackets with padded shoulders and wore her hair that lank way they had then.

I write your name and images of you tumble away, getting smaller.

'Elaine,' I write, and it's you, asleep in the back of the car, then some strange pub in the middle of nowhere. 'Elaine.' There! Behind that fringe of trees! Water. Some houses with big fronts. We turn into the sun and it blinds us.

What sort of images can I send you?

What sort can you send me? We blew it from the start. You started with a bad idea.

You kneel in front of me. I kneel in front of you. Outside it's sleet, wind. It's snow. It's snow all the way to the sea, pasted on to black buildings, small figures. Snow is falling on the pebble beaches; within an hour, twilight will fall on the snow.

We kneel to touch one another, naked in some upstairs room in some old house. Look out the window. No, don't look at me.

Look out the window while I do this.

Images of us go tumbling away across the landscape. We shed images which go tumbling away over the fallen snow. Images while I do this. Now you do this too, and I go tumbling away.

Do this.

Later, setting sun on ice, behind trees.

Black buildings, and a rim of ice at the edge of the sea. (I write, 'Elaine –' and we walk out from behind some wooden buildings by the sea.) Black buildings, bare grey boards, a fringe of reeds at the edge of a dyke, a fringe of masts at the edge of an inlet, some shabby old pub in the middle of the snow. Instead of watching TV we should have wrapped up warm, driven away, and faced the new year from somewhere out there in the dark, not even sure where we were. (I write 'Elaine,' and we're in Brown's, watching the wind fan snow-eddies down the road. Student waiters and waitresses turn up the music and dance in the snow, and you make the sign for wankers and finish your drink.)

Kneel here. Face me. Don't look at me. Don't tell me anything.

I'll kneel here if you don't talk. I'll come in your hand. You come in mine, biting your lip, staring out the window at the snow.

Let's give up language, make Egon Schiele figures in an upstairs room.

Let's not tell each other anything at all.

Let's be a black house.

Let's be pictures tumbling away across the fens, some forgotten couple walking out from behind wooden buildings – let's be a couple in a shabby old car, making a turn, picking up a hitchhiker, blinking in the sun.

What sort of images are these?

Elaine?

It's like being in a computer game. One moment you have needs, the next, quite suddenly, they're satisfied or sidelined. The field of vision seems empty. Then you detect this faint serpentine flicker as the fractals grow and boil, and new needs have replaced the old. Desire is desire. You can't talk your way out of it. It ripples off like the pleats of an old accordion from wherever you stand in your life, a kind of dusty but convoluted interior space. I think of that when people recommend, 'Go away and be for a while,' and invite you to come back when you are 'less needy'. They are really saying, 'Go away until you are less difficult to handle.' I'm not willing to be told that. I doubt that Wiffy or Spermy or the ageing ballerina were, either. Not until right up to the end.

Elaine never gave up her own house. About a month after she went back to pick up the threads of the life I had interrupted, I visited Ely. I had understood the escape kit. I had found the key to the bolt-hole: it was those lovers who stayed around. They performed a stabilizing function. They were there so she could go off her rails in reasonable comfort. Determining never to be one of them, I made sure she was in Liverpool and spent one Saturday morning painting the front door of her house black. I thought that would do it. Afterwards I wrote to a friend of mine:

'Her life is a performance. You're a support player, an audience, a theatre. She uses you not only on stage but as the stage. You become what she would call the "performance space". She wants you to fill the same role as all the others. Act this: someone who was warned, someone who burned himself on her through no visible fault of hers. Act this: someone who is willing to be reasonable, shelter her from his pain, stay around on reduced terms, claim his place in her story. I was unable to see this at first. My inexperience disoriented me. What made it plain was the note she left – all "I" and "What I need" – that, and the choice of Elizabeth Taylor novel she made from my shelves the night we first fucked. *Angel*. Of course. Am I slow? I am.'

While to her, in a letter, I wrote:

'I would do anything if you would come back.'

The Devil I Know
Liz Jensen

Lily, naked except for a push-up bra, was strangling away at her swimsuit to wrench out the chlorine-water. Cold always makes her vehement.

'I'm fucking well *sick* of telling you this,' she announced. I'd just been telling her about Mike. She flung down the swimsuit, which landed in the chlorine puddle, then shoved her dripping hair into a pile on her head and clenched it with a strange clip – it looked like a set of jump leads – and glared at me. 'You've *got* to try and see it from the *bloke's* point of view. You're like a *dog* waiting for them to throw a *stick*. You're *asking* them to mess you about. And then you go into a *bottomless depression*. Don't you think they get *bored* of you always nagging them about where the relationship's *going*? Like it's some kind of – *aeroplane*? You make me puke.'

'I know,' I muttered. I bunched my towel round myself and rocked to and fro on the slatted bench. 'I know, I know, I *know*.' (But she's wrong. It *is* an aeroplane. I get giddy with it, every time. This is your captain speaking; we are now travelling at a height of twenty thousand feet, on a steady flight path. Oh, Mike, Mike, Mike!) Hunger scraped at my innards. We'd done our lengths. Washed our hair. I was looking forward to my Maltesers from the machine. (I always have Maltesers after swimming. Lily goes for salt.) 'But – look, Lily. Can I just ask you one question?'

Lily straightened herself up, parked her hands on her bony hips. She looked absurd, her hair all wet and clotted up with the jump leads, her lips blue with cold. She's got the two kids as well as the marriage. Her life involves school runs, petitions about road humps in residential areas, dealing with verrucae (she's a chiropodist), and quite a lot of red wine. No wonder she's always so full of fury. 'OK,' she sighed wearily. 'What?'

'Promise you won't be angry?'

She didn't reply; just pursed her lips. Sometimes I think she actually hates me.

'Do you think,' I pursued, 'do you think that he *might* call me tonight?'

Lily rolled her eyes. 'You stupid cow,' she said venomously, pulling on a pair of lace knickers, grey and full of holes. 'Listen, Janey. How many men called *Mike*, or *Michael*, or *Mick*, d'you reckon you've been in love with, since we left school?'

'It's just a coincidence –' I begin.

'How many?' she commands. 'Just count them, will you, because I have a real feeling of *déjà fucking vu* with this conversation.' I did a swift reckoning.

'Five,' I mumbled. Then protested: 'But this Mike's different! He is!'

'And how many Johns?' she flashed, hopping about on one leg as she struggled with her jeans. 'And how many Simons?' Before I could answer, she'd pulled her T-shirt over her head and was lost for a moment. Then she popped out, hair still dripping, eyes blazing. 'And what about all those *Nicks*?'

I shivered. Lily is my best friend.

I have certain rituals. My swimming ritual with Lily (twenty lengths: ten crawl, ten breaststroke, Maltesers and salt afterwards), when we talk. Or my nail-varnishing sessions: fingers and toes, left side then right, in front of *ER*. A weekly date. ('Pathological,' says Lily.) Or my coffee ceremony: the dinky Italian percolator, the two scoops of Colombian, the one cube of brown sugar in the Diana mug. The seven stirs of the spoon.

The mating ritual. 'Hello.' My big wide smile. Lips by Revlon, eyes by Lancôme. 'I'm Janey.' I can switch on a certain mind-set that makes me feel like a woman in a glossy ad. Bed by midnight. The getting-to-know-him part is always the best. That's when the aeroplane takes off. A big lurch, and you're on your way to a new country. You can't beat the thrill.

But then, after a week, a month – a year, max – things always take a familiar turn. He starts to yawn, and complain about cabin pressure. Claustrophobia. The need to stretch his legs. We hit turbulence.

'Why didn't you ring me?' That's me, trying to suppress the hurt, but not succeeding. Letting that twang of misery, the twang that Lily assures me they dread more than the sound of their car alarm going off in the night, creep into my voice. I can hear myself doing it but I can't stop it.

'*That's* the moment when you should have put a cork in it,' advises Lily, as I rerun the doomed conversation for her over a pedicure and a bottle of Shiraz.

'I tried calling,' the man says. Or, 'I *wanted* to call.' Or, 'I called, but you must've been out.'

Lily's right: he's often called Mike or Nick or Simon or John. Sometimes he's Dave or Paul. Occasionally he's a foreigner – something like Enrique or Claude – or an American with a name like Brett.

'I was in!' I squawk. (*Subtext: See! You lied!*) 'And anyway, what's wrong with leaving a message on the answer-phone?' (This aloud.)

'Mistake, Janey! Mistake, mistake, mistake!' crows Lily, buffing away with the foot-sander. 'Haven't I told you a hundred times that they hate the sound of *need*?'

Yes, mistake. This is your captain speaking. We have begun our descent. The man's bailed out by now, either verbally or by parachute. A stab of pain, followed by a counter-stab of something else that says, *I knew it.* Yes; there is comfort to be had in ritual. My destination may have turned out to be shit, but as the plane bumps down on to the tarmac I have at least the satisfaction of recognizing the contours of the territory. This land is *my* land. Later, I find myself standing by the conveyor belt again, clutching my emotional baggage.

Heavy.

When I turned thirty I began to think I might need a new set of destinations, a new atlas of the world. By thirty-five, I'd been on enough aeroplanes to know that it wasn't just a new atlas I needed; it was a whole new globe.

And then I got one.

'Mirror-land' has become my private codeword for the sexual planet I visited that summer. It was a word that Lily used, in the one excruciating conversation we had about it. It stuck in my mind because, without realizing it, she'd summed it up. It was a planet I returned from the same but irreversibly different. Transmuted and soured. A place of disorientation and derangement. I've learned, since that conversation with Lily when she mentioned mirrors, that I mustn't talk about it with anyone, ever. If nothing else, it's too intimate and too likely to make people squirm. But it crosses my mind sometimes. I get a spasm of rage, that I ever visited the place. Then a rush of relief, that I escaped. Then goose-bumps, remembering what went on there. And then something lingering afterwards, that might or might not be regret. At which point I blush.

Suddenly, out of the blue, I had met someone different.

'Here we go again!' groaned Lily. We were doing our lengths again; I'd decided to tell her about my new affair (not all of it, of course, not the key detail) in the pool, rather than the changing room. It gave me the option of swimming off ahead of her.

'No. Someone *really* different. I mean, I'm actually quite nervous about it all.' I felt coy. This one was delicate. A man doing the butterfly stormed past us like a hovercraft.

'You mean he's married,' panted Lily. We were on length seventeen. 'Christ, don't you ever learn?'

'No, it's no one married.' My eyes were smarting from the chlorine.

'So, what, then? Mentally unbalanced? Broke? Some kind of sociopath?'

We swam on, reached the end, did our turn, checked our progress on the clock, pushed off. Lily gasped for air. She was having trouble keeping up.

'Another lush?' she called after me.

'No, not a lush.'

She put on an extra spurt and swam up alongside me. 'Have you been to bed yet?'

I quickly dunked my face under water. Then re-emerged and

said, not looking at her: 'Yes. Quite a lot.'

'And is that OK?' she interrogated.

I was embarrassed, but hoped that she wouldn't spot it through her goggles.

'Yes. It's very OK.'

'So – ' she plunged under to sleek her hair – 'you should be happy,' she accused, a hint of jealousy in her voice. 'Are you happy?'

'Well, yes and no. I mean, there are signs – ' I gulped some water, spat – 'that it might not work out.' This was true. As I expected, Lily looked satisfied.

'The usual signs?' She's so cynical. So scornful. 'I mean, are you doing your standard thing of pestering him for commitment and then howling at the moon when he says no?'

We swam a bit more.

'It's actually not like that at all,' I said, trying to sound dignified, which is hard when you're spluttering for breath. 'That's the thing that would surprise you. I'm behaving in a completely different way. You'd be impressed.'

'I am,' she said, turning her head to stare, but I couldn't make out her expression beneath the goggles. Disbelief, probably. Contempt.

'Look, I'm not sure I want to tell you about this. Actually.' I gulped another mouthful of water and half-choked. 'I mean, it's not what you – ' I swam a few more strokes. 'Hey. Look. I'll give you the gory details another time.'

Then I plunged under water, resurfaced and did the crawl for the last two lengths. When I next looked at Lily, she was floating in the shallow end, and the attendant was admiring her tits.

In the shower, we didn't discuss it any further. Lily was preoccupied with her eldest, Ben.

'He keeps drinking and peeing,' she said. 'Wetting the bed every night. He shouldn't be, at six. And he gets sleepy all of a sudden. The doctor's arranging for some tests.'

I didn't phone her. I couldn't. My affair continued, rockily.

Then I got an email from Lily saying she couldn't come swimming again for a while. Ben had been diagnosed as having diabetes. He was very ill. 'Sorry,' she wrote. 'But this is real life.' I emailed back saying I was sorry about Ben. But I was secretly glad that I wouldn't see her for a while. The affair I was having was so freakish that it was impossible to discuss. I was mad to have mentioned it at all.

Dr Per Lindqvist was a tall, blond, charismatic, intelligent, stimulating, probably married, highly educated, Swedish pharmacologist. We'd spent most of the week working together, and today's conference was the culmination of the Synapse Group's project on cell mutation. We'd both given our talks. And now, as the hall emptied, I was pretty sure that, given the sexual chemistry that had been simmering by the coffee machine all week, in particular on Wednesday, he was going to be –

'Oh *God*! NO!'

Suddenly gone. My eyes scanned the conference hall. One minute he was there, beside me, as potent and dangerous as a great humming chunk of uranium, shuffling his notes as the students filed out of the hall. And the next minute –

I slumped in a seat, and let my slides go crashing to the floor.

'Shit,' I said. Tears weren't far away. I'm always like that after a presentation. The terrible, yawning anticlimax of it. And then Dr Per Lindqvist doing a vanishing trick, like I'd just *imagined* all that chemistry.

Quietly, a woman in the seat behind me rose and began picking up my cell slides. I gulped back my tears. I couldn't let myself cry here. It wasn't professional.

'Oh, thanks,' I said. 'Sorry. God, I'm so clumsy. You needn't, really – '

She smiled. 'It's nothing.' She handed me my slides.

'Are you OK?' she asked. 'Can I get you a glass of water or something?'

'No, I'll be fine. Really. Thanks.' I looked at her. She was younger than me. And I hated to acknowledge it, but she was also seriously attractive, with a perfect oval face, not a trace of make-up, and, gallingly, no need for it.

It was as I was looking at her that everything suddenly fell into place. I get flashes of intuition like that. And I'm seldom wrong. She was Per Lindqvist's girlfriend. It was obvious. Or his wife. They lived in Stockholm, and at weekends they had sex on the deck of their boat, by moonlight, while the kids were asleep in the hull. And now she'd come to claim him. From *me*. I'd been hoping – oh never mind what I'd been hoping. The usual stuff I always hoped for and sometimes got but never for long. Yes; hoping, even when I'd dropped my slides in bungling despair, that he'd come up and silently put his arms around me from behind, grip me tight, and bury his face in my hair, like he so nearly did on Wednesday by the coffee machine. Even now, I could feel the heat of his breath on my neck. I was aching for him.

'I'm Jay,' said the woman, holding out her hand to shake.

'Oh. I'm Janey,' I said, still fighting the tears, and struggling to sound like a normal person. I shook her hand. It always feels weird and unnatural to me, shaking hands with women. Especially women I'm jealous of.

'I know,' she said. 'I heard your talk. Is Janey really Jane?'

'Yes.'

'Me too. Jay's short for Jane.'

Jane's one of those names. You want to dress it up as something less boring. 'I've always been called Janey,' I said. 'I don't associate myself with the name Jane.'

'Nor do I. Weird, isn't it? I've always just been Jay.'

I looked at the door. He might come back. Any minute.

'Well, thanks for helping me.' I forced a smile. 'Really. I appreciate it.' Eyes by Revlon, lips by Lancôme. *Now bugger off.* But she didn't take the hint. The conference hall had emptied – Oh *God*, where did he *go*? – and we were alone.

'So. Dr Lindqvist's abandoned us,' I said ruefully, half-joking, still wondering about their relationship.

'Lindqvist?' Her look of puzzlement got me thinking that my intuition about sex on the deck and kids in the hull might be wrong. 'Oh, you mean the last speaker,' she said. 'The pharmacologist. Yes. I think he left.' She smiled, unaware of my pain. 'Look, how about a drink? I'd like to talk to you about a study we're planning that might fit in with one of yours . . . ' She trailed off. 'Well, I could tell you about it over a drink, maybe.' She was steering me out of the conference hall. 'If that's OK with you?'

'Yeah, why not?' I say. Why the hell not? It's Friday. I'm miserable; he'd loaded his briefcase and his sexual charisma into a taxi bound for the airport without even saying goodbye. Bastard. A drink might help. I can even see myself confiding in her. She'll probably be a lot less brutal than Lily.

'I know a good bar,' I offer, flatly, unable to muster much enthusiasm. 'All Bar One.' Good as in, being somewhere I've met men in the past. The thought perks me up slightly. This Jay woman's attractive, after all. We'll be bound to pull.

We're in the bar, but there's almost no one there yet. Too early. The atmosphere's unusually low-key. We've had a couple of drinks, and talked in a desultory sort of way about cell structure, and realized that our paths of interest don't even begin to cross. She hasn't mentioned the study she's doing, but she's asked a lot of questions about me. Flattering, but a bit odd. A bit nosy. So I've started telling her about Mike, and how that ended. And Nick, and Simon. I've hinted at what happened with John, and –

Then I stop.

A man's walked in, and he's Brad Pitt. Or near enough. He's wearing a sleeveless T-shirt that shows off his arms. My first thought is that he's too beautiful to be heterosexual, but when he reaches the far end of the bar he catches sight of us and his eyes flicker from me to Jay, and from Jay to me, and then back to Jay, and then he smiles at both of us.

Hey. I smile back, then turn to Jay to share it. Her mouth twitches. I mutter, 'Yes please.'

He can't hear me, of course, but it feels like he has, and I giggle. I skipped lunch, because I was nervous before my cell talk, and now the wine's gone to my head. But Jay doesn't seem to register what's going on. Brad's still looking in our direction. He's focusing on Jay rather than me, of course. Reminder to myself: If you go anywhere with another woman, make sure she's less attractive than you. I find myself wishing I'd taken the time to put on lipstick before we came. I start fishing about for my make-up case in my handbag.

Jay's touching my arm.

I drag my eyes away from the man and turn to look at her. I say, 'Yes, what is it?' And think: *Yes: she's beautiful*, and groan inwardly. So here's the second defeat of the day coming up, I think. *She wins. I lose. Go on, then, Jay. Have Brad Bloody Pitt. He's all yours. Who's going to be leaving the bar alone tonight? Plain Janey! Muggins!*

But nothing's how I think.

'Do you realize I'm gay?' she blurts. She's squinting at me, her face serious, her greeny-grey eyes full of need.

Instinctively, I shunt backwards in my seat. At the other end of the bar, Brad orders a beer. He's still looking at Jay, but it's a different look this time. Like, she didn't return his smile, so now he's angry with her. Not as angry as I am, mate, I think. Her hand is resting now on my shoulder, so lightly that it's barely there. In my bag, I finger my lipstick, still conscious, in a side-compartment of my mind, that I'm waiting for Brad to turn away so I can apply it, and improve my looks by some twelve per cent. Burnt Cinnamon. It suits me.

A *lesbian*. Of course. Of *course*! Now everything's making sense. I mean, she hadn't so much as glanced at Brad Pitt. (God. He could still be mine. I clutch my lipstick tight. I could shake her off.) And all those questions about myself. It wasn't girl-talk. It was – well, why was she so interested? And then when I'd tried to tell her a bit about Mike, and recounted an anecdote about Nick, and explained how things had nearly worked with John, and why they'd failed with one of the Simons – why had she looked so bored, so weary, so impatient? Looked away?

'Gay?' I repeated. What was I supposed to say? I cleared my throat.

'Want another drink?' I said.

We were in her car, parked outside my flat. I'd nearly refused her offer of a lift home, because the conversation had become painfully stilted in the bar, once she'd told me. My brain had whirred off in all directions, and I'd started gabbling about how nervous I'd been before my cell structure talk, and how Ben was getting diabetes at the age of six, and how I always had Maltesers from the machine after swimming, but Lily-who's-a-chiropodist-and-also-Ben's-mum had something salty like crisps or Hula-Hoops, and how actually I wouldn't mind going home, as I'd recorded *ER* last night but hadn't had a chance to watch it yet.

'Well, goodbye then,' I said.

'Goodbye, Janey,' she said. She looked mournful and very beautiful, and I felt suddenly irritated, but I couldn't work out why.

And then it hit me. What pissed me off was that she'd pretty much wrecked my evening. Not actively, but passively. When she'd told me she was a lesbian, what she'd actually done was to *dump* it on me. I had duly reacted – and now I was confused.

Well, come on then, say something, or do something, I thought. *Stop pissing about*. But she just sat there, looking at me sideways. Silent. I felt oddly insulted. It had been quite a day for rejection. First Per Lindqvist. Then Brad Pitt (who'd left after one beer). And now – Christ, not even this lesbian wants me!

She was looking straight ahead now, through the windscreen.

And slowly, as we sat there, I realized two things: first, that she was blushing, and second, that – God, it was ridiculous – that she was waiting for something. *Expecting* something.

What?

Permission to be a lesbian?

For God's sake, you irritating woman, I thought. And suddenly all the frustration about Dr Lindqvist and Brad Pitt and the Nicks and the Johns and the Simons and the Mikes flooded over me in a great tidal wave of anger.

Someone's got to take charge of this situation, I thought. And I leaned over and grabbed her hair and pulled her towards me and kissed the lesbian on the mouth. Quite violently.

How soft she was. She tasted different from a man. She smelt of shampoo, and that fruit tea.

Girly.

I'll be honest; I was kissing Jay as an act of aggression, just to shock her. But I shocked myself even more when I felt a tingling jab of desire. Appalled, I pushed her back, her hair still tangled in my hand, and looked at her face. Her eyes were shut. She opened them slowly, languorously, and smiled. Is that what *I* look like, I wondered, when *I* kiss? Then she breathed out in a little groan.

'Do you know that I've been wanting you to do that all evening?' she whispered.

So she *had* been waiting for something.

'So what's next?' I blurted, bluntly, still clutching her hair. 'I don't get the rules of this.'

'There aren't any rules,' she said, and tilted her perfect oval face towards me again. Between my legs was still hot. It was a surreal and disturbing sensation, like being nuzzled by a casserole dish.

But when it's that strong, however incongruous it seems, you can only give in to it. It's that simple. So I pulled her towards me again, tugging her hair a bit on purpose, so that it would hurt, and kissed her again, hard, still angry at what she'd stirred up in me, and I tasted the fruit tea and smelt the shampoo and became aware of something else, more feral. And didn't stop and didn't stop and didn't stop.

When I woke up with her in my bed the next morning, feeling her flesh all soft against mine, like I had a twin, like I'd been cloned, the first thing she said was:

'Please – don't go. I mean, can I stay a bit? Please? I mean – look, you're not regretting anything, are you?'

The words, and the way she said them, sounded familiar.

Two months later, when the affair was over, I phoned Lily.

'Ben's on insulin,' she told me flatly. We talked about that for a while. Blood tests. A new kind of treatment. Sugar levels.

'Sorry I didn't ring you,' I said.

'I didn't notice,' says Lily. 'I was too wrapped up in Ben. Anyway, what's new?'

'Nothing much,' I say.

'Wasn't there some new bloke?'

'Well, there was the beginning of something with someone,' I begin. I'll have to tread carefully. Thank God her name was unisex. 'Someone called Jay.'

'So what happened?'

'It finished. We weren't compatible.'

'The usual?'

'No. That's the weird thing. Completely different.' It was all spilling out in a rush now. 'I mean, this – Jay – got too dependent. I couldn't stand it. Always waiting for me to phone, and then when I did, asking me why I hadn't phoned before. Always wanting to talk about our relationship and where it was going. Like it was some sort of *aeroplane*,' I said, quoting her. *Be careful*, I'm thinking. This is tightrope-walking. *Don't say 'she', don't say 'she'*.

'*What*? Doesn't sound like your usual type.'

'God, you can say that again. It was a real pain. I was the one who had to make the decisions about everything.' The memory churns about inside me uncomfortably.

'What about the sex?' Lily always wanted to know about the sex in detail. Married friends always do.

'Oh,' I say, remembering the softness of Jay's flesh, the unfamiliar familiarity of her scent, the feel of female hands on me. In me. The memory flushed through my entire body. 'That was – ' I drop my voice. 'That was OK. Amazing, actually. In some ways, the most erotic sex I've ever –' I stop. I'm blushing. I can't go on. The thought explodes within.

'Go on, then, tell me.'

'Well, the point was, there was a personality problem. I mean, it was like no matter how good the sex was, there was still – well, the next morning, Jay was always next to me on the pillow, being – *emotionally demanding*. Wanting stuff. You know, even wanting to settle down.'

I half gag at the thought.

Silence. 'Sounds like he wants the same things you do, then,' says Lily. 'Sounds like he's been giving you a taste of your own medicine,' she added, with a not very kind laugh.

'I hadn't thought of it quite that way,' I murmur. It's true. I hadn't.

'But anyway,' says Lily, 'you always *wanted* to settle down and – '

'Yes, but not with – this particular person!' I interrupt. 'Not with – Jay!'

'So it wasn't love, then,' says Lily slowly. She's not her usual furious self today, I realize; there's even a hint of concern in her voice. It must be Ben and the diabetes. *I'm* the angry one now. I've been angry for weeks.

'No. Not love. Jay was the wrong type. Absolutely the wrong type.'

'Well, at least you've *learned* something, then,' says Lily, sounding like she might have guessed something. 'At least you know what isn't your type,' she ventures. 'I mean, you can't have a future with someone like that. Someone who's not your type. It would be – against nature.'

'Absolutely!' I agree. 'I mean, there's just no way I'd go for someone like that again. They went for me, actually. I mean, it's not like I saw this person and thought – hey, this is the person I want to spend my life with. I didn't even look twice, in fact. It wouldn't have crossed my mind to fancy them.' And then I stopped, stuck. What more was there to say? But I felt uneasy, like I'd maybe said too much. Or not enough. There was a brief silence at the end of the line. Then Lily said cautiously:

'You haven't had a – a *Jay* before.'

'No, and I won't again,' I say. I force a laugh. 'I'll be sticking to Nicks and Mikes.'

'Sounds like a sort of mirror-land,' says Lily. She's talking to me very carefully now, like I'm a dangerous kid with a gun. *Just put the weapon down, Janey. I promise you won't be harmed.*

'What? Mirror-land, did you say?'

'Yes. Role-reversal. You know.' *Nothing will happen to you, Janey, if you just put the gun down. Now. Here. On the floor.*

I don't say anything for a while. I'm collecting my thoughts. Then what she's just said crystallizes itself, and suddenly I realize what Jay was, and what I'd seen in her. My God, we even had the same name! Lily's silent, too. Suddenly it unnerves me, this gaping telephone silence, and I feel the need to fill it.

'Look, I must go,' I say finally, glancing at the clock. I hadn't realized the time. 'My pathological date, remember?'

'OK,' says Lily slowly. 'Sure.'

'OK, so we'll go back to our swimming routine next week?' I ask. I'm trying to sound busy and brisk.

'Yeah. Fine.' There's an odd quality to her voice.

'Well, bye, then.'

'Yes. Bye. Er – Janey.' It's not brittleness; it's something else. Something I've never heard before. Something small and choked. 'Janey?'

'Yes?'

'So – ' I can actually hear her gulp – 'so you're not a lesbian, then?'

I miss a beat. 'No.' It comes out as a harsh croak. 'Definitely not.'

'Good. I mean you'd always be my friend but – ' But she can't finish. She makes an odd noise, that might be a sneeze or a sob, and hangs up.

★

Obviously, this can't, and won't, be discussed again.

In the kitchen, mechanically, I enact the coffee ritual. The dinky Italian percolator. The two scoops of Colombian. The Diana mug. The single cube of brown sugar. The seven stirs. Still on autopilot, I get out the nail varnish and settle on the sofa with my feet on the coffee table and my toes in the toe-divider. Then, feeling nothing, absolutely nothing, so much nothing that it's like a huge black hole consisting entirely of nothingless nothing, like I've just spent two months on another planet and I don't know who I am any more, I reach for the remote, flick on *ER*, and return to the devil I know.

The Next Files
D. F. Lewis

'Life is in itself a form of apprenticeship,' suggested tunicked Tom to this particular girl-in-every-port, as the tardy afternoon began to try on its evening wear. His words.

He was on shore leave: the Captain's favourite crew member, simply for his more than just a spark of intelligence compared to the rest of the sailors. He had often been invited to the officers' table, to spin a yarn or two, to plait a tale, to hold forth on all matters philosophical, spiritual and mundane. The port which the ship was visiting on this occasion was an occidental one, well beyond its beaten track, in search of new clients. The arrayed cranes, lifting in angles from the dockside, were huge stick insects: totems to some higher industry quite beyond the comprehension even of someone with uncommon nous like Tom.

His birthplace was tucked away cosily in the gleaming gulf of the Home Territories – a harder trip east than the ship's occidental clients could ever imagine. Thus, it was not surprising that these new recipients of the ocean spice-trail trade here in the waters of western Europe and the providers of such wares from the eastern Home Territories could never allow their cultures to meet eye to eye.

Tom had discovered the western girl lolling against a large bollard, mooning the time away till she could ply her own trade more properly in the darker-suited hours. Not his words.

He was immediately attracted to the uncanny planes of her face, in contrast to his own race's high cheekbones and sunken narrow eyes. Her eyes were wide and innocent-seeming; he read the lines of her features as he would a mandala or natal-chart at home. This dreamboat's voice, too, was deep for one so fair, with a lilt and dialect fit for a fairy-tale princess. He found it difficult to follow her drift, because of the quaintness of the speech rhythms; but he took it with a pinch of salt, as he tracked a deeper index within her. He was confident that her mental tackle would be able to trawl anything with which he chose to sow her feminine tides.

His lobster pot of a head beamed beardily, as he continued: 'And life being an apprenticeship, one should endeavour to learn everything one can before embarking on the voyage of death.'

'Eh, wot yer say, guv?' Her words.

Tom winced. This was the first time he had encountered one who answered so readily. It was off-putting to talk along the knife edge of such a sensitive audience. Her responses were so very much to the point.

Yet he resumed his diatribe: 'By logic, there can only be one religious faith, that which represents the belief in the positive aspect of death. A faith without this as its paramount tenet would not be worth the parchment it's written on. Accept that as an incontrovertible prerequisite, then all religions become a single faith. God is that faith. Faith is that God. Yet God is not an entity with omnipowers, not an anthropomorphic puppet-master . . . '

'Gor blimey, mate, has your brain swallowed your tongue?'

By now, the sun had risen elsewhere in the world, probably in the Home Territories, he surmised; the mist gathered apace, linking sea and land with translucent mountains of dream, the coloured deck-lights of Tom's ship bobbing spasmodically on the uncertain tide. A chill clung to his bones. He decided it was now high time to offer spice as a reward for her kind attention. After all, as well as the provocative esoterica of philosophy, it was also in the nature of tunicked Tom's breed to issue flirtatious cockadilloes to the local totties in new client lands. The spice would no doubt hotten her bland stews. He passed her a free sample packet, with a smile.

'I hope this complimentary gift supplements thy already warm heart . . . '

'Ey up, guv, is't bleeding hard stuff?'

She snatched the packet and darted off into the skid-marked underclothes of the night. No one's words.

Another day, another universe, she'd've refused the gift and probably stayed to make a match.

But as this particular moonstruck Tom rowed himself back to the ship, the gentle rippling of the oily sea as music to his ears, he determined to retain at least some of the girl's wisdom for the benefit of the officers' table . . . and for later life, when, by then, Old Tom's house in the Home Territories would be crumbling around him . . .

Old Tom nipped each problem in the bud, either by hiring a handyman or, at the last resort, actually getting his own hands dirty. Yet today, he felt like a little boy with a digit in a dam, as he stood in the garden probing the pointing of some external bricks with a chiselly fingernail. The whole place teetered on the brink of something far worse than collapse. Its wooden stilts were becoming as good as one with the morass whence they grew. And, with unaccountable abruptness, he remembered that European ex-girlfriend from the ancient days of his youth when at sea with the spice trade.

First things first. His wife had left him, but on second thoughts that was probably the best of it. Or, on first thoughts, was his wife yet to meet him? No, what really bugged Tom was the speed with which he seemed to be heading towards that selfsame death about which a younger Tom had been so coolly detached and philosophical. The house was simply symbolic of such personal ruin. The house was also instrumental. Entropy had a lot to answer for. Not that Tom understood such strange English words.

He removed his finger from the bare brickwork and sighed. The roof lifted up slightly where the gutter divided pantiles from stucco, revealing the grabbing paws of an oriental teddy bear: a giant version of the friendly old creature that had once shared Tom's playpen. It beckoned some Pandora to put her fingers in the toybox that Tom's house had suddenly become. Not that Tom was Pandora, nor tall enough to reach that far up. He realized that the loft was full of his old playthings. The rocking horse. The easel and paintbox. Whip and multicoloured top. Wooden hoop. Meccano set. Pick-a-stix. Jack-in-the-box. Spice rack.

He took one last look at the stilts, literally daring them to topple, and ran towards the French windows. But he was refused entry by a large tin soldier who creaked rustily as it aimed its bayonet at Tom, saying:

'This is private property.'

The soldier's grimace was painted on and his voice was more a thought process than that audible irritation of the air which speech tended to be.

'Yes, you are quite right,' announced Tom, 'it's mine!'

'This house belongs to the gods of dilapidation and decay. You no longer have any jurisdiction over it.'

This last statement was not the soldier's but a bouncier voice emanating from a closed box behind him. The soldier was equally startled by the intervention from such an apparently unviable source. How could boxes talk? Unless ... unless ... it was a Jack-in-one. And, no sooner contemplated, the lid flicked up and a rubicund clown-on-a-spring laughed up and down like a boomerang yo-yo.

Tom was at least certain about one thing. He was not dreaming. He did not need to draw blood from a pinched arm to prove that point. The whole episode was, in truth, nothing more than symbolic. And symbols were dreams made flesh. Metaphors had real meat. Similes actually were what they were like. Nothing could be simpler – or more complex. Even entropy took a back seat. Words taken as read.

Tom smiled as he proceeded with what he felt to be stilts down the garden path. Indeed, his face was on a swing-leg easel: a walking portrait that lived for ever, since the acid in the air was merely for things that breathed and for people who believed only in paintings that wore and tore. And as he reached crazy-paving's end, where fence divided real fairy-tales from false accounting, he turned round to admire his house. The girl on the roof was playing cat's-cradle with the television aerial: a girl he would recognize, if his old age were not now even older than the person it aged. His smile became the sob it was. He failed to realize that Pandora was the girl he'd once loved before he was her husband and she his wife, both failing to become the people they were meant to be – because metaphors kicked the bucket when they no longer meant anything whilst similes simply compared truth and non-truth, without coming off the fence. But the sentence was too long. A life sentence.

The teddy bear tried to regain the slit-eyed rag doll that he had once loved. Tom screamed from the island of his playpen for yet more toys. Playpens were worlds unto themselves. Doll's-houses, too. And the properties of life and death were private properties – both in law and in physical insularity. Occident met orient, in the same way as death met life, cancelling each other out. Not that Tom could now understand anything, let alone such symbols. He put anything complicated, and hence meaningful, as far from his mind as possible. He forgot, too, that, when he had looked again, he had witnessed the girl thrashing about as she was skewered on the TV aerial, her melted blood trickling into the gutters and down the soggy stilts. Her space was spice.

A voice pitifully gurgled: 'Blimey, mate, help me down!'

Tom shrugged. The girl was evidently in renewed birth throes. Left on the roof by a giant stork.

In his universe, opposites, once met, were male-merged and filed – and an Ex-Lover was always the Next-Lover . . .

'Pretty good, at his age, eh, sweetie?'

Jackinthebox words, not Pandora's.

Planet of the Exes
Pat Cadigan

Kit looked down at the postcard the very straight-looking man had handed her in front of the giant HMV on Oxford Street and felt her heart sink.

> Planet of the Exes
> A Place Where We Can Be Ourselves
> Come As You Are . . . ALONE

'What *is* this?' she asked. People had been handing her postcards, flimsies and handbills almost since she had come through the entry channel (with nothing to declare) at Heathrow. She had taken them all almost dutifully, thinking somewhere in the back of her mind that her simple acceptance of a slip of paper, proffered without charge or other obligation, would be giving meaning to someone's life with little or no inconvenience to herself. As a member of a society which involved the employment of people to distribute handouts on a city street, integrity of the most minimal sort demanded she participate (she thought) by accepting those handouts. She could dispose of them later if they weren't useful, something no more difficult than accepting them in the first place.

But most of the handbill/postcard distributors had been standing in one spot offering what they had in a nearly passive way to anyone who came within arm's reach – which on a busy afternoon on Oxford Street could be an amazing number of people, Kit saw. This guy, however, didn't look anything like someone who would distribute advertising for a living – his midnight-blue suit was immaculate and so well fitting it could have been *bespoke* (one of those British words she was fond of just for its quaintness), and his haircut looked almost as expensive. As well, he had made his way through the crowds on the sidewalk to hand the card to her specifically, as if he had recognized her, or had been waiting for her or someone like her.

'"Planet of the Exes"?' she said. '*Exes?*'

The man smiled in a kindly way; he was about forty or so and somehow she knew that the small lines around his eyes had been much more pronounced once. 'You know what we mean by exes, don't you?'

'Yes, but…' Kit turned the card over; there was an address on the back and a small map showing a tangle of streets. The only words that looked familiar to her were *Charing Cross*. 'What's this place supposed to be, "Planet of the Exes"?'

'It's a club. Like a nightclub,' he added. 'You're American, aren't you?'

'I thought the accent would make that obvious.'

'Not necessarily. Canadians sound like you people sometimes, especially Americans from northern Minnesota and northern New York.'

'Upstate,' she corrected him automatically. 'Why did you hand this to me?'

He blinked at her. 'It's a handout. Ergo, I'm *handing them out.*' His eyes twinkled.

'Yes, but…' She hesitated. 'The thing is…well…I was managing not to think about it for almost an hour. And then you come along and shove this at me. How could you know?'

'Oh,' the man said, and made a discreet gesture at something behind her. She turned to see an extremely tall, thin guy with what seemed to be two dozen piercings above the neck alone, concentrated mostly in his ear and nose cartilage. His head was shaved except for a patch on the very top. The hair had been dyed an electric pink and fashioned into a heavy twist of dreadlocks that fell to an area near his tailbone. His camouflage trousers and storm-trooper boots seemed to Kit to dare anyone to make something out of his penchant for pink.

'Well, he's unique,' she said, turning back to the man, 'but not really my type.'

'Oh, he's hardly unique,' replied the man, smiling even more benignly, 'and as to whether he's your type or not, I wouldn't presume to say. But I wouldn't hesitate to state that he's not someone who would be interested in Planet of the Exes. I doubt he's that kind of ex. Nor is she.' He nodded at a passing woman carrying two large shopping bags from a men's clothing store.

Kit couldn't help giggling. 'God, she's still trying to dress him.'

'My point exactly.' He was about to say something else when he suddenly stepped up to another passer-by, this one an anxious-looking man of about the same age, wearing a ponytail and holding a cell phone to the side of his head. He took the card without looking at it and tucked it into a pocket. 'Undoubtedly, I miss some people, and mistake some others, but in general, I think the cards eventually fall into the hands they're meant for.'

'How?' Kit asked.

'Oh, a sort of Brownian motion, combined with the laws of statistics, and lashings of serendipity.'

'Sounds like a recipe for something.'

The man's expression acquired a melancholy undertone. 'There's a recipe for everything, and everything is the product of a recipe. It's just that the outcome isn't always the one intended, is it?'

Before Kit could answer, he had slipped back into the crowds and, to all intents and purposes, disappeared. She turned her attention to the card again.

As a piece of advertising, it wasn't much – plain black print, albeit in a fancy typeface, on a white surface, and not even a glossy one. She stared down at it, oblivious to the people jostling her as they went in and out of the HMV behind her. The tall guy with the pink dreads paused just behind her to see what she had that was so fascinating and lost interest immediately at the lack of colour; she didn't notice. In the next moment, she kept thinking, she would crumple it up and stuff it in her pocket, or find a waste-can – damned scarce things in London, waste-cans – and forget about it. Had she really come to London for something like this, a visit to a divorcees' support group? *Hi, I'm Kit, and I'm a divorcee.* (Audience: *Hi, Kit!*) *I've been divorced for three months now, after a separation of a year and legal proceedings lasting about that long. It wasn't as bad as my friend Rhonda's — she has three kids — though it was more acrimonious than I thought it would be. It's taken me a long time to be able to say that I'm divorced without feeling even just mildly cheesy and tawdry. Don't ask me why. My deep fear is that the whole thing really is all my fault and I'm a horrid, evil person who destroyed the life of an innocent man by —*

She heard Rhonda's sensible voice in her head, just the way she had heard it that night when she had bottomed out and Rhonda had come over to save her from cheap gin with a decent whiskey. *Don't go there, kiddo — that way madness lies. And I do mean* lies, *because nothing like that can be true, of* anyone, *and certainly not* you.

OK. Kit took a deep breath and turned the card over to look at the address again. *It's a club. Like a nightclub,* she remembered suddenly. Not a support group. Not another 12-Steps programme, not group therapy for co-dependants who spent too much time in the psychology section of bookstores well stocked by shrewd buyers. A nightclub. Social stuff — music, entertainment. Mingling, small talk, sexual tension. Prelude to a date, perhaps. Or several, even. Who knew?

Uh-huh, sure. A whole club full of desperate, formerly-marrieds looking for a replacement in a hurry, someone to prove that they could, in fact, sustain a real relationship with someone, someone who was, of course, patient, kind, and understanding, not to mention normal, and not all neurotic and hung-up and dragging around a lot of stupid emotional baggage that —

Kit sighed. Suddenly she realized her mistake. She hadn't gone far enough away on vacation. It wasn't another country she'd been looking for but another planet.

Only not the Planet of the Exes.

From Oxford Street she went to Regent Street, rambled aimlessly along the fringes of Soho, looked for Chinatown only to find herself in Leicester Square, and spent most of the remaining daylight trying to find Soho again, only to end up circling Piccadilly Circus over and over. The *London A–Z*, which the clerk at the bookstore had insisted on pronouncing 'a to zed' seemed to be no help at all. This was a city with more roads and streets than should have been physically possible, and the various ways they all connected with each other —

or failed to – made no sense to her at all. She had to admit that she found it far more interesting than the locked-down suburban grid she'd been living in for the last decade, and it wasn't so bad to be rudderless in such a beautiful city, but finding your way around seemed to be a matter of random walking.

Brownian motion, combined with the laws of statistics and lashings of serendipity. Standing in front of a noisy, colourful arcade-mall kind of place called the Trocadero, she smiled to herself, forgetting for the moment that she had been trying to figure out which way to go for Shaftesbury Avenue. Maybe if she decided to look for Chinatown again, she would find Charing Cross Road. Arbitrarily, she let the crowds sweep her along to her left, where she eventually came back to Leicester Square for no reason that she could discern. And here was Charing Cross Road, also for no reason that she could discern. If this was Charing Cross Road, why was she standing near the Leicester Square underground station? What had happened to the Charing Cross underground station, where was *that* now?

Probably moved to Leicester while she was trotting around and around in Piccadilly Circus like a lost show-pony looking for a formation to join. A group of tall, beautiful young people swept around her, speaking French to each other over her head, and then were gone, closing ranks again without noticing. Kit stared after them, thinking that while you might feel conspicuous in a place like this, it didn't necessarily mean that you were. Except maybe to handbill distributors and pickpockets.

She headed up Charing Cross Road without any real destination in mind. Was it now time to wonder what Ed would have made of her adventures, or non-adventures? That was what you were supposed to do when you were having your first major episode as a single after ten years of marriage, wasn't it – wonder what your ex-spouse would say? Sure. Fate even dictated it, Fate or lashings of serendipity, by providing a timely handbill distributor to make sure that you spent no more than an hour not thinking about your ex-spouse and your ex life.

OK, Imaginary Ed. Strictly-in-my-head Ed. Do your stuff, she thought, pausing to stare through the window of a stationery store without really seeing anything but her own forlorn reflection. She managed to conjure an image of Ed standing just behind her, looking exasperated and bored. *Come on, Ed,* she prodded him silently. *You always used to have something to say about everything.*

In her inner eye, Ed's non-existent reflection rolled its equally imaginary eyes. *Oh, leave me alone, already – you divorced me to get away from my pronouncements. So give me a goddamn rest, why don't you?*

Startled, she turned around quickly, thinking that by some incredible synchronicity of events, Ed had decided to take a vacation in London as well, and had appeared behind her at exactly the right – or wrong – moment. But the face she found herself staring into wasn't Ed's; there was a superficial resemblance around the nose and mouth but that was all. The hair was completely different.

'Yes?' the man asked, and she realized he was also about fifteen years younger than Ed.

'Nothing. Sorry. I thought you were my e – someone I knew.' She brushed past him in embarrassment, moving quickly toward another shop, any shop further along, lunging for the first door she could see through a break in the endless streams of people going the other way.

Murder One, read the sign overhead. She was in a bookstore. She moved forward, past the display dumps offering her multiple Colin Dexters, to amble along the table where new hardbacks waited in uneven piles, their dustjackets blaring promises that sounded all too familiar. Strange, she thought, how everything seemed to make the same promises, whether it was a book, a movie, a fabric softener, a piece of candy. Or, yes, a relationship. Or a marriage. Maybe that was a kind of naturally occurring cosmic metaphor for marriage: you'll be on the edge of your seat; excitement every moment; prepare to be thrilled, terrified, changed for ever; you'll sleep with the lights on; you'll never look at the world in the same way again.

A rather large proportion of these, she noticed, involved serial sex killers in their promises, which seemed to be a new and rather unsettling development. Or maybe it was just that she was in a bookstore called Murder One. After all.

Still, if no one had ever gone broke underestimating the public taste or intelligence, then there was no telling how much money was to be made by combining something like the Twinkie Defence with the sweet tooth and coming up with Chocolate Cocoa Marshmallow Crunchies, Breakfast of Killers. The Serial Killers' Cereal. She suppressed thinking about the obvious pun. Good right out of the box. And no more absurd than, say, a club called Planet of the Exes.

She had reached the rear of the store now, where a slight man with very curly, greying black hair and sculpted features was talking with another man sitting behind a desk in an area so crowded with file folders, boxes of books, and stacks of paper that she couldn't see any way for him to get out.

'Everyone said her last book was an extended metaphor,' said the slight man. He was wearing a sweatshirt with the mysterious letters *pcl* on the left side.

'Yes,' said the man behind the desk, looking over the tops of his glasses. 'But I have to ask, a metaphor for what?'

Probably marriage, Kit thought. The two men turned to look at her in surprised curiosity. Horrified, she realized she had actually spoken aloud. Neither man seemed upset that she had crashed their conversation, but she was horrified all the same, especially when she realized that they were waiting for her to explain further. The one behind the desk opened his mouth to say something and she fled.

She hurried across the street, barely cheating death in the form of a taxi painted to advertise Snickers, and disappeared into the first vaguely side-street-like avenue she could find. Or hoped she disappeared. *Embarrassed the hell out of myself*, she thought bitterly, *just really stupid, what an asshole, now I can't ever come back here, they'll remember me, Brits have memories that go back centuries, they're still burning Guy Fawkes in effigy –*

Then she forced herself to stop and leaned against the wall to catch her breath. Now, what had *that* been all about – *really* all about? How many thousands of times in the past had she talked to strangers without a qualm? It wasn't like she'd ever been a prisoner of her own shyness, but she'd been acting funny ever since –

Yeah, ever since that weird guy had come up to her on the street and handed her a free ticket to Planet of the Exes. It was as if he had stripped her naked or put a mark on her forehead. Or both.

'Lucky guess,' she muttered to herself. 'Maybe.'

But now she had to go there, of course. She had to go to the Planet of the Exes and see what it was that had suggested *her* to the handbill distributor. Maybe there was someone there who looked like her. Or maybe he thought she looked like his own ex-wife. Maybe he'd just wanted to pick her up, and was counting on her being curious enough to go so he could buy her a drink?

If so, she thought acidly, she'd let him buy her a drink, but only so she could throw it in his face.

She found the card folded neatly in half in her trouser pocket and retraced her steps back to Charing Cross Road. Except it didn't look the same now. There was a theatre she knew to look for, and there it was, but in a completely different spot, at a different angle than she had been expecting. *Had* she retraced her steps, or had she gotten turned around while she'd been catching her breath and ruminating on her possible status as a bearer of the modern mark of Cain?

She looked down at the small map on the card. There was Charing Cross Road, or a small section of it anyway, as plain as anything…on the map. On the actual street in the actual world, she seemed to be standing a small distance up from what might have been a five- or six-way intersection – it was hard to tell whether some of the streets were actually streets, even with taxis jockeying for space on them.

Then she laughed, startling two girls with royal-blue hair the consistency of tinsel. Taxi. Of course. Taxis, the big ones, were supposed to know every single street in London, and they had to take you if you climbed in. She managed to flag down a relatively plain black one and showed the driver the map on the card.

The driver was a worried-looking man with wispy strawberry-blond hair and lots of faded freckles. 'Someone's having you on,' he told her, leaning over from the driver's side. 'There's no such address. No such place.'

'It's a phoney map?' she said incredulously.

'Phoney or wrong. But there ain't no such place in central London called Lisle Close.'

'Then could you take me to the nearest real street to that?'

He stared at her for a moment. 'What for?'

'Maybe it's the name of a building there. Or something.'

'What, you don't believe there's no such address as Lisle Close?'

Kit fumbled, trying to think of something to say. Then she shrugged. 'I don't know.'

'Well, I *do* know, miss. But your time is your own to waste, and that's fine. Only I'm not going to waste your money for you by riding you a few steps up Charing Cross Road.' He pointed. 'See there, up by that sign? That's Manette Street there. You want to get lost looking for a phoney address some con man's given you, turn left into Manette Street and go carefully.' He frowned at her. 'Ever think for a moment that what you've got is an invitation to a mugging? Or worse.'

She took a breath. 'I don't think so, actually. He was giving them to a lot of other people, too.'

'Accomplices,' the taxi driver said in a careless, knowing way.

'Well, I just thought I'd, you know, look. I came here to look around anyway. I know, I know – bloody tourist. Right?'

The driver shrugged. 'Have it your own way,' he said in a not-unkindly tone. 'Good luck to you, love.' He shook his head, put the cab in gear, and drove off.

She stared after him for a moment, trying to remember if she had noticed a wedding ring on his left hand, and then winced at herself. *Are you suddenly on the prowl, or are you just taking a census?* she asked herself silently. She didn't really expect an answer, which was good, because she got none.

Now she understood what the driver had meant – Manette was little more than an alleyway. It found its way narrowly between uneven rows of buildings to another, larger street, but as far as she could tell, the driver had been right. The map was a practical joke. Time to give up, find her way back to the tiny basement closet she was staying in just off the Piccalilli line, or whatever it was, and take a rest. Have tea at teatime, whatever that meant. Shop in those weird places to keep her mind off being a divorcee, and a very gullible one at that. If all else failed, she could stop in at that strange hairdressing place she'd noticed near the patisserie and see about having her hair dyed blue and made into tinsel. Hair like that would probably keep her from thinking about anything else for practically years.

Right, Ed? Only-in-my-head Ed?

For chrissakes, you divorced me so you wouldn't have to listen to my opinion, why are you asking me now?

'The perversity of human nature,' she sighed, and looked at the

Mexican restaurant that was roughly at about the spot Lisle Close was supposed to have been. Lisle Close. She should have known. The name was too British, even for London. What the hell was a 'close' anyway? Was it supposed to indicate that the buildings were close together? If so, then every street in town should have been called Close. Or maybe you were supposed to say it like *close* the door?

Maybe it was code, she thought suddenly. Or a password?

Did clubs still do that? Even really weird ones called Planet of the Exes?

Maybe she ought to try it, she thought suddenly. Walk in, wait for the maître d' or whoever and when asked if she'd be eating alone (*No, I've got my imaginary friend with me, of course*) she could say, portentously, *Lisle Close*, look wise, and hope she had chosen the correct pronunciation.

To which they would respond with something like, *Not even* close, *love. And* close *the door on your way out.*

There was a small box-office type of place just inside said door; the young man sitting behind the window had a barb through his septum and another protruding just below his bottom lip. Kit smiled at him tentatively and he smiled back, looking sunny and oddly innocent, even with the hardware.

'I think I'm lost,' she said apologetically. 'Or maybe I think, therefore I'm lost. I was looking for a place near here – ' She showed him the postcard.

His expression went from sunny innocence to sympathy. 'I see. Actually, it's downstairs.'

'Downstairs *here*?'

The guy shook his head. 'They draw the world's dodgiest maps, you know. See, it's not a street here, it's a room. Made a real pig's breakfast out of this one.'

Kit turned the card back toward herself so she could take a closer look. 'But I even saw a taxi driver take that for a road – '

'I would, too, I guess, from the way it's drawn. You'd never guess Lisle Close is the one who runs it, would you now?'

'Nope,' she said, laughing a little. She should probably just go back to her little-bitty room and see what was on Sky TV.

'Well, go ahead down,' he said, gesturing at the stairs. 'Be careful, they're a bit on the narrow side. Not got great big shoes now, have you?' He leaned forward to peer down at her feet. 'Nah. Good. Otherwise I'd have to warn you to step down the stairs sideways, like, because there's just no room on 'em for platforms.'

'You're very kind,' she said, tucking the card back in her pocket as she moved toward the stairs.

'You're welcome,' he said brightly. 'Have a good time.'

A cellar, Kit thought, *does not make a planet*. It did, however, have a nice bar.

It ran almost the length of the room and managed to look very British yet somehow suggest Mexican. There was no one else in the room, except for one plump woman whom Kit recognized as a Goth. She was moving around behind the bar doing preparatory things with glasses and bottles and more glasses.

God, Kit thought, *I'm so chic and hip I've managed to be the first person to land on the Planet of the Exes. This evening, anyway.*

She cleared her throat. 'Um, excuse me – '

The woman looked up from a sheet of paper she had been frowning at. Without a word, she pointed to Kit's left. The room was dark but in the light from the bar Kit made out a door labelled *This Way to the Egress*.

'Uh-huh,' she said. 'The egress, eh?' Oh, yeah. That was it. They were playing Fleece-the-Gullible-Tourist and she was It. She turned back toward the stairs.

'No, really,' the Gothic bartender said in a sincere tone that reminded Kit of the nice pierced man upstairs. 'It's through there. It really is.'

Kit hesitated; then she went over and opened the door slowly and carefully, ready to jump back if anything leapt out and tried to grab her. Nothing did, unless you counted the sound of many people socializing, chatting and laughing over the background noise of clinking glasses and tastefully vague instrumental music.

'Oh,' she said, and looked in. She could see, at the end of a short but very dark hallway, another room, a private function type of room, filled with people holding drinks in one hand and hors d'oeuvres in the other. There wasn't anything terribly ex-y about them that she could discern, but maybe, Kit thought, she just wasn't close enough. She looked back at the bartender.

'Do I just – go in?'

The woman nodded. 'That's what they all do.'

'Thanks.' Kit tiptoed down the hallway, feeling her way along the walls to catch herself in case she tripped over something. *Like what – some ex's body? Or some ex's ex's body?*

She emerged at the entrance to the room to hear a terribly jazzy and unmistakably retro instrumental arrangement of 'The Girl from Ipanema'. 'God,' she whispered to herself in awe. This wasn't just a cocktail party – this was *The* Cocktail Party, *The* Cocktail Party of Myth, Legend, and Proverb, where everyone drank Martinis and the only music was a series of variant arrangements of 'The Girl from Ipanema'.

'Children?'

She looked up. The tall man with the tray was dressed like a waiter, but instead of drinks or hors d'oeuvres, there were slips of paper fanned out in artful, multicoloured semicircles. 'Excuse me?' she asked, bewildered.

'Are you an ex with children or without?' the man said and nodded at the tray. The slips of paper, she saw, were small stickers; some read KIDS, others, NO KIDS.

'Oh,' she said, and winced. 'That's rather – I don't know. Like the way you'd describe a car – standard shift or automatic. You know?'

'Actually, I don't know,' the man said politely. 'But the guests here do tend to like being able to know whom they can talk to about divorce issues involving children. If you see what I mean.'

'Ah – it's more like a warning label,' she said, selecting a NO KIDS sticker and applying it to her right shoulder. The man took the backing from her and tucked it into a pocket.

'In your case, most definitely, I would imagine. The bar, as you can see, is over there. I hope you like Martinis, they're particularly good here.'

'Is that all you serve?' she asked anxiously as he started to walk away.

He paused. 'Oh, no. We serve lots of things. But Martinis are the only things they serve well.'

Kit moved uncertainly through the room, unsure of herself. People stood in little groups of threes and fours, sometimes as many as five. None of them spoke to her but she saw them all look pointedly at the NO KIDS sticker. It was hard to tell what sort of reaction she was getting. She felt as if she were wearing something that was a cross between a scarlet letter and a designer label. Most of the expressions were neutral. A few people turned away with stony faces, however, and all of them, without exception, were wearing KIDS stickers. Maybe it was some kind of status thing. *Real Exes Have Kids*, or something.

She reached the bar and took a space between a woman in a purple chiffon cocktail dress and a man in a dark suit. The bartender saw her immediately and came over. He looked like a standard-issue bartender from Central Casting.

'Martini?'

'Um . . . what else is there?'

He gestured. 'A whole bar's worth of whatever. You want a white wine spritzer instead?'

'God, no.' Kit shuddered.

'You tell 'im, babe,' said the woman in the purple chiffon cocktail dress.

'How about rum and Coke?' she said.

'Coming up,' the bartender said cheerfully.

Kit turned to smile at the woman and sneaked a look at her sticker. NO KIDS. 'You'll be sorry,' the woman said, sipping her own drink, which seemed to be a Martini. The glass was a classic Martini type of glass anyway, except that it was half as deep and twice as wide.

'Excuse me?'

'I *said*, you'll be sorry.' She didn't sound British, but then she wasn't quite slurring her words, either.

'What about?'

'About your drink.' She jerked her chin at something past Kit's right shoulder; Kit turned to find the bartender setting a rather small glass in front of her on a coaster. There was a less-than-crisp wedge of lime stuck on the rim.

'Three pounds,' he said cheerfully.

Kit handed it over apprehensively and picked up the glass. The woman didn't say anything else, so she tasted it.

'Love in a rowboat, right?'

Kit made a face. 'Well, it's pretty bad. The Coke's flat – '

'Yeah, what I said. Love in a rowboat. Fucking near water, that is. You can't water Coke that much and have it not go flat.' She definitely wasn't British, Kit decided.

'Which is their way of telling me to drink Martinis?'

The woman toasted her with what was left in her glass and finished it in a gulp.

'I *hate* Martinis. They taste like gasoline.'

'Tasted one lately? Anytime AD, that is?' The woman accepted a near instantaneous replacement from the bartender. 'AD – After Divorce. They'll taste better to you. Lots of things taste better After Divorce.' She dug in a tiny beaded handbag on the bar, came up with a pack of cigarettes, and offered them to Kit with a smile.

Kit fled to the other end of the bar, leaving her drink to its fate. She would have a club soda and then, if no one interesting to talk to appeared, she would slip out the way she had come in. Maybe ersatz-Mexican joints with Goth bartenders drew a better class of barfly.

This bar, however, was bigger than she had realized. What she had thought was the end was actually a curve; the bar made a curve and extended farther back – much farther back than she would have thought just from seeing it where she had first come in. It was like a whole other room back here – there were just as many people, but the sound of talking was livelier without being too much louder. Best of all, she could barely hear 'The Girl From Ipanema'.

She made her way through a loose group of men and women who seemed to be having a much better time than the woman in the purple chiffon dress, and found an empty stool at the bar. Sighing, she slid on to it, feeling her knees and ankles thank her. It was the first time she had sat down in hours, she realized.

The bartender who came over to her here was a woman about her own age, with hair an exaggerated but not unattractive red. 'You look like a margarita drinker.'

'Frozen,' Kit agreed. 'With salt.'

The woman winked at her and slipped off.

'Maybe *you* can settle this,' said a female voice behind her, and Kit turned around. Two women and a man from the group she had come through to the bar had adjusted their positions so as to open one side of it up to include her.

'Well, I – '

'Ah. I see you're a *NO KIDS*,' said the woman. 'Even better.' She was a handsome woman with dark hair and fair skin, and her sticker said *KIDS*. 'I've just been saying that if I'd had no kids, *I* wouldn't bother getting married – if I had it to do over again, you understand – and so when the relationship ended, I'd just walk out and there wouldn't have been all this messy divorce stuff to deal with.'

'And *I* say that everyone needs closure,' put in the second woman. Her hair was the same shade of red as the bartender's, and her sticker was *NO KIDS*. 'Divorce is as much a ritual as the marriage ceremony, and people need ritual.'

The man standing between them gave her a charming smile. 'I'm just the referee here,' he said, laughing a little.

Kit laughed with him. 'Well,' she said. 'Well. There is also the matter of legal protection – '

The group gave a sort of tidal-like surge in her direction and swallowed her.

Some time later, she found herself beached at a table too small for the group using it – six people? Eight people? More? Kit wasn't sure. At least none of them smoked, although there were times when she could have sworn some of them were about to pull out cigarettes. Maybe some of them were slipping off to some designated smoking area from time to time – the faces around her changed gradually over a period of time, but how often, or even what the period of time was, she couldn't have said. There was something pleasantly limbo-like about this place; something in the atmosphere made you feel as if time was suspended here, like you had stepped into some place where the intermission sign was permanently on.

When she discovered that her watch had stopped, all she could do was laugh. Another brilliant demonstration of synchronicity, she thought, synchronicity with a dash of irony. Not to mention those lashings of serendipity –

The topics of conversation bounced, revolved, rebounded, occurred, recurred, were dropped and then picked up later in some association. Kit couldn't keep track of everything that she talked about, or listened to, or who she was with at the time. It was all very eclectic, at least in the beginning, but somehow it always came around to divorce or divorce issues. Everyone in the world seemed to be either married, divorced, or remarried. With kids or not. Somewhere between what might have been her fourth and her fifth margaritas, Kit had an idea and turned to the man next to her, whom she thought she might be developing a crush on, if it was the man who had been talking about Roald Dahl and Patricia Neal earlier. Sometimes it was hard to tell.

'Don't you think,' she said, putting a hand on his forearm, 'that it's rather limiting just to divide people up as being married or divorced, with kids or not?'

Somehow, she had spoken during one of those lulls that sometimes falls into several neighbouring conversations simultaneously; her voice came out a little too loud and she was dismayed to find that she sounded slightly inebriated.

'What do you mean, "limiting"?' the man said after an excruciating pause.

Kit all but snatched her hand back. This wasn't the guy she liked; it couldn't be. The one she had been getting fond of didn't have that what-the-hell-is-with-*you* expression. At least, she didn't think he did.

'I mean, that, well, don't you think people are more than just – ' she looked around at the group. They were staring at her as if she were speaking in tongues or something. ' – people are more than just husbands and wives? Or someone's *ex*-husbands and *ex*-wives?'

People were trading glances as if she had suggested the world was in reality flat and had assumed they would all agree.

Finally, the woman who had spoken to her in the first place cleared her throat. 'Maybe that's true when you're ten years old, love. But you're on the Planet of the Exes now.'

They were all staring at her. She stared back, puzzled. 'That's a joke, right?'

'There are lots of funny things about divorce,' said a man across from her. Maybe *he* was the one she had been getting to like. 'But none of it's a joke.'

'I see,' she said, and started to get up. 'Excuse me.'

The man next to her caught her arm. 'Where are you going?'

'It's been lovely talking with all of you, but I think it's definitely time for me to go home now.'

'*Go* home?' someone said, and they all laughed quietly.

'Or *leave* home,' she said evenly. The margaritas were making her courageous, but at this point she didn't care where it was coming from. 'I've done that before.'

'Listen, my love,' said a gorgeous older woman with steel-coloured hair. Her sticker said KIDS in larger letters than Kit had seen on anyone else. 'Once you're married, that's it. You can be formerly married, but you're never *un*married again. It's like trying to get your virginity back.'

More laughs.

'And *I'm* saying that's fine, but that's not the only way to describe a person,' Kit insisted.

'Well, it's your legal designation, for the rest of your life,' said a young man with a ginger beard. 'Single, married, divorced, widowed. Try finding a form to fill out that doesn't have those boxes to check on it. Bet you can't.'

'That's not *all* I am,' Kit said, starting to feel a bit panicky. The man next to her wouldn't let go of her arm.

'Well, *actually*,' said a pretty blonde woman, and then giggled, covering her mouth with one hand.

Kit twisted out of the man's grip and backed away from the table. She bumped into another man standing near the bar who put both hands on her shoulders, perhaps only to steady her. But it felt more like he meant to hold on and she had a sudden vision of herself in five or ten or fifteen years' time, a regular at the Planet of the Exes. If not an outright gargoyle like the woman in the purple chiffon dress, then an ex in sheep's clothing, offering conversation that turned to quicksand –

She started to flee again, just as she had from almost everyone else she had met that day, and then forced herself to stop. Deliberately, she brushed the man's hands from her shoulders, first the left, then the right, and walked quickly but unhurriedly up the length of the bar to the curve. It felt like miles, and everyone she passed stared at her, some scandalized, others only puzzled. She made herself look back, and while she didn't exactly stare anyone down, it wasn't anywhere near as gruelling as she would have thought.

After what felt like an hour, she came to the curve in the bar and followed the turn around. In her peripheral vision, she saw the bartender put one of those overly wide and too-shallow Martini glasses on a coaster, and she knew she could have it if she wanted it. She kept moving. The woman in the purple chiffon dress was still sitting in the same place. Eyebrows arched, she held out the pack of cigarettes again.

Almost to the door, Kit thought, and kept going. The tall man was standing there, offering his tray to a lost-looking man who had just walked in. Both of them were staring at her. She nodded at each of them and then, as she passed, removed the NO KIDS sticker, tore it in half and left the pieces on the tall man's tray. Then she was in the dark hallway and out the other side, in the ersatz-Mexican bar again.

The Gothic bartender looked at her in surprise. 'Leaving so soon?'

Kit didn't bother looking at her watch. She knew it had begun running again and she knew it would be showing the correct time. 'Yeah. Not my kind of place.' She paused on her way over to the stairs. 'How long do people usually stay?'

The woman shrugged. 'I wouldn't know. You're the only one's ever come out the same way you went in. They must all go out the other door.'

'What other door?' Kit asked.

'Whatever. They must have another door.' The woman laughed. 'I mean, everyone who goes in there, they can't just *stay* there, can they?'

'I bet you'd be surprised,' Kit said, and went up the stairs.

Consummation
Conrad Williams

Wherever there was fire, she would drift towards it. It didn't matter if it was the starved flare of a match or something wilder. Any flame drew her, as though fire existed purely as her invocation. A promise of warmth and light that had previously been missing from her life. Perhaps I say this because fires meant a great deal to me too. They were my meal ticket and sometime confidants. How many times, as dusk slung its ochre cloak across the village, did I fuel the bonfires on my plot with whispered purgings scraped from the bitterest reaches of my mind? Darkness would take these ribbons of smoke, turning them to ghosts as they fled to the moors, bearing away my regret like rain.

People bring me their waste. *Burn this for me*, they ask. *Lose this.* They bring me uneaten meals congealing on paper plates. Dead pets taped into cardboard shoeboxes. They bring newspapers and ancient clothes in plastic carrier bags. I burn it all for them. I reduce the matter that makes them who they are to ash. Doing this lessens the faith I have in the people I meet and talk to. They become insubstantial as I burn their skins. They stand before me pink and fresh and renewed, talking of the future and how clearing their lives of clutter, tokens from the past, has cleansed them, given them a vacuum to fill with new experiences. I take envelopes from them filled with photographs and love letters. I burn their promises or threats of fidelity.

The first time I saw her, she was stumbling across the cuesta under a slow, crepuscular bleed. In her hand she was clutching a scrap of cloth as though it were a lifeline to heaven. She looked dazed, pale as the swatches of wool snagged on barbed wire surrounding the fields. Her dress was torn up one side; the gash revealed a band of pink fabric clinging to her left hip as she strode. Her other hand jerked up to her face every few seconds and fluttered there, a moth in distress. There was blood on her arm, a little more plashed across the cream V of her chest.

'Ho there. Lost?' I said, for want of a better.

She snapped her head up at me. 'Of course I'm fucking lost. Stupid fuck.'

Her hand whipped spastically to her mouth as though she were feeding herself titbits from her eye or, perhaps, from shock at her language. She paused and, leaning over, vomited casually, wiping her lips with the back of her hand on finishing. When she saw I was preparing a bonfire, she moved towards me. I'd been aroused by the violence of her language and moved to accommodate her, noticing in the fragmenting light how the right side of her face was twitching and sweating, its vermicelli veins in a grey-green riot against the skin.

She watched me from the juicy pulp of the eye sunken into this chaos as I snapped twigs and shaped the pyre. The sea was a non-committal blade of cobalt, arcing into the handle formed by the jut of headland far to the west. The sea was the flat colour of dead thoughts.

We didn't speak again until I had touched a match to the kindling. In those few seconds when the dry bundle of fuel took to the flame, she seemed to swell, a coral immersed. I imagined her absorbing the light and heat, feeding off it. Her face was twisted even further by the cruel spit of shadows, yet she was already relaxing into the moment and I could tell that whatever had seized her features was lessening, withdrawing beneath the skin.

'I feel very strange,' she said. 'I feel like something taken out of storage.'

'You don't look too clever, I have to admit,' I said.

'I'll look better, you wait.' She jutted her chin out. 'This,' she said, gesturing to the livid warp of her face, 'this is a cluster headache. Ten times worse than a migraine. Make your hangovers feel like a high.'

'Is that why you feel strange, then?' I asked. The fire was drawing me in. Caught between her and the flame, I was lost as to how I should share my attention. But the fire, always the fire won. I glared into its brilliant weft, marvelling at the way it would ripple and re-form itself into a sheet and then diminish as though the ground were inhaling the blaze into itself before bloating again. There is nothing like fire. It rages, seemingly more substantial than anything it comes into contact with, yet it is in constant flux, toying with the air, a ghost.

She had spoken and I'd missed it.

'Sorry?'

'I said that the headaches are only a part of it. I feel spent, like I've been asleep too long.'

'What's your name?'

'Laugh and you'll be sucking on those ashes.'

'No. I won't laugh. Go on.'

'Ligeia. Ligeia Mutch.'

'Jesus,' I said.

She stayed until the fire had burned down to indistinguishable remains. Sometimes she'd be so motionless and quiet that I'd forget she was there. When she spoke, I'd wonder at how I could have ignored her. As darkness fell, so the tension in her face withdrew, allowing her face to find its natural cast. Her eye still leaked and appeared sore.

'I'm always so cold,' she said.

'Where do you live?'

She looked at me blankly and didn't answer. The fire dwindling, she seemed to lose interest and moved away, her confusion still apparent.

'Where will you go?' I called out. 'I thought you were lost.' No answer.

She sank into the dark like something absorbed. I wanted to say something, to ask if she would like to have supper with me, but it would have felt perverse. I didn't know her; she didn't even know herself.

I left the embers seething; looking back at them half-way up the hill, they resembled a sprinkling of spice on a cut of black cloth. A row of cottages rose out of the gloom, white fronts writhing. The living-room window of my own was a block of soft pink. A thin, sour paste bound itself to the roof of my mouth as I fumbled with the keys.

I entered the room, expecting her to be gone, but she still clung on, despite the lack of anything to live for. I sat by the bed and took Helen's hand. Her face appeared famished and hollow in the light, tiny purple veins sprawled across her forehead. Her eyes fixed on me and I detected moments of the old Helen move across her vision, like breaks in cloud cover.

I talked to her for a long time, long after she began to cry. I gave her some medication, kissed her on the mouth, then pulled back the sheet and bit her breast. No response.

Upstairs, I masturbated in the shower and thought of Ligeia. She merged with Helen, until they were a seamless being, the perfect parts of them I was drawn to knitting together to form an imperfect Prometheus. Ligeia's small, bird-bone hands. Helen's thick, steak-red mouth. Ligeia's blanched eyes. Helen's hair, blonde and bountiful.

Helen, in the days before she ended us, had been flourishing like a freshly planted flower. Under the sun of a new lover, she was opening up while I was cast away like a corrupted seed rotting in a mulch of shadows. She moved around our home, chased by sunlight, opening up room after room to the scouring winds of a new beginning. Yet she could not dislodge me, no matter how vigorous her cleansing. I was the part of her past that would not yield to her dustpan and brush.

'But we're finished, Ben,' she sang, one morning in that lalling voice of hers as she prepared to go out to meet this new man. 'We're finished.' She said it in the same way a person might point out the first robin of winter. In the inexorable, she would discern no understanding of pain. She anticipated my refreshment too in her banishment of me from her life.

'But I don't want us to be finished. I want us to be married. I want us to be for ever.'

She had laughed. Her back to me, naked, she bent effortlessly from the waist to slide open a drawer. Her neat little cunt split gummily open like a horse chestnut spilling its oaken centre. Sunlight painted dull stripes along the meat of her thighs. The dipped horizon of her buttocks became a well into which seven years of my past had vanished. She had absorbed me, she carried all the vigour I had spent upon her in that time. A few tears on her part might have been enough to satisfy my poor, bastard soul.

'You don't care,' I said, redundantly.

'Not any more, no. I'm sorry.' She straightened and turned the top half of her body so that her right breast swung lazily into view, its peak quivering at the termination of her movement as it had in those long, glutinous hours when I'd gripped the generous base and squeezed her stiffened tip towards my mouth. Our lovemaking had degenerated into a series of accidental collisions as we tipped out of sleep, reaching for the remnants of our fantasies. In every kiss, she bore a code of distance in her spittle. The soft suck of her body became a wasteland. At her climax, one hand would grip me tightly while the other would be pressed against my chest, pushing me away.

That I was never going to have her in any capacity other than a sour memory made me feel sick.

'Who is this man you've met? Why haven't I been introduced?'

The first stirrings of anger. She wouldn't even feel bad about this; she was justified in a light rage, she'd been so patient with me. I saw how easy it would be to grab her by the throat and press my thumbs into that suprasternal notch where I had lapped at her during her gurgling climaxes. Squeeze until her windpipe collapsed; the sound of a polystyrene carton giving way.

'Ben, we are finished. We will *never* sleep together again. Enjoy this show now, because this is the last time you'll see me naked. I have fallen in love with another man. You don't need to meet him. He has nothing whatsoever to do with you. He is everything to me.'

'Why couldn't it have been me?' There, I'd done it. The first yield, the first question that was an acceptance of what had happened. The child's question, the recourse to 'me'. Sensing that she'd gained control, her anger levelled and she smiled at me, not without warmth.

'We tried, love,' she said. 'But it takes two happy people to make a relationship. I'm not happy with you and if you search yourself a little bit, you'll realize that you weren't happy with me either. It'll come to you, eventually.' She came to me, her arm shielding her breasts, her black briefs making a no-entry sign of her body. With her free hand she ruffled my hair. She kissed my cheek and I smelled all the ghosts of our hours locked together come screaming at me out of her hair. Never had she looked more desirable. She was content with the detour of our conversation. She could sense closure, she could sense a Hollywood ending. Music swells as she finishes dressing. A pause as she turns at the door, a hand raised and is that a tear, right on cue, a moistening of the eyes as she gazes at me fondly?

'I wish you well, Ben,' she says.

Fade to black.

Four months later Helen slipped during a walk by the cliff's edge. She and her new man had been drinking wine most of the afternoon, a cosy picnic on the bluff. Tartan blanket, wicker basket, all the usual clichés. If I hadn't been there watching them, I might never have seen Helen again. I did what I had to do and within half an hour I was powering my Volvo through country lanes, trying to keep the RAF helicopter in view as it transported Helen to hospital.

The top five vertebrae in her neck had been crushed, compacted like one of those plastic collapsible Evian bottles. She was in a coma for three weeks and when she came out of it, there weren't too many people around who believed she'd make much of a recovery. The general consensus was that she'd be in a persistent vegetative state for the rest of her life.

Are you the husband? they asked me. I told them I was her fiancé. Over the weeks we talked about what should happen. They suggested switching off life support but I was against that. I'd look after her, I told them. Smiles all round. One of the nurses kissed me.

I watched as Helen emerged from the mire of near-death. She yawned often – just a primitive reflex, the doctors opined – but it made her look more real than I'd seen her since she had been carted senseless on endless journeys from CAT scans to the operating theatre to Intensive Care. Yawning softened her features and made her look like the woman I used to wake up next to. At any moment she would sleepily open her eyes. A clotted murmur: 'Cuppa tea, toast 'n' jam. Gizza kiss.'

Layer after layer, the coma was sloughed off. She responded when the doctor pinched her clavicle, twitching her head toward the pain. Her eyes blinked when the doctor thrust his fingers at them. By late summer she was opening her eyes when she was asked to. Slowly, she returned.

She was paralysed from the neck down. I was taught how to keep her limbs active, to prevent them from withering. I learned the best way of washing her without expending too much energy or putting my back at risk. Never leave her alone, they said. She could easily choke. They installed an alarm system in my living room when we got her home. I could be summoned from anywhere in the house if she triggered it with her chin when she needed me. As soon as the nurses and the doctor left, I dismantled the alarm, fucked her gelid, unresponsive carcass and went up to the Postern Gate to get mortal. It was a satisfying time.

But now, Ligeia.

I couldn't stop thinking of her. I took to walking the gravel beaches around the village and down in this natural wind-trap, the only sign of life being the church steeple rising above the bluff and the treacly black remains of my own beach fires, I would consider gambits and entreaties that I recognized would never pass my lips, envisaged couplings that could only ever remain blueprints for the masturbation sessions I undertook in my own house. I believed she was too separated from my own life to become a part of it. *I* was too separated from my own life, for God's sake.

A slew of copper leaves skirled into my path from the trees fringing the coastline above me. The trees appeared shocked by something, branches flung back in horror, away from the raging winds that swept in from the North Sea. All along the coast, the trees were balding; the village losing its shield against the sea's bite. It would be a cold winter.

Up ahead, a twin helix of smoke rose from behind a shoulder of rock, stroked away to nothing as soon as it met the wind. I picked my way over the stones, trying unsuccessfully not to make too much noise, and saw Ligeia Mutch, naked, hunched over a pathetic nest of twigs, trying to get a flame to hatch.

Horrified, I hobbled over to her, shrugging the fearnought from my shoulders. Even through a heavy coir jumper and my thermal underclothes I could feel the bitter reach of October as it bid for my flesh. She must be numb, on the verge of hypothermia, but when she saw me approaching, she smiled sheepishly and shrugged. At first I thought this was due to being seen in a state of undress, but then I realized it was because of the pitiable condition of her bonfire. She must be hallucinating, I thought, as I thrust the coat at her, my cheeks burning at the sight of her kindling-thin limbs.

'I'm okay,' she said, but took the coat and eased it on, probably more to rescue me from my embarrassment than assuage the cold she must undoubtedly be feeling.

I picked a way through the rocks, pausing occasionally to make sure she was following. Her hair was streaming in the wind like a shredded standard and I was affected again by her famished state. Even though she was swaddled, she looked little more than a stain in the air.

As I made to move off, I noticed she was trying to say something.

'Fire,' she murmured, her voice barely carrying on a wisp of steam from her lungs. 'Make me a fire.'

'Later,' I said. 'We're going to get you dressed, get something warm to drink.'

I led her up the steep cobbled lifeboat ramp by the harbour. A couple wearing bright yellow raincoats held hands as they stood on the harbour wall, looking out to the North Sea. They were the only people we saw on the way to the pub but seeing them made me hang back and take Ligeia's hand, wishing I'd done so earlier when she'd needed it. I thought of Helen at the beginning, how she had asked me to cuddle her for a change as we lay in bed. 'You're a bull, stampeding all the time,' she'd said, not without affection in those days.

In the pub, William, the manager, gave me an askance look when he saw the state of my companion but he didn't say anything. I was burning bags of photographs he had taken with a hidden camera over the last ten years of his barmaids changing for work in the utility room, or on rare occasions, taking their boyfriends back there for handjobs or quickies against the safe. Why he hadn't burned them himself, I couldn't fathom. Perhaps he came to me for some kind of silent absolution. I never judged anybody by the contents they wanted torching.

I bought Ligeia a cup of sweet coffee and we sat by the window.

The gravel bay swept out under separate concertina rock faces pressed into each other. Where they met, a giant split had formed. From here, I noticed uneasily, it looked like a huge vagina. The sea spent itself on the leading edge of rocks, grey spume dribbling into shore, carrying dead birds and drinks cartons, empty bottles of engine oil and plastic netting. I could see redshanks, woodcocks and jack snipes picking through this soup. Later I would comb the beach and build a fire of this jetsam. I wouldn't feel comfortable until I had reduced the real to ash. Somehow it made me feel more alive.

'I wanted to go for a walk in the woods,' Ligeia said. 'I was at the edge of the trees, about to go in, but I couldn't. As soon as it seemed I was entering the first fringe there, I would be emerging into light, having turned round without realizing it.'

I tried to soothe her and offered to take her there myself but this seemed merely to distress her even more. I felt a sudden, staggering sense of coercion but from a source I couldn't pinpoint. Here I was, sitting with a woman I didn't know, my coat around her shoulders, already the two of us involved in her uncertainties. I cared but I didn't know why. Surely it wasn't Ligeia who was influencing me; she was too concerned with her meandering to understand the new set of codes that were now governing her life and mine. Determined, I gripped her hand. 'Drink that, then we're going for a walk. To the woods.'

She acquiesced quietly, her rising fear waxen in her face, resigned.

'I'm getting a headache,' she said, rubbing the stiff white flesh around her eye. 'Another bastard.'

'You'll be okay.'

Brackets of coffee at her lips when she took a last mouthful. I kissed them away. Close up, in the cold flame of her stare, I read the pain that had followed her through life. I wanted to ask her its source but I guessed she wouldn't know. She drifted, a core of hot energy, like a dust devil seeking something to latch on to. Chased by the formless shadow of her grief, she could neither codify nor clarify her situation. I imagined that she was almost grateful for her headaches, a substantive into which she could load all her free-floating anxieties.

'What do you dream of?' she asked. 'I mean, I don't want to pry. I wondered if you slept well.'

Not since meeting you, I nearly said. All my dreams were hot and airless. Into them she would sail, her body fragmented and billowing like torn sheets. I would lean into her, my body tight and swollen with need, but there was nothing for me to grab hold of, no hook to keep me close. The dream would disintegrate, Ligeia spinning away from me, and I would be pressed down into the black, feeling its impacted granularity cosy up against me, filling my nose, my mouth with soil. Eyes too, but not before I glimpsed the pale, sightless eyes of my malformed neighbours; babies reaching out to me through the earth.

'I dream of being buried,' I said. 'Come on, we can talk while we walk.'

I borrowed a pair of wellington boots from William, and Ligeia slipped them on. Outside we struck out across the gravel shore aiming for the thick nest of trees just visible above the bluff. Ligeia didn't attempt to turn back.

'I dream of being buried too,' she said. 'And sometimes I seem to find another layer of sleep. An even deeper sleep that gives me faded scenes of childhood, in this very village, only there are tall ships with large sails that come into the harbour. And postmen who deliver on horses.' She laughed. 'When I'm awake. Times like now, I can't remember anything of my youth. Funny, isn't it?'

Her humour sank back into the collapse of her face. Her eye had become an ember, puckering the flesh around it. At any moment I fancied it would burst into flame.

'Only dreams,' I said softly, squeezing her hand.

Twenty feet away from the woods, she closed her eyes and allowed herself to be led. Her breathing slowed; at the end of every exhalation, a thick buzz of sound came from the pit of her chest as though there were something animal there that wanted to be set free. I thought I saw the affected half of her face actually lift from the boss of her skull. Her cluster headaches were like sandfish, flat against her skin, indistinguishable from the surface colour and texture. They were poised, ready to wind the flesh of her head tight around the eye of its violence. It was hard to reconcile the lurch of her mask of pain with the open, fresh creature that wore it.

Five minutes or so into the wood, the air turning spiced with pine, the light becoming a leaden coating for the trees, I asked her how she felt.

'Hollow,' she said, her voice as light as a child's. 'Old.'

It was cold and uncomfortable on the floor, but we fucked. At one point, just before she opened her eyes and loosed a chill, cloacal breath across my face, her fingers scorched a trail across my chest. I pressed her back into the loam and she sank into it. In a second I was kneeling on pine needles, seed jetting thickly from my cock, my hands splayed against an area where her breasts had yielded beneath them. And where her raging eye had been, a white flower stood proud, a blood-red stamen at its core.

I sat Helen up in the bed, spending patient minutes trying to stop her head from lolling over on to her wasted chest. I couldn't be bothered mopping up the drool. Now she could see him. Her dentures oozed from her peeling lips like maggots questing from carrion. I went to him, splayed across the chair, and combed the crisp remains of his hair. What didn't come off in the teeth fell back against the purple-green expanse of his taut, shiny head. On the day of the accident, I had tried to burn him but aborted when he wouldn't catch. I had stopped coating him with varnish some weeks ago and he was beginning to spoil. It was easier to look him in the face now that his eyes had liquefied. I left them for a while and walked through the village to the harbour. Boats rode fast swells belting in from afar, powered by the black band of cloud pressing from the horizon. A shock of wind at my face. I stood there a long time, until the storm swung in across me, drenching me in a second. A minute or two later and it was gone, chased by a broad sweep of late afternoon sunlight.

An old woman emerged from the pub and clapped her hands together. She was laughing. 'Daft one. Why didn't you get out of it?' she said. 'Some steamroller that, wasn't it?' Then she went inside, clucking happily. She hadn't recognized me. Six months ago she had brought me a small cyst wrapped up in polythene. She had excised it from her armpit with a pair of scissors, too afraid to go to hospital. Her father and her husband had died under anaesthesia. She had drunk half a bottle of rum before digging it out. That it might be malignant, its roots still festering inside her, bothered her not at all. It was out – she must be okay.

I remember I had burned her cyst on Crucible Hill, overlooking the village while I ate ham sandwiches. Whenever I make a fire, I feel split in two. The front part of me is hot and dancing with light, the back like an ugly figure in an impatient queue, pressed hard against me from behind, wishing it could get in front. I love it.

The smell of her burning was like a peppery incense. I had smelled much worse.

I struck a match. As ever, the carefully constructed cone of tinder took well to the tongue of flame. I could not meet Helen's eyes and left, before the fire could reach her. I didn't look back, even as the flames grew, in my wake, lifting my shadow into a jumping, elongated sprite that drew me towards the wood. She was coming, my Ligeia, lured by the primitive heat. I would do all I could to chase the cold from those old bones of hers. I would try to make amends. But she moved past me, as if I weren't there, as if I were the stain in the air that she had seemed to me in the first few days of our acquaintance. A light smile played on her grey mouth. I watched her approach the conflagration and sit at the edge of its reach where the light met the border of night. Halved by this clash, she rocked on her haunches, eyes never leaving the blaze with its brick mask. She stayed there for ten minutes, I too, until the roof caved in and fire soared like a flare. We waited till I was sure the house would topple. Thin sirens looped into the sky as fire engines powered through the dark from the nearest town, five miles away. I said Ligeia's name maybe half a dozen times but she didn't acknowledge my presence. I had the feeling she would wait there for as long as it took. Longer. Suddenly, she sighed and clapped her hands softly. I backed away from the fire, trying to convince myself that it was the heat that was becoming unbearable, as the carbonized door gritted open and the sheet of flame behind it gathered form.

Near midnight I carry the metal box up to Crucible Hill. It was all that was left of the fire. Something Helen must have hidden away from me. I found no body. The grass here is still damp from this morning's storm but it doesn't matter; this will catch. I tip the letters and bone-dry photos, a flurry of sepia and ancient violet ink, into a hollow. Out of their box they make a pitiful mound. A corner of one photograph, showing two young women smiling, wearing petticoats and shaded by parasols, takes the flame lustily, as though it has been waiting for nothing else across the years. The flame moves in from the edges, curling the photograph into itself so that, at the last moment before it is consumed, the faces of the women are pressed together. Everything burns. It takes a minute, if that. The last thing to catch is a small card, stained by time. I can just make out a few words before blackness descends. *Darling Helen . . . love you with all . . . for ever . . . Lig . . .*

Here I'll sit, in the grass above soil packed down through the centuries, a bed for time's lovers and slayers. Here I'll sit and wait for them to come.

Mind the Gap
James Casson

On Saturday morning, the day after her eighty-second birthday, Sally Sugden looked out the bedroom window and decided that enough was enough.

'I can't be doing with this any more,' she said to no one in particular, and resolved to dress up and take a bus into Bradford to mark the change.

Striding down Heaton Park Drive, she felt a new sense of purpose and with every step some of the weight she had been carrying slipped away. Half-way down the hill a cat noticed something was different.

'Oh, so I get a smooch this morning, do I? Well, don't brush too hard, I'm keeping myself nice for morning tea.'

The incorrigible Catholic boys were smoking in their favourite corner at the end of the playing field. But instead of returning home to phone the headmaster Sally gave them all a cheery wave.

'Keep the home fires burning, boys. Just be careful you don't make yourselves impotent.'

The sun and a gentle breeze did battle with the smog and won, five sheepish boys stubbed out their Marlboros and there wasn't a trace of new dog waste on the footpath. Sally was reminded of one of those awful American car-window stickers she had seen recently, 'Today is the First Day of the Rest of Your Life', and so it was. For the first time in recent years crossing Heaton Road was a doddle and Mrs Sally Sugden was almost skipping as she made her way down Firth Street to the bus stop. She had nearly forgotten that simple pleasures could be so sweet.

But of course they're not and Sally's nemesis lay on the pavement in Wilmer Road, right by the bus stop. She felt one foot slip from under her and the other was not nimble enough to save the day. However, she didn't fall hard and it happened in slow enough motion for her to spot the banana skin and be tickled stupid at the absurdity of such a thing happening so early on the first day of the rest of her life.

Strangely she had no urge to get up but gave in to the moment and imagined how it would seem to the neighbours. Fifty-six years a respectable married woman and look at me now. Down by the waterworks in Wilmer Road, rolling around with my legs in the air, laughing my silly head off. This is me faffing around at the bus stop like a schoolgirl just about to wet her knickers and I don't even care.

Robin Kendal spotted her as he rounded the curve and weighed up whether it was safe to stop. Although a stranger in town, he knew Bradford was reputed to be dangerous. Yet she hardly looked like the decoy for a teenage gang and she may be having some kind of fit or seizure.

'Can I help at all?' A pretty inadequate response, he thought, to someone who's hysterical. 'Would you like me to call someone?'

She struggled to get him into focus and this set off new waves of mirth.

'I'm sorry, I can't stop ... it's so silly ... you must think I'm ... It was kind of you to stop ... it's all right ... I'll be all right, it's just so ... It's so ... '

Without warning the laughter turned to tears. They were the deepest sobs Robin had ever heard in his somewhat sheltered thirty-nine years. He wanted to offer her a clean white handkerchief like they did in old movies, but this was 1997 and so he retrieved a stand-by Kleenex and checked it for pocket rub.

Sally was grateful for the thought and tried to pull herself together but only managed to sit up far enough to lean against the brick wall of the waterworks.

Standing guard over the crumpled figure on the pavement, Robin thought it could have been his mum, or even his gran, except they would never carry on like this in front of him. The tears dried up and Sally sat there exhausted. She was saying something to Robin but it was in such a drained little voice he had to squat beside her to hear.

'Thank you. Don't let me hold you up. I'll just sit here for a while. Thank you.'

She reached out to take his hand in a gesture of thanks and to his surprise Robin found himself sitting alongside her on the pavement. It wasn't as though she pulled him down there. It wasn't as though she took his hand and wouldn't let go. It was, and this was the surprising part, Robin himself who had taken the decision to initiate this intimacy. Dispensing tissues and support to old ladies in distress was the compassionate act of a good Samaritan, but holding hands in silence, sitting on the footpath and enjoying the sunshine with a strange woman, was a mildly dangerous and totally new experience.

A double-decker bus, the number 680, swung round the corner and slowed down a fraction but Robin decisively waved it on. Sally closed her eyes and took stock.

Look at me holding hands with my young man. Is this what it's like to have a toy boy? It isn't a bad hand, a bit soft compared with Arthur's, but a well-intentioned hand. And very calming, which is what I need after all that silliness. But it wasn't all my fault. Deciding to make a new life and then slipping on a banana skin just confirms what I've always known. Someone up there's got a nasty sense of humour. But thank you for Sir Galahad just the same. He must think I'm quite daft, but he seems a nice young man. Quite happy to be there just for me and goodness knows that has always been a rare quality. I could tell him about Arthur, about his illness and about the guilt at feeling so much better when he died. About making a fresh start and about someone up there who sends you a banana skin to make you laugh and a kindly man to make you cry.

It took Robin a while to realize that his hand was being stroked. It was almost imperceptible but she was stroking his hand with her thumb. He tried not to think about it. Probably a post-traumatic reflex after all the crying. Quite likely little old ladies of her generation did it all the time without realizing. But it was a soft hand and a caring hand and to his great alarm Robin found himself experiencing a stirring which could hardly have been less appro-priate. Fortunately she started talking and Robin was able to think of something else.

'This isn't me at all. At least not the usual me. The normal me would have been so embarrassed she would have jumped up and brushed herself down and you would never have found her all in a heap. But today it doesn't seem to matter. If I want to fall around and see the funny side of things as well as the sad, does it really matter? It's a very unusual feeling, me not caring if I make a spectacle of myself. A bit like sliding into a nice warm bath and letting go of all the mess of the day. Perhaps dying is like that. Perhaps I fell harder than I thought. Perhaps I'm gone already, or I'm lying unconscious in Wilmer Road waiting for the ambulance.

'Am I dead? Are you anyone who appears in the literature? What happens next? Am I transported on wings of angels or do we just hail the next 680?'

And then she saw his car.

'Well, that says it all, doesn't it, the angel of death come for me in a silly little three-wheel hearse!'

And although Robin would strenuously deny having anything to do with the afterlife business, fate had brought him round the corner of Wilmer Road minutes after picking up the newest vehicle in his collection of three-wheelers, a low mileage '87 Reliant hearse.

'You're not getting me in there! I may be a little old pensioner widow lady come to an undignified end but I still know what's what. My contributions have always been up to date, so you just go back to the garage and get a proper one.'

But a group of women from the tapestry club appeared at the top of the hill and Sally was very glad to jump in the hearse and be transported, sitting not lying, back to Heaton Park Drive.

'We haven't got anything like it in Australia,' he said. 'The three-wheelers. Reliant's always been a favourite of mine. And they still make them in spite of all the changes of fashion in the last fifty years. It could only happen in Britain. And as for some enthusiast extending the Rialto van and turning it into a hearse for use on Sark, that was a masterstroke. My Dad's an Anglophile, which is probably where I get it from. When I was a kid he was always setting the alarm so we could get up and watch old Ealing comedies on late-night TV. I don't recall seeing a three-wheeler in any of them, but it's just the sort of bizarre thing you might expect. This almond tart's very nice.'

The tea flowed in Sally's kitchen and she learned that the Reliant company had been going since 1937 and Robin had actually been to the works in Staffordshire. It seemed that a lot of three-wheelers ended up in Yorkshire because they ran all day on a gallon of fuel and the locals reasoned that it was extravagant to pay good money for four tyres when three would do the job just as well. Robin was an Australian electronics engineer who worked in Lincoln. He spent all his spare time looking for offbeat three-wheelers which might grace the ground floor of the church in which he lived.

Sally had been curious whether Robin had a wife and children but the picture he painted of the church and his passionate collection of strange cars left no space for partners of either sex, let alone children. How sad, she thought, for a nice young man like this to spend his weekends in the solitary pursuit of bubble cars and the like. What awful trauma would cause a man to turn away from a normal life shared with family or friends? Bad enough to banish oneself to the other side of the world, but to become a recluse surrounded by automotive follies of the fifties was very sad. His father, the Anglophile, sounded a bit strange. Perhaps he had something to answer for.

'Well, Mr Kendal, I'm flabbergasted. I had no idea there were such goings-on in Emm Lane. Yes, I've passed the garage on many occasions and I've seen the little cars lined up out the front. But I would never have guessed it was part of such an exotic...sub-culture. Fancy, all over the North, every weekend, every day off, single-minded young men seeking out riches in places like Heaton. There's a lesson there, I'm sure. You live for eighty years in the one place and you think you know all there is to know, but it's not until fate serves you up a banana skin that some things are revealed. Now if I can persuade you to delay your return south a little longer, I might find some home-made soup and you can tell me all about Isetta, Bond, Rialto and Robin.'

So the lentil soup and the baps were defrosted and a meal was shared. Robin found himself relaxing into the fabric of the kitchen and becoming uncharacteristically talkative. It was so easy to be the life of the party with Sally opposite, totally enthralled by the tough little 848cc alloy engine's removable wet cylinder liners.

However, it was not just accounts of needle-roller swivel-pin bearings that had turned Sally into the perfect audience. She had been transported to another time, while Arthur was away, during the war. And there was another young man, one who wasn't called up because he worked in Sally's office in an essential occupation. He had a passion too, for clocks, and although married himself, his walking and talking barely masked the most painfully respectful worship of Sally.

Robin paused, concerned, that with the sliding contact-breaker points on the camshaft-driven distributor, he may have gone too far.

'Have I lost you?'

'Not at all. You actually found a part of me I thought I'd lost.'

'I get a bit wound up sometimes.'

'So do I. You reminded me of someone I haven't seen for fifty-five years. There was an unusual mood during the war. A mood that allowed things to happen that would never have done in peacetime. Young men spending their last days. Women presented with situations and opportunities that would never come again. You probably saw it all in your father's late-night movies. But I thought, Robin, and I still do, that one should never fall in love with a married man, or even one who is spoken for, if it comes to that. I know it's a double standard but it's up to women not to let it happen. He wrote me notes and took me to the cinema, we went for walks and he even issued invitations. But throughout it all he was a perfect gentleman. Yes, there was a chaste kiss or two and even a cuddle and I may have imagined I was in love with him, but it was up to me not to let anything happen.'

The place of reinforced glass-fibre in the development of the three-wheeler seemed unimportant now and Sally suggested Robin take her for a spin in the hearse up to the top of Fox Lane. If Robin had anything waiting for him in Lincoln, it was pushed aside by the chance to watch kites flying on Baildon Moor, to ride up a wooded slope in the old tramway to the top of Shipley Glen, to walk through Saltaire village and hear the story of the enlightened Titus Salt and his model mill.

As they stood on the bank of the River Aire watching the rapids she took his hand.

'Thank you, Robin, for a lovely afternoon.'

'Thank you, Sally, for showing me all these new places.'

Robin's instinct would have been to let go of her hand now that the pleasantries had been observed, particularly as she was looking at him warmly and the inappropriate feelings were stirring again. At this point the old Sally, too, would have released his hand and moved away, but the new person wanted more.

'I'm having a right good time,' she beamed at him. 'And, young Robin, I'm going to do something I've never done before in my life. Why don't we have a meal out on the terrace of the Waterman's Arms? And don't you worry about being late back to Lincoln, because I've got a bed made up in the spare room.'

'Oh.'

'Don't be shy, we're both doing things we've never done before. That's one of the advantages of a family of three-wheelers, you don't have to rush home to feed them or take them for walks.

'What do you say?'

Black pudding with onion rings, Caesar salad, leek and blue Stilton pasty, grilled trout. A pint of Theakston's for the gentleman but nothing strong for the lady because she's already high on the fantasy of things that never happened fifty-five years ago. Coffee, liqueur, why not?

Robin Kendal saw himself sitting in the gloaming, by a gently gurgling river, smiling into the mischievous eyes of a woman old enough to be his grandmother and he was amazed. What most confounded him was not the difference in their ages, but the realization that he had never done anything remotely like this before.

Sally Sugden returned from her dreams, looked carefully at the young man sitting opposite and thought of child abuse. He was so trusting, so open to influence, so inexperienced and to her astonishment and shame, so very desirable.

'Robin, can you lean closer? There's something I want to tell you and I don't want the whole terrace to hear.'

Sally smiled as her young man cast a nervous glance over the whole terrace before leaning a fraction closer.

'Robin, I may have to arrange for you to stay somewhere else tonight. It's not that we don't get along right grand. In fact it's just the opposite. If you're under my roof tonight, I fear I may do something embarrassing. I may not be able to resist making a pass.'

Sally saw his serious face break into a cautious grin and his brown eyes light up.

'I thought you'd been making passes at me all day.'

'Oh, I am sorry. That just confirms my fears. If you come home with me, I may become impossibly forward. Do you see what I mean?'

'Yes, I do.'

'Good, I'm glad that's settled.'

'Is it? I thought we should go home and put it to the test.'

The Sugden family discussed all options, including whether to have their matriarch sectioned on the grounds of diminished mental capacity, but late blooming love has a power all its own and Sally was duly borne off in a Reliant Robin to take up residence on the mezzanine floor of a church in Lincoln. The house in Heaton was let, furnished, to a French teacher from the school across the road, and Sally hoped the family would eventually get used to the idea of visiting her in Lincoln.

She made them welcome and was at pains to show they still mattered even though she now had a new family of assorted three-wheelers, many of which were older than her partner. Jenny, her youngest, who worked in community health, was the most regular and in some ways the most difficult visitor.

'Mum, there's no use beating about the bush. I need to talk to you about sex. No, not me, you. What if Robin had too much to drink one night and wanted to do it?'

'Would there be a problem?'

'Problems? You must be joking. Where do I start? Broken bones. Lubrication. Vaginismus. Heart failure. Stroke. Without even touching on hepatitis, herpes or AIDS.'

Sally was tempted, but resisted the wicked urge to tell her that she and Robin had signed up for a tantric sensuality workshop.

'Thank you, Jenny, the family's concern is a great comfort to me.'

Peter, the eldest and her only son, tried hard to be supportive.

Of course they all wanted her to be happy, particularly as she had stood by Dad so patiently and loyally when he was being difficult. She deserved a little happiness. No one would deny her that.

They just didn't want her to get hurt. After all, this Robin was an unusual sort of a chap. What if he took it into his head that they should get married? Sally reassured him that marriage was quite out of the question, although they were taking a little honeymoon in September, the twenty-day 'Romantic Europe' tour.

Robin's father, the Anglophile, celebrating his most recent divorce by paying a visit to 'the old country', was more accepting.

'Sally, I can't tell you how glad we are that our Robin has settled down at last. Talk about a slow mover. When he turned thirty without any sniff of a lady-love I thought he might be gay. And you can't very well ask them, can you? We always said there was nothing wrong with Robin that couldn't be sorted out by the love of a good woman. And I personally put my money on an older woman, very likely a widow, so there you are. And don't you worry about the cross-cultural implications of your liaison. His mother's a Pom and a very good woman she is too. Far too good for me, but that's another story. And if fate was going to bring you two lovely people together before the millennium, it could only happen in England. For all I love this country dearly, I have to say that if you need a banana skin to make it happen, come to a filthy place where the locals sling their rubbish all over the footpath. Anyway, Sally, cheers, God bless and may you both have many happy years together. By the way, strictly off the record, was he a virgin?'

Sally and Robin took their 'honeymoon' and even started a joint photo album with all the happy-couple shots the romantic Dutch had insisted they purchase. Late into the night they lingered over shared memories of canals, castles, cathedrals, lakes and mountains. And the unspoken thought was there between them and it wouldn't go away. Was this their first holiday or their last? Robin wanted to celebrate the success of their relationship against all odds by getting married, but Sally's perspective was more down to earth.

'And I would like to marry you too, Robin. I think we touch each other deeply where it matters and the joy I feel at finding you is only tempered by the sadness that we both had to wait so long. And the certain knowledge that one day you'll wake up and find yourself stuck with an angry old woman raging at her incontinence, her immobility or her tumour. And if dementia sets in, I won't even know what I'm raging at. I've seen it happen and I could never risk doing that to someone I love.'

'I can't accept that. Our love has to mean more than that.'

'Yes, it does. It means that I was sent to help you discover all the lovely parts of you and bring them out of their shell. It means that in the larger picture of your life as a loving, relating, maybe even family man, I am just a prelude. I was a rite of passage. The rest is up to you.'

It was not easy, but Robin recognized a spirit even more stubborn than his own. His love hinted at illnesses held in remission during their heady summer. She alluded to the prior claims of children at times of crisis. Put bluntly, she was going home to die. But Robin, in his own quiet way, had a persuasive streak too. Sally was persuaded to stay another night, share a bottle of the best Australian fizz and all the most expensive dishes from the best Indian takeaway in Lincoln.

They ate to excess and laughed themselves silly. They drank to excess and cried themselves silly. They went to bed and laughed in the face of all the illnesses that were supposedly easing them apart. And they clung to each other unbelievably tightly because there was no tomorrow.

'I won't change my mind,' she whispered in his ear just before they slipped into the deepest, longest sleep. Robin wondered if that was a challenge, but was left in no doubt next morning when he woke up next to Sally. He was quite alone.

Sombrero
Geoff Dyer

About fifteen years ago, just after I left Oxford, I applied for a job at the famous Lucy Clayton Secretarial School in London. Two days a week, one teaching English language, the other literary and cultural stuff. Anything really. I also had some teaching at a crammer and this flexible combination of well-paid, part-time employment suited me well because I had only just moved to London and was very into nightclubs which, back then, were very different – a lot less fun – to how they are now. You stood around and looked. The job at Lucy Clayton was like being in a nightclub in that there were many opportunities for looking. I was the envy of my friends. I was the envy of myself. The girls were aged between sixteen and twenty-two; most were eighteen, had left school after A-levels. Some badly wanted to be secretaries but I liked the ones who had been sent there to get straightened out after taking too many drugs or having abortions at some public school or other, the kind of girls I saw at nightclubs.

I resigned after a term for awkward practical reasons and was then free to chase after one of my former students, Claire, the most expelled, attractive and fashionable of them all. She spent part of the year in the Caribbean, where her mother was developing tourism on an island, Anguilla, which has since become a millionaire resort. In London we went to nightclubs and slept together and took acid – the first time for both of us – and in the summer I went with her to Anguilla.

We flew to a big island in a big plane and then to a smaller island on a smaller plane and from there we flew to Anguilla on a very small plane. Two days earlier I had never been on a plane and suddenly, in the space of twenty-four hours, I had been on three.

I was not used to travel and although the island was idyllic I became bored quickly. The sea was perfect and though I was bored then I would not be bored now. Back then I missed nightclubs too much. We did acid a couple of times and I remember the pelicans being like pterodactyls and the waves sort of going backwards. We had strange conversations. Claire would say 'Have you got shattered nerves?' and I would say that I did or did not depending on how I was feeling.

One day we went out on a boat to Sombrero, a rock in the middle of the sea, about half a mile across. There was nothing on it except bird shit and a lighthouse, and once every fortnight a boat arrived with supplies and a new shift – perhaps the right word is 'crew' or 'team' – of lighthouse workers. We went out there and I sat on the bow sprit (the front part of the boat, the part that sticks out over the water), hanging on to the rigging as the boat lunged through the water. Claire was seasick and one of the crew chucked a bucket of water over her to clear up the vomit. There was a group of about five of us and when we got to Sombrero we crossed to the other side of the island where there was an inlet. The sea entered this inlet through a very narrow gap of maybe ten feet. Then it widened into a circle, a pool almost. You could jump off the cliffs – about the height of the top board in a municipal pool – into deep water. Then, if you swam out beyond the little gap in the rock, you were in deep blue. The waters were shark-infested. One of the people we were with, Lorrie, had a spear gun and he harpooned some fish which alarmed me because I was worried about sharks being attracted by the blood-scent. Then I stopped caring, because I was so happy jumping off the rocks into the pool.

At first we jumped cautiously, inching tentatively towards the edge. Then we began taking running leaps, in pairs, holding hands, waggling out legs and arms in the air and whooping like Texans at a rodeo. I liked jumping off the rock but I also liked snorkelling along beneath the water and seeing people come crashing through the blue in a white surge of bubbles. A couple of times I swam out between the narrow gap in the rocks, into the fathomlessness. It was a deep experience. There was nothing but blue in every direction. It was lovely but you felt so utterly out of your depth that it was easy to become frightened. We were in the sea, there were sharks in the sea. As soon as I thought about sharks I swam in again, but then, because it was so beautiful, I swam out again. Then I swam back in and looked at the others all jumping in off the rock and I climbed up and jumped off again myself. We kept doing it over and over.

I am thinking of all this because, a few days ago, I looked in a large atlas at a friend's house in Rome and found Sombrero quite easily. I felt almost proud that this little rock had achieved such recognition – global recognition, you might say. There it was, this place where, all those years ago, I had spent an afternoon jumping into the sea. I wasn't able to recognize happiness back then. I was capable of experiencing it but I could not put a name to it. It had not acquired the definitive cast that it has now. I looked at Sombrero, that orange-coloured rock in the middle of the pale blue sea, and it was lovely to know that I had been there, that it was still there.

I went back to England about two weeks after our trip to Sombrero. Claire stayed in the Caribbean and we lost touch. I heard that she was getting into trouble there as she got in trouble, eventually, everywhere. She had an affair with a rich photographer, possibly a cousin. Then she moved to Dublin and I visited for a few days. Either before or after that I also spent an afternoon with her, in the Cotswolds, where her family had a house. The last time I saw her . . .

Something urges me towards a sentence beginning with those words, but I don't remember the last time I saw her. It could have been Dublin or the Cotswolds or it could have been some other brief meeting in London. Certainly it was not in Anguilla, but that is when I remember seeing her for the last time, at the little airport, wearing her red sunglasses, while we waited for the little plane that would take me to the larger airport and a larger plane and so forth. Ours was the only car in the car park. The only people to be seen were airport staff, waiting. Somewhere off to the west a hurricane was building up. Already a strong breeze was blowing. The car radio played calypso at a low volume and we sat and listened and waited for the latest hurricane warnings. I knew nothing about hurricanes, but I was sure I could feel it closing in. The breeze whipped litter across the yellow grass. Grit swept across the tarmac. There was the noise of corrugated iron. I looked at the dials on the dashboard. Claire smoked a cigarette and seemed on the verge of speaking. Several times I thought I heard the sharp intake of breath that precedes speech but she said nothing. A voice on the radio said the hurricane was still too far away to be dangerous.

An aeroplane tilted in from the west and came in to land. An airport official came out and raised his arm and shook his head to indicate that it was not my plane. A few minutes later some people emerged from the immigration office and stood around until a car swung into the car park and picked them up and drove off.

I looked at Claire's hand resting on her leg. Her nails were painted red. She ran her other hand through her hair and began saying, 'Red sunglasses, red nails through red hair. Red nails through red hair, red sunglasses and red hair. Red nails and red sunglasses.' She kept saying it, with variations, over and over. 'Red nails through red hair, red sunglasses and red hair, red nails.' Softly and hypnotically. 'Red nails and red sunglasses, red nails through red hair . . .' And then again. 'Red sunglasses, red hair, red nails through red hair. Red sunglasses . . .'

I looked out at the trees beyond the airport. The light had grown metallic and in the east was a wall of emerald black cloud. Claire opened the car door and eased herself out skilfully (at Lucy Clayton there had been a mock-up of a car and the girls practised getting in and out without showing too much of their legs or underwear). She walked a few yards and then came back and leaned on the bonnet.

The music on the radio changed from calypso to gospel and the voice between songs soothed and urged. No mention was made of the hurricane but families on the island who were in difficulty were singled out for some words of comfort.

I got out of the car and rested my elbows on the roof. No other passengers had arrived, the car park was still deserted. There was another burst of enthusiastic singing from the radio inside the car. At the end of the song there were more dedications and appeals for the needy. At last the voice said something about the hurricane but I did not hear what was said.

I looked across at Claire, hoping she would speak but she had turned away and was gazing out to the eastern horizon where a black speck was becoming a bird, with silver wings, and then, just audible, a steady drone.

The Willow Pattern
Joel Lane

A few days into the New Year, Richard's father phoned me. We'd only met once, five years before, so I knew it wasn't a social call. He told me Richard was dead. 'He had an accident while suffering from depression.' I asked what had happened. 'He took too many sleeping pills. He was drunk. No letter or anything.' I said I was sorry. 'I know you and he split up. But your name was still in his address book. I wondered if you'd like to come to the funeral.' I said yes, and thanked him for getting in touch. When I put the phone down, the flat seemed colder than before. Light was shifting in the sky, as if on the surface of water. I went to find Carl. He was in the kitchen, cooking. I told him what had happened. He embraced me without saying anything.

The funeral was in Macclesfield, where Richard's parents lived now. A metallic, functional town. I sat uneasily through a service Richard would have detested, in a grey church where light sifted the dust high overhead. Lack of sleep made my own grief feel heavy and impersonal, like a cold. I felt that I'd already mourned his loss, years before. His death made me feel hopeless, not bereaved. At the graveside, there seemed to be a disproportionate number of male relatives – possibly cousins – who looked like younger versions of Richard. The sky was overcast and brittle. The empty grave made me think of a cavity in a row of teeth. I didn't stay long at the reception. Being Richard's ex-lover would have been awkward at the best of times. I shook his father's hand; his mother kissed me on the cheek.

Afterwards, I wondered why none of our mutual friends from

the old days had been at the funeral. Maybe Richard had lost touch with them. But hadn't he lost touch with me? The next couple of weeks were pretty hectic at work, which stopped me brooding over it. The company had committed itself to a huge range of new product, and I had to design all the catalogue pages and leaflets. I was working into the evenings, sometimes coming home to find Carl had already gone out. I hadn't told him much about Richard. In my experience, it's better not to lay chapter and verse regarding your exes on a new lover. Even one who's moved in with you.

What happened then was partly due to work pressure. I'd been drinking late, vodka, to help me get to sleep. One Friday morning, I heard the alarm nagging through a haze of deferred stillness. Despite the cold, I was sweating. Taking care not to wake Carl, who didn't need to get up for a while, I slipped out of bed and put on my dressing gown. Then I went into the kitchen, put the kettle on and made some breakfast. I was drinking coffee and wondering whether the post had come when I glanced at the timer on the video. It was seven minutes past four. I was almost three hours ahead of myself. For the first time I registered that it was that much darker, that much colder, than even a typical January morning. Perhaps the video was wrong. I crept back into the bedroom and checked the alarm clock. It showed ten past four, and was set to go off at seven. I hadn't switched it off.

Carl and I didn't get out much. Living and sleeping together was as much of each other's company as we needed. He was a quiet lad, with close-cropped hair and eyes that seemed to reach back into the night. There was something inarticulate and physical about him that coloured our relationship. I remember the first time we went to bed: how he curled up under me, pulling his knees up to his chest, and drew me into him until we formed the two halves of a closed shell; how he gripped my hand and moved it from place to place on his body; how his dead eyes opened and stared through me as we shuddered together. Soon after that, we both had blood tests and, on getting a negative result, started having unprotected sex. I'd never done that with Richard, because he'd never been faithful to me for long enough.

The sleepwalking incidents got worse. Nearly every night, I woke up out of bed – curled up on the floor in the freezing bathroom, on the sofa watching a blank TV screen, standing at the front door trying to find the keys in my pyjamas. I'd always double-locked that door for safety; now it had the added purpose of keeping me in. There was nothing very strange about my dreams. I was always just going about my life, getting up, preparing to go out. I was expecting to see someone. Then when I woke up, it was like falling out of normality into a damaged world. The pattern breaking up. Maybe I was getting out of bed so I could wake up alone and cold. Once or twice, I felt a pressure in the air, a stillness, and wondered if God was about to speak to me. I don't believe in God, but that was how it felt. The intake of breath before the words came.

One Sunday afternoon in late January, I decided to walk into town along the canalside. Carl was away visiting his sister. He didn't like walks anyway. It had been a freezing night, mist stuck hard to the windows; but today the sun was shining through a glassy layer of sky. The canal walkway began in Yardley, opposite a Victorian cemetery full of milky-white angels. The water surface was frozen over, a faint pattern of ridges turning the ice into a pavement. On the far side, the backs of derelict factories had been sprayed with Technicolor designs: soft letters, clouds, lightning bolts. The glass in the high windows was broken, revealing darkness. On the path side, leafless trees and shrubs were etched against blank walls. I had a chill from the nights, a nasty cold coming on. But I kept walking.

Why had Richard died? It didn't sound like an accident. But I couldn't believe he'd gone out hating life or himself. He wasn't like that. He enjoyed his own pain too much. It had to be something unbearable, something in particular. Like AIDS or cancer. But if his family had known anything, they hadn't told me. It wasn't like I had a right to know. I was only his ex. We'd hardly spoken in three years. My strongest images of him were from the early days, back in college. And the nights. Walking up the long, straight Manchester streets, across the parks, litter poltergeisting around us. The subways, the canals. Kissing against a wall in the golden streetlight. Richard's mouth open, his long hair breaking up around his face.

Further along the canal, a ruined doorway in the brickwork led through into a disused factory yard. Several rotten doors lay face down on the frozen mud, grass stretched across them like wire. Scraps of wallpaper and torn-off paint were grafted on to the uneven dirt. As if someone had dreamed a house and let it decay as only dreams can. I took a few cautious steps beyond the doorway, then crouched and blinked at the eroded concrete walls. Suddenly my eyes were flooding and I couldn't move.

Richard was one of the first friends I made at university. We used to meet up between lectures, go to the bookshop or the record shop together. On his own he'd always wear a concealed Walkman. The Doors, the Velvet Underground, the Bunnymen. He usually wore a black denim jacket which matched his hair. Early on, we kept running into each other at the same societies or events: concerts, films, a Poll Tax demo, a lecture on telepathy, a performance of Pinter's *Betrayal*. One evening I cooked dinner for him. We shared two bottles of red wine. It got too late for him to leave, since his lodgings were a bus ride away. No confessions or seductions were needed: we made love. I wasn't his first partner, but I was the first boy to fuck him. That happened a few weeks later, on his red duvet in sunlight. He gave it to me too. Strange how these things can give a framework to your life. I didn't just need any more. I belonged.

It was too early, of course. In more ways than one. As we grew up, we broke the chrysalis of our imagined twinship. But it lasted four years, on and off, well into the first year of real life. We even lived together for a while, and spent a week camping in the hills of North Wales. Those platform shoes were a disaster on muddy ground. We shared music, politics, a love of bass notes and darkened rooms and plain chocolate. We walked home along busy streets in the early hours of the morning, holding hands. We were so close that sex between us felt like masturbation, like incest. Richard used to say that we belonged together without needing to behave like a couple. He was right. That was the problem.

Maybe what he wanted with me was more than love. He was heavily into astrology and fringe religion at that time. We both joined a parapsychology group and spent many pointless evenings sitting round Ouija boards or trying to project images under *Ganzfeld* conditions. None of it ever worked. But he used to talk about sharing dreams, touching the astral body with the fingers of the mind. We never did meet in a dream, not really. Once I dreamed I was following him through a wood. I could see his naked back and arse moving in front of me, but when I reached out all I could feel was wet bark. The sound of rain blurred my voice, like static on a radio, and he didn't hear me. Richard's dreams often had to do with canals. Him trying to dredge furniture from the mud under yards of still water. Old chairs, beds, sofas. He'd get stuck trying to pull something free of the weeds, start drowning and wake up in a cold sweat. He wanted me to help him release the memories. I understand that now.

He was always in search of new experiences, whether physical or mental. Sometimes he'd go into the city alone and just explore – maybe spend the night at a rave, which was quite a new thing then, high on speed or E. Maybe get sucked off in a park or an alley in the dead hours between clubtime and dawn. He told me things a few times, but I made him stop. Sometimes there were marks, bruises or bites. In retaliation I went out with other blokes, usually students. But we always came back to each other. One night I walked him along ten miles of canal walkway between Manchester and Stockport. He'd been smoking heroin and was in danger of passing out. It was a June night, but Richard was shivering. 'Are you cold?' I kept asking. He said, 'I'm cold inside.' When we finally got home, I undressed him and let him fall through my arms into his static, waterlogged dreams. Richard wasn't into drugs. They made him panicky and ill, and he never got addicted. Except to alcohol, of course. That was something we had in common. Neither of us could get along with people who didn't drink.

Richard eventually left me for a woman. Or rather, his affair with her made me leave *him*. I'd never seen him in love with someone else before. It made me wonder if he'd ever loved me. They were only together a few months, but by then I'd moved to Birmingham and decided I didn't want him back. We stayed in touch, by phone mostly. Over the next couple of years he made several attempts at going steady with men or women, but it never lasted. He was too intense in some ways, too careless in others. From a friend in Manchester, I heard about him sometimes turning up drunk in Rocky's nightclub and trying to pick up the drag queens, a quick shot of quasi-hetero sex. Even his ambiguity he wanted given to him on a plate.

As I stood there in the derelict yard, sunlight wriggling in a net of cloud overhead, one particular story came back to me. It was something he'd told me from his childhood. I went back on to the canal towpath and walked on towards Small Heath, thinking about it. The light traced patterns of flaws and ridges on the ice surface; they seemed regular and abstract, like the image of a perfect world. Then I came to a bridge that had been designed to contain a fan of granite supports, with the bricks worked in above them. The granite pieces were too long; the builder had cut the ends off some of them, and made the bricks fit using odd pieces of brick and lots of mortar. It was a hideously botched job, despite the elegance of the design. I smiled, and felt Richard laugh quietly inside me. The sky was clearing.

He couldn't have been older than nine. It was a bank holiday, probably Easter; the morning had been bright and cold. Richard's father had gone out to visit a friend for a game of chess. After lunch, his mother put on her make-up and jacket. 'Come on, Richard. Let's go out for a walk before your father gets back.' They took the bus out of town, to an area Richard hadn't seen before. Streets of terraced houses broke up around factories and tower blocks. When they got off the bus, his mother held Richard's hand tightly. She was wearing thin leather gloves. Her face was set hard, even paler than usual. A patch of wasteground by the side of the road was heaped with refuse, mostly food cartons and bottles. All the flats behind it were derelict, their windows either boarded up or smashed in; except for two flats which had curtains and washing lines, and flowers in their window boxes. 'Poor sods,' his mother said. 'Why do they hang on? They're as crazy as the vandals.'

The sun came out, breaking the pale sky into silver-edged pieces. A high brick wall surrounded the local reservoir; the gates at the near end were open. They walked across a bridge where, obviously, there had been a fight and it hadn't rained since. Dried blood was spattered across the tarmac surface and hand-smeared on the wooden rail facing the water. Down on the footpath, weeds and rushes were mixed with normal grass and shrubbery. You could still see the grey factory chimneys smoking above the trees. Richard's mother stared at the water surface. Her eyes were wide, as if trying to collect every scrap of light. When Richard looked at the water, he imagined the sky was down there and felt momentarily dizzy.

At the far end of the reservoir, the bank was a flat marsh streaked with red clay; the water was black. Richard's mother let go of his hand and stood looking at something close by. There were tears on her face. Her arms, crossed over, were shaking. Richard tried to see what she was looking at. He couldn't see anything there except a willow tree, its lowest twigs reaching the ground. It trembled slightly, like its own reflection in the still water. Eventually, his mother walked on, and Richard followed until she turned and took his hand again. There was another gate at this end, leading back on to the main road.

When they got back to the house, Richard's father greeted them with a frozen stare. 'Where the fuck have you been? I've telephoned the police and all the hospitals.'

She stared back at him, then laughed quietly. 'No, you haven't. Don't be childish. You're trying to make him afraid of me, aren't you?'

'Don't laugh at me, you fucking cow.' A few seconds of stillness; then his mother walked upstairs to the bedroom and slammed the door. It was a typically blank, impenetrable ending to the trip.

In that year there'd been a number of fights. They often tried to ignore each other, but that was impossible at night. Sometimes they'd sleep in separate rooms and end up going back and forth to shout at each other. Once he tried to drag her downstairs from the bathroom; at the top of the stairs, she scratched his face, and he staggered all the way down backwards, wiping the blood from his cheek on to the handrail.

Another time, years earlier, Richard's mother threw a set of ornamental plates at the living-room wall — one by one, lifting them slowly back. For weeks, pieces of the willow pattern kept turning up in corners and behind the furniture. There was one plate left, standing in the cabinet, undamaged.

Stories within stories. Dreams within dreams. The cold caught up with me after that walk. I tried to fight it off with paracetamol, but it sank from my head down into my chest and hung there. Pressure of schedules kept me at work, coughing in feverish spasms that made the words dance on the little screen. By the end of the week, my lungs felt like wads of tissue paper. I was sleeping so badly that Carl, on my insistence, relocated to the futon in the living room.

One of those nights, I dreamed I was a canal. Locked in by stone, unable to move, I felt something move inside me. It shifted around, freeing itself, then slowly came to the surface. I saw a hand without fingers, a tongueless open mouth. As it crawled across the bed and the towpath, I saw it was a sleeping child. Then I woke up and the room was dark. Something moved off the edge of the bed and fell clumsily. It was more than an hour before I could find the courage to switch on the bedside lamp. The child was slumped in the corner, watching me with eyes of mud. He was three or four years old, naked, his skin a pale shade of grey. I couldn't hear him breathing. After a while I fell asleep with the lamp still on.

The child didn't go away, but he moved about. Sometimes he was in the bathroom, hugging the radiator with his large flat hands. Sometimes he was in the hall, as if waiting to be let out; when I opened the front door, he didn't move. Usually he was in the bedroom, somewhere just at the edge of my view. By daylight or full electric light he was translucent, the way a baby's ear or finger-webs can be. You could see the light through him, but nothing else. He reminded me of photographs of myself as an infant, walking along low walls in Leicester. Carl didn't seem to notice him. I tried not to.

That weekend, Carl and I got drunk on red wine and lay together in the living-room, half on the futon and half on the floor. Apart from the gas fire, the only light was the red signal on the stereo. The long drum rolls of Gallon Drunk's 'In the Long Still Night' shuddered around us, the slow piano chords giving an undertone of fragile tenderness. We undressed each other and floated in a haze of fatigue and desire, exploring patiently with our hands and mouths. He asked me to fuck him. I spread his body out beneath me, my face beside his, and felt him press up as I entered him from behind. My hand stroked his lower belly, then gripped his cock. A dark heat spread from my chest into my face, and I tasted blood on my upper lip. I couldn't stop; it was like being a passenger in myself. As I reached the climax, blood poured from my nose on to Carl's shoulders. I hoped he'd forgive me. The combined effect of sex, fever and loss of blood made me come like never before. For a few seconds I couldn't move. Blood trickled into my mouth and I nearly choked. Then I lifted myself, pulled away from Carl and took a deep painful breath.

Carl didn't move. 'Are you OK?' I said. No answer. I stood up and reached for a box of tissues, to clean the blood from his neck and shoulders. Cold pressed in around the gas fire's nest of warmth. Something crept from behind the futon into the shadows. I bunched a mass of white tissues in my hand and knelt beside Carl. The blood had eaten through to the shoulder blades, exposing the pale knobs of his spine. Where I'd coughed over his ear, only a ragged fin was left. I dropped the tissues against the back of his ribcage. Already he was losing shape, blurring into the dark fabric of the futon. When there was nothing left but a charcoal sketch in the air, a folded shadow, I turned the gas fire off and went to bed.

I lay there in the dark, redrafting my memory. It was like waking from a dream and not knowing quite how things stand. Had this been going on for weeks? Or had it begun and ended now, and all my memories of going out with Carl and living with him were false? But not even mortal terror can keep a man awake after sex. I fell asleep and didn't wake up until early dawn, when something else was trying to pull away from me. He was nearly my own height, a teenager, a thin double. I heard him sleepwalking around the flat, blundering softly into things.

The next night, it was a newborn baby. I could just feel his soft breath on my fingertips. Since he couldn't move around by himself, I picked him up and put him in the empty cat basket. I was between cats. His eyes didn't open, but I could see the eyeballs moving under the whitish lids. On Monday morning I woke up with all three of them around me. The baby at the foot of the bed, the child perched on the windowsill, the adolescent sitting at the bookshelf and leafing through a book without seeing it. Being unable to wake up was not enough to keep them still.

Then I thought of Richard's funeral, and the penny finally dropped. Again I felt that stillness in the air, like the pause before someone begins to speak. It was such a waste. A terrible, miraculous waste. He'd broken through after all. But somehow we'd not been in touch, and it was too late. A few words from either of us – a phone call, a visit – might have made all the difference.

I keep a baseball bat near the bed in case of a break-in. That morning, I destroyed the sleepwalkers with it. The teenager first, then the infant, then the baby. They had no bones or flesh, only form, and their bodies quickly dried out once broken. I gathered the brittle husks in a bin liner and kicked it until it was nearly flat. Then I carried it out to the row of dustbins at the side of the building. The way they had cracked apart made me feel awful. But memories have a lifespan, like anything else. Sometimes you have to help them die.

Outside in the street, people were on their way to work. I could see their paths intersecting, weaving around each other, making patterns. Was any pattern real or just something imposed by human need? All the patterns of Richard, the contradictions, the duality, came down to one final paradox. Richard's absence was all I had of him. Once I stopped missing him, he'd be gone.

Glisten and Beyond Herring
Tim Nickels

Once upon a day in a century that never really happened . . .

. . . Do you remember the triannual mermaid count here in Mare Selene?

Well, it *is* an institution lost to us way back when – and anyhow it's hard to imagine needing one these days, with mermaids being so scarce and all. Think of the occasional pale example cowering at the back of the Downmouth aquarium; shrunken mermaid tails used as swizzle sticks in executive minibars . . . And of course there's the rather more successful Californian variety with their jacuzzied lifestyle – force-fed pasta and vanilla milkshakes to gain that special snowy sheen so beloved of the underwater-world cognoscenti. No Hollywood pool should be without one. Do you recollect that special feature in *Hello!* magazine last year? Of course you do . . .

Ah, but back then . . .

Back then . . . in a century that might have happened (but no one can quite remember it), our West County village of Mare Selene was a different place to what it is today. Fishing didn't figure so heavily in the scheme of things. Irish boxes were items not much talked about in polite society and quotas was a game played out of doors by those with not much else to do.

Mare Selene was a place of creation, not catching, then. Not buildings (although there were quite a few of those) but boats. Proper boats. Wooden boats. Brigs, brigantines and barques and barquentines; schooners built, dry-dock fashion, into the quay – their bowsprits crossing over the main street and into the open windows opposite. And when those schooners were finished, the shipwrights would hack away at the sea sand cement and release the vessel – and start building again . . .

So much is known . . . but so little is only half-known of the mermaids of Selene Haven. *And* their voices . . .

. . . The sweet mer-voices as the angels of the sea hit the surface, their wide wonderful mouths open and crooning to equalize the pressures of their native sea-bed home with the strange alien outside. *Our* outside. The outside of the clumsy walking humans, barely able to talk and breathe at the same time; and wearing their strange, strange clothes – and they were even *stranger* back then.

The mermaids used to come up at dawn and dusk, the midday sun too much for their large sea-lion eyes (think of that cowering shadow at the back of the aquarium . . .). And the heat too – which they hated, but had to endure – on their once-every-three-year crawl up Sunny Cove to lay their dark strings of eggs. *Imagine*: the sun of June on those shimmering tails – dulling and shedding themselves to pieces in the lunchtime glow.

And it was here that the Mermaid Census-takers would wait . . .

The Census-takers would sit on their shooting sticks and tea chests (with their clipboards and bumph from the Ministry of Wrecks & Mermaids and their Victorian equivalent of datatags) and would watch their seaward cousins crawl slowly up Sunny Cove.

The mermaids feigned to take no notice. But they could hear, of course: modern research shows us that the mermaid sonar system is extraordinarily sensitive and capable of detecting a pilchard yawn ten leagues distant. And the dry-air scrape of those Victorian pens on Census paper must have resembled an especially distant and very sleepless fish indeed.

So the mermaids would wriggle ever on, grubbing out a nest at the head of the beach with their webby, barely fingered hands. And when their work was finished – when the precious egg-strings were secure beneath the dry sand – they would worm off back to the sea and its rising tide of coolness and welcome.

The Census had come about soon after the Reservation of the mermaid race. The battles between humankind and merfolk are well documented. Indeed the first official mention of Mare Selene in the County Records of 1360 refers to the conflict:

> *The fishar town of Marre Selene lies between two hoar stones at the west side of the Haven, and is much troubl'd by the curious seafolk who steell ashore and do take sheep and turn gryvestones upon themselves a-plenty . . .*

And the Breton raid on the village (led by Le Comte de la Marche in 1403) was said to have been piloted into the Estuary by:

> *. . . Three sea devyls, fish women of hideous shimmeryng aspect . . . and they did reek . . .*

By the beginning of the Victorian Era – as every schoolchild forced to breathe on dry land knows – the sea nation had been forced into five Reservations, the largest spanning right across the mouth of the Selene Estuary from Finale Bay to the mouth of the Awning River. The Royal Navy ringed the area with buoys suspending sulphur flares beneath their bellies. And the sailors sometimes scattered mustard pellets if they considered the folk below were getting boisterous – or occasionally dropped fresh pilchard over the side if it happened to be a Sunday or if one of the cooks was getting married.

Such was the curious behaviour of human beings in that century that might never have happened.

Such has been the curious behaviour of human beings always.

But the mermaids had a community friend in Mare Selene . . .

The shipbuilders and crabmen of the village would happily accept the Queen's Census shilling every three years: but they would undertake their task with kindness and consideration. The womenfolk – thrust to the background in this imagined century as in any other – would make up great cooling buckets of wet muslin . . . And the men themselves would bring spades to help the exhausted seafolk dig their nests . . . And even the odd pilchard pasty too.

The mermaids had an extra-special special friend in a gentle shipbuilder called Glastonbury Baskingvivian. They called him

Glisten in Mare Selene because he *listened* and *glistened*, but it was easier to say one word. He *listened*: his ears were always open and his mouth remained closed until something was required of it. And ever so occasionally, perhaps on the night before midsummer – or maybe in the cold morning after All Hallow's Eve when the wind blew strangely in the rigging of the boats moored in Quarantine Bay – boatbuilder Baskingvivian might be seen to *shimmer* slightly, to *glisten* in an otherworldly manner.

Oh, he had such a *way* with the mermaids – some said he could even understand their haunting dawntime shrieks – that many said (in the sniggeringly superior city of Downmouth mostly) that he was half-seaboy himself. Which was pretty strange because – as you know – there are no such things. Mermaids are alone in their gender: supremely, magnificently alone. True, legends abounded of the occasional male aberration or hermaphrodite – and many curiosities had been netted ashore in Hopeless Cove – but these remained food for gossip-pots.

Baskingvivian was *the* boatbuilder on the Estuary, far surpassing the work of Pupperell and Watey and Blonker or W. Plant in Dukesbridge, further upriver. His barquentines were much sought after for the fruit trade, his schooners crossing many distant oceans... And all of the marvellous ships that Glisten built in his yard (that lay where the Selene Hotel stands now) came safely to harbour. And all said it was Glisten's witching way with the seafolk that kept his vessels safe for the crew and their stockholders . . .

Still, Glisten dwelt quietly in one of the handsome new villas up on the Cornish road – the ones that are all holiday flats and Velux windows now. He lived sparely and without fuss and was much respected by the God-fearing flock of Mare Selene – in spite of his *magickry* with the pagan mermaids.

Now this story might have been even simpler than it is – but Glastonbury Baskingvivian had a neighbour called Miss Mariella Lowdrop.

Miss Lowdrop was an unamiable woman of mean aspect who enjoyed autumn and disliked seawater. Popular opinion – *does any other sort matter?* – concurred that Glisten and Mariella would one day be man and wife. No one could quite remember when the gossiping seed for such a union had been sown, especially as the two seemed *so* ill-matched.

But as well as her unwinning ways, Mariella Lowdrop had an additional problem.

She possessed a Trained Voice.

The Voice didn't scurry about with its fellow voices at the Women's Guild and after church on Sundays. It didn't canter wildly down to the saloon bar of *The Crabber's Hitch* with the others ... You see, Mariella Lowdrop's Voice was *trained*. Some said (in Downmouth perhaps ...) that Mariella had a precious Italian jewelled purse in which she kept her Voice, along with small change and old arsenic lipsticks. The Voice didn't like lipsticks much. Well, the Voice wasn't terribly fond of lips really – lips being on the final stage of things. Lips could pucker and make the voice rather smaller than it wanted to be. Lips could even become *affectionate* on occasion. And it wasn't even as if Mariella had trained the Voice herself; her Voice had been sent off to Switzerland while Mariella matriculated her way through a crammer in Hopeless Cove. So the truth of the matter was that the Voice was just downright better than Mariella. Here's another truth too: she didn't own an Italian purse and actually imprisoned the Voice in an ancient shoebox without air holes. Therefore, if Mariella was jealous of a part of herself, it was hardly surprising that she was madly jealous of the sweet *natural* voices of the mermaids. And of Glisten and his *curious* way with them ...

So when Census time came rolling around again, Mariella Lowdrop refused to prepare cooling buckets of damp muslin or queue up outside the baker's to buy pasties to stuff pilchards into ... *Instead* she prepared to moor herself (and a dinghy) off the Hellstone – a grim rock at the mouth of Sunny Cove Bay – so she could see what Glisten (the *man* who *might* be a *mer*man) was Getting Up To. Christ! She was a bitter woman as she shoved her dinghy off from the municipal quay, muttering to herself in her Trained Voice, telescope dangling from a neck scrawny with jealousy.

She became aware of the mermaids below as she reached mid-channel. They were slick night shapes beneath the planking, dozens and dozens. They moved very quickly, like swallows, seeming to swarm and circle the dinghy as if their motion had some master plan; as if the mermaids were linked by a strange telepathy. Seagulls hovered low, eager for the fish that the mermaids left behind.

And even though it was midday, Mariella swore she could hear the hypnotic howling harmony of the mermaids far out in their Government Reservation. And her own Trained Voice – her one precious if hated thing – seemed to shrink inside its cardboard shoebox without air holes, shrivelling into silent invisibility.

On the beach, at the nesting site that the humans call Sunny Cove – and known to mermaids as *Bright-Beach-That-Burns* – Glastonbury Baskingvivian readied himself to meet his old friends. He and the rest of the Selene men had crossed over to the beach with their Census boards on George Dustin's penny row-ferry.

Now Glisten stood apart from the upright hairy forms of his race, overdressed – it seemed – in the heat of June. And almost casually he noticed a disturbance out by the Hellstone: a figure – hour-glassed as was the fad then – *mostly* upright in a tipping dinghy as seagulls tried to steal her telescope . . .

But now the mermaids were coming ashore.

Quietly, almost unnoticed, they slipped in – easily at first on the slick, semi-liquid sea sand of the low-water mark . . . And then with greater difficulty as the dry white of the beach proper rose up like a hazy-heated snowdrift . . . *Bright-Beach-That-Burns* . . .

As ever, Ma Hipple came first: she was Glisten's oldest friend and a veritable mer-matron. It was Hipple who had first spoken to Glisten as he strolled the shores of one of the estuary creeks and dozed by the lime kilns there. He had thought it was a sea lion watching him – as is often the way – until the mermaid began juggling grey mullet and reciting risqué limericks about Atlantis. Hipple looked the same today as she had looked then. 'You're only young once,' she had said. 'But some of us are younger longer than others . . .'

The Teasetail Sisters came next, five mermaids with tails that *never* moved. They had perfected the *Tailless Drive* and mermaid lawyers were fighting copyright battles over their case. The Teasetails were followed up the beach by their bickering Aunties; knitting crammed under one arm, copies of *Waterwoman's Own* stuffed under the other. Next, Maria Weedpoppins: sad Maria Weedpoppins – the mermaid who had wanted to walk on dry land and wear clothes and go shopping – and had lost her voice crying out to the crabbers to haul her in ... Following on eccentrically, Jiggery Halfshell – whom no one knew too much about and were afraid to ask.

And now Ma Hipple's daughters.

Elvereddy who crawled with a swagger: the arch-wannabe seducer; the subaqua sauce-pot of Starfire Bay; combing her hair and covering her sea-lion eyes with Marilyn Monroe sunglasses and smiling up *awfully* at the coastguards there ...

And her sister Kelptrep: so full of it, almost an *un*beautiful mermaid with her unending whine and dull dislike of humankind and its two sexes: a non-believer, a reluctant egg-layer on the shores of *Bright-Beach-That-Burns*. You're only young once – or sometimes not at all if you can wriggle out of it ...

And *finally* ... Glisten sighed as he always sighed as a dark shape double-somersaulted itself out of the offshore water, touched nose to tail and almost had a chance to wink at him before plunging back in.

Beyond Herring ...

Glisten felt himself swoon as he recalled the name.

Beyond Herring: the true angel voice of the ocean – the youngest daughter of Ma Hipple with all the attendant coddlings and favouritisms ... Beyond Herring: *not* the owner of a Trained Voice – but rather a partner with a voice that could really sing and really *wanted* to ... Beyond Herring: a mermaid who saved her singing for the full moon at midnight when the *ghosts* walk: when all the ship-wrecked sailors find their shore at last; when all fogs lose their mystery; when even the ships of the invading Bretons find their way to our *Marre Selene* and are welcomed ...

Beyond Herring wriggled like a five-foot silver cormorant on to Sunny Cove; her ears foaming slightly after her acrobatics, her mouth pulled back revealing a hundred white-white tiny teeth. And her eyes – Glisten sighed and started again like he knew he would – her *eyes* were *blue*. Clearly madly violetly blue like a stained-glass window, light seeming to fall out of them from the inside ...

Beyond stared her blue stare at Glistening Glastonbury on the burning beach, as Glisten absent-mindedly wrung out and rewrung the wet muslin in his bucket. And Beyond Herring winked again, the blue iris disappearing ever so briefly – but long enough for that first spell to be broken ...

Glisten glanced over at the other men as they laid their own wet muslin on to the boiling backs of the mermaids. All the seafolk looked the same to them, he realized. The Teasetails, Elvereddy, Kelptrep, the voice-starved Maria Weedpoppins and even the enigmatic Jiggery Halfshell ... All the same to the surface dwellers. Only the catalogue-tags told them that these mermaids had crossed this beach before. But Glisten knew – almost unconsciously as one human simply realizes and recognizes another – every one of these oceanfolk. These very good friends ... these sea-*sisters* of his ... *perhaps* ... *maybe* ... in a century that never happened ...

Sunny Cove was moving now. The white sands had been replaced with the dull aquamarines, the shining silver pinks, the underwater rainbow tails of mermaids. It was a strange, strange sight. And Glisten was not alone among the human men in thinking they had entered ... *dreamland* ... (*An unbuttoning of Sunday trousers; a seeding of eggs as they slithered into their sandy nests ...*)

Glisten, midway up the beach, reawoke to the snaking form of Beyond Herring, all blue eyes and gleaming greyness of tail as she wriggled up towards him. And her head was ... moving. Her head was ... *shaking* ...

Beyond turned on her tummy, pivoting around to face the sea again. She always did this: every three years for the last nine. Glisten closed his eyes tight and prayed – as ever – that the other men didn't notice.

Even on that busy beach, there seemed to be only silence. Glisten kept his eyes closed: *you're only young once, you're only young once ...*

He opened one eye a crack. Beyond Herring had stopped moving back towards the waves. In past years she had kept on going, her brief flirtation seemingly enough. But now she twisted her head awkwardly over her shining shoulder and opened her mouth to speak ... And when she spoke, everyone in Mare Selene stopped what they were doing; and the upriver bells in Dukesbridge held on to their clappers, catapulting their ringers half-way up the church tower. And on far Downsmoor, the sheep and ponies looked up and sniffed the salty air coming in from the sea ...

For when any mermaid speaks she is singing too. And when Beyond Herring spoke even the mermaids stopped and listened and put down their pilchard pasties. And Beyond Herring said to Glisten there on *Bright-Beach-That-Burns* . . .

She said . . .

She sang . . .

And when Beyond closed her mouth at last – and the bellringers of Dukesbridge slipped down their ropes (and wondered if it was a story they could get away with in the pub that night) –/ Glastonbury Baskingvivian found himself with his feet in the waves, the water rising about his legs and suddenly his chest, his senses dulled but rejoicing as he followed a somersaulting shape with a dash of blue out into the sea . . .

And on her Hellstone mooring, Mariella Lowdrop reached deep inside herself and found her Trained Voice and threw it over the Selene sand bar on a green foam of jealousy . . .

Time passes by if you're not looking after it too carefully.

Especially time out of mind, if minds can ever remember a century that never really happened.

Changes came to Mare Selene. The rest of the world intervened. Between 1864 and 1890, the number of trading vessels working from the village fell from ninety-seven to just twenty. The new century brought the bustle of iron and steam to the world's oceans. But the wooden ships lived on for a little while, finding curious berths or graves – some even ending their years in the home estuary, their hulking forms fossilizing into the mud of minor creeks.

The yard of Glastonbury Baskingvivian was bought up when its owner failed to return from the Mermaid Census, and Halfshank Ivy – former landlady of *The Crabber's Hitch* – built her famous hotel there.

Glisten's friends gathered around his memory and preserved it. Although nothing was discussed of that strange June day on Sunny Cove in a century that never happened – or only happened to those who lived in it.

And oddly – or perhaps not so oddly – there were fewer mermaids to count when the next three years came around. And in six years there were fewer still. And by year eighteen – or maybe year twenty-four – only *one* mermaid was crawling ashore to lay. And if any of the land-dwellers had known – and of course they didn't –

they would have recognized old Ma Hipple as she wriggled up the beach, looking – *always* looking with her sea-lion eyes – for her youngest, bestest and most beautifully singing daughter. The midnight moontimes had been quiet since Beyond Herring had taken her Glisten into the far oceans.

But what of the Trained Voice? And what of its Owner, the hater of saltwater? Mariella Lowdrop paddled out to sea around Prawn Point and just kept going.

She lived for years sustained by her jealousy; decades passed as she fed on her dark hatred of the mermaid race and its loathsome *naturalness*.

And eventually the Voice slithered from its cardboard box, leapt over the side and deserted her. Mariella had assumed it had departed on a search-and-sing mission – until it failed to return, leaving the empty shoebox as a metaphor for her tortured vacuum soul.

Mariella became truly monstrous then.

She whistled up whirlpools with her silent screams and conjured the plummeting descent of kamikaze seagulls on to the world's picnickers. She visited hideous fogs on the Mare Selene Regatta. It rained every day in every July and August for the next two millennia and she cursed every umbrella to be made of rice paper (and they wouldn't open anyway). And every shoe to have a stone in it and every ice cream was cabbage flavour and every playground was turned into a *factory* that *built* playgrounds very noisily and every song sung in a singalong was sung *without* a song (unless it was a sad one) and laughter was less than a memory and chortles were not remembered at all. Only sniggers and sneakering things were permitted in the world of Mariella Lowdrop. Only things that she thought were less than herself.

And as the decades passed and the grim century that we call our own came calling, so Mariella's actions lowered in morality and dropped in compassion. Her vengeful hurricanes began to widen the ozone hole. She globally warmed through the sheer multihued vulcan super-heat of her invective (*and* by farting like a trooper). Oil slicks were sent to engulf the wayward couple (whose existence had long fallen away from popular memory). The litany of darkness: *Torrey Canyon*, *Exxon Valdez*, Milford Haven – the slick, slick oil flooded over the waters, strangling everything in its way – but not the souls or bodies of Glisten and Beyond Herring . . .

And so Mariella Lowdrop found herself in our own poor decade; the decade that kisses the millennium with an enthusiasm normally reserved for an old sock or seldom-seen relation . . .

She was worn out with travelling, her hour-glass figure a frayed memory. Mariella had rowed across the world's oceans a hundred times and was herself wearying of rice-paper brollies that refused to open. Mare Selene was an alien place to her now – and yet curiously familiar. It held *ghosts* . . . As she moored up to the garbage pontoon she could still see the silhouette of the town she remembered.

The municipal quay had gone, replaced by the big fish factory owned by a consortium from the Continent. And there seemed to be a large number of dormer windows and balconies facing the sea (whereas in her own day folk hadn't cared for the view *over* much). And when she had taken the water taxi ashore, Mariella found that the little alleyways she had once walked freely from the main street to the water now sported *fancy* flower baskets – and PRIVATE signs on *fancy* iron-worked gates with *ever* so discreet padlocks on them. And the main street itself was busier, with many a horseless carriage charging through and threatening to crash into postcard shops, scattering their contents like glib confetti.

Mariella left the centre of town and walked upriver towards the creeks where the yards used to be. The old boatbuilding smells of wood and pitch had been replaced by those of diesel and fibreglass resin.

The main creek had a boatpark and a reclaimed road; but it still had its two lime kilns – one tucked way behind the new tarmac, the other the same as it had always been on the shingle beach opposite. The same as it had been when Glisten had first heard Ma Hipple reciting her Atlantis limerick all those years ago . . .

There was some commotion over by the kiln, the sound of children's voices and . . . *Mariella Lowdrop grimaced* . . . laughter. Then it came again – and at that second burst of giggling, the venom seemed to seep out of Mariella's soul. And when a joyous tittering rose up from the water, she seemed to feel a great weight rise from her.

An object landed at her feet.

She glanced down into the creek just in time to see a dark shape with blue eyes slip back beneath the surface. Mariella might even have said a *manly* dark shape . . .

Presently, several figures appeared in the shallows by the lime kiln on the other side. And – pausing only briefly – they slipped out of the water on scaly feet and scurried up the beach to be lost in the woods of Quarantine Bay. More blue eyes – Mariella couldn't help noticing – and with a certain *glistening* way about them.

And perhaps now I could tell you the tale of Glisten and Beyond Herring. (Of their adventures in the wide oceans; of their personal audiences with narwhals and sea serpents and the ghost of Jacques Cousteau; of their beachings on tropical rocks and icebergs and oil rigs; and of their wonderful children; and of their perfection of the rice-paper-free self-opening umbrella; *and* of their strange and curious return to the port of Mare Selene . . . And *maybe* I could speak of how mermaids and men can become free of both land *and* water, slipping easily between them . . . needless to say, a matter of some magic and magnificence . . .)

But for the moment . . .

. . . Mariella reached down and picked up the cardboard shoe-box that the almost-mermaid had left. She opened it carefully because it *wasn't* the shoebox she was used to, with its pale underwater beauty . . .

And so you might hear the bell of the Hellstone buoy clanging on stormy nights. And you can think of Mariella Lowdrop – tired but happy, disgruntled but ecstatic with her new love of seawater – as she clings on to the Hellstone and saves her glorious if *second-hand* Voice for the perfect midnight moontimes when even the mermaids – those that are left – will stop what they're doing and swim in from their secret places to listen to the song of Beyond Herring – even if the song slips from the lips of a stranger . . .

Not that there's much time for listening, now that our own noisy century's winding down (you're only young once but some of us never grow up). A century so terrible and wonderful that it might have well and truly happened.

Matter of Fact
Madeleine Cary

Steve turned over on the lumpy mattress and flung an arm out to wrap around Jenny. But he felt only a soft indentation where she'd once lain, her absence shocking him like a cold corpse. In six months he was still unused to living alone. He even missed the babies' screams. If Jenny was back with him now, he'd never complain again when the twins started up their nocturnal duet, howling like banshees. He'd even get up in the night to soothe them.

A shaft of sunlight pierced through the moon-and-stars fabric that acted as curtains on the big bay window. The beam cut through the room with laser precision, highlighting the dancing dust that whirled like bacteria. Steve kicked at the duvet then curled into a foetal ball. And that's when he heard it. A shuffling, a rustling in the corner of the room.

He turned, dragging his bristled cheek on the pillowcase, and peered at the mess in the corner, the mound of debris from six months of self-pity and sloth. Everything that Jenny would have once consigned to the rubbish bin or the wardrobe or the cupboards, on to the shelves or to the kitchen sink, was now abandoned in a sordid jumble that had already spread half-way across the room. Steve concentrated, listening for the sound again. But he heard only his stomach rumble. He lay back and stared at the ceiling, where dust and cobwebs blackened the ornate Edwardian mouldings. And then, at the very edge of his vision, something stirred. It was the mess in the corner. It had moved. He could swear it had moved. His eyes darted back just in time to see it heaving, then resting in stillness again.

He crawled under the gamy duvet like a mole. Moments later he peeped out again and held his gaze on the untidy heap. But there was no more movement. He had imagined it, of course. God, he thought, what was I on last night? Time to stop if I'm starting to hallucinate. Perhaps I should get this place cleaned up.

'Slob!' Jenny had called him on that last day. 'Slothful slob! A stone around my neck. An unpaying lodger. I've enough with two babies on my hands without having you to clean up after.'

'Go and find yourself a bank manager then,' Steve had ranted as he watched her struggle with the double pram and a hold-all out on to the landing of the flats. 'Someone who can put you up in luxury. I always knew you wouldn't be able to hack living with an artist.'

Perhaps he'd been a little unfair. But she'd been so different before the kids came along, he thought. She'd been a free spirit. Yes, really cool, that had been Jenny before she had the twins, letting Derwent and his mob hang around the flat for days on end; giving Steve all the space he needed to practise his guitar after that pub landlord had offered him the Sunday afternoon gig in exchange for free beer.

And then she found out she was pregnant.

She couldn't open her mouth after that without mentioning nesting instinct. She'd bought some rubber gloves and gone through the place like the demented housewives in the ads, leaving smells of disinfectant and cheap polish in the air. Steve had almost set the place on fire he lit so many black coconut joss sticks just to make the place smell normal again. And when Abraxas had her kittens, Jenny cosseted the little creatures like they were her very own and started spending their dope money on steak and fish for the cat and catnip toys for the kittens. If those kittens hadn't come along then perhaps they'd still be together. For things went downhill after that business about the mushrooms.

Steve stared at the mess in the corner. It was just that. A mess. An inanimate heap. No movement. No sound. He closed his eyes and was about to drift off to sleep again when suddenly he heard another sound, this time coming from outside the bedroom. He half lifted his head. If he hadn't known it was impossible, he would have sworn it was the sound of crying babies. There it went again. It was a faint chorus of high-pitched screams coming from the kitchen. Birds? he thought. He staggered from the bedroom across the hallway into the kitchen.

The noise had stopped. There was nothing there. Only the growing pyramid of dishes around the sink and several empty cartons and cans littering the work surfaces. Like everywhere else in the flat, it looked worse in the morning sunlight. Jenny's pride and joy, the spider plant on the shelf above the sink, was decaying in a dried-out pot. Only his dope plants, the five little green shoots that rewarded his loving care with a prolific growth every month, were bouncing with life. They were. Literally. Bouncing, that is. At least that's what Steve thought. There were no windows open. Why, then, he thought, are these little plants trembling on the window sill? He reached for a dirty glass and ran it under the tap, splashing water on to grease-soaked crockery and a jigsaw of food scraps that had lodged in the plughole. When he turned to the plants with the water, they stopped trembling and he fed them with care.

'There, my little lovelies,' he said, 'you grow nice and big for Daddy.'

Steve returned to bed. He hadn't had his quota of sleep yet. Since Jenny had left he'd become a nocturnal creature and was usually only getting up when the sun was past its midday arc.

He stretched out and thought of his little plants. Jenny had banned him from growing the stuff after the mushroom fiasco. He still felt bitter about her unreasonable behaviour. He'd always insisted it wasn't his fault, but Jenny never forgave him. She'd been at an ante-natal class – Steve should have gone with her but he'd been too tired to get up – when Derwent popped in with some mates who'd just found a crop of magic mushrooms on a school playing field. They spread them out on newspaper in front of the Calor Gas fire and left them to dry. Steve couldn't remember at what point the kittens woke up and started exploring, for Derwent had brought some excellent blow and time sort of stood still. Besides, they weren't exactly as keen on the cute antics of the kittens as Jenny was. Which is why, when she returned home and found the kittens dying from poison, she went ballistic. Steve had protested. How was he to know they were really toadstools? And, no, he couldn't remember seeing the kittens nibbling at them. Then Derwent made things worse by saying it was like in the mines when they take birds in cages down to see if there's enough oxygen and if they die it saves the men.

'I'd rather have all of you dead in a cage just to have one of those little kittens alive again!' Jenny had screamed, storming out of the room.

When she'd gone all the men agreed that her hormones must be doing a song-and-dance act.

Jenny had banned Derwent from visiting the flat after that. Then Pico, then Drac, then Widgit and his latest woman, some lady with a Gaelic name who liked drumming on Widgit's bald head. And then there was the argument about names for the twins. Once they found out they were having two, Jenny insisted on using old Anglo-Saxon names and came up with Twitchell and Marden, but Steve objected, pointing out they'd end up being called Twit and Mard. When the boys were born, one with her dark swarthy looks and one with his gingery fairness, she met him half-way and settled on Lysander (Greek) and Barlow (Anglo-Saxon), and then blamed Steve when everyone started calling the boys Lice and Ken.

But it was the domestic arrangements that finally got to her. Before she'd walked out on him, she'd screamed: 'I hope you stew in your own mess!'

And now it looked like his own mess was stirring with a life of its own, for there, in the corner, the pile of rubbish was quivering again. Rats? Steve thought. He'd have to go and borrow someone's cat. Jenny had returned once after settling in with her mother and claimed Abraxas ('Even a cat isn't safe in your company. You'll forget to feed it!') and all those books by women writers she'd been reading in the past year ('You wouldn't read them anyway – they're beyond you!'), so he'd have to borrow a cat from a neighbour and chase out the vermin. No worries, he thought. If it's rats, I'll get rid of them, then maybe it's time to clear away the mess. New beginnings and all that.

And then he sat bolt upright. For this time the noise was louder. A muted sound, somewhere between a hiss and a moan, was coming from inside the mountain of debris. As Steve focused his incredulous eyes on the corner, he saw the clutter move again. This time he fixed his stare like a marksman; yes, he thought, it's shuddering!

He crept from the bed and placed his feet on the floor cagily, as though a bogeyman were hiding under the bed waiting to reach out and grab them. Then he dashed to the curtains and tore them open, so sunshine hit the room like a spotlight. Forget rats, he thought, watching the heaving mass, listening with repulsion to the disturbing sound. This is something bigger. As he crept towards the corner, he grabbed his didgeridoo – a home-made job from a plastic drain pipe – and held it up ready to attack.

'Look mate,' he said. 'I don't know how you got in here. I'm not that bothered. Just get yourself out of here and piss off. No questions asked. Are you listening?'

Steve had trouble remembering what he'd done when he'd left the pub the previous night. Perhaps one of the homeless kids who hung out round the all-night kebab shop had followed him home. Perhaps it was that young girl with the mauve hair who looked anorexic, the one who swore at him that time he'd said there was no need for someone like her to starve out on the streets.

'Come on, love,' he said, a serene smile spreading over his face as he waited for her little purple head to pop up out of the debris. 'Don't be scared. You must be suffocating in there.'

And then the movement stopped and the jumble was silent, inanimate again. Steve suddenly felt foolish, then angry. He lurched at the pile of rubbish and started digging through the mess, pushing through the rancid chaos and flinging items around him in a frenzy. And then he saw it. As he leaned forward to inspect it a prickle ran up and down his spine like a hairy insect and he clenched his teeth till they ached.

For there, palpitating in the sun, was a patch of grey-green mould.

Steve worked slowly then, removing every item delicately as though taking bandages from a festering wound. And the more he cleared away, the more mould he revealed, until he'd uncovered a weird but beautiful bulk of organic mass, a metamorphosis of six months of neglected rotting food and drink, that throbbed with life. Like a beached sea monster, the gigantic mould heaved and shuddered. Steve gazed in awe at the thing, watching how its furry surface muted from white to green, green to grey, grey to a blue that was almost black. In parts it was semi-opaque and non-organic objects sat in the gelatinous blubber like fossils – a plate, a glass, a can, an ashtray. Steve noticed with fascination that his Thai bong, the one he'd been looking for for several weeks, was crystallized in there. He sat back on his heels and gawped.

'Amazing, man!' he said.

And as soon as he spoke, the thing started to undulate, then with a great effort, waddling awkwardly like an overweight walrus, it shifted its bulk and moved towards him. Steve laughed out loud, 'Wicked!' and then the thing settled its throbbing mass next to him and extended, like a snail's antenna, a small blob which rested, eventually, on Steve's knee.

Before he thought about what he was doing, Steve stroked it. It wanted to be his friend. It was, like him, alive. Alive and living with him in the empty sad apartment. He was no longer alone.

The amorphous mass was soon moving with ease, writhing, rolling and squirming round the flat. Like an amoeba it could flatten itself, extend narrow promontories or curl into a giant ball. Steve followed the thing around, watching it investigate the flat. It seemed to like windows and doors, reaching long tentacles out along their edges and around the locks. It was some time before Steve realized it had left a gelatinous matter behind, sealing up all the escape routes.

In the kitchen the giant blob went into a paroxysm when it discovered the overflowing rubbish bin, shuddering as it pushed the bin over, then covering all the half-eaten scraps and decaying foodstuffs that fell out on to the floor. Steve stepped back when it devoured them, recoiling from the squelching, sucking noise. When it finished, there was no sign of the organic matter it had imbibed, only a pile of tin, plastic and glass containers covered in a gooey slime. Steve knew now the thing had an appetite for organic matter. He looked at his own pathetic white feet and wished he had steel-toed boots on. He'd have to think of a way to protect himself. Suddenly, the mould started to extend its form like a giant slug and sucked its way up the kitchen wall, hovering over the little dope plants. Steve froze.

'Please, don't touch them,' he cried. 'Don't harm them. They're only little innocents. Please!'

Through the greasy window, the sun dipped on to a smoky horizon. Steve felt panic rush through his veins like bad speed. But the thing suddenly withdrew from the plants, slithered down the wall and re-formed into a wobbling bulk. Steve was relieved. It seemed to understand him. Perhaps he could talk it into letting him out of the flat. He wondered if he could appeal to its reason, or perhaps to its compassion. Did it have reason and, if so, was it the same as his? And compassion? It wasn't made of the same stuff as him, so why would it be able to empathize? He decided on another tactic.

He stroked it slowly, telling it how nice it was, how handsome, how strong. He explained how it didn't need to harm his little plants to show its power. It had already won. And then the thing pushed at Steve gently until he fell back and sat in a chair by the kitchen table. From its dense mass it spewed out a cellophane package containing several old decaying roses and nudged it across the floor to Steve's feet.

Steve picked up the flowers. 'They're fantastic, mate,' he said.

The mould bristled in satisfaction and stroked against his leg. Steve winced in revulsion. He wanted to run but he knew the thing could overwhelm him if it wanted to.

He cradled the flowers and remembered the day he'd given them to Jenny. It was the morning after that terrible night when he'd no longer been able to put up with her objections to sex. He'd got used to her complaining about how he was usually too drunk or stoned to make love properly; how his breath smelt, his sour sweat made her gag, his heavy weight crushed her till she couldn't breathe. But that night, even though the babies were screaming for a feed, he couldn't control himself any longer and, anyway, he remembered his dad always told him that when women say no they mean yes. And by the morning she was calling him a rapist and telling him she'd had enough. The dozen red roses had cost him a fortune but they hadn't pacified Jenny, who'd flung them, unopened, into the corner of the bedroom.

The mould rolled away again and writhed towards the living room. Steve followed. The thing was lurching towards his guitar and shuddering as though laughing silently. Suddenly the guitar was covered by the trembling blubber.

'No! Don't break that,' Steve pleaded. 'Please!'

But it was too late. The thing belched out a chord. It had ingested the instrument.

Steve ran to his bedroom, locked the door then jammed the wardrobe up against it. He kicked at the redundant phone on the floor, wishing now that he'd paid the bill and not been cut off. He could always smash the window to get out, but then he was four storeys up. Suddenly the little screams started up again from the kitchen. He realized now – it was the dope plants. They were calling for him.

There were some Temazepam on the bedside table – sleepers. Maybe he could drug the evil thing? No. It was easier to drug himself. If he popped a few he could probably sleep the whole nightmare off. For, it couldn't really be happening, could it?

'Pull yourself together, man!' he said to himself.

And at the very same moment, the wardrobe toppled over and the bedroom door was pushed with such force it fell off its hinges. The giant mould was palpitating in the doorway, two dark fungal patches widening like lustful eyes. Steve's feet carried him backwards as he tried to work out what to do. The window – he could dive through the window. Anything would be better than... But he stumbled backwards and fell on the bed.

'No! No!' Steve yelled.

But the thing was upon him within seconds, crawling over him on the bed like an eager lover, pressing its putrid dampness into his mouth and ears. Its soft panting turned to a rasp as it fixed itself like a giant leech on Steve's body, pressing and kneading. Then came the grunts, the dark phlegmy sounds, as it writhed and squirmed. It was having fun, Steve knew. And when it finally shuddered and released a burning slime over Steve's body, he felt the first searing pain of decomposition. He tried to scream but his mouth was gagged with a blob of furry mould that filled him like an angry tongue. And as the torture of slow disintegration began, his body being softened to a stew before it was ingested, he heard his little dope plants crying out for him. Howling in the night like banshees.

Vanitas Vanitatum
Nicholas Lezard

gaze at yore strange unnatural beauty – nigel molesworth

They met again (everyone in London meets again; it gets tiresome) over, would you believe, the frozen vegetables in Brook Green Tesco. Their hands achieved a momentary unity as they reached for the same bag of sprouts. They lifted their gaze, and their eyes saw each other once more.

– Well, well. If it isn't my ex-better half.

An onlooker, had one chosen to be there, would have seen two very different-looking men, one of them looking very awkward, the other with the relaxed assurance of the depraved. The awkward man was unshaven, chaotically dressed, and pushing a small child in a flimsy buggy. The other was impeccably turned out: a dapper suit (odd, as one does not normally wear suits to Tesco's), hair nicely crisped and modulated.

– Having a nice . . . *family* Christmas, are we? he said.

– Er . . . yes. And you?

– Just a few friends round. Remember Tammy, and Dean, and Roger and Angela? Thought we'd have a pleasant dinner. I thought I'd cook a goose this year.

He looked disdainfully at the frozen turkey in the other's basket. It spoke of a hectic, forgetful last-minute dash.

– So: how have you been? It's been a while. I can see you've decided to reproduce yourself. What's her name?

– Hannah.

– Very modish. What a sweet child.

Hannah, who, like a smoking volcano, had been threatening to go off for some time, now did so.

– And how old is she?

– Eighteen months.

– And a poor sleeper, I'd say, judging by the state of the bags under your eyes.

– Observant as ever, said the other, to the state of other people's infirmities. Give my regards to Tammy and the crew. I don't suppose they miss me much, do they?

– My dear boy, they hardly notice you've been gone.

– Well, that figures.

– Look, let's just nip over to that ghastly café area over there and have a little breather. We can have a natter about old times. And you can soothe little Hannah. Look, she's upsetting all the other happy shoppers.

– I don't think that would be a good idea. I don't really want to have a natter about the old times.

– But of course you do. And we're not going to be bumping into each other again. I'm leaving the country after Christmas for good, and you . . . you're not going anywhere.

Which was true enough.

– Leave those sprouts in the freezer. They'll wait for you.

While the one anxiously tried to soothe the purple-faced Hannah with the infallibly useless technique of pushing the buggy back and forth, the other stirred his milky coffee urbanely, and sized up his ex-lover. Lover? No, more than that, much more. There was a time when, strictly speaking, they had been one.

– I know what you're thinking, said the father. You're looking at my hair, my clothes, the fucking bags under my eyes, and thanking Christ we split up when we did.

– *Au contraire*, my little cupcake, I am absolutely riven with jealousy. Your life represents an impossible ideal which I shall never be able to attain. And how is . . . oh dear, I seem to have forgotten her name.

– Delia.

– Delia! Of course. Like that sweet little cook on the television.

I imagine motherhood suits her down to the ground.

He thought of his wife as he had left her at home, lying on the sofa and weeping, asking him to take the brat to the fucking supermarket before she went out of her mind.

– More than you could imagine.

– Don't be so brusque with me. We will probably never see each other again. And we had quite a thing going, didn't we?

– The best.

The well-dressed one's manner changed suddenly.

– Don't be a silly cunt. It was the worst, and you know it. Look at me. *Look at me.*

Their eyes locked once more, and, for an instant, it was if nothing had changed.

It was the purest, most sensual, most fulfilling relationship imaginable; and yes, it had been imagined, in song and legend, thousands of years before he had been born, the most poignant love story of them all: Narcissus and his pool, and his own reflection.

He discovered the potential of his own reflection around the age of puberty. It was one of the first times he had got drunk. He had thought, at first, he was going to be sick; but as the nausea passed (to be replaced by a feeling of triumph, as of a rite of passage successfully endured) and he felt able to remove his head from the toilet bowl, he looked into the mirror of his parents' bathroom cabinet and noticed, as if for the first time, the strange unnatural beauty of the face looking back at him. It was if he'd seen himself across a crowded room. As sensational and as banal as that. It was sporadic at first; to awaken the recognition he had to be quite deranged, whether on drink, or drugs, or feverish illness; but then his image would take on a reality of its own. They did not need to talk: their love was contained in gesture, in the inflection of an eyebrow, the quarter-turn of the head, the sudden flaring of a nostril.

Eventually that changed, and he could gain satisfaction in any place with a reflecting surface; the windows of parked cars, shop windows. On trains, or the underground, he would whenever possible take a seat faced by an empty one, so that he could contemplate himself with all the serenity of a couple, exhausted by a Saturday afternoon's lovemaking, looking at each other in bed, spent and content. One day he had an idea and, as a treat, went into a photo booth and took some snaps of himself (always with the option of four different poses; full on, unsmiling; full on, quarter-smiling; seven-eighths profile, stony-faced; other seven-eighths profile, smug leer) without there being any need to surrender any of the pictures to a tube pass or passport office.

Ten supremely happy years passed like this. Time could hardly be said to have meant anything; they were so happy together. It was a love based on the idea of improvement; they would go to the best movies, read the most rewarding books (when, stuttering and grim-faced, he managed to finish *Ulysses* after five attempts, he bought himself a bottle of Piper Hiedsieck to celebrate), eat at the most exquisite and sought-after restaurants (even the fanatically exclusive could squeeze in a table for one at the last moment).

And the sex . . . well, every relationship worth the name has to have a sexual element to it, and theirs was no exception. How he learned to caress himself, to bring himself to the brink of orgasm and then leave himself there, twitching and gasping, before it was safe to touch himself once again; the fantasies conjured up, the indescribable internal orgies, the safety of the lover's trust . . . 'On se comprend,' he said to himself whimsically, after he had pleasured himself in front of his first proper purchase for the first flat of his own he moved into – a full-length tiltable mirror. How he – they – he – scorned the ordinary couples they saw, those pitiful dyads, their fretful reliance on each other, anxious with concern or frozen with indifference, doomed either to stay together or to fly apart. Which, he wondered, was worse? And who cared? He was indivisible.

And it would all have to go wrong. You can always date the precise moment of love's collapse, the moment it caves in on itself, or the instant when each little reverse ceases to be itself reversible, when the siege engine of difficulties becomes structurally secure; when the entries in the register of grievances become written in ink instead of pencil. One night, reeling in from a night of regular debauchery, his head alternately swimming from booze and fizzing from cocaine, he caught himself in the mirror as he brushed his teeth.

– Try turning your head this way, said the mirror, and brush your teeth in this manner. Perhaps with a hint of a snarl. I think it would look quite fetching.

– I'm sorry, he said, I'm not in the mood.

– I beg your pardon?

– I said I'm not in the mood. Now I'm going to have three Valium and go to bed. It's a work day tomorrow, in case you'd forgotten.

– But we have all night! Call in sick.

– I have to go to work tomorrow.

– Why? asked the mirror – and knew the answer as soon as the question was expressed.

– There's someone, isn't there? Someone else.

(In went the pills.)

– It's that new girl, isn't it?

Sighing, he pulled the cord. The room went dark.

And, in the dark, in bed, he turned over and over again the image of that new girl – Delia – who had started at the office at the beginning of the week. He could, quite literally, not stop thinking about her. Six inches shorter than him, hair a different shade of brown, the face structured in a way quite different from his own, the arrangement of the limbs . . . it was extraordinary, shocking, that he could think of someone in such a way. That he could think of someone at all. He rolled over on to his stomach and felt, with a familiarity that suddenly made him feel sick, the first stirrings of an erection. To touch, to hold, another person's body, to feel strange contours, to sweep one's hand over a thigh and only feel the sensation in one's own hand – that was how people lived, how they saved themselves from despair. To familiarize oneself with another mind, instead of having it on a plate, like having the same meal day after day . . . His erection, if you could call it that, wilted, the Valium soothed his racing heart and softly pulled him down a long dark tunnel into sleep.

After that, everything was different. When he shaved he looked at himself with sturdy utility. He moved around the house with the bogus purposefulness of someone making a point. He was civil. If he brushed against himself he apologized. His conversations became perfunctory, routine, then stopped altogether. On his own, he felt himself becoming less substantial, a person fading like an old fax message. Which was why he was so happy to see Delia, to spend time with her. He began to feel like another person. So to speak.

– You never touch me like you used to, said the mirror.

– Fuck off, he said.

– This is intolerable, said the mirror, after weeks of this. I'm leaving.

– Fine, he said, and the next time he looked in the mirror, it was as if he didn't recognize the face that looked back at him at all. He liked that.

So now they stared at each other over a cup of revolting coffee.

– Tell me about married life, then.

He had managed to pacify Hannah with a small carton of Ribena, which she was now squirting out of the straw with tentative little spasms.

– Married life? You should try it.

– Oh, very funny.

– I would think that it's something you couldn't possibly begin to imagine.

– Which is why I'm asking you all about it.

– Well . . . it can be hard at times. But it's terribly rewarding. (He thought of Delia, at home, still on the sofa, her arm over her face, like a cat's, so that her nose rested in the crook of her elbow.)

– I mean, there are times when you think you can't carry on with it any more . . . but those are the bad times. Mostly it's wonderful. It's all about . . . it's all about sharing.

– And how long have you been together now? Four years?

– Yup.

– It took you four years to come up with a miserable string of clichés like that? Come on, you could say something a little more original, surely. In fact I know you could. But you just can't be bothered to, can you? Or at least not to me.

He shook suddenly, and pulled Hannah roughly on to his lap.

– Listen, pal, is your alternative any more interesting? Sitting there wanking yourself into oblivion and then if you're lucky having a fucking flower named after you? I don't think so. This is real life. This is something worth living for. I know you couldn't grasp it if you tried, but there it is.

– *Touché*, my old mucker. That's more like it. Now would you like to hear about me?

— Not really.

— I thought not. So you really don't want to know about my free and easy lifestyle, my jet-setting trips to New York, my mistresses so numerous that I can't even remember their names?

— Spare me. I happen to know that when I'm not around, you don't even exist.

— This is quite true.

They finished their coffee at the same time, and with the same grimace.

— So you don't miss me? I always loved the way that the French say that the other way round. '*Tu me manques*' instead of '*je te manque*'. It suggests a dissolution of individuality, a lack so profound that the very boundaries of personality become blurred, amorphous. How did Plato put it? That we were all once man and woman in the same body, but that we were then torn asunder, and have spent the rest of time trying to make ourselves whole once more. Oh, don't roll your eyes like that. I'll tell you something I've never admitted to anyone: no one ever made me feel things so intensely as you. No one.

— That's very sweet of you, but I think I have to go now.

He put Hannah back into her buggy.

— Now she's stopped crying, she really is adorable.

— Yes, she's terrific. She's just getting over a bug of some sort, that's why she's been so fractious.

— Really adorable. Do you know what? I bet lots of people have already said this — but she looks just like you. You're like two peas in a pod.

And now, the onlooker, if she had stayed to watch (we imagine her as a woman on the far side of middle age, passing the time in casual speculation about the people around her in the supermarket or the bus queue, wearing a frumpy woollen coat and glasses which really should have had new lenses put in some time ago), would have seen one harassed man, clumsily putting his daughter in a cheap pushchair, and then picking up the scant, last-minute basket of provisions for a modest Christmas meal. Her heart might have gone out to him, for he looked exhausted and unhappy; but then her gaze would have strayed to the little girl, and she would have smiled, in the way everyone smiles when they notice that father and child look exactly alike.

Freshwater Fishing
Nicholas Shakespeare

There's a splash. A white face breaks the surface. It's the larger of the two girls. She treads water, laughing. Then an arm comes out of the lake and flings something on to the dock, bright blue – a bathing suit.

I watch her for a moment. From the Copacabana you have a good view of the dock. The Indians watch too, their eyes expressionless like the water. The thinner girl stands against the dirty waveless lake, deciding whether to dive in. I'm waiting for her to make up her mind when the lounge door opens and the Indians smile and I know with a true weight in my heart who it is.

'Hello, Richie!'

I turn and squint. For a moment he's indistinguishable from the coats and shadows. And then I begin to make him out. He's standing in a black rubber diving suit with his hair wet and he's holding a pair of yellow goggles and some flippers of the same colour and an oxygen cylinder. I won't ask why he's dressed like that. I don't even want to know. There's nothing to dive for in that lake. Unless he's after lost watches – or bathing suits which have missed the dock.

'Hello, Silkleigh.'

'How are you, old soul?' he comes back at me as if I'm his best friend.

Silkleigh plonks his diving gear by the door where it starts a sizeable puddle and goes over to the Indians. He's the only white I've seen cross the floor to chat with these Ojibwa. He pinches Plywood Pete's purple, drink-ballooned cheeks and says a few words as though he's speaking Pete's special language, but I don't believe he is. He's only been in Kenora four months. If you ask me, he's just old-souling them.

They laugh at Silkleigh and then he squelches to the bar trailing water and a whiff of England like sulphur, and without a blush he asks Ned for a pint of Molson Golden, the girl's beer.

'And a packet of Humpty-Dumpty crisps.'

Ned comes back from the store room and he's telling him he only has Old Dutch Ripple, when there's a shout.

Silkleigh follows the trajectory of my stare. We're both looking down on the dock where the small girl is standing in her Speedo bathing suit. She has a farmer's tan: shoulders white, arms brown as if she's wearing long dark gloves. Her friend waves from the water urging her to jump. They must be girls from the city. Local girls don't swim off the dock. The water is full of diesel fuel and rainbows.

'Richie, old soul,' says Silkleigh, all conspiratorial, 'that's the one ship I'll never sail in. A relationship.'

That's how Silkleigh is. I say nothing. I'm hoping he'll dive back into the lake, but he dins on.

'Temperament has a lot to do with size, Richie. The smaller they are the more you've got to watch out.'

He sips his girlie beer and waits to see if I've taken his bait. By the set of his chin I can tell he's thinking an enormous thought which no one in the Copacabana shall prevent him from sharing.

'I know it's traditional to suppose that what happens to us is scrawled in the stars . . .' Noisily, he tears open his Old Dutch Ripple.

I'm in the middle of establishing Silkleigh's drift when he says: 'Crisp, old soul?'

'They're called chips,' I tell him.

Silkleigh gazes at the small thin girl on the dock. She curves her back and prepares to dive. Seeing her neat form strike the water like a match going out, he suddenly looks very tragic as if he's remembered something quite awful. Beneath the surface her white legs catch the sun, but Silkleigh is no longer smiling. In fact, he's all in a heap and lonely.

'You know, Richie, old soul, you and me are both men of letters.' I am seriously content to leave our conversation at this, but he wrist-wipes some beer from his lips and swivels to me and says with an urgency which I have not observed before in our acquaintance: 'You're probably the only person in Kenora who has the smarts to understand this.'

'Understand what?'

He waves his hand in the air like it's surrounded by flies. '*You* know, old soul. Of course, you do. How people can separate or stay together for the most tenuous of reasons.'

I look around for Ned, but I hear him in the storeroom stacking bottles. I tilt my empty glass, waiting for him to reappear but Ned's a sensible fellow. 'Not sure I know what you're talking about, Silkleigh.'

'Shall I tell you, Richie, the secret of the sexes?'

With two Molson Ex under my belt I am equipped to study him. Silkleigh, to be brutal, does not look like someone who can tell the difference between the sexes.

'No,' I say.

You have to hand it to him, he's uninsultable. 'Tell you all the same, old soul,' he says. 'Women hope men will change. Men hope women will stay the same,' and he leans so close I can smell the sour cream and onion. 'They never do.'

I'm investigating the top of Ned's bar through the bottom of my glass in a contemplative, microscopic way when Silkleigh says, 'And can I tell you something else, Richie? Something I've never told anyone.'

'Ned!' I call.

'Coming . . . ' Ned answers, but that's a lie. He stays in his back room clinking the empties busy-busy while Silkleigh starts to tell me what he's never told anyone. I'm not listening to be honest. Being a nice guy, I'm nodding, but what I'm really trying to do is to glance at the dry bits left in my paper. Anyways, I gather it's about some squeeze Silkleigh was once married to and how she left him pretty soon after, which does not shock me in the way, evidently, he thinks it should.

'Terrible,' I manage. Ned may have told me Silkleigh was married, I can't remember. Everyone gets married in Kenora at some point.

'You're bound to have met her father, old soul. Bound to.'

'Who is she?'

'She's basically a very selfish woman,' says Silkleigh and then adds, 'She doesn't love me.'

Here I can relate. 'Name?'

He scrunches up his chip bag, claps his hands and tells me.

'You were married to her!' I say, much astonished, and Ned's dog starts barking.

'Don't be such a pain,' says Silkleigh and he caresses the top of its head.

'Stella Fotheringham,' I repeat.

Now all I know about Stella is that she's supposed to be bright as hell and beautiful with it. The only other thing I know, she works up north with animals. Two weeks ago I was up at her father's Lodge for an article I'm writing about Big Business on the lake. Stella wasn't there, but the office was hung with pictures of a lovely-looking woman standing in the snow beside no one and certainly not beside Silkleigh.

'I had no idea Stella was married.'

'Wasn't,' says Silkleigh. 'Until she met *moi*.'

He peels the rubber down his wrist to reveal a swanky-looking watch. 'See this?' He holds it to his ear and when he listens his face positively ticks with joy. 'She gave it me. Wedding present. Water-resistant to three hundred metres. "Like you, sweet," she said. But that's just the Silkleigh cover. I can tell you, old soul, I was a bit leaky after she left.'

'Why did she leave?'

'Now you're asking too much,' and he sits there all in black and dripping, like he's mourning.

But I want to know. 'Silkleigh, that's not fair. You were about to tell me.' And seeing he's undecided, I make a vicious appeal. 'One man of letters to another.'

At this he drops his wrist and all of a sudden it's the face of hurt I'm looking at. 'She left me . . . ' says Silkleigh and I'm not sure if he will continue, but he manages to find the words, ' . . . because I took her fishing.'

They'd met on a ship in some fiord. Stella, as it happens, is an Arctic mammologist with a Ph.D. from Tromsø. 'She hated everything south of the sixtieth parallel and that, in the end, included me,' says

Silkleigh. 'But not in the beginning. Ah, the beginning . . . '

Eleven months of the year, she lived by herself in Nuuk, tracking walruses and their cubs. The other month, she gave lectures on adventure tours for rich folk who wanted to see the North. She talked about reindeer, polar bear, walruses. Nobody talked to her. 'Too intelligent, old soul.' Except one night on deck as they sailed into Tromsø, Silkleigh.

'We had the wilderness in common, and one thing led to another. I will not detail how she took her comfort, but when she danced the waltz that night she almost carried me in the air. I was arse over tea kettle about her, old soul,' he whispers. 'Arse. Over. Tea. Kettle. But there was just one problem.'

'Tell me.'

'I wasn't a walrus. Not that I knew this at the time. At the time I was tumbling gaily into the old freefall. "Want to come diving in the Gibraltar Straits?" I whispered as we danced. "Why not?" she said. We stepped off that boat and flew to Abyla, cold to hot. She thrilled at the idea of it, just as she thrilled at the idea of me. Contrast, old soul. Women love it. And all that cold, it melted in the Mediterranean Sea. I showed her giant turtle and squid and cuckoo wrasse and if I could get her south once more it would happen all over again.'

I'm gathering from Silkleigh that Stella was, as I have observed her to be in her photographs, small and compact. 'And beautiful?' I ask, to be sure.

'Does a fish swim!' says Silkleigh. 'But she didn't like to be reminded of her physical attraction and so I never did. "Beauty. Skin deep," I observed after one of her squalls. "Lucky I'm thick-skinned," she snapped back. And Stella was that, which is one of the things I discovered in Abyla. Most people filter unpleasant things out. She filtered everything in. She was like a Dutch slaver, old soul. Miserable. On our honeymoon I had a name for her because she looked so sad. Viejita, that's what I called her. Little Old One.'

I'm about to say that I don't recall her looking sad up at the Lodge, but Silkleigh grabs my arm. 'Know what Stella's mother told Stella on her deathbed?'

'No.'

'"If that's how you kiss a man, no wonder you don't have one."'

And her mother was right. She saved every endearment for her bob-sleigh team. Old soul, you can't imagine. The terrible cruelty of animal lovers . . . '

At this moment, I notice something move into my line of vision and ever so slowly a hand curls around the doorframe and then a nose appears, followed by an eye, some whiskers and an ear.

'Ned!' But he vanishes and all I hear through the renewed clinking of bottles and the dog barking is Silkleigh's unstoppable voice.

'Which meant,' Silkleigh went on, 'that she had no interest in my writing. Couldn't cope at all. Can you imagine, old soul? She wanted to go to the top of a revolving restaurant or put out forest fires. Anything but read my work-in-progress.'

'So where does fishing fit in?'

'Ah, fishing,' says Silkleigh, as if he might have forgotten the reason why I sit here nodding. 'Well, this part will especially fascinate you, Richie, being a wordsmith. I bet you're the same as I am. Never happier than when sixty miles from a pavement. We writers, we're like the Indians, I reckon. We need our space. When we're in the woods with our .22 and our sleeping bag, no sound but the cry of the loons and the low-pitched rumble of the ice talking to itself, that's when we're at home. That's when we're at our peak, isn't it? I can see it in your face. So, Richie, you of all people will understand why not long after we married, I took this houseboat in Minaki to write my book and left Stella behind at the Lodge.

'I ought to say that since the honeymoon there'd been a teeny-weeny bit of tension. We hadn't been fighting, but things were a mess. Which is why I was careful not to say too much when I left for Minaki. No home is broken by an unsaid word, old soul. That's what my housemaster told me.

'Well, there I am in the woods, scratch scratch scratch. I suppose you'd call me one of the last of the old-fashioned autobiographers,' and he spreads his fingers and glances from his hand to mine. 'Tell you're a calligrapher, too, old soul.'

'No, I'm on a computer.'

He looks from the back of his hand to the palm, closes it. 'And when I finish my chapter I ring her. As it happens, this chapter's taken longer than I thought. It's the writing bug. Once it gets you, you don't notice the time. But how do you explain that to someone who runs a Walrus Alert Team in Nuuk? I can hear on the line she sounds a trifle subdued when I explain that I've got myself to prep school and only thirty years to go, ta-ra. But I do understand. It's hard to be married to an artist and I expect she's missing me. So I say: "Viejita, don't be like that. I'm going to give you a big treat." You would have thought she'd be delighted to hear this, but she goes on in this voice and that's when the old Silkleigh sixth sense ought to have clicked in. You see, she was using words she'd never used before.'

'What kind of words?'

'Words like "touched". "I'd be touched if you took me out to dinner." Poor Viejita. She's never been touched in her life. So I say, knowing what an animal-lover she is, "No, I'll do something much better. I'll take you fishing."

'You know that island opposite the Lodge? Smoke-coloured pines on a pink rock. Well, that's where I decided to take her. I wanted to make it a day she would remember and to this end I stopped off in Kenora to buy her a present.'

'What do you buy a girl in Kenora?'

'I bought her a spanking new split-cane rod and a lure.'

'Just what she always wanted.'

'What I didn't tell her was I'd forked out every penny of my publisher's advance to give her this treat. But that's how you are when you love someone. The old do-re-mi doesn't mean a thing. So I row her to the island and tell her how lucky we are. It's a beautiful day for fishing, overcast, with the ice melting in a tinkle and the sun invisible behind the beaver-stripped trees. I start to put up her rod and she sits on the rock, pulling on a jersey. I'm just sorry she's not saying much, that's all.'

'Didn't you lay it on the line, Silkleigh?'

'When you're having fun you never lay anything on the line. And the rod is lovely, a twelve-foot state-of-the-art cane. I hand it to her and I say, "You know, Viejita, how mayfly live twenty-four hours? When I look at that rockface, I feel like a mayfly." Well, she stares at the rock as if she has twenty-four things she'd prefer to do and she suddenly becomes inexpressibly sad.

'"Don't say that, Silkleigh. Don't call me, Viejita. It's everyone's inevitability."

'By now, I'm tying on the lure. I've bought her a Five of

Diamonds. Actually, if I wanted to be critical, I could say Viejita was a bit like that lure, bouncing along all shiny on the surface, glistening with hooks, but lacking in the what-it-takes to land a fish. But in the right hands, the Five of Diamonds can be lethal. As I tie it on, I do a little demonstration so she can appreciate the science. Biophysics, I understand, is one of the subjects she studied in Tromsø so she'll be pretty interested. I show her how the lure doesn't revolve, flips back and forth, does a full turn one way, then a full turn the other. "So you can use it all day without twisting the line," I explain. Still she says nothing. Just sits on the rock and holds the rod and looks at the lake. I'm thinking all she needs to be Britannia is a helmet, and decide maybe the best thing is to educate her more about the lure, which is named after a metal-worker from Alberta who was gassed at Ypres. I tell her how the doctors told Len that he needed a year of exercise and fresh air and how he took his sleeping bag and tent and went off into the woods. "Rather like me," and I bowl her a Silkleigh special, a smile normally which works a treat. And how, I go on quickly, not being able to afford fishing tackle he got hold of some kitchen spoons and cut their handles off and drilled holes in them so they revolved in water instead of going back and forth.

'"You wait. You'll catch everything on the Five of Diamonds," I promise. "In fact, my darlingest, I should be hiding behind a tree doing this so the fish don't jump out."

'What I'm saying must strike a chord, because she says, "How do you know, Silkleigh? You've never fished a freshwater lake."

'And that's when I see it. As I finish tying the lure, a big fish rises about thirty yards from the rock.

'Stella looks at the ripple, concentrating for the first time. "I wonder if that's a pike." It would have to be a pike or a muskie. She only likes things that are big.

'"Probably a trout," I say, and I start to tell her about the first trout I ever caught, out of a Christmas tree in Hungary. "I was so excited that I hoicked it from the river into the branches – "

'The fish rises again, a little further out.

'She stares at the disturbance. "Or could it be a sturgeon?" Her voice suggests that even if it was a beluga and she happened to catch it, she couldn't really care. But I do have a feeling she's more interested than she wants to be.

'I show her how to cast and she casts in a dutiful fashion for about ten minutes, but there's no further sign of the fish. She returns the rod. "Here. You have a go," and as I take it the fish rises again and I can see it's a nice one.

'I can also see the fish is heading out slowly into the lake. I try to cast beyond it, but the lure falls short in the grey water. I reel in the line and throw the rod harder.

'"More to the left," she says at the splash, and I'm excited. "I said you'd get a taste for it." The lure bounces out of the water and a little further off I hear another rise.

'A wind blows in from the lake, fanning water on to the rockface and beside me Stella shudders.

'"You watch. I'll get it this time." I'm so afraid the fish might swim out of reach that I back-flip the rod and with a special effort hurl it forward and that's when the wind catches the lure and the Five of Diamonds instead of dropping into the lake buries itself in Stella's arm.

'I put down the rod, run to her, peel up her jersey. One of the hooks curls dark under her skin.

'"I can cut it out," I say. "I could boil a knife."

'"No," she says firmly.

'I row her to the Lodge and drive to the hospital in Kenora and by the time we arrive two hours have passed. The nurse takes her away and I wait outside until the nurse comes to find me. "Boy," she says. "Your wife's mad at you."

'That night, I take Stella out to dinner. Since we're in Kenora I've booked us a table in the revolving restaurant. I thought she'd appreciate that. We go up in the lift and find our table. But when we're seated I have to admit the old sixth sense is relaying to me that maybe she doesn't have every oar in the water. Even though she insists her arm isn't hurting, I can see she's all churned up about something.

'I bowl her another Silkleigh special. "Share?" I say. Not that I expect her to. She's close like that. Put it this way, old soul, I have by now ascertained that Stella isn't someone to wear a matching curling jacket with "Silkleigh" on the sleeve.

'"Order anything you like," I tell her, ascribing it to hunger, but she just asks for a children's portion of pickerel cheeks. When the pickerel cheeks arrive she looks at them and after a while she picks up the pepper pot. Then she looks at me and she says, "It's not working."

"'No, my darlingest, it's a grinder. Give it to me," and I'm reaching out for it when she says, "I want a divorce."

'I put down the pepper-grinder and I can tell you, Richie, it takes a second to sink in, this bolt from the absolute blue. Then I meet her gaze.'

Silkleigh plucks at the skin under his chin as if it's not me who's looking at him but someone else, and he picks up his glass. 'Know something else, old soul? While we're about it, I might as well tell you. Hatred is not the reverse of love. Indifference is. She had a look in her eye that I'd only seen before in wolves. I've come across them in packs on the ice. They look at you for a second out of curiosity, a very intelligent look, and then walk on. That was the look on Stella's face.'

Silkleigh finishes his beer.

'That was the last time I saw her. As a wordsmith, I know what's going through your mind. That Five of Diamonds in her arm was a symbol, the final straw. That's what I thought, too. To begin with I even tried to blame myself. I know, I know. But one does. In fact, there was actually a moment when things got so squiffy that Silkleigh here nearly had himself shrunk. Shrunk, old soul! Then I thought: "That's ridiculous" and for a while I blamed the old stars in the sky. I spelled it out to myself. There was nothing you could have done, Silkleigh. N.O.T.H.I.N.G. It was inevitable. Unpreventable. And then not so long ago I started to ponder. If we'd caught that fish … If instead of her arm I'd hooked that fish and we'd had a beautiful day on the lake, would not Stella Fotheringham and I still be man and wife? I tell you, old soul, when you bother to think about it, our happiness, our misery, hangs by a nylon thread. And then I thought, if I could just get her south again, under the sea … '

Silkleigh's words are lost in the noise of an engine revving.

Outside the Copacabana, it's getting dark. A girl arranges her legs on the back of a motorbike and I see it's the thin girl from the dock. Her hair hangs in a long wet rope down her back. She lifts a bare leg high over the exhaust pipe and her skirt falling over the tail light of the motorbike glows red.

' . . . but I'd do it all over again. The writer in me, I suppose. Remember what our brother Nietzsche said about artists, old soul?'

I watch the girl disappear down Waboden Avenue and dwindle into a hot dot. 'Remind me.'

'We never learn.'

Ari's Hands
Hilaire

Molly wept.

Ari hadn't called round for over a week.

That Thursday evening as she prepared her dinner, clear tears had flowed out of her eyes and dripped on to the kitchen bench. Molly was slicing an onion into rings. She felt the water pouring down her face, but her eyes weren't stinging. The knife sawed through the white bulb as she counted back how many days it was since she'd seen Ari, flicking through a mental calendar. Monday last week. At what point would she decide he was gone for good?

She pushed the onion rings into the frying pan and they began to sweat and sizzle. Molly continued to weep, but she was not sobbing. She felt calm and very empty as she poked at the frying onions with the wooden spoon. She was about to switch on the extractor fan when she realized she could smell nothing. Momentarily puzzled, she dismissed it as an early symptom of flu, but later she would remember the odourless onions as one of the first indications that something was wrong.

Molly took her plate of spaghetti bolognese through to the living room where she had a fold-out dining table. When she first moved down to London she had been lucky to find an unfurnished flat in the basement of a grand old Victorian house. Intensely private, she was glad to have her own entrance. Her first months had been taken up with decorating and furnishing the flat, creating her little retreat from the world. She felt secure there, cocooned from the pressures of work and the daily grime of London life.

She lit some candles and opened the fat paperback she was reading. As she tucked into the spaghetti a chill settled around her shoulders. Ari's absence. It was behind her, in the room, an awareness she couldn't shift.

They had met one October morning. Following her usual route to work, Molly had been knocked off her bike by a car which had suddenly turned left without indicating. Ari was cycling in the opposite direction but stopped and crossed the road to make sure that she was OK. At first her anger shielded her from the shock. She stood in the road and waved her fist and shouted at the car, which accelerated down the road. But as soon as Ari placed his hand on her shoulder and led her to the pavement, her stomach turned to jelly. Molly couldn't stop shaking and the shaking released huge sobs, as if all the gunk she had ingested over the past months, all the build-up of stress, was being dislodged.

Ari stayed with her, checking over her bike, spinning the freewheel, squeezing the brakes, until the shock passed through her body and she was calm again.

Then they shared a cigarette, squatting on the pavement of the quiet side street, hazy autumn sunshine filtering through the plane trees. The leaves were just starting to turn.

– *I'm going to be late*, Molly said, glancing at her watch.

– *You're not going to work after an incident like that*, Ari countered. Instead, he walked her back to her flat, wheeling their bicycles beside him as if they were cows being led home for milking.

Molly started to explain the route but Ari pre-empted her with a nod. – *I know the way*, he said quietly. She did not question him. Already she had noticed his long slim hands. Solicitous hands. And she knew something fundamental was changing.

Ari locked his bike to the railings before carrying Molly's bike down to the basement. He ran a bath for her and as she lay back in the bubbles Molly imagined his slender, bony hands washing her. She felt drunk; wanted to invite him into the bathroom but did not dare. When she emerged, a Japanese wrap tied demurely around her, Ari had brewed a pot of Earl Grey tea. Ever since, the oily hint of bergamot reminded her of that morning.

In the following days and weeks Molly discovered the pleasures of Ari's dark and salty skin. She delighted in his long toes which were like fingers. Ari could cross his toes, make them click in syncopation to her jazz records, pick up cigarettes with them, tease and pinch Molly's nipples as he reclined languidly on her bed. His hands and feet fascinated her. When he kneaded and pummelled the tension from her neck it felt as if he was reaching deeper, right inside her. Then he would trace his fingertips slowly along the contours of her body and Molly's mind would pulsate with new and exotic images, brain prints of Ari's thoughts and emotions.

Ari was elusive. Molly never learned his surname, where he lived, what he did. He would arrive on his bike and stay for a night or a few days or even a week at a time. Then he would disappear, unexplained, but never for as long as this.

Sometimes when she got home from work his bike would be chained to the railings but there would be no sign of him in her flat. She would be reassured, though, knowing that he was nearby. As she sat reading or constructing boxes at her workbench she sensed his presence in the flat, as if he were asleep in the bedroom, exchanging oxygen with her.

About two months after they had met Molly was setting off for work after spending the night on her own. As she carried her bike up the stairs she noticed Ari's bike locked to the railings at the front of the house. Something, a slight fluttering of the curtains in the ground-floor flat, or a quiet laugh which floated out into the cold grey morning, brought to the surface of her mind what she already knew. Ari also visited her neighbour Vadim upstairs.

Molly swivelled her feet into the toe straps of her pedals and coasted down the street. The jigsaw of that first morning was now complete. No wonder he'd known the way back. He'd been cycling towards her street, towards Vadim.

Up until that point Ari had not mentioned Vadim. But, although Molly said nothing, it was as if he knew she knew. He began to casually drop Vadim's name into the conversation, until Molly felt she knew more about Vadim than Ari.

— *Vadim's from Transylvania, you know*, Ari said once, before sinking his teeth into her soft neck and sucking hard. Molly remembered devouring orange segments at half-time during a netball match; these flashbacks often came when she was with Ari.

But now Ari's bike was gone; Ari was gone.

★

The second time it happened Molly knew something was wrong. She'd laid two rashers of bacon in the frying pan and turned the gas up high. The bacon spat and hissed, the fat shrivelled and the pink meat darkened, but Molly's mouth was dry. There was no aroma to make her salivate. And yet, ten minutes ago, when she'd gone out to buy the Sunday papers, she'd smelled the newsprint. As she walked home across the common she had registered the smell of wet earth, and, passing the betting shop, the stench of urine had been overwhelming.

Without its redolent, smoky odour her breakfast was tasteless. For the past couple of days Molly had been suffering a heavy headache which had never quite broken into a migraine. It felt as if the whole weight of the house was pressing down on her. Something or someone was sucking the air out of the flat and taking all the aromas and scents with it.

Usually on Sundays she worked at her boxes, assembling disparate objects, feathers, broken glass, a champagne cork, into 3D collages. However, now that she had become aware of the absence of smells in the flat she couldn't concentrate. As soon as she unscrewed the lid from the tube of glue she missed its chemical tickle. The scrap of driftwood she picked out of the mound of junk on the bench lacked even the slightest whiff of the sea.

Molly ransacked the kitchen, sniffing bottles of bleach, a jar of coffee grounds, a chunk of Parmesan cheese. Nothing. What had previously given her pleasure was now textureless. The olfactory dimension had been erased from the flat and her distress was the same as if her surroundings had suddenly been drained of colour.

The throbbing in her head was unbearable. Molly had the sensation that her brain was being vibrated by something external, a pressure or force being exerted downwards through the ceiling, right through her body. It was causing her to choke and she fled the flat, grabbing her bike and hoisting it up the stairs despite her breathlessness.

Out on the street she realized she was trembling. But there was air and a sudden assault of different fragrances, petrol and damp leaves, which rushed her nostrils. Swinging herself on to the saddle she set off, glad simply to be mobile, breathing freely.

The motion of cycling allowed Molly to disengage her brain.

She cycled aimlessly for hours, criss-crossing London, afraid to stop lest the pain in her head returned. Until she found herself half-way across Putney Bridge. She dismounted and stood staring down into the river. It was low tide. A mud-caked shopping trolley was partially buried in the silt, as if it had dived head-first into the river.

Molly remembered encountering Ari once at exactly the same spot as she was cycling home from work. He was looking out over the river, towards Hammersmith, and she had studied him from the other side of the bridge, his muscular back and toned thighs revealed by his cycle clothes, before crossing over and joining him. The image of Ari's back, of him turned away from her, gazing into the distance, contained his mystery, everything she loved about him.

Now she waited for the return of the river. By the time it had crept back under the bridge and spread out between both banks night had fallen. Molly told herself that what she had experienced earlier had been a strange type of migraine, nothing more. She listened to the water lapping inland. It was time to head back home.

Waking was a nightmare. The weight of the house pushed down on Molly's chest, her eyelids were stuck together, she could not raise her hands to lift the duvet. In panic, she thought she had been drugged; how else to explain this leaden feeling?

Then she heard again the sound which had kept her awake until three a.m. Up above, a dull *pop, pop, pop*, like someone bursting bubble wrap. *Pop, pop, pop*, all night long. It would stop, and then, just as she drifted towards the edges of sleep, *pop, pop, pop*, insinuating itself into her head, a slow PacMan virus eating her brain.

As she'd carried her bike down to the basement the previous night, Molly had glanced up and seen Vadim letting himself into the house. He was, as usual, wearing a black polo neck and a dark suit, clothes which emphasized his alabaster complexion. They rarely crossed paths. Occasionally, on a Wednesday night, they would bump into each other as they hauled their bins out for collection, and murmur a hello. Molly had not asked him about Ari, nor, until this point, had she felt jealous. How could she, when Ari had already been involved with Vadim before he met Molly?

Vadim's key glinted as it slid into the lock, and Molly caught a subliminal image of a knife entering flesh. The notion that Vadim was implicated in Ari's disappearance came to her with a jolt. And here she was, smothered in the flat below, being subjected to the aural equivalent of the Chinese water torture. *Pop, pop, pop.*

With a supreme effort she flung off the duvet and forced herself up out of bed. She got the broom from the kitchen cupboard and banged it on the ceiling three times. She would not let herself be controlled by Vadim or whatever other energy was at work in the house. But even as she formed that defiant thought it rang hollow, as weak as the taps she had made on the ceiling. Her muscles had gone slack; defeat had got a foothold in her heart.

The structure which now held her together was the routine she had previously detested. Work was her sanctuary. Her flat had become a strange, unfamiliar place.

Clicks and pops rattled through the walls and ceilings. Some mornings when she woke her arms would be pocked with burns which faded over the course of the day. Once, as she ate her bland and odourless dinner, a bolt like lightning had shot up through her feet, knocking her off her chair to the floor. It left a singed, metallic taste on her tongue, like licking a battery.

Molly could not envisage a way out of her situation. She had no friends in London, nowhere to go. More than this, though, if she left her flat she would lose any hope of ever seeing Ari again. Sometimes she would return from work determined to counteract what was happening. In the dead of night she placed a knife on the front doorstep, aimed towards Vadim's flat. She shook talcum powder on to the stairs down to the basement. On a sheet of paper she wrote Vadim's name over and over before burning it in the flame of a candle. Her efforts only exhausted her.

The morning after she'd scorched her fingers on Vadim's name, Molly woke with a rash across her chest. The flat was stifling, though the heating hadn't been on for days and outside it was frosty. Before she realized it she was scratching like a flea-ridden cat, trying furiously to gouge the itchiness from her skin. A hound's-tooth pattern of blood soon overlaid her chest.

As she got out of bed a wave of heat rose off the floor, *whoosh*, and she sprang across the flat to the bathroom as if she were traversing an expanse of baking-hot sand to the cool sea. She lay in the bath and as the water gradually covered her the itch abated.

Pinching her nose, she submerged herself briefly, eyes shut, and wished she could stay there for ever. For a long time she remained in the bath, floating her arms on the surface of the water, watching trickles of pink curl out from her bloodied chest. Calmed at last she yanked the plug out with her toes, remembering with a tug of desire Ari's long sexy toes.

The tepid water drained away. Molly tried to get up but her body was stuck to the bath. Pulling on the handles at either side of the bath she managed to prise her back away from the tub with a sickening squelch. Her legs seemed to be melded to the enamel. Panicking, she grabbed the taps and peeled herself forwards, her skin ripping away from the bath as if it was an enormous plaster, until she was upright. Only to find her feet similarly suckered to the bath. The thought that the soles of her feet might have mutated into fleshy suction cups repelled her, so she visualized instead two heavy, gold-leafed Buddha feet. She took a deep breath and with both hands hoicked first her left leg, then her right, out of the bath.

Molly was broken. She sat at the top of the basement stairs and cried. Ari was gone and her flat no longer welcomed her. Her lacerated chest hurt but it was nothing compared to the pain in her heart.

She felt someone standing behind her and she hoped they would shove her down the stairs. Instead Vadim squatted beside her. He offered her the cigarette he had been smoking. Molly hesitated and then took the cigarette, sucked hard and filled her lungs with nicotine. Feeling dizzy, she rested her head on her knees.

Vadim put his hand on her shoulder. – *Would you like to come in for a cup of tea?*

Molly turned to look at him. His eyes were dark, very dark, as if he had not slept for weeks. In the middle of each ivory cheek was a smudge of red, which deepened and spread as she continued to stare at him. He held his hand out and helped her to her feet. His hands were almost translucent and he wore heavy garnet-encrusted rings.

He led her inside, into his flat, shutting the door gently behind her, and went through to the kitchen. Molly blinked, adjusting her eyes from the daylight outside to the gloom of Vadim's flat. For a second she thought she must be dreaming. Everything was grey. She moved around the room, touching the furniture, the books, the vases of colourless flowers.

Vadim came back into the room carrying a tray with the teapot and cups and saucers. She saw that his complexion had become pallid. The blush in his cheeks had evaporated and his suit had faded. He poured the anaemic tea and its citrus scent hung paradoxically in the room. Vadim spread his hands out. – *You see, I am also bereft.*

– *Do you know where he is?* Molly asked.

Vadim shook his head. – *The last time I saw him he was watching the river, near Richmond. He seemed so absorbed I didn't want to disturb him.* He stirred a spoon listlessly in his tea, then added: *I always worried about him cycling too fast, weaving in and out of the traffic.*

Molly thought about the hill in Richmond Park, the road swerving down, how easily you could somersault off your bike. It was still light outside. – *Come for a ride*, she said, reaching out for Vadim's pale hand. – *I'll give you a lift.*

Handfast
John Burke

He waited a decorous month after Rachel's death before going to bed with Marion.

It was a rather unnecessary formality. That first week he had felt winded, with a sort of sick emptiness in the guts; but he had no cause to feel guilty. There was no question of a heartbroken Rachel committing suicide because she sensed him reneging on their covenant. The explosion which killed her had been due simply to a faulty gas cooker in her kitchen. If he had been with her that evening, he might have been killed as well. He spent a few pensive, nostalgic evenings looking back over what had been and might have been, and then shook himself out of it and allowed himself to succumb to Marion.

It was only a fancy, a guilt he had no reason to feel, that in his head he should hear Rachel's accusation: 'You ought to have waited. The year's not up yet.'

She had been so beautiful, yet so difficult. Marion wasn't difficult. Marion was easy and insatiable. Very good for a man's morale. He could hardly be expected to honour a pledge laid down by someone who was no longer alive to fulfil her own part of it.

Marion opened her legs, threshed madly in his arms, and raved words and non-words in his ears. Enough to drown out that ridiculous reproach: *The year's not up yet.*

After that first delirium of fulfilment with Marion, without questions or doubts or frustration, it was another fortnight before Rachel came out of the shadows of memory and began stalking him.

At first he was only vaguely aware of her when he crossed a street or got into his car. Then he glimpsed her at the head of the riverside steps as if waiting for someone to accompany her down to the towpath. Next day he was almost sure it was her silhouette against late afternoon sunlight on the bridge.

Which was nonsense.

The following Monday she was outside the post office as he passed, not joining the pensioners' queue or heading for the slot to post a letter. He hurried along the pavement and stood right beside her.

'What are you doing here? You can't be here.'

'You should have waited.' This time the voice wasn't in his head, yet where else could it have come from? 'The year,' she said fervently, 'isn't up yet.'

He tried to reach out to her, but all at once she was swallowed up in the mist from the river. Yet the next day she was back again, drifting across his path, staring greyly at him.

She had once been so dark. The slenderness of her long, ivory-smooth neck had been emphasized by black hair pushed upwards from a fine arrowhead in the nape to a tight casque which in some lights could be almost raven-blue. Now she was wispy and insubstantial.

How long would it take her to fade away altogether?

Making love to Marion, he tried not to make comparisons. Rachel's dark nipples had been like purple bruises. Marion's were a babyish pink against glowingly babyish skin, and there was a fresh grassy smell in the corner of her throat. Her hair was a golden riot on her head and a golden bush way below, with a swathe of golden down running between her shoulders to the base of her spine.

And with Marion it was easy and uncomplicated right from the start. No awkwardness, no 'I'm sorry, truly I am, Alan', no 'Please give me time, it *will* be all right, I promise.'

Only it had never been quite right and now never would be.

Yet still that wraith expected him to wait?

You couldn't accuse a man of being unfaithful to a woman who had stalled over marrying him, and now was dead.

It was a warm, blue-hazed afternoon when Geordie Johnson came to sign the documents and pay over his cheque for a new tractor, one of four bright red and green monsters below Alan's office window overlooking the Tyne. 'I'll send Harry along to pick it up tomorrow.' Johnson sounded pleased as he left. Alan watched from the window as the farmer patted his new tractor in passing, as if formally patting a newly acquired horse to establish his authority from the outset.

This side of the river, glossy painted metal and one enclosure of rusty, dismantled trucks clustered below the board advertising the twentieth-century presence of VANTRAC: Commercial Vehicle and Tractor Services. On the ridge across the river, twisted blackthorn hunched against the north-east wind, and the stump of an old pele tower was almost obscured by summer foliage. In winter, from this vantage point it would be a clear ragged stump, and he would be able to see the scattering of stones on the slope like tiny grey and white sheep.

Among those stones was one he preferred not to remember.

This side of the river was today. Marion's world. Across the river had been Rachel's world.

Suddenly he knew she was standing at his left shoulder, but was not there when he twisted his head round to look at her.

'Why couldn't you have waited?'

'It's not *my* fault I didn't hold to the promise. You *died*.'

'That's not *my* fault, either.'

This was grotesque: on the verge of arguing with a ghost about the safety standards of her gas cooker.

Alan shuffled invoices desperately and made a string of telephone calls. Business was real. His own future was real. His and Marion's, the way things were going.

On a Saturday evening he took Marion to a concert of Northumbrian pipe and fiddle music high up in Hexham's ancient Moot Hall. The announcement of one Northumbrian folk air 'arranged by the late Rachel Robson' was in danger of conjuring her up again.

'Wasn't that your old girlfriend?' said Marion with breathy curiosity.

'I knew her, yes.'

'What was wrong with her? Why didn't the two of you . . . '

The music started and he didn't have to answer. The spell of the melancholy pipe melody was like a life-giving injection to Rachel. She was at his shoulder again, fitting a lyric of rebuke to the melody. He stared resolutely ahead. She would soon ebb away from his imagination.

Or not until the year was up?

Marion was fidgeting. Music meant nothing to her. She rubbed the legs of her tights together in a scratchy, conflicting rhythm. Her right forefinger plucked away at the corner of her thumbnail. When he put his hand on hers in the hope of soothing her into stillness, she began tugging it across her lap and between her legs, impatient to get back to bed.

Which Rachel had never been. Promising to be so one day if only he was patient, but wretchedly having to fake the shudders and pulsations of an orgasm just to please him.

He had been patient. Because he loved her. He loved the lilt of her voice, loved the unhurried hours sharing music and laughter and the long walks by the river and over the moors. Except for that one block. And that would dissolve eventually, and everything would come right. They both said it would come right. That was why he had played along with her eager conceit about the handfasting, coaxing her and carefully urging her towards the decision she simply had to make when the year was up.

Which she had not lived to make.

Rachel Robson was a musicologist and adviser to the Folk Music Faculty of the Border Marches Academy, and Corresponding Professor of the Fort Rouge Ethnic Music College of Manitoba. She wore the titles lightly, pursuing her researches out of love rather than professorial earnestness; though not many were allowed close enough to feel the warmth of that passion.

She had become the acknowledged expert on ballads and folksong on both sides of the Border – the Northumbrian pipes and the Scottish small pipes, the fiddle tunes and country dances, the significance of old customs no longer observed in the countryside but preserved in song and verse. Some men were put off by her intensity. It took a man like Alan Storey to enjoy basking in the glow of her enthusiasms and her sheer concentration when on the trail of some half-forgotten scrap of melody or bringing together the fragments of a poem and music which her instincts told her were meant to blend into one.

In her flat in a September twilight he gave her a CD of a new recording of the Bartók Third Piano Concerto. She leaned contentedly against him on the couch, rapt and still, her hair tickling his cheek only when a faint breeze from the open window stirred a few strands. The eerie night sounds of the second movement flowed over them and into them. Alan was lost in the music itself; Rachel took an extra joy from it because it so resonantly paralleled her own researches into old airs and rhymes of the Marches. She recorded with more sophisticated equipment than Bartók had known in his wanderings through the wilds of Hungary and Romania, but her commitment was as intense as his had been.

When the last exuberant flourishes of the final rondo had raced headlong to their conclusion, she sighed. It was over. Neither of them had wanted it ever to end.

Alan said: 'I love you.'

She tensed, then let herself sink back against him.

'Oh, dear,' she said.

'I love you,' he repeated. After a silence that was taut and strained after those moments of perfect ease, he said: 'It can't have come as much of a surprise. Can't you say anything?'

'It's . . . not easy.'

'Not easy to say you love me? Fair enough, I suppose.'

'No, Alan, it's not . . . I mean . . . oh, hell, I'm not much good at this.'

'There's somebody else.'

'No.' She gripped his hand fiercely. 'Of course there isn't. I couldn't love anyone else. If it's anyone, it has to be you.'

'But it's still *if*?'

'Alan, I can't imagine being without you. Truly.'

'And that's the best you can do?'

'The best I can do right now. Please give me time. When I can say it, I'll say it.'

'Let me persuade you.' He got up from the couch and tugged her to her feet. 'It's all so easy, really.'

She did not protest or try to push him away when he led her into her bedroom. Silently she shed her clothes and lay back on her double bed with its single pillow, and in a lilting whisper said, 'All right, Alan. I'll try. Dear Alan.' But she was tight and unyielding. At the same time she whimpered with the effort to please him and herself. The greater the effort, the more intense her stiffness and misery.

'It'll get better,' he assured her. 'With us two, it just has to.' He put his right arm round her and drew her head down to his shoulder. 'I love you. In the morning . . .'

But she didn't want him to stay until morning. She was not used to sharing a bed, certainly not for an entire night. She was not ready to change. Not yet.

'Alan, be patient. Please.'

They spent a holiday in Shetland, revelling in the swirling unison of the Shetland fiddlers. He made love to her, and she apologized so sadly for not being loving enough. Back through the long nights and shifting daylights of Orkney, they made their way down through the Highlands and old Border battlegrounds to the banks of the Tyne again. They shared music rather than passion; but one must eventually lead to the other – there had to be a resolution, a perfect cadence, at the end of their *liebeslied*.

At a performance of Janáček's *Cunning Little Vixen* at the Theatre Royal in Newcastle, acquaintances nodded at them and muttered knowledgeably together in the bar. They were a couple – an item, in current jargon.

In his flat he poured her a glass of Chilean Chardonnay, and they sat back under a watercolour of Windy Gyle, high in the Cheviots, which he had bought a few weeks earlier. They were relaxed, happy. She put her glass down and rested her hand on his. It ought to be so natural, so effortless. His fingers curled round hers; strayed; began touching and stroking her. In the end she made another gallant pretence of uncontrollable frenzy. Neither of them believed it. Next day they went to her flat, watched over by her favourite gouache of a sad clown and by shelves of cassettes and CDs. And he said, 'I love you,' and when he was sunk in her she smiled and breathed 'Alan' with unfeigned affection, but could shape no other words.

He said: 'Rachel, will you marry me?'

'Oh, Alan, no.'

'I want you to marry me. You've *got* to.'

'Alan, I wouldn't be any use to you. I'm not up to it.'

'Everything'll be so much simpler when we're married.'

'I've . . . wondered. But, no. No, Alan. I was engaged once. Over a year ago. It came to nothing.'

'Thank God for that.'

'It didn't work. My fault. And I don't think I'd be any good for you, either. And I couldn't bear to let *you* down.'

'Think about it.' He was as close to anger as he had ever been with her. 'I mean, really *think* about it. Because you're going to marry me. You may as well get used to the idea.'

She laughed, and unaffectedly kissed him, and he went out to collect a Chinese takeaway.

It was on an early October afternoon, as they picked their way around tumbled stones and walked up towards the ruined pele tower, that she said: 'Once upon a time this was a Robson pele, you know?'

'Your old family mansion?'

'Long ago. When the Border was torn apart by reivers and murderers and blood feud. You needed strong walls to keep the raiders out in those days.' She sauntered a few yards and stared down at the stones in the coarse grass. 'They used to hold a handfasting fair here.'

'A what?'

'A couple would clasp hands and pledge themselves to a year's trial marriage.' Her dark green eyes were shining with pleasure in a past as real to her as the present, a richness of tradition which would never quite drain away from these haughs and fells. 'Shall *we* make a troth?' She was playing with an idea, the way he had so often seen her play with a theory about a snatch of overheard melody, a scrap of old manuscript. All at once it became overwhelmingly important to her. 'A pledge for a year, and after that . . . '

'After that?'

'It'll depend on how it goes.'

'Look, I've already told you I – '

'I will handfast you,' she said.

She stooped over a large lump of whinstone with a hole eroded through its centre. Experimentally she eased her hand and wrist through it.

'During the next twelvemonth I promise to come to you, and

only you, when I fancy the idea,' she said, 'and you can come to me and only to me.'

'Not so very different from the way it is now. Except that I'm the one who does all the coming.'

'But it'll be different.' She was very serious. 'Don't you see, it will be . . . a commitment.'

He shrugged. 'Shall we choose an engagement ring?'

'No tokens. Only the pledge itself. When the next fair came round a full year later, either party could renounce the agreement unless the woman was pregnant or had given birth. If so, but one of them still wanted to break the bond, reasonable arrangements had to be made for the care of any child resulting from the . . . the . . . '

'Say it.'

'From the . . . liaison.'

'From the lovemaking,' he corrected her. 'Lovemaking, Rachel. Copulation. Intercourse. Gorgeous raving lust, my love. Or to put it bluntly – '

'We pledge ourselves for a year,' she said. 'And if it still isn't a true match, we freely unclasp our hands.'

Her mind was dancing to a measure which elated her but made little allowance for the appetites of her partner.

He said: 'You mean you'll come and live with me for a year.'

'Oh, no. No, Alan. For some that was how it was. But do it my way – please, do it this way – and in the end it'll all come right. I know it.'

With anyone else he would have said she was a prick-tease, but that wasn't true. She was sincere and beautiful, and he would do anything to make it do just that – come right. He went down on his knees and laced his fingers in hers through the whinstone ring. He swore to be true for a year, and she swore to be true for a year, at the end of which she would answer him. Then they both laughed, the way they so often laughed together, and walked back into town and listened to a tape of riotous Geordie music-hall songs, and went to bed.

And still it was awkward, and she kissed his shoulder pleadingly and pretended, and it was no better than before.

'It *will* come right,' she sobbed as his fingers tried to inflame her. 'It will, Alan, truly it will.' It was like the repetitive chorus of an old ballad, always ending on the same phrase.

Her mind willed it, her body denied it.

And then he met Marion Elliot.

Marion's mouth was wide and ravenous. From the moment she came into Alan's office as secretary to her uncle, a seed merchant wanting to do a deal on a new crop sprayer, the instinctive nibbling of her slightly overhanging upper teeth on her lower lip was a calculated provocation.

But he had pledged a troth. And he loved Rachel.

Until she died, and what was left of her exquisite yet un-responsive body was converted into ashes, and the music of her voice was silenced.

Silenced but for those whispers seeping back into his mind.

He was in desperate need, and Marion was warm and inviting and uninhibited. No problems, no awkwardness. Everything easy and delightful.

Apart from the fact that music now had become no more than background music. If he played a tape or disc while they were eating supper or sitting back finishing the wine, Marion would talk over it – Mozart, Bach, Bartók, it was all one – or even ask sometimes if it wasn't a bit loud. Strolling round an art gallery or museum with her, he had to get used to her attention wandering, beguiled only when she came across a statue or painting of a naked man or of lovers entwined. Then she would pluck at his elbow and hurry him back to his flat, which was rapidly becoming their shared flat. She moved into it without protest, without conditions.

He supposed that he really ought to propose to her.

But not until the handfasting year was up.

Which was crazy. He wasn't still under Rachel's spell; couldn't go on being subject to that discarded fantasy.

Would Rachel fade away entirely on that date in early October?

You ought to have waited.

When he next saw her, on the river towpath, Marion was with him but saw and heard nothing. Yet Rachel was drawing closer and closer: a shadow wreathing closer not to Alan, he abruptly realized, but to Marion, twining the filaments of her web to shadow Marion's face in a fine caul which might have been a widow's veil – or, when the sun suddenly brightened it, a bride's.

Then the shadow fled. Marion brushed her cheek as if a strand of hair had tickled it. He hurried the two of them back into the familiar streets. Marion was very quiet for once, glancing back a couple of times with a puzzled frown.

It was only a week before the year was up.

Next morning, as Marion got out of bed and went into the bathroom, he heard her humming a complicated variation on a tune from three centuries ago – 'Jockey Stays Long at the Fair', clear and lively as the day it was created. Then when she had run the shower and come back in with her golden hair as damp as it often was after their lovemaking, she was humming without a wrong note the opening piano motif of the Bartók concerto.

He said: 'Where did you pick *that* up?'

She blinked. 'I . . . I don't know. I just sort of . . . well, heard it inside.' She laughed, delighted with her own cleverness in appealing to him in this unexpected way; and somehow in harmony with her laugh was Rachel's, faint but unmistakable. 'I will try, Alan. You wouldn't want our baby to have a tone-deaf mum. So I *will* listen, and it'll all be all right. Truly.'

From an infinite distance came another echo of Rachel. *It will come all right, Alan. I know it will.*

But that wasn't the important bit. 'You're going to have a baby?'

'Are you cross? I'm sorry, Alan.' But Marion was still laughing. 'No, I'm not. I'm over the moon. And if you don't want to have anything to do with it, I'll understand, and – '

'Haven't I already had something to do with it?'

'Oh, yes. Yes, indeed. But you don't have to worry. We don't have to get married.'

'But we do,' he said. He dragged her into his arms. 'Oh, yes, we do. As soon as possible after next Tuesday.'

'What's next Tuesday got to do with it?'

'I don't know,' he said hastily. 'I'm just talking rubbish. Haven't got a clue. Take me time to get used to the idea.'

On the Tuesday, the day when the handfasting ended – as if such an absurdity mattered any longer – he considered staying at home, or working late in the office. Not that he was as stupidly superstitious as folk who tried not to venture out on a Friday the thirteenth. But nor did he fancy any sentimental pilgrimage, any likelihood of some perversity in his own mind conjuring up a last reproach before his succubus faded and released him for ever.

If he didn't show up, would Rachel come in search of him?

He crossed the river and trudged up the long green slope.

It ought to have been a relief to find the area round the hand-fasting stone deserted. Yet somehow he was irritated. He had come up here to do the decent thing, ready to put an end to the pledge in just the way she had told him it should be ended, and she wasn't here.

A cold wind blew disjointed tunes through the gaps in the pele tower ruins, half whistling, half coughing. He looked at the dark mouth of the crumbling doorway, and saw a shadow forming, elusive grey against black.

He took a step towards her before realizing that the blackness behind her was moving. Shapes of men crowded behind her, waiting and watching.

He said: 'Rachel.'

She smiled. 'Dear Alan. You couldn't bring yourself to wait, could you?'

'Let's be honest.' It was absurd, having to justify himself to a figment of his own imagination. 'You know that I've met somebody else.'

'Of course I know,' she said wistfully.

'And we're getting married. But not until I've been up here to agree with you that this hasn't worked. On the terms that you yourself laid down, we free each other from the pledge.'

'But there has always been one stipulation.' She sounded sweet, affectionate, yet determined. 'If a handfasting is to be ended, provision must be agreed for any child of the union.'

It was not just the wind that chilled him. 'Look, Rachel, I ought to tell you that my . . . that Marion is pregnant.'

'Yes, I know that, too. And so was I when I died.'

'You . . . ?'

'Pregnant, with your son.'

'A son? How could you know – '

'I know now that it would have been a son. Just as your Marion's child will be. That I know, too. So you will have to make provision for both of them.'

'But that's crazy. How the hell can I make provision for

someone who ' – how did you put it delicately? – 'someone who doesn't exist? I'm sorry, but – '

'I'm sorry, too. And Alan, I forgive you. But my family won't forgive you so easily.'

He recalled that she had sometimes visited a mother and father living in London, but had never suggested that Alan went with her, or suggested that she had spoken to them about him. So why should he need the forgiveness of total strangers?

Without waiting for him to ask the question out loud, Rachel went on: 'I mean the old family, of course. The true blood line. And their blood feud.'

He saw the spectres behind her thicken menacingly.

'You're a Storey,' she said. 'Your Marion is an Elliot.'

'That's right. But what the hell – '

'There has always been blood feud between Elliots and Robsons, throughout all the time there was a true Border. Through days when it was March Treason, punishable by death, for an Englishman to consort with a Scots lass, or a Scot to marry an Englishwoman. And now today, for a Storey to reject a Robson in favour of a Scottish Elliot, and not honour his handfasting to the letter… I'm sorry, Alan' – she was rueful yet implacable – 'bitterly sorry, but my menfolk will come for you and your Elliot woman.'

'In this day and age? Spooks playing old games – '

'Not games. Old customs, Alan. Not to be defied.'

'I'm not listening to any more of this. Must be out of my mind. I came here to end the charade. And it's ended.'

He turned and strode down the hill, nearly turning his ankle on a cluster of stones. The wind through the tower jeered after him. He refused to turn and look round. Whatever he had read to put such crazy notions in his mind, the sooner he shed them the better. The real music of Rachel's voice had died months ago. It was high time to dismiss tantalizing echoes.

Not until he reached the foot of the slope, still without looking back, did the hideous discords begin in his head.

There was no respite. No music loud enough to drown the inner cacophony. His favourite Northumbrian pipe tunes crept in to taunt him, as if Rachel herself had chosen the programme; and then were annihilated by bestial screeches of clashing tonalities which even Bach could never have woven into a rewarding pattern. Trying to drown the infernal dissonances, he played tapes and discs at such a volume that Marion clapped her hands over her ears and fled the room. He clapped his own hands over his ears; but still the persecution continued. The theme of the Bartók Third, wantonly distorted, mocked him. They knew how to strike at his most vulnerable point.

It was impossible to concentrate in his office. Leaves were falling from the trees and stripping away the cover of the pele tower, and from his window across the river he could see that it was occupied again – by Robson men, watching him, destroying him.

Impossible to relax at home.

Impossible to make love to Marion.

She said: 'Darling, gone off me all of a sudden?'

'My head.'

'I've heard of women pleading a headache, but – '

'It's non-stop.' He had to tell her; had to tell someone. 'This jangling inside my head, it's driving me round the bend.'

She put her head sympathetically on his shoulder. 'Isn't that what they call . . . oh, I've read about it somewhere.'

'Tinnitus. No, nothing like that.' Not the torment of tinnitus which had driven Schumann and Smetana mad: this was a deliberate campaign to drive him mad.

'You've got to see the doctor.'

The doctor said that he would make an appointment with a specialist. Perhaps hypnotherapy would help. In the meantime, he prescribed a course of tranquillizers.

Impossible to tell a busy general practitioner that you were being blackmailed by ghosts, impervious to tranquillizers of any kind. The noise went on, rising and falling in a tumult of crashing waves which scoured the world away from under him. An exorcist would be more practical than any medical man or hypnotist.

No. He would fight them on their own terms. He went to the library and spent an afternoon in the reference section, digging out yellowing histories of the region and March customs. He began to be hopeful that he was on the right track when he sensed Rachel at his shoulder again, directing him which volume to reach for, which page to turn. He was warmed by the knowledge that she was still at his side, anxious to protect him against the brutal fatalism of her family.

And here it was. Day of Truce. A day when enemies from both sides met at a Border rendezvous to settle their differences, paying for transgressions in blood money or by surrendering a malefactor to judgement by the injured party.

'A Day of Truce,' he said aloud, alarming a young student at the far end of the room.

He was quite sure that the message had been received and agreed on.

Autumn was being hustled into winter. The wind grew stronger over the fells, and each day there were bouts of thin, stinging rain. When Alan trudged up the damp slope, the bleak tower was dripping with moisture, and a fine drizzle blotted out any memory of Rachel bending gracefully towards the trysting stone.

But she was there, waiting in the doorway like any walker caught out in a storm, sheltering from the rain.

He said: 'All right. What must I do?'

The shadows stirred behind her. He could have believed that a moment of wintry light caught the glint of a lance, but when he edged under cover of the doorway the dark shapes backed away – just a few feet away.

'It's so simple, my dear.' Her voice was tender and, on this cold day, so warm. 'You must bring up my son as your own – which, after all, he is.'

'Bring him up? But we already know he's . . . I mean, he was never born. I'm sorry, but – '

'He was never born,' she agreed. 'He was alive, but never born. You gave him that life. You must continue to care for him.'

'How the hell can you expect me to do that?'

'I shall be with you. Alan, my love, I still can't imagine being without you. I won't be. I'll be with Marion and her baby. You'll have two sons, and we'll all three bring them up together. Your Marion's son will watch over his brother and comfort him. They'll be like twins, understanding each other without having to speak. But in their own way they *will* talk together. And you must encourage your flesh-and-blood son. Not tell him he's being silly, or just daydreaming. Not a fantasy brother — a real brother. And you'll not call in exorcists or doctors. Do I have your pledge?'

Making provision for an unborn child through an eternity in limbo? 'It can't work,' he protested. 'It can't possibly work.'

There was an ominous shuffling in the recesses of the hall.

'If it doesn't,' Rachel pleaded, 'the noises in your head will return. Alan, my love, don't ask me to hurt you. Love your children — both of them. And I shall occupy Marion.'

'Occupy her?'

'She won't know. But I shall be there, playing my part in the upbringing of your boys. And enjoying our lovemaking. And you and I can listen to music together, and she'll never know. But gradually perhaps I can make *her* listen, too. I've started already.'

'Yes,' he said shakily. 'So I've noticed.'

'Dearest Alan, we still have so much to learn.'

Yes, he thought, we have indeed.

Behind him, Marion said: 'Who on earth are you talking to?'

The only sound in the shell of the tower could have been wind, or a fluttering bird seeking shelter in a cranny within the walls.

Alan stood back to let Marion peer into the interior.

'I could have sworn I heard somebody in there talking.'

In a secluded embrasure Rachel was laughing contentedly.

'All right,' he said. 'It's a deal.'

Marion turned to stare. 'What are you on about?'

'Talking to myself. Dizzy with relief. All that racket in my head has stopped. And it's not going to come back.'

'How can you be sure of that?'

'Oh, I'm pretty sure.' He took her arm and steered her away, round the handfasting stone. 'But what brought you up here?'

'You looked so odd. I wondered where you . . . who you were going to meet and . . . Oh, I don't know.'

He kissed her. 'Getting suspicious already? Following me, even before we're married? Expecting to find me in the arms of another woman — on this wet grass?'

She shivered, and laughed, and stumbled closer to him.

At the foot of the slope he glanced back for a brief moment.

The misshapen windows seethed with men long dead yet clinging to a terrible life. The Robsons were back in their old stronghold. A flicker of half-hearted sunlight across the doorway lintel sketched the shape of a woman's head, tilted yearningly to one side — a dark-haired princess of legend waiting to be rescued, but knowing she would wait for ever.

Still she would cling to existence, and watch — watch other people living out their lives in the world, in the flesh; and inch her way into that flesh and remotely learn, too late, to enjoy its pleasures.

Marion was humming a melody. He recognized it as the haunting lament of the fiddler Niel Gow for his dead wife. Melancholy but entrancing, it eased away the last, lingering discords.

Rachel was fulfilling her part of the bargain. The rest was up to him.

He had a feeling that life from now on was going to be a lot less simple than she had made it sound.

Pleas
Christopher Kenworthy

When I woke up, Sarah was hogging the single bed we'd crammed into. In sleep, her dry mouth was open, each tooth dented with the molten black of a filling. Moving to the foot of the bed, I opened the window, heat rising from the radiator, mingling with cold air from outside. A narrow street of labs and offices was made colourless by the weather, the cars armoured with snow. Tree trunks had turned glossy black, their branches and twigs holding impossibly thick ledges of white. Even the icicles hanging from gutters were opaque with a roughening of flakes. There were no sounds of dogs or traffic, no car doors or footsteps. All I could hear was snow falling on snow, like the sound of blinking.

I moved back to Sarah, kissing her back and neck, a habit of giving her attention. Her hair smelt of smoke, making my guts wrench. She yawned, her breath pungent with old wine, and when her eyes opened she stared as though drunk and put a palm on her forehead.

'Fucked,' she mumbled, holding her tongue out to show me how stale it was. I passed her the water and she gulped at it, wincing. I was trying to think of a way to make her leave, when my phone rang. In the hallway, still naked, I curled up against my legs to avoid the cold.

'Chris? It's me,' the voice said.

Sarah sat up in bed to watch me, wide awake now, her mouth a quizzical pout.

It was the first time I'd heard from Wendy in two years, but I could only say, 'Oh, hello.'

'Can I see you?' She was shivering, and from the quality of the line she must have been in a phone box.

'Yes, all right.'

'Your voice sounds different. Are you with somebody?'

'I'm afraid so.'

'Can you get rid of her? Chris, I need to see you now.'

She slotted another coin into the phone, waiting for me to speak.

'Are you in Leicester?' I asked.

'Yes, by the park, at the end of your road. Can I come round?'

'I'll meet you there as soon as I can.'

Walking back to the bedroom, I had three seconds to think of a way to make Sarah leave. I knew that hints and suggestions would fall flat. When we were at her place, she'd crouch on all fours over me, grinning, insisting that I stay. If I refused, she'd lie on her back, showing her stern profile, folding the duvet around her like a shroud. I'd find myself making excuses, saying sorry as I left. To avoid another scene like that, I took the direct approach.

'You have to leave, now,' I said.

'I don't think so.' She grabbed at the duvet as though it could hold her in.

'Yes you do. I have a friend who's in trouble.' I threw Sarah's clothes on to the bed. 'Get dressed. Please, for once Sarah, let me get on with my day.'

'Who is she?'

'She's an old friend.'

'Girlfriend?'

'Yes, but so what? You have no right to be cross.'

'Which one?'

'Please, get dressed.'

'I'll wait here for you,' she said, smiling as though nothing was happening. It was her last attempt at being happy before she'd switch to bitterness.

'Just get dressed. I'm *not* going to argue with you.'

'I'll tell you something, Chris . . . ' she snapped, rummaging to get her knickers on under the covers. For once, she was stuck for something to say. She got out of bed, rushing her last clothes on faster than me. I felt giddy with the relief of getting rid of her. She put her coat on and set off down the stairs without another word.

The park was nothing more than a square of grass, bordered with trees and benches. Behind those, main roads and houses, their curtains left open to reveal lamplight and early Christmas trees. Wendy had cleared the snow from a bench, and was rubbing her gloveless hands together, blowing into them. The ends of her blonde hair mixed with the snow on her shoulders. She looked at me as though she was sorry for something; there was no smile left in her face. She stood up, brushing the snow from herself. The whites of her eyes were so webbed with red, I thought she must have been crying.

The first thing I said was, 'Are you all right?'

'I just wanted to see you.'

She started crying. I expected her to lean on me, but she lowered her head into her hands and sobbed, the breath of vapour passing from her fingers. Behind her, a blackbird left its branch, snow breaking free beneath it.

When we made it back to my house, I put the kettle on, switched on the Calor gas fire, and took her coat. We sat cross-legged on the floor, drying out. It felt as though we could spend the whole day finding out about each other again.

When I met Wendy she was nineteen, still living with her parents, and trying to come to terms with the fact that she hadn't gone to university. She'd wanted to study music – she was a horn player – but her dad wanted her to find something more secure. His idea of compromise was to let her do what she wanted, so long as she paid her way. For the past year she'd been working in Waterstone's, trying to save up. 'And now I don't even practise enough,' she said, 'so what's the point.' It was unusual for a first conversation to be so doubtful; people are usually keen to show you how well their life is going.

She didn't want to go to pubs or back to my place, but asked me to drive her into the surrounding countryside. There wasn't much to see, especially at night, and we had to go slowly once we left the salted roads. I parked by the reservoir outside Sheepy Magna; the sky was clearing, the moon appearing at odd moments, lighting up the snowy landscape, its wide glare spread on the water.

I wanted to get out and walk, but Wendy said it was too cold, so we stayed in until the windows had steamed up and frozen. She spent so much time in town, getting out was something she cherished. During those first weeks, we spent all our time in lay-bys, eating at service stations, driving down windy roads. We didn't go to a single pub or restaurant, or to see a film; she was happy to sit with me and talk. It suited me, because she made me laugh, and I got the feeling this was simply a delaying tactic, a way of getting to know me before we slipped into normality. Although we'd kissed, it had been reserved, a brief punctuation to our conversation. I'd never touched anything more than her ribs through her jumper, and given the cold, I hadn't wanted to put my hands directly against her skin. By mid-January, a thaw had set in, and I moved to a larger room on Regent's Road, next to the university buildings. I never knew why, but that seemed to make a difference to her. As soon as I'd moved in she said, 'Aren't you going to invite me over?'

I met her at work, and it was raining so much that we stopped off at a gaudy pub near Leicester's train station. Frequented mostly by businessmen, it was empty when we arrived, with almost too much space for us to be intimate, but soon filled up as it went dark outside. She held my hand and said that she loved me, before kissing me. Later, in my room, with the sound of heavy rain falling on to the pavement outside, we undressed each other.

In the morning we drove down the motorway, to get breakfast at a service station. Both wearing yesterday's clothes, we looked un-washed and tired. Instead of sitting opposite me to talk, Wendy shuffled in next to me, her hands between her legs, blowing on her coffee to cool it. It was cold outside, but the windows made the sunshine feel hot. I worried out loud that she might be pregnant.

'A baby,' she said, 'imagine that.' She looked puzzled, rather than worried, as though the thought of such a change could excite her.

I rambled on about responsibility, and how many lives it wrecked, and how she had to pursue her own life first. Wendy nodded solemnly.

'I know I couldn't really cope.'

'And if you're not pregnant?' I was hinting about contraception, but she missed the point.

'I need an outlet,' she said, though it wasn't clear for what.

Three days later, her period started while we were making love. At first I thought it had embarrassed her because she pulled away from me, but then she stripped the bloody condom from me and threw it aside. She lay on her back, legs spread so widely it looked painful. 'In me, in me,' she said, her eyes tightly closed. Her face remained clenched with wrinkles while we made love, until she came, when her jaw opened like somebody shocked by cold water. I felt her fists draw me into her, and she continued moving until I came. I waited a long time before trying to withdraw, but even then she held me in place. I wanted to say how relieved I was to know that she wasn't pregnant, but whenever she heard me breathe in to speak, she shook her head.

When we both had the time, we'd spend whole days in bed. We watched the grey rain sharpen the light on the red ivy of the university labs outside my window. The clouds pearled and spread, until they revealed the sun when it was low enough to lower into twilight. At night, we'd go out for takeaway food, bringing it back to eat in bed, then, too restless to sleep, we'd stay up all night talking.

One of Wendy's habits was to question me with bizarre insecurities.

'Would you still love me if I lost a leg? What if I was disabled? Would you still love me if I was disfigured?'

It was a peculiar way to test me, and I didn't like to think about it. Why do we stay with people? At first, it's out of joy, rather than responsibility. She was asking me whether I loved her enough to stay with her, even if doing so was unpleasant. It was like saying, 'What if I'm no fun any more, what if I bore you? Will you stay with me if I'm bad-tempered and angry?' I'd joke my way out of it, as far as I could.

'Even if you were a brain in a bottle, I'd stay with you.'

'What if I was paralysed? Or burnt?'

'Yes, I suppose so.'

She paused, streetlight gleaming on her pupils.

'What if I was pregnant?'

It took a long time for her to convince me she was joking.

★

In February, she left her parents' house, finding a room two roads away from mine. 'It'll eat into my savings,' she said, 'but at least I'm moving on.' She put Monet posters on the walls, bought a few plants, and made her mattress the centrepiece of the room.

The first night I went round, the pavement had frozen into fern-shaped patterns, glittering like tiny lenses. After we'd made love, we lay with the curtains open, a streetlamp outside so close to the window that we needed no light. It was cold enough for my breath and her breathing to show in the air, occasionally moving into sync. The traffic outside was a constant rush of noise, but sometimes it would clear, and for a few seconds there would be silence.

A calm came over us. For the first time, we began to make plans. If she went away, I could move with her. We could find the time for each other. Being together, we decided that night, would be better than being apart.

We made love into the morning, sleeping for an hour, waking while it was still dark, watching the dawn through the ice-laced window.

The long night must have taken its toll, because I caught a cold. At Wendy's request I stayed at her house, so that she could look after me. My throat felt like it was cut, and my head ached constantly with the pressure of mucus. It was a pleasant week, though, passing the hours with reading. I enjoyed the anticipation when she was away, waiting for her to appear at lunchtime, then again at night, bringing food and medicine; all her returns made me smile. It was only when she came back one lunchtime with a pregnancy-testing kit that I felt uncomfortable.

'Are you late?'

'Only about five days.'

'You didn't seem worried.'

'It only occurred to me this morning. I got this so that we don't have to worry.'

She pissed on to a plastic stick, which was pushed inside a chemical holder; we had to hope that it would come out white. If it looked slightly blue, we had a problem. It took two minutes, and we counted down the last seconds out loud. When the stick was withdrawn, its tip was the deepest, richest blue, a thick drip of blue water hanging from it, trembling with the shake of Wendy's fingers.

I felt like I'd been winded. Wendy put her fingers into her hair, then touched her heart. For a moment she took on the expression of crying, but it was replaced by a blank, pale stare. She touched her stomach, her palm resting there gently.

She began to distance herself as soon as she agreed to have an abortion. Even after she'd booked an appointment, I didn't let up with my insistence that she get rid of it. She was too young for a baby; it would ruin her life; it was such a responsibility. She didn't want me at the clinic with her, and the last thing she said to me before leaving was, 'Don't worry, I'll go through with it.' She rang me afterwards to say that it was done, and asked me to give her space for a few days. I was so relieved, I didn't complain. A letter arrived a week later saying that she'd moved to London. 'I'd better start taking myself seriously, at last,' it said. Her writing was tender, but she said she couldn't bear to see me yet. 'The decision was mine, but I have to say that you influenced it.'

I wrote back via the PO box number she'd given me. It was a long, disjointed letter, full of the apologies and kindness I hadn't offered when she needed it. I didn't hear from her again until June, when she sent me a postcard of the BT Tower. She wrote about her new job, a friend she'd made, her horn practice; things were looking up. At the bottom she put her phone number. I didn't wait for the cheap evening rate, but called that morning. Our conversation covered the basic pleasantries for less than a minute, and then we established that we were both still single.

'Did you give me your number because things are getting better, or because you're missing me?'

'Both,' she said. 'I missed you the whole time, but I couldn't be with you while it was all so close to my surface.'

'And what do you want now?'

'To see you for a while. That's all.'

I went down that Friday evening, the train drawing into London as the sky began to yellow. I half hoped she'd be waiting at the station for me, but headed straight for the Northern Line, with its distinctive smell of oil and hot paper. By the time I got out at Tooting Bec, the sun had set, so I caught a cab to her flat. She lived on the eleventh floor of a white tower block, one of three identical buildings set across the road from Wandsworth Prison.

Wendy's hair had grown, which was the opposite of what I'd expected. When people go to London for a new start, they usually trim down for efficient city life. I wanted to touch her, but she didn't even hug me hello. Instead she showed me round the small rooms of the flat, led me out to the narrow balcony for a good view of the prison. I suggested eating out, but she said there was nowhere nearby. She didn't mind cooking, she'd been practising. I offered to go out for wine, but she said it was too far.

'Let's just stay in tonight. I'll show you round town tomorrow.'

She was serious throughout dinner, and when I tried to make her laugh, she'd look off to one side, trying to work out what I meant. She became happier when I grew tired, lighting up enough to say she was glad I was there.

We went through the motions of pretending we'd sleep separately, even making up the bed-settee in the main room. When I borrowed her toothbrush, I felt unexpectedly pleased to be using it, knowing that it had been in her mouth that morning.

I got into bed, and listened to her brushing her teeth, washing her face. There was a long silence after that, and then she came through. 'I don't think I can sleep yet,' she said, so she sat at the edge of the bed. I let her make the first contact, touching my knee through the covers, then without looking at my face, she wrapped her arms around me, pressing her head against my solar plexus. She turned so that her face was closer to my skin, and kissed. The soft spread of her hair excited me, but she seemed desperate to hold me still. No matter how I stroked and kissed her, she just held on to me.

We slept in that position, and in the morning we made love. When she came, she made a sound so loud and intense, it didn't look enjoyable. Afterwards, her forehead was tight, and she appeared irritated with my conversation. I brought her breakfast in bed, and she smiled; I was often amazed at how quickly her mood could change. 'You're so kind to me,' she said, but in contrast her face regained some of its reluctance.

After that weekend, I went down every few days, spending so much money on train fares it would have been cheaper to move in with her. Sometimes I'd travel home on the morning train, only to have Wendy ring me up in the afternoon, asking me to go down again that night. Even so, it was never clear whether or not we were going out with each other. If we talked about the future at all, she would prefix every sentence with, 'If we stay together . . . ' At other times, she seemed so eager for me, I couldn't believe she could accept a future apart. There was one night when I arrived late, keen to talk, but she undressed before I'd even put my bag down. She laughed briefly, but looked anxious as she pulled me towards the bed.

'Please,' she said, looking so unhappy it was difficult to become aroused. 'I'm really trying, Chris,' she said afterwards, which helped her into sleep, but kept me from mine.

We hardly ever argued at first, which was a useful habit, but it meant that when we did bicker, the insults carried more weight. As a result, I would keep my distance if she appeared angry, because one misplaced comment could make her insecure for days. Weeks after I'd say something insignificant, she'd bring it up again, and admit that it had been eating at her. By November, we were arguing more often, and I became impatient. As soon as I felt a row brewing I'd say, 'Do you want me to leave?' but she'd say that I should stop threatening and just go if I meant it. I was never sure why I stayed. Was it because going would make me feel worse, or because I didn't want to hurt her? Even when I was trying my best, she could lapse into a mood. There were a few times when I thought back to how much fun she used to be, and almost found myself saying, 'You never used to be like this.' I never voiced this thought, because I didn't want to remind her. If she once started blaming me out loud, it would never stop.

Some nights we wouldn't talk at all, but watched television. I was surprised when, part-way through an obscure Swedish film that I'd lost interest in, Wendy's face contorted. I thought she was in pain, but she was crying. When I asked her what was wrong, she couldn't think of an answer.

The next morning we caught a series of buses to Alexandra Palace, for the sake of somewhere to aim for, as much as for the view. It was a perfect winter's day: no snow, no wind, no rain, just watery cloud and thick sunlight. The leafless trees were a shiny grey. That night she was particularly tense. She went for a bath, and I guessed that it was more to be alone, than for its soothing effect. She snapped at me when I went in without knocking, which wasn't something that would normally bother her. When she was dressed again she came into the front room with a book, biting her lip in concentration.

'I can't carry on like this,' I said. She didn't answer so I got straight to the point. 'Should I go?'

'Stop *threatening* me.'

Her eyes were teary, but I couldn't prevent myself from saying, 'Why should I stay? So that you can sulk at me all night and ruin a good day?'

'You don't give me enough room to recover.'

I was shocked by the momentum of the argument, so tried to calm her.

'If you have problems, fine, share them, but please don't take them out on me.'

'Then stop threatening to leave.'

'Why should I stay?'

'Because you love me?' It was definitely a question.

Cruelty is more difficult to resist, when you know it will really hit home.

'When you're like this,' I said, 'what is there to love about you?'

She started to say something, but I cut her off.

'I'm not interested,' I said, going out and slamming the door. There was nowhere to go unless I left the flat, so I sat on the edge of the bath, wondering why she wasn't coming after me. There was already a tinge of regret, immediately countered with justification; we couldn't get anywhere if she insisted on blaming me.

There was a loud noise, like a door being slammed, and then Wendy's voice, somewhere between moaning and screaming.

I ran back in, and saw her kneeling in the centre of the room; her mouth was a distorted hole, her face redder than I'd ever seen it. She looked terrified, more than upset. Behind her, there was a hole in the window.

'What did you do?' I asked, the sadness in my own voice making me want to cry. I had never seen anybody look so despairing. I found myself saying, 'Please,' unable to believe I had brought this on. She looked so afraid, so utterly lost, that I immediately knelt to hold her. The relief that flooded off her body made me feel worse. Even at that point, she'd thought I was going to carry on being mad at her. That, more than anything, made me want to help her.

'I had no idea,' I said.

This time, when she cried, there was no restraint, and it went on for minutes. Over her shoulder I looked at the hole in the window, the trails of fracture spreading a few inches around it; the window itself was largely intact. Cold air blew in through the hole, making my eyes water.

When she went to get tissues I stepped out on to the balcony, to see what she had thrown. Amongst the shards, there was a drinking glass, still whole, not even chipped. It felt fragile and light. I couldn't imagine how it had passed through the window and on to the balcony without shattering.

Wendy came back, blowing her nose, and I showed her the glass. 'I don't even remember doing it,' she said.

I sat with her for hours, apologizing over and over again, for being thoughtless and taking her for granted.

'I just couldn't understand what was wrong. I thought today was lovely, that was all.'

'It wasn't today that hurt me,' she said.

Before she slept that night, I made promises that seemed plausible. I promised to think of her feelings first, to be there when she needed me, to accept the extent of her pain. I would even understand her anger.

It surprised me as much as Wendy, that I was unable to cope, and broke those promises within weeks. I simply couldn't live with what I'd done to her.

Perhaps sensing how badly it was affecting me, she said, 'It was both of us, Chris. It was circumstance as much as you.'

In the week leading up to Christmas, she kept asking where I was going to be over the holidays, and how much we were going to see of each other. Her need hurt me, not because of its depth, but because I knew I might not satisfy it. Most of all, I was worried about my capacity to hurt her. I couldn't bear to see her so broken. A few days before Christmas Eve I told her I wouldn't see her again.

She said something at the time, so calmly that I should have seen the truth in it. 'You regret it as much as I do.' My reaction was to insist that she'd misunderstood me; I only regretted the pain her abortion had caused. In recent weeks, I've begun to wonder.

*

When she turned up yesterday, two years after we last spoke, she was reluctant to talk at first. It was as though she was thawing out, and when the colour returned to her cheeks, so did the smile. Enough time had passed for me to remember what brought us together in the first place, rather than the difficulties that separated us.

It snowed for so long that all the trains were cancelled. We could have found a way around that somehow, but I welcomed the situation and told her that she could stay. With that commitment made, it was easier for us to relax. We talked until the early hours, so that when I finally slept, my dreams were intense. I woke an hour ago and sat looking out of the window. The sky has cleared, the unlit bulb of a streetlamp illumined by the rising sun.

My dreams are coming back. I have a vague memory of taking Wendy to the station, waiting with her on the platform, letting go of her cold hand. She was pleading with me, and because she was pleading, I had to say no. Her skin became so blue, her eyes so sunken, that I knew she was a corpse.

Can our actions really have such drastic consequences? I never wanted that sort of responsibility; I only ever wanted to spend time with her, to enjoy being together. But I can't get the image out of my head, of her eyes sinking into her skull, because they are liquid and rotten. Something tells me that that future is probably our truth, but for now I'd rather believe that I can look to the side and see her in sleep, with one hand on her stomach, rising and falling with the waves of her breathing.

Hard Times and Misery
Laurie Graham

I'd just like to say I've been a hard-working man all my life. I had to work hard to get born, on account of my mother lying down on the job, and I've been working ever since. I've always put my best foot forward, shoulder to the wheel and nose to the grindstone. I've burned the candle at both ends, rose early, went to bed late, and did everything I could to improve the shining hour. I'm no slouch. I've always been known for my briskness, alacrity and promptitude. Also for my way with words. Still, and in spite of that, I've been laid off, retrenched and let go more times than I can count.

When I was thirty-nine years of age I was appointed to the post of under-manager on the Silver Bullet Wild West Supplies stall in Ely Market, sole proprietor, my Aunty Rene. My dear mother had recently passed over, not entirely unexpected on account of a floating rib, a rumbling gall bladder and pressure so low her blood barely drug itself round her poor suffering body. Aunty Rene said to me, 'Clyde – ' my given name is Alan Bernard Markham, but since Aunty Rene took up with the Texas Moon Toe Tappers, everybody's been Glenn or Chuck or somesuch – 'Clyde' she said, 'you're near enough forty and you've never got nowhere yet.' That was as may be, but I'd got there by work of the hardest kind. 'Clyde,' she said. 'Time to pack up your wagon and head on out.'

So that was how I come to Ely and how I come to meet Shirley Elaine Kerslake. I was married to Shirley Elaine and her two sisters for one year, five weeks and three days, five weeks and three days of which me and Aunty Rene were just waiting for those lawyers and judges to sign the papers and release us into sweet freedom, and still it was harder work than anything I ever done theretofore or heretosince.

First time I seen Shirley Elaine, she was handling the goods on Aunty Rene's market stall and not leaving things as she found them. We had a first-class stall, me and Aunty Rene, with a fine selection of authentic Western and Line-Dancing wear. We carried Stetson hats, buckles, belts, collar points, shirts, skirts, boots, flags, waistcoats, holsters, spurs, guns and ammo, replicas of course, badges, scarves, handmade boots and a whole lot more.

Aunty Rene was away fetching tea and bacon rolls, as she was inclined to do some time between 10.40 and 10.55, when Shirley Elaine showed up and started rifling through the bolo ties. Now, a swatch of bolo ties is easily tangled and keeping them hanging nice can be a full-time job, so I come round the front of the stall to tidy up after her, and thinking back, in my hurry I may just have stood a bit closer to her than I generally would with a lady of the fair sex.

She said to me, 'You got a car? You coming to the Dance Ranch Saturday?'

When I mentioned the Dance Ranch to Aunty Rene she was all for it as a wholesome and decent way for a man of my years and a newcomer to town to find himself a bit of pleasant company on a Saturday night, and she even allowed me to pick out a Rawhide belt and matching collar tips, as a token of her goodwill, until she heard I was figuring to meet up with Shirley Elaine Kerslake, upon which she made me give it all back. According to Aunty Rene, the Kerslakes were a bunch of halfwits, except that Pammy didn't even have half a wit, and Shirley Elaine was known as the village bike in Coveney and Witchford, and probably Wardy Hill as well, and Gwenny wasn't so green as she was cabbage-looking, not when it came down to money.

Still I did go along to the Dance Ranch because I'm not a man to be pushed around by a woman like Aunty Rene, nor to condemn a person such as Shirley Elaine if she sometimes loaned out her bicycle. We danced the Cotton Eye Joe, the Cowboy Cha-Cha and the Honky-Tonk Stomp and many more besides, and when it was over Shirley Elaine pressed herself up close to me. She smelt somewhat of Marmite. Or Bovril, it could have been. And she pressed herself up to me close as a man and a woman can get, and I must say, it was an experience that was by no means unpleasant.

Wednesday she was round at the stall, measuring up for a pair of ladies' cowgirl half-boots, white leather with fringing, £49.99. She said, 'Well, we'd better be naming the day,' and Aunty Rene clipped my ear for not having more sense and shook her fist at Gwenny and Pammy because she'd spotted them, lurking, as she put it, between Reg's wet-fish stall and the stall where the coloured gentleman sells T-shirts.

Of course, at that time I wasn't acquainted with Pammy and Gwenny. Only what Aunty Rene had said, and she had a tongue on her like razor wire.

So the way things panned out, the following Saturday me and Shirley Elaine went to the Boot Scootin' Nite at Prickwillow, musical accompaniment by Doug's Desperadoes, and she showed me the engagement ring I'd bought her from the Argos Catalogue Store. When we'd done dancing and I was all in a sweat and gagging for a nice cold orangeade, she did that business again, pressing up close. Three weeks later we were man and wife. Might have guessed all that rubbing and squeezing would lead to complications.

We went to live with Gwenny and Pammy, being as how Aunty Rene had said, 'Over my dead body.' I promised and vowed how I would work hard and do what I had to do to be a good husband. I bent over backwards, knuckled down, and studied up every way I knew, but I'll tell you, understanding the ins and outs of married life and getting along with those Kerslake ladies was the hardest work I ever did.

I took all my worldly goods to that house, which amounted to five cardboard boxes, eleven Tesco carrier bags, a holdall, a duffel bag and three plastic bread trays which I was intending to take back just as soon as I'd done borrowing them. It was no red-carpet welcome, and that's a fact. Shirley Elaine was in the bath making herself ready for me, and those two halfwit sisters were watching *Countdown*, so I never got a lick of help, but every other mortal soul in Bryant Crescent found the time to walk past and say 'How do?' or lean on their gate and give me a cheery wave. I must have made a nodding acquaintance with fifteen or twenty friends and neighbours and shook hands with a good few too, and some of them might have been kin, because one or two of them had the exact same haircut as Pammy and the same wall-eye too.

Anyway, they never so much as opened that front door until I was through unloading and I banged on it a while. That was when they loosed that Princess on me. According to Gwenny, Princess was a pedigree smooth-haired poodle with Jack Russell terrier on her father's side twice removed and royal corgi blood in her too, but I'd bet good money she was a small pig. By the time I got my goods and chattels inside that door, Princess had made a meal of my trousers, and it's a well-known fact that pigs will eat anything. Also, she had a tail curled tight up and over her back, which is a sure sign of a porker.

Shirley Elaine came down the stairs smelling of talc and other such lovely lady smells. Gwenny said, 'Put him in the boxroom, if you must.'

Shirley Elaine said, 'We should have the double. We're the married ones.'

Gwenny said, 'I'm the eldest. I choose.'

And all the while Pammy was grinning at me with her hands up her jumper, and standing too close. Gwenny was the only one of those Kerslake sisters that didn't stand close up to me and I was always glad of that because she had a hairy mole on the end of her chin. If there's one thing I abhor it's a hairy mole.

Pammy said, 'Into the boxroom! We're the eldest!' And that was what happened. Shirley Elaine showed me the way. She said she'd soon talk Gwenny round to giving us the double. She said she'd tell Pammy there wouldn't be any little babies if we didn't have the double, and then Pammy would beg Gwenny and we'd all be happy ever after, but to tell you the honest truth, I was having second thoughts, specially when I saw the boxroom because it only had a camp bed and at Aunty Rene's I'd been accustomed to a three-quarter divan and a candlewick bedspread.

For tea there was fish with black skin in parsley sauce. Gwenny said, 'Why does he eat so slow?' I was just minding out for bones. They cleared away while I was still eating and that worked to my advantage, because I'm not fond of fish in sauce. I fed it to the pig, with the intention of slipping out for chips and a battered sausage later on, which I didn't, as things worked out, because Gwenny turned off the electric when she went to bed at nine o'clock, and I stayed in my camp bed waiting for Shirley Elaine to come and lie on top of me. I was hungry. I could have ate a monkey with the measles. And that Pammy made matters worse, sitting all the while with her tin of chocolate bars, counting them out and reading out the titles and putting them away again and never offering anybody so much as a Rolo.

'All mine,' she kept saying. 'All mine.'

Gwenny said, 'Has he been told about rations?'

Pammy said, 'Tell him about rations.'

Shirley Elaine said to me, 'Mind how you go with the toilet paper, sweetheart. We have to watch the pennies.'

I had noticed, when I attended to a call of nature, that the Izal had been taken out of its box, had numbers written on its sheets and then put back again.

Gwenny said, 'Tell him properly. Two squares is enough.'

Pammy said, 'Two squares is enough. Tell him two squares or there'll be trouble.'

I said, 'Me and Shirley Elaine will make our own arrangements. We'll buy our own and use as many squares as we please.'

Pammy said, 'They'll use as many squares as they please.' That woman was like a Polly parrot, repeating every mortal thing a person said. But Shirley Elaine gave my arm a squeeze. She was proud of me for standing up to Gwenny, I could tell. And after the dimwits had gone to their bed, she came and fetched me to her room and showed me her true love and devotion. That camp bed never would have stood it. Shirley Elaine was no sparrow. She was no piece of thistledown. I didn't get back to my boxroom till nearly midnight, and even then I was a long way from sleep, thinking up ways of working hard and fixing things for me and my bride to have a long and happy life together. Also I was pretty much in need of attending to another call of nature, but that side of bacon was stretched across the passage, showing her fangs to me every time I so much as looked out of my door. I lasted till three. Then I just had to get my old pecker out and relieve myself out of the window.

It was the same story the following night and every night thereafter, but when Gwenny's hydrangea plant turned yellow and died, certain accusations were made, and looking back, I'd say that I didn't get the hundred per cent loyalty a man should get from his lady wife, and that was when they started turning Shirley Elaine against me.

Sunday morning Gwenny said, 'Tell him that hydrangea cost twenty pounds and it's to be replaced.'

Twenty pounds!

She said, 'Tell him he's a disgusting specimen and he'll be thrown into the gutter where he belongs.'

Pammy said, 'Disgusting specimen. Into the gutter!'

Well, my blood was up. Truth to tell, I'd had about as much as a man can take. My money had been cut, on account of oversleeping one morning. Two or three mornings. Also Aunty Rene had whispered to me that Shirley Elaine was still lending out her bike, though I'd seen no evidence of that, and there was no sign of the dimwits giving up that double bed so that we could have a little baby come to live with us.

I stormed out of that kitchen like a white tornado, and bolted myself in the convenience till I was good and ready to come out, didn't matter how many times they rattled the door. I stayed there till I heard them go to chapel, and I used sheets 37 to 49 of the Izal.

The rest of that day they carried on like I was the Invisible Man, smiling and chatting and passing round the *News of the World* and never saying a word to me, even when I asked Shirley Elaine if she'd like to practise the Achy Breaky ready for the next Dance Ranch. That night Shirley Elaine never asked me into her bed, and when I ventured out to the convenience to do what a man has to do, which I only did because I didn't want to hear another word about twenty-pound hydrangeas, and which I was only able to do by throwing the wild boar a full-size Mars Bar to keep her tusks away from my ankles, my wife's door was shut tight and there was a notice stuck on it, said PRIVATE KEEP OUT.

I won't have anybody thinking I'm the kind of lily liver that gives up without a fight. All my born days I've never throwed a towel in, and no man ever toiled harder in the name of lawful wedded matrimony.

I chopped firewood, brought in the coal and took out the ashes. I lugged home twenty tins of baked beans in tomato sauce, when they were on special, cleaned out the guttering on a ladder that had seen better days, and put my arm round the U-bend to unblock the convenience more times than I care to remember. When Pammy had tightness of the chest and the motor wouldn't start, I walked seven miles there and back to Ely for menthol rub and her ladies' magazine, and as for the many kindnesses I did for Gwenny, not to mention enduring that wart hog called Princess, I could be here all day reciting a list. Then there was Shirley Elaine, who ended up a turncoat. I always took her dancing and brung her some nice little thing from Aunty Rene's stall. I studied up on Toe Fans, Hitch Turns and Heel Splits, so I could be a worthy partner, and I never raised my voice to her no matter how sorely I was tried. All I did for those women, and still they kept me stuck in that boxroom when by rights me and Shirley Elaine should have had the double bed. But the bedroom thing wasn't a skeeter bite on an elephant to what transpired at the end.

Came one Wednesday, my last night as a paid-up live-in married man as it turned out, and all three of them had gone visiting the Cleggs. The Cleggs were just another pair of dimwits, according to Aunty Rene, but then Aunty Rene was born and raised in King's Lynn, and city slickers never have got the time of day for country types. Anyways, them dimwit Cleggs had come up on the lottery, and Gwenny said they needed advice of a financial nature. She said Shirley Elaine should go along with her because the Cleggs had a boy who'd always liked her and now he was going to be a millionaire, practically, which was no way to speak to a married woman with her husband standing right there in the same room.

Gwenny said to me, 'You're not invited.' And then the Polly parrot said, 'Not invited!' Course, she had to tag along. Being a person of differently abled learning disabilities, she couldn't be left.

So that left me in peace to watch the football without Gwenny switching it over all the time to programmes about jellyfish. That left me all on my own with Pammy's chocolate bars, and the double bed, and Shirley Elaine's catalogue with pictures of ladies' brassières. When you keep an animal on a short rope and he gets loose, way I look at it, he might go either way. He might start running and just run and run and you'd never catch him. Or he might have forgot how to run, except just round and round in a little circle, like the rope was still holding him.

Me, I ran and ran. I had half a loaf of toast with as much jam as I pleased, and I drunk milk straight from the bottle. Then I went through all Gwenny's cupboards and drawers, but I swear I never took anything except five pounds that was mine by rights anyhow because she cheated me out of it for a new teapot when the old one had a crack in the handle anyway. I had a Lion Bar, two Milky Ways and a Curly-Wurly out of Pammy's tin, and snagged my finger on the lid, and I had a look at all their insurance and their certificates, which was how I found out Shirley Elaine wasn't thirty-four at all, nor had been for quite some time. Then I answered a call of nature on to that hydrangea and I was just looking for secret compartments in the hall dresser when they suddenly came back and smelt the chocolate on me. Also, I'd been enjoying myself so much I'd clean forgot to put my old pecker back where he belonged.

Gwenny said I was a thief and a snoop and a sex fiend, which was a pack of lies but nobody'd ever contradict her because it was her name on the deeds of the house and her name on the bank book, as I'd happened to notice when I looked in her bureau for Elastoplast. But whatever Gwenny said was gospel. If Gwenny said the man in the moon had been thieving from her biscuit barrel, Pammy'd take her word for it and so would Shirley Elaine.

They chased me out of that house just in the rags I stood up in, but not before I'd put up a fight. Shirley Elaine held me fast so Gwenny could go for me with her handbag and her great clodhopping feet, must have been a size seven or an eight, and felt like they were filled with concrete. 'Fetch the police,' she was shouting to the halfwit, but all Pammy did was run round shouting 'Fetch the police' as well. Then, when she spotted the Lion Bar wrapper she started howling like a prairie wolf, and they had to worry about her instead of beating me within an inch of my life, so that was when I made my escape. I had to leave behind everything I had in the world, including my Paul Gascoigne shin pads, my digital alarm clock and my Billy Ray Cyrus and Travis Tritt albums, and it was as black as pitch walking to Aunty Rene's, apart from when cars came along, blinding me with their headlamps and near enough running me off the road and leaving me for dead.

Me and Aunty Rene get along just fine again now, running the Silver Bullet stall and taking it in turns to go for the tea and bacon rolls. Shirley Elaine sent a lawyer's letter asking for the shirt off my back, but Aunty Rene said if she understood me right it had never been any kind of a marriage anyway. Course, the word got round Coveney and Witchford, and probably Wardy Hill too, that I'd taken chocolate from that retard and made vile demands of Shirley Elaine. No mention of the five pounds though. Gwenny doesn't want folk knowing she's got paper money rolled up in her drawers.

In some respects I do miss Shirley Elaine, like when she used to press up close to me and we used to pick out the names we'd give our little baby, if ever the dimwits let us into that proper bed. I can't smell Marmite nowadays without feeling choked up. Bovril too. But Aunty Rene says it was never meant to be. She says best to put it down to experience. Apparently Shirley Elaine's been lending her bike again, so maybe she's right.

As for what Gwenny Kerslake claims I did to that Princess, hell, they've never even found the vicious little porker. Besides, a man has the right to remain silent.

Descent
James Miller

I'm standing in the toilets, swaying quite badly as I try to piss. Nothing seems to be happening and I realize I'm staring at my shrivelled-up penis and wondering what's to blame for that. Nearly midnight and the evening has unravelled around me, too much skunk, coke and beer and I'm not even sure what I'm supposed to be doing in this club, except outside there's this girl I've been talking to and I even bought her a drink and now I'm wondering what I'll say to her when I go back out.

I don't know how long I stand at the urinals staring at my dick waiting for something to happen but it's long enough to start feeling paranoid because the other men waiting behind me might start getting the wrong idea. I'd expected another quiet evening down the pub with the usual crew and an early night. Instead Steve turned up with a gram of fucking sharp charlie and an eighth of Purple Haze and he's always been a bad influence on me. I'd been watching *EastEnders* on the broken-down sofa in our front room, waiting for *The X Files*, which is pretty much the only programme I can be bothered to watch properly these days, when Steve appeared.

'How was your tute?' I'd asked, knowing it would be fine because Steve works much harder than he lets on.

'Brilliant,' he replied, all wall-to-wall smiles as he sat down.

'Oh, so we're brilliant now?'

'Last tute of the term.'

'I know, I haven't got anything left to do either.'

'Guess what I've got?' and he'd reached into his jacket. 'Fancy going out tonight?' We did a line and I still didn't feel like going out, but Steve suggested a spliff and then, seeing as it was still early, I went to the shop and got some beers. We drank them pretty quickly and Steve kept harassing me, 'DJ Blag is at La De Da's tonight and I can get us in free,' whilst I tried to choose between *Gardeners' World* and a moronic game show. 'Come on, Robert . . . Look, we haven't been out for ages and it's not like we've got to *do* anything tomorrow. Crazy shit could happen, could happen tonight. You've got to stop pining over that girl, start getting out more, start enjoying yourself. I mean, what you had with her, that was crazy shit as well, but, you know . . . '

'It's nothing to do with her,' I'd protested. That girl: Lucy, my summer love, my summer runaway. No one else understood. Steve can always zoom in on my weak spots, unpeel my defences. A bad influence.

'Well then, let's go out.'

'A little enthusiastic tonight, aren't we?'

'Might I suggest another line of cocaine, dear sir?' So it goes.

I step back into the club. The smoky darkness seems thicker, almost solid, a heavy embrace after the harsh exposure of the toilet's bright lights and broken taps. I close my eyes for a moment, dissolving. The club is packed, the walls sweating and everything melts past me. I look into people's faces, into luminous, glowing eyes and everyone seems almost familiar and I'm aware how wasted I am, a bit of my mind floating upwards and turning retrospectively to gaze upon my more disorientated, spontaneous body. I try to judge whether another drink would sort me out or not.

'Robert.' Steve appears out of the darkness, one hand on my shoulder. 'Where's that girl you were talking to?' I flinch as hot, beer-thick breath tickles my ear.

'I don't know. I was just looking for her, I had to piss, except . . .'

'Come on.' He pushes into the crowd and I follow. He keeps glancing back, speaking to me, but I can't hear a word against the music. Earlier, funkier break-beats have been replaced by a relentless, oppressive house rhythm rotating over and over, broken only by sudden washes of drum-machine rolls and a voice repeating again and again, *'everybody feel the love, everybody feel the love . . . '* Despite myself I realize I'm grinning at Steve, grinning at anybody, because

I'm happy to be here and very glad Steve dragged me out: and he's right, I must stop thinking about *her*, must move on, new pastures and all that. We walk down from the bar area to the dance floor and I catch glimpses through the light and smoke: bare shoulders bathed in white light, shining blonde hair, a group of girls dancing close together, expensive trainers, glowing contact lenses, dozens of hands all saluting the air, a couple standing still and kissing, their bodies forming a single stationary figure against the vibrating throng. Someone knocks their cigarette against my arm as they squeeze past, sparks cascading on to the floor. Some people just sitting in the corner, looking around with wide, sad eyes; others dancing slowly, surreally out of time to the music, moving their arms and legs as if they're trying to swim through the air. Darkness and light. The music is the same frantic loop. Everyone looks the same. I close my eyes for a moment, lingering spots of light, and see her through these decaying images, but faintly, like the last haze of twilight on the western sky. My dearest Lucy: how lost she would be in a place like this. I imagine her image projected against the walls of the club like an old, time-fraught film. Sun shining through her dress as she walks along the beach, slender fingers tucking auburn strands of hair behind her ears. Distant. Someone pushes past me, three pints of beer balanced against their fat stomach.

'Isn't that her, over there?' Steve grabs me, twists me to the left.

The girl, whom I sort of know from lectures, called Lisa, waves at me and keeps dancing. She's taken off her shoes and her bare feet tread little circles as she spins round, dropping down, letting her hips lead the dance, knees bending to the sudden climaxes in the music. Then she turns away from me so I can watch her naked back, her shoulder blades rubbing against the straps of her dress, hands furling and unfurling, fingers teasing the air. The DJ mixes in another tune and I think it's got bongos in somewhere and if I wasn't off my face I'd hate this sort of music but she's dancing faster now and her tight, marine-blue dress seems to glow in the light and I sense it's stuck to the curves of her body by sweat alone and maybe her legs are a little heavy but they still look great as they bend and twist the body above them. She keeps flicking her short, bleached-blonde hair and it falls over half her face and her dress is tight against her breasts, pushing them upwards towards the jagged planes of her collarbone, the glistening hollows of her throat. I look round to Steve to get his opinion but he's gone over to the DJ and is probably trying to introduce himself.

In two strides I'm across the floor, next to her.

'Hiya.'

'Hey, where did you go?' she asks me, putting her mouth up to my ear so I can hear her against the music. Her hair brushes against my cheek, tickling, and I'm acutely aware of the wet heat of her body next to mine. She steps back, sort of dancing and I don't think she hears my reply.

'Lisa.'

'What?'

'You're a great dancer.'

She doesn't say anything but keeps dancing, moving towards a couple of her friends, leaving me wondering if I should start dancing with her or just stand about looking awkward. Her eyes seem to say *come on* as if she wants me to join in but the music is too repetitive, too constant, a barrier keeping me back. I'm still too lucid, I think. I look at her again and for a sudden, prolonged instant wonder what it would be like to kill her. To dismember the body beneath the dress, strip away the hairstyle, the make-up, to hew into the raw flesh, tearing her apart with my teeth and hands; then I recoil against the thought, appalled at myself. '*Feel the love you know you're gonna take me high-er, you know you're gonna take me high-er*' the music is howling and I wonder if I'm starting to go mad, if other people imagine killing their friends and family, raping and terrorizing their girlfriends and sweethearts, or if I've just been reading too many pretentious contemporary novels trying to exploit some sense of *fin-de-siècle* confusion.

I walk up to her again and take her hand, holding it for a moment as I shout into her ear, 'Stay here, I'll be right back.'

I find Steve standing by the wall near the DJ.

'Steve – '

'What a wanker, I'm telling you, he doesn't know shit. I asked him if he had . . . '

' – Steve, can I borrow that coke? I'll pay you back.'

'It set me back nearly sixty quid . . . '

' – Just a couple of lines, you know, please.'

'All right.' He pushes the wrap into my hand. I slap him on the back in a way that's meant to be manful and comradely and hurry back to Lisa.

She's standing still now, smoking a cigarette and sharing a cocktail with one of her friends. She sees me but it's too dark and hectic to work out her expression. She tilts her head so I can shout in her ear. 'Do you want to do some coke?'

'Do you mean cocaine?' she shouts back at me. 'I don't think I've ever done that before. Shall I?'

'Well . . . yes.'

'OK.'

'Well . . . ?'

'What did you say? It's very loud.'

'Toilets.'

'What?'

'We'll go to the toilets.'

She seems to agree and puts her shoes back on. Her acquiescence helps us do something free of the bright embarrassments coded in speech. In this place there are only so many things we can do. She leads the way from the dance floor, threading effortlessly through the crowd. Everybody seems to block my way as I hurry behind her, half annihilated by the music, forcing routes through the heaving wall of people. A horrible, gabbling noise, like a wah-wah guitar having a nervous breakdown is gradually mixed into the grinding, monotone beats. Through the smoky light I keep my eyes on the shape of her blue dress.

At the toilets she turns and says, 'We should go into the gents, there'll be a huge queue at the ladies.'

'OK.' Now I lead the way. I try not to think about what's happening, or how things are meant to work out. I want to stay at this razor-hot intensity, this vanishing point.

There's one man in the toilet, pissing. He sees us coming in and smiles but doesn't say anything. I see us in the tissue-flecked mirror above the sinks, our flushed faces glistening with sweat. My eyes are red and haunted, stained with an uneasy desperation. I smile at my reflection, at this other person wearing my skin, my comrade in arms. The only one to share all my secrets. I remember Steve telling me how a girl gave him a blow job in the toilets at a club once. 'Half-way through,' he said, 'there's this banging on the door and I heard someone say, "There's people shagging in here." All these people cheered us when we came out. She was a dirty fucking bitch, man, she really was.' I push open the cubicle and turn on the light whilst Lisa closes the door behind me and locks it. There isn't much room and she keeps giggling. 'This is exciting,' she says. The floor is wet and littered with soggy paper. Cigarette butts float in the bowl.

I close the toilet seat and use it as a table on which to spread the coke. 'It isn't mine,' I say, 'we can't take much.' I look at the white powder in the central crease of the magazine which it has been wrapped in.

She peers over my shoulder. 'I've never seen coke before.'

'Looks just like you'd imagine.' I put my wallet on the toilet seat next to the wrap and dig out my credit card. My hands are shaking slightly and I'm breathing hard. I'm not really sure what I'm doing. I scrape about a third of the coke out of the magazine and on to the toilet seat. I'm terrified of spilling it. Steve would go crazy. Carefully, I fold up the rest and put it back in my wallet.

'What happens if I die?' she says.

'You smoke fags, don't you?' I use the card to split the third and roughly drag out two thick lines.

'Yeah.'

'Well, then, what are you worrying about? Everything kills you.' I lick the sides of the card and take a fiver out of my wallet.

'This is funny,' she says.

'Not the most romantic of venues.' I start rolling up the note.

'Have you finished work for the term?'

'Yeah.'

'Me too. When you going home?'

'End of next week some time. I'm in no hurry.' I bend down and snort up the first line.

'Is it difficult?' She giggles nervously.

'Easiest thing in the world.' I sniff again and re-roll the fiver, passing it to her. I'm close now, I think, reaching the limit, teasing it. She fumbles, almost drops the note, giggles again. 'Oh my,' she says. She has vague, grey eyes. I realize, as if seeing an element of myself in her lopsided grin and flushed cheeks, that she's very drunk. 'I'm sure I'm going to do this wrong.'

'It's easy.'

'You won't think I'm not cool or anything if I do it wrong, will you?' With one hand she lightly touches the top of my chest, letting her hand rest there, as if steadying herself.

'No.'

She smiles again and squats down, muttering something about 'the disgusting floor'. She leans over the coke and I'm rushing, champagne gold sparks tingling my fingers and tongue, my hands running through her hair to the dark roots, massaging her neck and shoulders as she snorts it up. She bends her head and coughs before standing up slowly, using both her hands to steady herself. She says something like 'hmmmurgh' and gives me back the fiver.

I can hardly fit the note into my wallet. My hands have gone all numb and fizzy. I slouch back against the toilet door, hearing it knock against the lock. I shut my eyes, giddy golden waves of dizziness exploding like stars in the darkness. 'Shit,' I say. I think I'm smiling. The light in the toilet is thankfully dim and the space in the cubicle seems deceptive, as if the walls are shadows leading to darker rooms and tunnels. I'd be happy to stay here for the rest of the night.

'I can taste it, I think I can taste it,' she keeps saying. One of her hands rests against the wall, the other teases the air as she speaks, as if she can conjure flavours and scents out of nothing.

'Do your fingers and teeth feel tingly, and on your tongue?'

'Hmm, yeah, yeah they do. I feel good, I like it.'

'It's good stuff, I'm fucking wasted.'

She laughs again. 'But it's all so funny. Look at us. Imagine this happening to me.' I don't know what to add to this but she saves me the trouble. 'Oh, but Robert, I can't possibly snog you in a *toilet*.'

Back in the club we split up quickly. I find Steve trying to light a cigarette by the bar and give him back the rest of the coke. He says something but I go away, waiting for Lisa to come back. The music sounds the same but different in a way I can't work out. I can't even remember what it sounded like before. The lights are low and red now and the place seems cavernous, satanic. I catch a glimpse, between people, of this girl, standing behind some tables. Only for an instant. Then someone blocks her from my view. But, in that half-second of sight I'm sure it's Lucy, that she looks like Lucy. I remember her near the sudden end that neither of us wanted or could stop: her face, pale beneath her tan, and her blank, lonely expression as she watched me eat in an Athens fast-food restaurant. The heat was incredible, a wave, a fracture. Made me angry, made her sulk. She sat there looking so lost and so young. So heartbreakingly alone, despite me. The girl moves forward, talking to a guy in a red shirt and she's nothing like Lucy, nothing at all. Then Lisa appears. 'Katie had my purse,' she says. 'I had to get it back.'

It's cold outside, the streets stretched and starched, the old buildings scratched out against the darkness, brushed by orange streetlights. Lisa talks and walks quickly and I hurry to keep up behind her. I agree to go back to her house, 'five minutes away'. I try to remember something we were talking about earlier in the evening, after I'd rolled up with Steve, still riding the icy wave of our first coke hit, but nothing comes. She pumps questions at me about college and where I live and I say a few things in reply. The fresh air and flickering, passing cars sober me up slightly, or make me realize how fucked I am, one foot stumbling in front of the other, and I notice Lisa is hugging herself with her bare arms, shivering. With Lucy the nights were warm and we would sit on the beach, the constant hiss of the sea soothing our silences. But that happened to another person, in another lifetime. I can't even think of her as my ex-girlfriend: the words are all wrong, ugly and jagged, like scratchings-out, like dissections. I wish I could ask Lisa, 'What really makes you happy?' or 'What do you really hope for from life?' – something that would stall her drunken chatter and make us stop, as if there was a way to fix this evening, like a shard of glass from a broken window, with meaning, with radiance.

But she really does live five minutes away and we're at her house and I lean against the wall whilst she fiddles with the front-door key. She keeps laughing at her attempts to open it and I join in; but I'm apart from the scene, watching myself suddenly playing a part I hadn't anticipated. I almost think I'll have a cup of tea then politely leave, but I'm at her house, of course she wants me to pull her, she'll probably be deeply offended if I don't and it wouldn't be very fair of me. I wanted to kiss Lucy the first second I saw her. We spoke for hours, a conversation of lingering pauses and brilliant connections and she had been so strange and unknown to me that the kisses, when they first came, were slow and delicate, an opening not an ending.

We go into the house and Lisa tells me to come up to her room because 'nothing's downstairs'. I follow her up the dark, narrow staircase, stumbling near the top, my hand brushing her ankle, grabbing at the step above. 'Shhh,' she hisses at me, then laughs weakly as I pull myself up.

'Are your housemates in?' I whisper.

'Don't know, but keep quiet anyway,' she answers, pushing open her bedroom door. 'Look,' she says, 'double bed,' and points at the large mattress on the floor. She switches on a small lamp on her desk and I glance about the room: clothes spilling out of a wardrobe, a towel and underwear spread over the floor, an overflowing ashtray, an expensive hi-fi, a handful of crappy CDs, a stack of files on the desk, a large, dusty mirror, a make-up box. The bed is neatly made, covered with a blue duvet. 'Isn't it great?' She makes as if to sit down then pauses. 'Do you want anything? I think one of my housemates might have some pot in his room. I could go look if you want some?'

'No. I don't want anything.' Photos are stuck on the walls. I see groups of tanned, smiling girls sitting on a beach, all blonde hair, bare legs and blue skies. I can't distinguish Lisa from her friends. We're standing by the bed and she pushes back her hair and I look at the sweep of her long neck, the top of her shoulders, her pink, soft skin, her eyes flickering back and forth, drunken, edgy. Fuck it, I think, she is pretty. I step forward and she opens her mouth and I can taste Hooch and saliva and my face feels numb as if everything is happening under water. I kick off my shoes and we lie on the bed, adjusting our bodies, trying to get used to what's happening, finding ways to fit our mouths together. I shift away to get more comfortable and her tongue squirms in the space between us, searching for my mouth, her eyes closed. I lean down again and resume kissing her and the room spins slowly around me like we're stuck in a sinking submarine. She reaches round with one of her hands, grabbing the back of my neck, pulling my face closer and all the time I'm kissing her it's distant, my body too limp and dulled to feel anything, the rest of me wondering if she expects me to have sex with her, what I'll say to her in the morning, if she'll want to see me again, if I'll kiss her goodbye when I leave. The drunkenness and coke are dissolving, merging into tomorrow' s dark hangover. I listen to the wet sound of our mouths.

She gets up suddenly and I lie back, squinting against the dim light which seems too bright. I can't get comfortable. My eyes burn when I close them. She switches on her hi-fi and tacky house music like the stuff in the club comes back on, except at a very low volume, and she flops down next to me, the mattress sagging, and I start kissing her again because it's easier than talking. Time passes and because I suppose it's what I'm meant to do, because maybe it'll wake me up a bit, I fiddle with the straps of her dress whilst kissing her, but can't get anywhere; her body pressed too close to mine to reach for her breasts, which I can just about feel, crushed against my shirt. My hand moves up her smooth legs and over her thighs before slipping inside the tight space of her dress, tugging at her panties, my palm pressed between soft fabric and hot flesh. I try to push her dress up over her hips. She squirms and looks uncomfortable so I take my shirt off, to balance things out, and my head feels thick and I'm sweating badly. My throat is dry and all I can taste is the chemical aftershock of the coke and her saliva. I kiss her again, squeezing her breasts, her nipples hardening, tight against her white bra which I can't seem to pull off either and she digs her hand into my pants and roughly tugs at my half-erect penis and this goes on until she moans and starts breathing faster. I can tell she smokes too much, a rasping, unhealthy edge lacing each gasped exhalation and I remember telling her everything kills you then I guess she comes, my cheek wet with her saliva and I move away from her, pulling my pants back up instinctively, trying to find a cool patch on the bed. The tape clicks to a halt and the silence of the night seems terrible and over-whelming. She rolls over, turning her back to me. I get up and go to the toilet. I can finally piss. My head swims, reeling, spun out, legs weak. When I get back into her room the light has been switched off and she's changed position in bed. I lie still for a long time, sweating into the darkness. The silence is finally broken by a distant car alarm that howls and howls. Eventually a faint grey light seeps in around the curtains. Lisa twists about, pulling the duvet tight around her, moaning in her sleep. I try not to move. My heart is beating too fast. When I shut my eyes I see little shapes, spinning away.

With Lucy the mornings were different, a delightful surrender to the blue washed sky of consciousness. She would sit up in bed, pulling her hands slowly through her heat-blonde hair, her body breaking the sun as it seeped in through the window. Leaning over me, strands of her hair shining in the morning light, falling down, golden shards on white sheets. I could taste her in the warm air, the gentle cone of her presence. Leaning over me like a perfumed kiss, like golden light falling through the windows of the village's little orthodox church. With her nothing was left to remember.

Time passes, grey and silent. Lisa wakes up coughing. She pushes down the duvet and sits up, rubbing her head. Her eyes are puffy, tired. 'I'm going to have a shower.' She pulls a towel around herself and leaves the room. I look at my watch and it's nearly eight o'clock. Whatever that means. I put my shirt back on and pull open one of the curtains, letting weak, pasty light creep into the room. I look at some of the photos on the wall again, trying to pick Lisa out from her friends. I see pictures of an empty white beach, a sea shadowed sky. It could be Amorgos, the Greek island where I stayed with Lucy. There's a couple of pictures of Lisa, tanned and slimmer, with a man I've never seen before, both of them beaming at the camera. I wonder what sadness haunts her empty days, her quiet hours. I wonder what I'm supposed to do now. In the hour after dawn, when the air was still fresh and cool, Lucy and I would leave our small rented room above a bar on the seafront and cross over to the beach. Lucy led the way to the sea and I followed behind, my feet erasing her footprints. One morning we found hundreds of dead crabs, upturned and rotting in the glistening hinterland between sea and beach. Flies swarming over their bodies, screeching seagulls slashing down like white blades to tear them apart. Twitching yellow claws and empty Coke cans caught in the wet sand. I stood back but Lucy simply lifted her white dress above her knees and waded into the ocean. She kept going until the water swallowed her slim waist and her dress billowed out like a huge jellyfish. She swam away into the diamond-bright sea. I tried to spot her head bobbing against the sliding shadows of the sun-split waves. Around me circling seagulls were dropping crabs on to rocks to bash their shells open, their yellow bills biting and pulling at the pink flesh beneath. There was something of a dream about the morning, a thin veil of clouds blunting the sun, and something of a nightmare. I couldn't go into the water. Later, the afternoon heat peeled the bandages away from the sky and we hid in our room. I could taste the sea when I kissed her wet and salty places. The solitary whir of a small fan by the bed marked the silence, wafting cool air over our sweating bodies. When I lifted up my head I would see her cloud-pale eyelids closed and lips smiling, as if to approve our miniature, naked republic. I wanted her body to be the only border, her kisses the only law. But she talked about her home in England incessantly, stumbling monologues like stories of herself to fill all the hours when I wasn't working in the bar, when she wasn't waitressing, when we tried to pretend we weren't like the other tourists. It was as if she wanted to remind herself of who she was. I was afraid she would peel away the layers of her brilliant mystery, the occult territory that enthralled and blinded me. Later, as the sun set, I went to the beach alone. The birds were still there, pulling the bodies apart.

I put on my jeans and shoes. I find my top on the floor over some of Lisa's underwear. Scraps of her clothes scattered all over her small room, one-night-stand shrapnel. I can hear her in the bathroom next door, shower hissing, water kicking through the pipes. Saying goodbye to Lucy: the ferocity of her kisses in the airport, her arms tight around my neck, one hand clutching the ticket that took her from me for ever. I can't remember what I said to her in those last minutes, my throat tight. She squeezed my hand before she left, one last time. Then she was gone, disappearing into the departure lounge. I remember the electric doors folding shut behind her, the nightmare-bright loneliness of the airport. I sat outside by the yellow Athens taxis, crushed by the heat, trying to remember everything. There was no longer anywhere to escape to. I go downstairs and no one's up so I let myself out into the quiet hysteria of another morning. And I've missed something, I know it: I've missed something. Another day and I'll forget her. Another day.

The Earthquake
Elisa Segrave

The first night they had raw fish. Purple octopus legs, transparent unnamed flesh, squirmy brown jelly, 'smelly' fish which had been salted and left in the sun for four days, raw mussels and finally crunchy wormy things in a pink sauce which they couldn't eat.

Their host was on a diet but this hadn't stopped him sampling every dish and enjoying it, even the crunchy wormy things which Laura and Bernard, who had been married for three years, found disgusting.

The next morning, the three of them swam in the harbour among efficient Japanese fishing boats equipped with powerful lights for night fishing. The host told the couple how octopus were attracted by the lights, swam up to the boats and were caught. He stretched out his enormous body on a rust-coloured lilo and lay on it in the black water. He warned the couple to be careful of the iron boat hooks which lay at the edge of the sea. Once a child had been impaled on one. It had died.

After the swim the three of them sat on the stones and drank Bloody Marys. The host pointed across the bay to another small cove which was just a heap of black rocks.

'That used to be a sandy beach but last year the villagers asked everyone living here for a contribution then they covered it with those rocks. They don't want tourists. Why should they? The women alone earn forty thousand dollars a year diving for abalone.'

There was a rumbling noise. Above the bay where he was pointing, red rocks and earth fell down the cliff.

'There's a road there. I hope there are no cars on it,' said their host casually.

Slightly drunk, they walked up the path to his house, passing a little grocer's shop. The Japanese shopkeeper bowed politely as they went by.

In the garden there was brilliant sunshine. Huge yellow irises stood beneath a kumquat tree. The bright green grass was deliciously soft under their feet, like wool. The host placed a folding table and three chairs on the lawn, saying he was going to cook barbecued sausages.

Bernard and Laura had been travelling together for three weeks. They had been invited to Japan by Bernard's uncle, who ran an office in Tokyo. Since they had arrived from England they had not been separated once.

Bernard's white skinny body now seemed to Laura like that of an English schoolboy, compared with the host's big brown one. As he barbecued the sausages the host told them how, as a young man, he had had a job collecting wild animals from zoos all over Africa and the Far East. He had even kept a leopard in his house in Bangkok. The easy way he padded round his house and garden reminded Laura of a big jungle animal.

Bernard, in contrast, seemed protected and timid. He had hardly travelled, although he was thirty-five. He had a quiet, gentle manner and was considerate of Laura, which was partly why she had married him. He was also witty and offbeat, and she admired the way in which he debunked pretension.

When he was courting her he had taken her to a musical evening where the guests had shown off by shouting out the names of obscure Russian composers. Bernard had yelled: 'Russ Conway!'

He was a cartoonist and had had some success with a weekly strip for a satirical magazine. But the strip had suddenly been discontinued and instead of asking the editor why, Bernard had accepted the decision passively. Laura wished he was more aggressive. She sought explanations for why he wasn't. She knew he was the ignored fifth child in a family of six and had been bullied by his father. His uncle in Tokyo was the only person who had consistently paid attention to Bernard since he was a small child, giving him special oil paints for Christmas, taking him as a teenager to London art exhibitions, and, now that the uncle was based in Japan, inviting them both to visit.

From the moment they had walked off the plane, when they were presented with a timetable by Bernard's uncle's company chauffeur, Bernard had obeyed his uncle who, it transpired, had pre-planned almost every moment of their holiday. Laura was shocked by her husband's acquiescence. Aged thirty, she had often travelled on her own and didn't like to be told where to go. She had persuaded Bernard to go for three days to an island in the south of Japan where, she had heard, there was an intriguing mixture of Buddhism and Christianity. Even on the Bullet train going there, Bernard's uncle had telephoned to give Bernard orders.

Chet, their host this weekend, worked for the same company as the uncle. Originally from Chicago, he had lived all over the Far East and Africa before settling in Japan. He was six foot four and his best friends in Tokyo were a French chef, three single women journalists and an international jazz trumpeter.

Bernard and Laura sat on deck chairs on the lawn while Chet went in and out of the kitchen. He was an excellent cook and prefer-red to do everything himself. The Japanese gardener, who had been stooping over a flower bed, stood up, sweat running down his face.

While they ate lunch, Chet talked about his house.

'I'm the only foreigner in this village,' he told them proudly.

He took them inside and showed them pure-white walls, simple wooden bookshelves containing books on music and an expensive-looking CD player. He loved classical music.

An empty birdcage hung from the ceiling. A canary had been in it but Chet had recently moved it to his tiny flat in Tokyo.

After lunch, Chet fell asleep in his own part of the house and Bernard and Laura went swimming. The tide had risen in the bay, obliterating the iron spikes. A hideous floating apparatus had come right into the harbour and they had to swim around it. Chet had warned them of sharks beyond the breakwater so they stayed close to the shore.

Why weren't they making love instead of swimming? Laura thought irritatedly as they breaststroked timidly up and down the little bay. She thought of their host alone in his room, his loose-limbed body draped in a Japanese kimono, or maybe he was wearing nothing. She recalled the first night she had spent with Bernard in her bedroom in London; he had simply lain there on his back without moving. She had found it puzzling and insulting. However, she hadn't been able to make the first move herself since she, like him, was afraid of being rejected. It was one of the aspects they had in common but it also drove them further apart.

Even on this holiday she and Bernard had not made love successfully. His pale, gangling presence did not make her feel secure; it made her anxious. On the nights when he would try to make love to her his nervousness made her even more nervous. Instead of being sympathetic, she found this infuriating. When Bernard did succeed in penetrating her, she was seized with a feeling of panic, as though she were drowning.

When they returned from their swim their host was sitting in the garden in a rocking chair, his eyes closed, listening to music.

Later he prepared a bath for his two guests. He lit the bathroom with fat candles and sprinkled gardenia blossoms over the water. He changed the record on his record-player to Handel's *Water Music* and turned it up so that they could hear it in the bathroom.

The fact that Chet had prepared the bath for them made him seem to Laura a powerful omniscient figure. It was as though she and Bernard were not lovers but brother and sister or even members of the same sex. She remembered a married friend of hers saying that her husband was at his most sexless in the bath. Bernard, in the circular Japanese bath with his knees up and his wet hair clamped to his head, annoyed her, and when he tried to squirt her with the shower she was furious. When he got in he had displaced a lot of water so the lovely gardenia blossoms were washed over the edge.

When they came out, their host was drinking whisky. He had changed into white denim jeans and a brown silk shirt with the neck open, showing the yellow curling hair on his chest. (Bernard's chest was hairless.) He offered them whisky also and began to talk about the gardener they had seen earlier.

'He made four girls pregnant while he was still at high school,' said Chet. 'Now, besides his wife, he has three mistresses in this village.'

'Is his wife allowed to have lovers?' Laura asked.

'No,' replied Chet. 'That's why there's so much lesbianism in Japan.'

Bernard said little. He seemed overawed. He too had put on white trousers. His wet hair was slicked back behind his ears and he was wearing a new pair of glasses. Laura hated the way her husband was dressed. He looked too buttoned-up. He wore a very high collar, which made him look as if he had no neck and emphasized his pouting mouth. His blue blazer, she thought, made him look too smart and allowed him no freedom of movement. When he wore these clothes she associated him with a certain type of behaviour – he was too soft and good-mannered, trying to please everyone to the point of insincerity. She wanted her husband to be more robust.

She would have liked to ask Chet more about the customs of the local men and women but he said it was time to leave. He was going to drive them to the nearest town for dinner.

There was a high wind blowing. The main road was fenced off, because of fallen rock. They could see the new red earth where the landslide had been. Small tremors shook the ground all the way to the town as they drove there on a lower road.

'This peninsula is well known for earthquakes,' their host remarked. He did not appear to have said this to frighten them.

The local town was a spa. Japanese men walked around the streets in thin dressing gowns called *yukatas* which they wore after taking hot baths.

'They're looking for women,' Chet observed.

At the restaurant they were welcomed by a lady in a pale orange kimono who threw her arms around him. Laura had a sense of Chet's other life, lived on this peninsula at weekends when he had no guests. Maybe he also took hot baths and walked round in a *yukata* looking for women. The thought disturbed her. She was also envious of his sexual freedom.

Inside the restaurant it was warm and friendly. The proprietor in her orange kimono didn't seem perturbed by the earth tremors. Dish after dish of beef, tongue, raw cabbage and dumplings arrived. They washed it all down with sake. The fact that this was served warm, in tiny cups, made it seem non-alcoholic.

Chet was angry when Bernard tried to order beer as well as

sake and drink them alternately. Bernard said he had seen his uncle doing this in Tokyo.

'Well, if he did, he's wrong. I've lived here twenty years and it's simply not done,' said Chet.

Laura drank only sake. She too was angry with Bernard, because he drank faster than she and Chet did and kept holding out his glass for refills. It was the custom in Japan that no one was supposed to refill his own cup. You had to wait until a waitress or your companion offered you more. A few times Laura deliberately omitted to refill Bernard's cup when he held it out. She did not want him to get drunk but there was another feeling which she did not fully acknowledge – why should he do a 'macho' thing like get drunk when he was unsatisfactory in bed?

By midnight the three of them had drunk over ten bottles of sake. When they set off home the host told them to look out for the turning to his own village. It was beside a sign saying 'Love-Hotel'. This was where Japanese men could go to have sex, he said.

But when they reached the 'Love-Hotel' they saw it too late and he missed the turning.

'Damn! Serve me right for talking too much.'

He reversed the car abruptly. The road was ill-lit.

'Look out!' Laura screamed.

The back wheel of the car was hanging over a ten-foot drop. Bernard, who was in the back, tried to open the door nearest to him. As he moved, the car tilted dangerously.

'Get out!' the host roared.

He ordered Bernard to edge back along the seat and get out of the right-hand door. He made Laura move up close to the steering wheel, to avoid any possibility of the car tilting to the left again, then he told her to sit still while he decided what to do.

Laura was conscious of his enormous body close to hers. She could see patches under the arms of his brown shirt and she smelt his sweat and the sour smell of his breath from the sake. He ordered her to move up even closer, to avoid any possibility of the car tilting again. She felt their thighs touch, then he told her to follow him out of the driver's door.

They saw that most of the back of the car and the whole left back wheel were hanging over an empty parking lot, at least twelve foot deep. If they had reversed another foot the whole car would have toppled into the pit.

The three of them stood uncertainly on the dark road. A Japanese man drove up in a sports car and Chet hailed him. He stopped but there wasn't much he could do as his vehicle wasn't strong enough to pull them.

At last a big truck drew up and its driver agreed to tow the car out if they could find a rope.

Bernard peered under the back wheels, trying to help.

'Perhaps we could use your belt as a tow,' he suggested to Chet.

'The best thing you can do is keep out of the way,' said Chet savagely, as though the accident had been Bernard's fault.

Chet and the truck driver then found a rope in the truck. They tied it to the car and, with a couple of tugs, the car was on the road.

'Well, after that, we must have a drink. I know a little bar near my house,' said Chet equably.

The bar was small and quiet. The tables had Space Invaders games on them. Chet and Bernard drank beer. Laura asked for a banana milkshake. The childish taste of the drink reassured her. She asked for another but neither of the men took any notice.

Chet still seemed irritated with Bernard, who nervously tried to make jokes. But that only made their host more annoyed. Laura began to see Bernard as she imagined the host saw him, blundering and inadequate. That night she refused to make love with him as they lay together on the tatami mats on their floor.

Next morning it was raining. The bay was streaked with fog. A few figures in raincoats could be seen trudging up the Nature Trail over the cliffs. The harbour was now crowded with fishing boats. They looked to Laura as if they had come close together to be safe.

The earth tremors started again later that morning while they were reading in the front room. The floor shook periodically, but no one made any comment. Bernard went on doing things wrong. A long-time bachelor, the host was neat and particular. He liked shoes left in a row inside the front door. Bernard kept forgetting to take off his shoes before he entered a room and when he did take them off he left them in the way, so that the host tripped over them, cursing. Bernard also left the sliding doors open into the garden, though Chet had asked him to keep them closed so that mosquitoes didn't get in.

Chet did not find fault with Laura, however.

In the afternoon while Chet had a rest Bernard and Laura went for a walk. She wore Chet's plastic sandals which squelched in the mud. The thongs cut into her feet. Carrying oily Chinese umbrellas, they walked along the Nature Trail. There was no one else on it. They passed bushes of drenched blue hydrangeas and came to a long bridge over a ravine. The sea swirled madly underneath.

'What if there was an earthquake when someone was on the bridge?' asked Laura.

She did not think that Bernard had much physical courage. Once he had refused to go into her flat in London when he thought a burglar was there.

When they returned, their host was still in bed. Laura went to rest herself, taking all her clothes off and lying down on the floor of their tiny bedroom. Bernard stayed in the other room reading a book.

Laura was restless and worried about her marriage. She often enjoyed Bernard's company but did not see how their sex life could improve. They made each other more inhibited than they already were, more than they would be with other partners, she was sure. Bernard had told Laura about his former girlfriend, with whom he had had no sexual difficulties. But he said that the passionate nature of their physical relationship had made him feel closed in. Also, he didn't have the same feeling of companionship that he had with Laura; they didn't share the same jokes. When he had met Laura, for the first time in his life he didn't feel lonely. He talked about his solitariness as a child and as a teenager, how his older brothers had referred to him as 'The Mad Boy' and how, when he had first come to London, he had walked for miles round the East End in the evenings on his own.

Laura was woken by an earthquake worse than any they had experienced so far. The light walls of her bedroom shook and there was a sound of china breaking in the kitchen next door.

She grabbed a sheet and ran out of the house. Bernard was already on the lawn. He looked terrified. Laura was furious that he had not even shouted her name.

Chet was still upstairs in his own bedroom. They could see his big silhouette moving about upstairs. Then he too came into the garden, laughing and saying that his part of the house, which was new and more fragile, had been badly shaken. His bed had collapsed on one side and the staircase had come loose. He too had been asleep when the earthquake had started.

Then the telephone started ringing and he went back into the house to answer it.

Bernard and Laura stood together on the lawn.

'How could you abandon me in there?' she demanded.

He hung his head, silent and ashamed. Then he too went inside.

Laura stood alone in the garden, still wearing only a sheet. She was aware that some decision had to be made, but what? She thought of what Bernard had said in Tokyo, when she had complained once again of his timidity.

'You know you've married the runt of the litter.'

He had made it sound as though he could not change and that, because she had chosen him, any defect was now her responsibility.

Chet now came back into the garden, saying that the phone call had been from Bernard's uncle. He had heard about the earthquake on a newsflash.

She was standing on the soft green grass where they had had the barbecue the day before. Now, after the rain, the yellow irises had drooped and their petals were torn.

Chet was looking at her. She took in his large feet in light brown shoes, his ankles, surprisingly white, his wrists covered with thick brown hair and his pale brown eyes, with odd flecks of yellow. When he went on staring she realized that the sheet that she still had on had slipped and was showing part of her right breast.

Suddenly he moved. Snapping off one of the irises, he strode with it across the lawn, then threw it high over the garden wall. She watched the dead flower arc towards the sea.

Then he turned back to her. All at once, he was relaxed and laughing.

'Go and put your dress on instead of that sheet! Then we'll go down into the main street and see what everyone's up to.'

Very soon, the three of them were walking down the path into the town, Bernard, still looking shame-faced, several steps behind.

Enough Pizza
Michael Marshall Smith

I first saw him in the lobby, on the Friday afternoon.

I was sitting sipping the last of my tepid Coke, leafing through the convention brochure and planning when to attack the book-dealers' room. I'd decided that Saturday morning would probably be the best time, swaddled in what I assumed would be my first hangover of the convention. I like buying books when I'm hung-over. It's very comforting. I was running through an internal checklist of the items I'd be looking for when I happened to catch sight of a small group of people who had just entered the hotel through the unpredictable revolving door. An elderly guy in a good suit, a tall and fluttery young woman holding a sheaf of folders, and a porter carrying a single battered suitcase. The old guy came to a halt for a moment, looked around the foyer with an expression which was difficult to interpret, and then set off at a reasonable pace towards the registration desk on the other side of the room. The woman followed somewhat chaotically, eyes darting in all directions, as if expecting an air attack at any moment. The porter waited impassively, waiting to be told where to go.

For a moment I wondered why I was noticing all this, and then with a rolling feeling in my stomach I realized I had just seen the man who was my reason for being here in the first place.

'Here' was *Smoking Gun IV*, a crime-fiction convention being held at the Royal Plaza in Docklands, a hotel so appalling I imagine the only group of people who actually enjoy attending events there are sado-masochists. More likely just masochists, because the hotel's staff are drawn from species so far down the evolutionary ladder that I doubt it's possible to make them feel any real pain, as we understand it. If the barman in the lounge had greeted my earlier request for coffee with just an ounce more insolence, I might have tried to find out. Instead I'd rather meekly settled for the Coke.

Crime fiction is my passion. I have an insanely dull job in computing, and there are times when the knowledge that I can go home in the evening and immerse myself in a fictional world is the only thing that prevents me from seeing how far you can push a hard drive up a client's arse. I'm not obsessive – I don't stand in my bedroom in an old mac and tilted hat, firing my finger into the mirror and quoting lines from old movies in which people get over-excited about stealing sums of money which wouldn't pay off my overdraft. I don't even go to conventions very often. They're all the same: you go to some anonymous hotel, listen to people talk and launch books, meanwhile drinking glasses of cheap white wine and eating small slices of free pizza while wondering who everyone else is. This convention was different, however. The very morning I received the flier and read the guest list (I'm on a couple of mailing lists, from specialist bookstores), I wrote a cheque and put it in the post, even though I'd been to the Royal Plaza before and knew what I was letting myself in for.

The man who was now standing at the registration desk, favouring the sullen woman behind it with a raised eyebrow which would have sent most people into a decline, was Nicholas Price. Chances are you won't know the name, but believe me – thirty years ago you would have done. Without Price's novels, most of the crime fiction that people read nowadays wouldn't even have been possible. Back in the 1990s he plunged a big stick into the genre and gave it a stir which changed the flavour for ever, bringing crime into the mainstream in the way Stephen King had done with horror twenty years before. For two decades Price was one of the biggest wheels in crime, never quite achieving true pre-eminence or stellar book sales, but very much the man in form. And, judging by the small press biography I'd read, rather a handful as well. The author of the booklet had discreetly referred to him as a 'bon viveur', but the real story was there between the lines: he and his group of cronies, between them making up most of the big names of the age, had drunk a good many bars dry before they'd even got into their stride for the evening. A representative anecdote tells of how Price and his wife Margaret had once been discovered in the ornamental fountain outside a convention hotel in Houston at half past nine in the morning, having retired there only two hours before. The fountain was in full working order, and the pair were somewhat wet. Half an hour later, after a change of trousers and with a small Scotch in front of him, Price was on a panel concerning techniques for using flashbacks in crime narrative. History does not relate how telling or otherwise was his contribution to the debate.

That was half a century ago. Later his novels became less frequent and began to feel like reworkings of earlier material. Younger guns came to the fore, unknowingly building on foundations Price had laid. It doesn't matter how good you are; sooner or later you're going to be yesterday's man.

There hadn't been a new Nicholas Price in twenty years – in other words, since I was ten and not reading any books, crime or otherwise. But now there was a new novel. *The Days* was going to be launched at the convention, and I was going to be first in line to buy a copy and get it signed. I discovered Price six years ago, through an awed reference to him in an introduction to a book by a contemporary writer. I tried one of his early novels – not easy to get hold of, but then neither were the later ones – and I was hooked. I read everything I could find, and I'm here to tell you Price was the best. The absolute best.

The tall young woman was involved in a heated discussion with the girl behind the hotel's registration desk. I could guess the subject. Despite the fact that check-in time was three o'clock, and it was now gone four, Mr Price's room wasn't ready. I'd been through the same thing myself, and my bag was currently stowed in the room the porter was now carrying Price's suitcase towards. Price himself had evidently lost interest in the dispute, and was gazing serenely into space. His minder fired one last salvo at the apathetic troll behind the counter, then turned to Price and gesticulated apologetically as she led him in my direction.

I held up the convention brochure again, feigning deep interest in its contents, and watched from behind. Price walked slightly ahead, the woman consulting notes from her file. By now I'd worked out that she was from his publisher's PR department, and something told me this was her first experience of author-wrangling. She looked nervous and distracted, as if her head was so full of things she was reminding herself not to forget that she couldn't remember what any of them were. Price looked far from nervous. It wasn't so much that he exuded confidence, more that he could have been anywhere. Walking down a street, on a stroll in the park, crossing his own living room. He didn't look left or right as he walked, checking out the delegates standing and sitting all around, as most people would have done. He headed straight for the bar. His suit was charcoal grey, of modern cut, and fitted well, and he was wearing a white shirt and a dark tie. For an old guy he looked pretty sharp.

But he also looked old. He had every right to. He was eighty-four, and if I'm still moving around under my own steam at that age, and doing so with a publishing person at my side rather than full medical back-up, I'll feel I'm doing better than OK. Price's eyes were clear, his grey hair was neat and his tie was knotted immaculately.

But his skin was pale, and papery, and despite his best efforts to hide it, he was heavily favouring one leg. It was hard to believe that this was the man whose mind had mapped the brutal worlds of China Sofitel, Bill Stredwick and Nicole Speed – not to mention the countless minor characters who had moved through his fiction with damaged grace. Apart from what I'd gleaned from the thin biography, everything I knew about Price had been intuited from between the lines of his fiction – as if his narration placed him in a permanent present tense in the company of wild people in dangerous places. Now he stood at a characterless and danger-free bar in a Docklands hotel, a couple of fat and bearded members of the convention's organizing committee converging on him from behind, and a blank-faced barman in front.

'I'd like a coffee,' Price said, reaching in his pocket for his cigarettes. The barman immediately embarked on the kind of dismissive dumb show he'd used on me earlier.

Price ignored him, and turned to his PR person. 'Would you like a coffee?' She shook her head.

Price winked at the barman. 'Just one then.'

The barman, provoked to speech, said that coffee was impossible.

Price raised an eyebrow. 'Impossible? How so?'

The barman looked away. The exchange was obviously over, as far as he was concerned. The two convention organizers stood sheepishly behind Price, knowing they ought to do something but evidently realizing they'd have no better luck. I empathetically shared their embarrassed fury at being shoved around by someone who's supposed to be serving you.

'Listen, Jean,' Price said mildly, evidently having read the man's name off his tag. The barman turned to him, ready to be affronted, but his face turned to caution as he caught Price's eyes. 'This is a bar. Behind it I see all the paraphernalia of coffee production, namely a coffee machine, milk and sugar. I notice that many of the bar mats bear the name of a prominent coffee manufacturer, and that a price for a "cup of coffee" is displayed on the badly punctuated sign behind your alarmingly bulbous head. Coffee is clearly not only *not* "impossible", but a feature of this establishment. So serve me a cup.'

Jean, full of injured innocence, explained how it simply wasn't feasible that he do so, on account of the fact that he had no cups, the cups were in the restaurant on the other side of the lobby – a journey of about ten yards – and he had no back-up to prevent a riot in his absence. He was sure the customer saw how it was.

'I do,' Price agreed. 'And this is the way it is. You're going to get out from behind that bar and go fetch a coffee cup. Bring a couple, so the problem won't arise next time. Then you're going to pour my coffee into one of them, in return for which I will give you some money. The alternative is I stand here waiting until the queue gets so long it stretches out the front of the hotel. Eventually it's going to go across the road, and when it gets dark, someone's going to get run over, and their relatives will hunt you down and avenge their kin with fire and pointed sticks. I have a great deal of time. It's your call.'

Jean stared at him. Price smiled gently, lit his cigarette and looked away.

Jean lifted the hatch and walked stiff-backed out from behind the bar. 'And don't you be a slowcoach,' Price advised, 'or when you get back this bar won't be nothing more than a few broken bottles and an empty till.'

Shouldn't have worked from a man in his eighties. But it did. Jean scooted across the lobby.

I turned away from the bar, to hide the broad grin on my face.

The highlight of the afternoon's programme was Price in conversation with the convention's Chairman. I sat about four rows back. I had a slew of questions I wanted to ask, mainly about the China Sofitel series, but also about some of the short fiction.

I didn't get a chance, but I didn't mind. Most of my questions got answered anyway, in a fascinating, often hilarious conversation that overran by half an hour. Price lounged in his chair on the stage, whisky glass in one hand, a cigarette usually in the other, and turned the Chairman's carefully planned questions into a freewheeling discussion of crime-writing that, a few days after that weekend, led to me starting my first short story.

I wish I'd taken a tape recorder into that session, and preserved it for posterity and myself. It was Price's last convention panel. He died three months later.

Midnight found me back in the lobby bar. In the meantime I'd been to dinner with a gang of acquaintances, drunk an awful lot of red wine, and had a long and mildly flirtatious conversation with an American fan I'd never met before. She was called Sheryl and came from Kansas, and at eleven had abruptly announced that she needed to go to bed. I was still buoyed up by the way I'd dealt with the waiter in the pizza restaurant, and said I hoped it wasn't my company which was provoking her departure. She explained that it wasn't, but that she had to go throw up, and we arranged to meet for coffee the next morning.

I wandered into the part of the bar which overlooks the water, and sank heavily into a chair. I had most of a pint left and intended to drink it. There weren't many people around, and none that I recognized, but I didn't mind. I'd had a good day and it was nice to be out of the normal rut. I didn't need company to enjoy that feeling, and when I realized that someone was standing behind me I didn't turn and bid them a cheery hello. Everyone I knew had gone to bed, and you can get into some very dull and mood-destroying conversations with strangers at conventions.

I heard the sound of a cigarette being lit. Then:

'Mind if I sit here?'

I turned. Standing behind me was Nicholas Price.

'Christ yes,' I said, completely flustered. 'I mean no, go right ahead. You're very welcome.'

'You may change your mind. I've had a certain amount to drink.' Price sat gingerly in the chair opposite me, and placed his glass and cigarettes within easy reach.

I struck around wildly for something to keep the conversation, such as it was, going. 'Impressed to see you're still smoking.'

Immediately I regretted it. It sounded like I thought he was old. All I meant was that it was good to see someone who'd resisted society's moral and emotional pressures to give up; and to give up for their own good, of course, though it's strange that people don't feel able to order complete strangers to give up fatty foods or alcohol or hang-gliding – for their own good.

I dithered, wondering whether I should try to explain this or if it would just get me deeper into trouble.

'Always meant to stop,' Price mused, no offence taken. 'Never got round to it. Just as well. Last time I tried was when I was thirty-five. Do you have any idea how galling it would have been to know I could have spent the last fifty years smoking? Margaret used to say there were smokers and non-smokers, and everyone should work out which they were and be willing to pay the price.'

I knew who Margaret was, of course – and Price had just used her name as if I had a right to know. I was sober enough to realize it meant nothing, that he obviously just used her name instead of saying 'my wife', but I still felt dangerously excited.

Nonchalantly: 'She's not coming this weekend?'

'No. She left me nearly ten years ago.'

Aghast, I tried to apologize. 'I'm so sorry.'

Price smiled. 'It's OK. So was she. It was cancer she left me for. Came and swept her off her feet, charmed her away from me. Now she doesn't even write. Still, that's ex-wives for you.'

He was quiet for a moment, and then continued. 'We were together from the age of twenty. She smoked then, she smoked all her life. She made her choice. There are three types of decisions you can make in life. Good, bad and unavoidable. In the latter, reason plays no part, no matter how much you think it does. Emotion or circumstance or pure that's-the-way-it's-got-to-be makes the choice, and it's those decisions that shape your life and build the house you live in. All the good or bad decisions ever do is change the colour of the walls.'

'I'm not sure I understand what you mean,' I said.

He laughed. 'Neither do I. Just thought I'd try it out. Came across that little observation in a notebook of mine from back when I was fifty. Obviously meant something to me then. Sounds like complete gibberish now.'

'I really enjoyed your panel this afternoon,' I blurted.

He looked at me levelly. 'You're not going to ask me about my work, are you?'

'Oh no,' I said, immediately shelving my first question, and the fifteen subsequent ones.

'Never used to talk about my work,' he said, looking out across the dark river. 'None of us did. Now it's all anyone ever wants to hear about. What did I mean in this story, what was I saying in that one? Who cares? Chances are what I was saying was just what it occurred to me to write, on that particular morning, with a hangover and a deadline. You want meaning, ask a tree. Work's just what you do to pay for your life.'

'It must mean more than that,' I ventured.

'Sure. I can go into the study, look at the books on the shelves, know I'm not going to leave this place entirely unmarked. We didn't have any kids. We had books instead. Plus I liked some of the characters in them. They were just imaginary, but then so is everybody else these days.'

We sat in silence for a few moments. I sipped my beer slowly. I didn't want to finish it too quickly, because then I'd need to order another – which would involve going over to the bar and dealing with a barman – and Price might take that as a signal to leave.

'What time is your book signing tomorrow?' I asked, eventually. Weak, but the best I could do.

'Eleven,' he said.

So much for that gambit. 'I don't know anything about the new one. Does it have any of the old characters in it?'

He shook his head. 'Couldn't find them,' he said. 'Went away, no forwarding address. Maybe even died.'

Then, for no reason I could see, he raised his right arm. Jean the barman appeared from nowhere. 'Yes, Mr Price?'

'I'm going to have one more Scotch,' Price said. 'And for my friend here . . . '

Jean accepted my order, inclined his head, and then turned on his heel and scooted off. 'How the hell did you do that?' I asked Price delightedly.

'It's a knack. Spend the rest of your life in hotel bars, chances are you'll pick it up. What is your name, anyhow?'

I told him, and he nodded. 'Sorry to abandon you after this one,' he said, round the end of another cigarette, 'but I got to be in reasonable shape for tomorrow afternoon.'

'Why? What's happening then?'

'I'm getting an award.'

'Really? I didn't know that.'

He winked. 'I'm not supposed to know either. Actually, nobody's said that I am. But I'm getting it, sure as hell.'

'What for?'

'Lifetime achievement. What else?'

'Well, congratulations in advance,' I said. 'That's quite something.'

'Yes, I suppose it is,' he said, looking away. 'You ever hear of a guy called Jack Stratten?'

'He was your best friend, wasn't he?'

'Yes,' he said, appearing pleased. 'That's exactly what he was. If I asked most people here what I just asked you, they'd probably know the name. They've read a book of his, or heard of one, watched one of the dumb movies. Seen his name somewhere, or heard about that time he punched his editor out in Chicago.

'But that's not what Jack was. Nor Geoff McGann, though yes, he did write a lot of good books and made a sight more money than me or Jack. Nor Nancy Grey, though she was my editor. They were my friends. I liked them and they liked me and we had some good times. *That* was my life achievement, not the fucking books.'

I waited, feeling a little cold.

'And so tomorrow morning I'll get up and put on a suit and go sign some more hardcovers. Jo from the publishers will be there, and she'll make sure I'm OK, and I'll sign books for a lot of strangers who probably weren't born the last time I did a line of coke. Then in the afternoon I'll sit in the banquet and people will be polite to me and I'll probably get this award. I'm pretty sure I will. They were awfully keen I came, and most people don't get too excited about me any more. So I'll get a statuette with my name on it, which is supposed to be a big thing, and it is, except it's too late. Who's going to hold my hand when I get back to the table? Who's going to see it on my shelf except me?'

He stared at me, his eyes bright. 'I don't want an award. What I want, for just one afternoon, is to have them all back. Margaret, my friends. The people who knew me when I had a life, instead of a bibliography. Who'd seen me walk fast, deal with hangovers, throw up or make people laugh because I'd been funny, rather than just out of respect. People who'd always be surprised to see me with grey hair or walking with a limp. Someone who'd tell me to stop fucking smoking.'

He stopped, and I swallowed, not knowing how to react.

Jean appeared and politely placed our drinks in front of us. I noticed that Price's hand shook quite badly as he signed the room-service slip, and racked my brains for something to say.

Price watched Jean walk away across the lobby. 'It's like breaking in a horse,' he said. 'Trick is to get their respect, and then tip big. Works every time.'

I laughed and realized I didn't have to say anything.

'So,' he sighed, sitting back in his chair. 'Ask me your questions about what I wrote.'

'I don't have any,' I said.

'Yeah, you do. Ask them. I'll do my best to come up with some answers.'

I did, and he did. After he left I had one small nightcap, then slowly walked up the stairs to bed.

I met Sheryl for coffee at ten o'clock the next morning. This went well enough that we toured the book-dealers' room together afterwards, and it was only when I found a very battered copy of Nicholas Price's first novel that I realized I'd missed his launch.

I checked my watch. I was definitely too late. 'Expected somewhere?' Sheryl asked, suddenly appearing at my shoulder.

'No,' I said, keeping the disappointment out of my voice. It was the truth anyway. Price wouldn't be looking out for me. I still wanted to get the new novel signed, but at the launch I'd have been just another stranger in a queue.

'Good,' she said, and linked her arm through mine.

I saw him twice more before the end of the convention. The first time was at the banquet. Sheryl and I were sitting at opposite ends of the room, the seating plan having been put in place before we'd met. I was on a table with the people I knew, and had fun, though I felt strangely anxious throughout the dinner.

When the speeches started I realized I was nervous for Price, though I had no right to be. He was sitting at the top table, and seemed to be having a reasonable time, nodding when the people either side asked him questions. He started smoking before the dinner was over, but nobody seemed to ask him to put it out.

After the speeches came the awards ceremony, which took half an hour. Best short, best novella, best novel; best this, best that, best the other. And at the end, Life Achievement. Best life, I guess.

The Chairman got up, and before he was two sentences into his speech I knew Price had been right. The applause which greeted the eventual revelation was tumultuous, and our table was one of the first to stand. Price got to his feet, wincing slightly, helped by those on each side. He made his way to the lectern where the presentation was to be made, watched carefully by the organizers. He was given the statuette, several people shook his hand, and then pointed him to the microphone. Everybody else sat down.

Price stood at the lectern, and looked slowly around the room. 'What a pleasant surprise,' he said, eventually, and someone at the back of the hall cheered. 'Thank you very much for this award,' he continued, 'and for treating me so well. Thank you also to my publishers, and to Jo, my publicist.' He smiled at her, and she blushed.

Then he turned and stared ahead, at the far wall or at nothing at all. 'Most of all I'd like to thank four people, without whom none of it would have been possible. Jack, Geoff, Nancy. And especially Margaret. Thank you all.'

I could see several people craning their heads, trying to see the people whom Price had been referring to. Nobody seemed to realize they were imaginary now.

After the ceremony there was a drinks reception in one of the other rooms. I latched up with Sheryl and we stood by one of the walls, working our way, in a roundabout fashion, to suggesting to each other that we hang out together for the evening. At last it got said, and agreed, and we relaxed: sipping complimentary white wine and nibbling on small slices of free pizza.

After about an hour I saw Price on the other side of the room, and told Sheryl I'd be back. I gently pushed my way through the throng, getting gradually closer. The bookroom was shut and I didn't expect Price to be carrying a few copies of *The Days* on his person just in case the need arose. I'd found a piece of blank paper and was going to ask him to sign that instead. I was only a few yards away from him when I saw something.

Price was standing alone, Jo-from-the-publishers momentarily in conversation with one of the convention organizers. The head of Price's award statuette was sticking out of his jacket pocket, and he was slowly panning his eyes around the room, listening to the noise of a hundred voices, watching the groups of people.

He saw something which made him smile – a cute couple maybe, or someone on the way to being spectacularly drunk – and turned to one side to say something. But he turned the opposite way to where Jo stood, and tilted his head very slightly down – as if to speak to someone a little less tall than himself. He framed the first word, and then he remembered, and his mouth slowly shut.

I froze in place.

Price raised his head and took a sip of his wine, as if nothing had ever happened, but his eyes looked flat. After a few moments his publicist extricated herself from her conversation, and turned back to face him.

'Hello,' she said warmly, as if greeting the grandfather she secretly preferred. 'You must be ready for another glass of wine by now.' This was said sweetly, a nod in the direction of the reputation she must know he'd had. I realized that Jo was probably better at her job than might at first appear.

'No, thank you, my dear,' Price said quietly. His voice sounded very old, and unsure of itself. He put his glass on the table and looked up at her. 'I'm tired,' he said, 'I've had enough pizza, and I think I'd like to go home.'

*

When I checked out of the hotel the next morning, I was puzzled to find a parcel waiting for me at the registration desk. God knows how something left by one guest for another, with the name spelt correctly and everything, had actually made it to that guest – but it had. I would have thought its getting lost was a mere formality. Someone in the hotel was obviously slipping up.

I paid my bill, haggling briefly over a small cache of entirely fictitious charges hidden on the second page, and went to sit and wait for Sheryl. She wasn't flying home for two days, and I was going to show her some parts of London. Including, I'd been given reason to suspect, the inside of my flat.

As I waited I opened the package. Two things were inside.

The first was a copy of *The Days*. It was signed to me, with best wishes. I read it soon afterwards and it's not a bad book, but it's not vintage Price. The second object stands on the shelf above my computer, where I can see it as I write.

A small statuette, a monument to an ex-life, given to me by a man I once had a drink with.

Aquiqui
Bernie Evans

I was off the plane and on the train leading into Barcelona. I was in a period of recovery, having gone through a cycle of relationships where I was either the fuckerover or the fuckeroveree; and I was really tired. After finishing college, I'd been with the same woman, Hannah, for a while. We got on well and I liked her, but she wanted more than that; and I couldn't give it. On holiday she slept with another bloke, and I used that as my cowardly excuse for an exit.

Within a week I had fallen in love with a big mistake of a woman I met in a nightclub. She was a long-haired bisexual, with a large nose, who I couldn't make come. I fell hopelessly, even though I knew she was trouble; she broke my heart. After Hannah I suppose I deserved it. I got into this old pattern of suffering, interspersed with picking up women, shagging them and dumping them. Inevitably I was picked up, shagged and discarded, as these things tend to go. So I lost all contact with myself, abandonment in the most unhealthy way.

That's why I was on the train, just before Christmas.

I arrived smack in the middle of the Ramblas. Although it was cold, the sky was blue and the people were out promenading, as they do. That's why it's called the Ramblas. I found a small hotel on the street, and though I wanted a balcony, I was put in a back room that was very quiet, but at least it had a double bed. The concierge was Italian. She had those dropsy legs where the ankle is as thick as a kneecap; it hung over a worn court shoe. She had popolly eyes, severely myopic, wearing thick glasses with clear frames, her eyeballs pressed against the lenses like pickled eggs in a jar. Her hair was frizzy white, dyed black; she wore a mantilla. Her office, I could see from the top of the stairs, was a converted cupboard. In it she sat in front of a table with bread and foodstuffs, and a bowl of oranges on it; above, on a shelf, a television with a coat-hanger aerial and a plastic radio. Both were on. The radio turned up, tuned in to a Catalan music station; the telly turned down, with what looked like a games programme taking place, its contestants mouthing soundlessly like carp in a blizzard.

She was not unpleasant.

It was four in the afternoon. I unpacked my bag, lay on the bed and slept for a good few hours, until the evening, when I woke in a darkened room, wondering for a moment whether I was with anyone. I got up, washed my face in the basin in the room, listened to the radio in the hall. I decided to put on one of my suits. Normally when I travel I carry few items of clothing: T-shirts, good shirt and trousers, shorts and jeans, sandals and boots stuffed in a holdall. This time, because it was soon to be Xmas, I decided to bring five suits, in a suitcase. I intended to stay over the Xmas period and have a 'grown-up' holiday, although I hadn't got enough money to stay in a posh hotel.

I chose the grey broken pinstripe zoot suit, with three-quarter-length jacket. I put on a red silk shirt, which looked nicer than it sounded, flipped the collar over the jacket collar, in a 'John Travolta stylee', no socks, Gucci copy slip-ons with chain. To complete the outfit I fastened a long chain to the belt and let it drop with the fall of the baggy trousers to my knee and then back into my pocket. I ventured out, got one or two stares, walked.

Young girls and boys ambled in gangs up and down, sometimes with their families and relatives; people out taking the twilight air; noisy; happy. There were a few stalls selling mainly newspapers and cigarettes; crippled vendors selling lottery tickets. On the stalls porn magazines were mixed in with the daily papers, no censorship now, post-Franco. I resisted the temptation to buy some, because I didn't want to spend all my time in my room whacking off; which is what would have happened.

I had decided I wanted to smoke on this holiday, so I went to buy some cigarettes from one of the stalls. To my surprise and pleasure they had Capstan Full Strength, a brand I hadn't smoked for years. I bought two packets. At the end of the Ramblas heading towards the port, I turned off the main drag and into a quiet side street. I had hardly gone two blocks before I was hassled by a man, a gypsy.

'*Allemaine?*' he said.

'No, English,' I replied. He drew closer.

'Ah, you want drugs, hash? You want girls?' He paused to look at me. 'Boys?'

In true Englishman-abroad fashion I said, 'No, thank you,' and carried on walking. He walked with me, put his hand in my pocket from behind. I pulled away, his hand stayed there. I turned again, noticing the street was empty apart from two guards who stood on the corner, saw what was happening, then turned away; walked away.

'Fuck off,' I said to the man. He smiled, a very nasty smile, his fingers went to grip my throat at the Adam's apple, but before they could I quickly brought up my elbow and caught him under the chin. His front teeth broke like sucked Polos, his gums filled with blood. He gave a high loud whine and stepped back holding his mouth, blood coming through his fingers. Aroused by the noise he made, people began to appear, to see what was happening. I walked quickly away, then ran down a side street on to the Ramblas and melted in. Relieved he hadn't followed. On the street I felt shaky and excited from the adrenalin. I walked along until I came to a bar called the Opera, which looked busy, and went in. Waiters in full-length white aprons bustled behind the Gaggias; the customers ranged from opera-goers to young, beautiful men and women; sitting, talking, laughing, flirting. I took a seat, ordered a beer, looked around, wondered why people, things, catch your eye. Sat and thought about my theory that a man can spot a shard of a fuckbook at twenty yards from a moving bicycle; thought, 'I'll test it out some day.'

At one of the tables to my left I noticed two striking-looking women. One with short hair, cut close in on her neck; the other Indonesian with long black hair. The woman with short hair kept turning around to look at one of the waiters. He would smile at her, then share a word with the other waiters, who would also smile. A fat guy at the till glanced over lazily; he looked as though he could just as easily beat her as fuck her. You couldn't tell from his glassy eyes what the choice would be. I stared at the Indonesian woman; she stared back at me.

Some beers later, the noise level had increased and the bar had become even fuller, but I was still managing to keep her gaze whilst her friend rubbernecked. I went over and sat in the seat opposite. At first they said nothing to me, but I started to talk to them anyway, because I knew they were Dutch and likely to understand English. Slowly we began to have a conversation. I told them about the incident in the Ramblas, omitting the fact I had chinned the guy, because I didn't know whether it would put them off. Before long I was talking and laughing with the Indonesian woman whose name was Anneka; her friend was called Martine. I discovered they were both on holiday in Barcelona until after Xmas, and were staying in a hotel, not too far from mine. Anneka said they had come to have some fun. Martine was kind of hyper because she had the hots for the waiter, who was called Ramón. She had been trying to get off with Ramón since they first came to the bar three nights before, and Anneka said she was getting bored with this, because she didn't fancy any of the other waiters. By the end of the evening we were getting on well, but I was too tired to chat her up any more so I said goodnight, and said I would see them in the bar the next night. Walking back I decided to use the Opera bar as a base while I was there, and to try and get some cockfun with Anneka.

As I climbed the stairs to my room, two black guys were coming down, going out. They looked African, were speaking loudly in French, wore Gaultier chequerboard jackets. They said 'Hi', as they bowled past. 'Hi,' I said back and nodded. At the top of the stairs the concierge was still on duty in her cupboard, she turned from the snowbound television screen, and looked at me. '*Moolies*,' she said, looking around the doorframe and pointing with her chin down the stairs. 'Good boys,' she said smiling inoffensively, 'good boys.'

'*Buenos noches*,' I said to her, and she dipped her head, returning her gaze to the screen. I unlocked my door, took my clothes off, lay on the bed and went to sleep, wondering what '*Moolies*' meant.

Four days later, relaxed, attempting to order breakfast in Spanish, roaming the city in bright winter sunshine, I went back to my new room at the front of the hotel, which had a balcony facing out on to the Ramblas. The double room I had been in was now rented to a German couple, and although I was disappointed at losing the double bed, I comforted myself in the knowledge that if the will was there,

there was nothing you could do in a double bed you couldn't do in a single; apart from get a good night's sleep that is.

In the afternoon, I walked down to the seafront, then back through the streets to the student quarter of the city. I was sat at a table drinking beer when suddenly I felt a hand on my shoulder and looked up into the tanned smiling face of Hannah. She kissed me on the forehead then introduced me to her new boyfriend Mick. They were staying in a hotel nearby, run by a drag queen; 'It's very lively,' Hannah said, arching her eyebrows and giving a dirty laugh.

Knowing Hannah the way I did, I got the impression she and Mick were trying to work something out in their relationship, and it was obvious they had come away to sort it out. It didn't look as though things were going too well as they sat there talking, taking care not to step over whatever boundaries or rules they had set themselves before coming away.

Hannah had a sturdy sexuality. I often fantasized about her playing netball or a sport in which the wearing of short skirts was compulsory. It was a tight, hard-packed, muscled little body. Mick was slacker, young and good-looking, but had pasty skin that looked as if it might accommodate another forty pounds in the not too distant future. The boy was going to be fat unless he did some serious gym.

As we sat there the mood picked up, because they had an opportunity to step outside of their own shit, and shoot the shit with me.

I ordered some beer, and then some more. Hannah talked about her new job at a magazine, doing subediting. Mick was an industrial designer and an SWP member. He tried to engage me in political conversation. I said jokingly I was far too decadent, and even though I recognized the revolution was imminent, sadly I was on my holidays and didn't give a fuck. I felt I was getting the eye from Hannah, and as Mick continued talking about politics, I realized what the problem between them was about.

Basically they had been together since not long after Hannah and I split. He had left college a year ago and was working for some shite firm over in Kentish Town, which designed vacuum cleaners for use in developing countries. They were cheap, robust and a waste of fucking time. The genius behind this idea was an SWP member, who had persuaded Mick to join the party. He was now a convert but Hannah was not. I could see it was a problem.

Hannah asked me what I was up to. I told them a little about my relationship problems, 'the work I was doing on myself', how 'I had come away alone, to work things out'. Hannah looked secretly pleased that I'd had a rough time, but said it was brave of me to come away alone and that she was glad I no longer took my relationships with women for granted. As she said this she looked at Mick, who looked away.

I continued to tell her how I used to compartmentalize everything but was now looking for a 'more flexible approach to relationships'. She warmed to this like an egg in hot butter. I looked in her eyes every now and then to make a point about a 'deeply felt' belief, throwing eye movements to Mick as well, wanting him to be complicit in the seduction of Hannah that I began to plot after thinking about her in a tennis skirt.

As we drank into the evening, Mick became maudlin, went off, came back, went off again. First to change some money, which he spent on more beer for us all, then because he wanted to be alone. Hannah said she would see him back at the hotel, I shook his hand, stood up and gave him a hug, waved at him until he was out of sight, then turned to her and said, 'Do you want to shag me?'

She looked at me and laughed. 'Yes,' she said.

We left the bar, turned into the alleyways. She didn't want to go back to her hotel in case Mick was going straight there; she thought it would be safer to go back to my room. We stopped to kiss in the first quiet, secluded doorway we could find. I had a hard-on, she pushed herself against it; the kisses got juicier. 'I'm wet,' she said and started at my button fly jeans.

She quickly got my cock out, putting her other hand around my back and slyly slipping a finger up my arse. She yanked me upwards, pulling it like a rope; it hurt. A man came out of a doorway with a bucket of fetid water, threw it into the alley; he didn't see us. Hannah crouched down, spittled on to my knob end and down the shaft. She hooded it briefly with her mouth, then turned round, lifted her skirt, and pulling her knickers aside at the leg, put me in. It felt like warm, ripe fruit.

I could see people walking past the top of the alleyway, we were hidden in the shadow of the doorway, in the failing sunlight. She pushed hard against the door with both hands, backing on to me up to my balls. I held her hip bones and we rode each other and came quickly, feelings heightened because of the erotic danger of discovery.

We finished and disengaged. She took off her knickers, threw them away; I put my soaking cock back into my jeans. She smiled, patted me at the front. We stood looking at each other, with stupid grins; she gave me a hard kiss, biting my lip, rubbing off briefly against me; then pushed me away, began to walk back to the street. I followed, post-jissom; in space.

It was hard to walk, without touching her.

Knowing this, she stayed slightly in front, carried me along in her wake. When we got half-way down the street, she stopped. At one of the stalls, Mick was buying a couple of porn mags; he noticed us, looked shocked, tried to be casual.

She said, 'What the fuck are you doing, Mick, buying this stuff?'

He shrugged, began to say something; suddenly, out of no-where, she slapped him hard on the side of the head.

'You wanker,' she said, then walked off, looking at neither of us. I looked at him and shrugged, said, 'Don't worry, she'll get over it.'

I looked at the magazines in his hands; *Blanco y Negra*, *Teenage Sex*. I couldn't see the cover of *Blanco*, but *Teenage Sex* had a picture of an old hooker, with bunches and a shaved fanny; she was propellered on a man who looked like the waiter at the till at the Opera bar. I looked at Mick; he looked away.

'Better go and talk to her,' he mumbled. 'Sorry you got stuck in the middle of this.'

'No problem,' I said. 'I'll be at the bar later, if you want to talk about it.'

'Thanks,' he said, and moped off.

I turned back to the stall, picked up a copy of *Teenage Sex*, bought it and went back to my room. There I undid the staples in the centre of the magazine, spread the photos over the bed, closed the blinds, took off my clothes. I rubbed my cock to get the taste of her on my hand, licked my palm, spat in it, rubbed it over my face, closed my eyes.

In the semi-darkness, with the sounds of the street coming

through the open window, I lay naked amidst the pictures, thinking about the cum I had seen glistening on the inside of Hannah's legs as she walked away. Wondering whether Mick had noticed it too; and if he had, what he would do about it.

The Garden of Eden Rainwear Catalogue
Elizabeth Young

For WS – A Memoir

Like many old and wealthy institutions, Verity's boarding school had been able to refine its private cruelties over many decades. Its stately buildings, so picturesque as to seem parodic, gazed serenely over barbered greensward, tennis courts and copses, knolls, ponds and roller rinks.

Verity – or rather, Verry – has been left outside the monolithic main building. She is eleven, frail and frightened, standing beside an old-fashioned steamer trunk, her red-and-blue marbled hands pushed deep into her sleeves. The damp September wind blows the leaves into clots on the shallow steps. It is not the first institution she has known.

That night in a huge dormitory with iron beds laid out like racks, Verry is trying to read by moonlight. This is tricky, because of the clouds. It is late, long past two. Another new girl, Jane, a tiny, bony child, appears by the bed. She is crying. She says she is homesick and has eaten all her Aspirin. Verry wakes the girl in the next bed – Nathalie – and whispers to her. Silently they get up, put on their dressing gowns and slippers and walk Jane down the long, dreaming corridors where the lights blaze always. The big front door to the Junior House is unlocked and they step out into the cool, black autumn night. They know they should be wearing their rubber overshoes but haven't got any idea where anyone has put them. Jane is barefoot on the gravel.

Holding Jane's hands, between them they drag her over to the Sanatorium. They know where it is from a tour earlier in the day. Timidly Verry rings the bell. She and Nathalie try to hold Jane up. She is limp by now. Yellow drool is coming out from both sides of her mouth. She has wet herself. After a long, long time, Verry rings again. They hear noises. Nurse comes to the door, strapping on a huge man's mackintosh. She is red in the face and seems very angry. She is a squat, ex-army bruiser with a tight grey crew cut and hog bristles on her chin. They tell her Jane is ill. Nurse grabs the child violently by the upper arm and pulls her roughly up the stairs. Verry and Nathalie trail behind. Nurse smells funny. Vinegary, smoky.

In the Surgery, Nurse smacks Jane in the face. 'Silly girlsh . . . shilly little girlsh . . . alwaysh shamming . . . ' Jane falls down. Nurse lurches over to a cupboard and bangs it open. She comes back with a bottle of Aspirin. She pulls Jane to her feet, opens her mouth like you would a dog's and shakes some pills into it. Nurse picks up a beaker of dusty water and pours some of that in, then she holds Jane's mouth forcibly shut. Jane retches and chokes. Her eyes bulge out. The tears are still pouring like liquid mercury down her cheeks. She swallows. Nurse starts pulling off Jane's long Viyella nightdress, mumbling about what a bad, dirty girl she is. The last Verry ever sees of Jane is from the back. She has a livid, red bruise on her upper left arm and her shoulder blades stick out like knives. She is wearing thick, navy-blue knickers and her feet are trailing. Nurse's big paw is clamped to the nape of her neck. Nat and Verry slip back to their beds without speaking. A few days later Jane dies of liver failure. No one ever asks the two girls anything.

In the Children's Home, when Verry was very young, men would rumple and tousle her. Doctors, carers, relatives. Bribes – a chocolate watch, a sprig of rowan berries. Thick fingers force their way under her knickers. They are too tight and the elastic bursts suddenly and for the rest of the day one leg flaps strangely against her flesh as if it were sighing to itself at intervals.

That first year at boarding school Verry becomes a sexual autodidact. She is extremely well informed on the subject through reading novels. She was able to enlighten the others. Judiciously. Lubriciously. Her audience was almost opalescent with rapture. Their need to know was terrible. They would have sucked these impossible-to-imagine pictures from her by force if they could. Verry knew everything. She knew all about it. She knew that you couldn't have a baby without boiling a kettle. She knew that during intercourse both partners lay together completely motionless in a miasma of inconceivable bliss, which was why, not much later, she concussed Nathalie's first boyfriend with a box camera in a tent outside Marseilles. But at age twelve Verry was still the mage, the avatar.

She writes and illustrates a book called *Willy with the Ten-foot Willy*. They put it in a sponge-bag and hide it in a bricked-up fireplace in the classroom. It is found and the headmistress, her lipless mouth stretched in fury, gives Verry a book on unusual sports such as kayaking.

Behind the warehouses, in the rain, a man exposes himself to a group of schoolgirls wearing blue gabardines. The girls split up and start to flow back down the wet street with the slippery abandon of a spreading ink blot. They are giggling hysterically but Verry is short-sighted. She thinks the white thing is the man's umbrella handle and walks on.

When she was small, Verry liked to pee into the tooth mug, knowing people would use it later. Much later, when she grows up, she sometimes puts menstrual blood in her lovers' food – it is an old voodoo trick – to ensure they will never leave her.

That first summer Verry, Nathalie and Fi-Fi were down by the railway, getting the trains to squash pennies into huge, flat moons when they met some boys from town. One of them had tiny skulls with green glass eyes on his jacket instead of buttons. This made Verry fall for him despite his narrow, sour face and bandy legs in tight, oil-stained jeans. They promised to meet the boys the next afternoon in the orchard garden. They had to push through the currant bushes in single file to reach the assignation point. Nathalie was in the lead and suddenly she screamed and turned back towards the others, her hand over her mouth. Peering past her they too saw the wet, used sanitary towel left hanging from the walnut tree and now flapping in their faces.

There is something about the way her father talks about her girlfriends that makes Verry feel all crawly inside. 'Nathalie – mm, she's going to be really something one day . . . Fiona, now that girl's a tease...' He never uses that unctuous, suggestive tone when talking about Verry. With her he is sarcastic, cold as a scalpel.

The next year Verry starts her periods in the Christmas holidays and turns thirteen in late January. February brought the annual, institutional torment of Valentine's Day: the post was distributed as usual at breakfast by that month's letter monitors but not until anything that was obviously a card had been separated out and sorted into piles for every form. After breakfast and cleaning – polishing duty, each class assembled in their home-room to receive notices and instructions for the day. For St Valentine's sake the class mistress greeted her charges coyly or grimly depending on the depths of her own disappointments. Once the girls were seated she would read out, one by one, the names on the pile of virgin envelopes on her desk and each girl summoned would walk up to the front and receive the card to a muted chorus of giggles and jeers. It was a brutal lesson in reality that brought humiliation and terror to those who, knowing they would be neglected, had to beg fathers, brothers and uncles not to forget or, *in extremis*, post cards to themselves. This particular year the mistress glumly announced 'Verity Sayles' fourteen times; it was as if a pack of hounds had caught the smell of fresh menses and was tearing after her in full cry. Verry's record popularity was further confirmed by a subsequent flood of brief letters in cramped, careful writing from boys at their brother school on the other side of town, begging to be allowed to walk her back from church on Sundays.

The adults at boarding school were swollen with assurance. They had no sense that their days of absolute power over their prisoners would not endure for ever. They did not see the first tiny cracks in their idyll of abuse – the amphetamines, haggled over at dusk with town kids by the door to the walled orchard garden; the radios, so minuscule they could be concealed and, late at night, transmit their insistently erotic rhythms; new, miniaturized contraceptives, sugar–coated, deceptively quiescent in their silver packets and hidden in the textbooks of the older, bolder girls. All the girls could sense the new combustible sexuality in the air with its promise of release from stains and ignorance, shameful secrets, virgin brides and paralysing embarrassments. But this glowing river of youthful honey was taking a long, long time to serpentine its way into every crack and crevice of little England. Meanwhile, in just such boarding schools, in just such provincial tourist towns, prosperous in their conventions, Verry and those like her waited for the change that was going to come. They waited for release.

Verry had passed from being a sad, pretty child with hair like cream and short-sighted green eyes into an equally appealing dark teenager whose misery was only apparent in her torn, bleeding fingernails and hesitant stammer. These were not serious handicaps, she knew, in the vicious race for social success. By now her cynicism and sophistication regarding all matters sexual had reached such heights that she was convinced the whole business was a con and in reality a synonym for status. The prettiest girls got the cutest guys and the most respect. That was it.

Feigning indifference Verry sorted through her piles of letters, notes and Valentines, shrewdly calculating the odds. It had to be someone older who was not in their equivalent boys' class. Sam Hershey emerged ahead on all counts. He was nearly sixteen. He sometimes wore dark glasses in church. He played in the boys' school rock band. He had very long legs, his bottom was much admired and three forms of girls, in ascending order of age, ached for him. Her friend Nathalie was completely obsessed by Sam but had been rebuffed when she asked him to dance at Christmas. He was rumoured to have wickedly decadent London girlfriends who wore spiked heels like daggers. He was tanned from the holidays in Colorado and his hair was the colour of cinnamon. He had never asked anyone from the girls' school out before – in fact had been known to describe them all as 'dullards, dogs, dumplings'.

The year before, when Verry realized that people spat into each other's mouths prior to intercourse, she suggested that they should all have some rehearsal. So they took oranges and tore off a piece of the skin to make a mouth and then they practised French kissing on them, exchanging juice for saliva and plunging their tongues deep into the raggedy holes.

Verry wrote Sam a line, as formal as a sick note, and sent it across town with one of the girls going over to study physics. Nathalie wept. Status, power, status.

Such courtships were rigidly structured. On their first date Sam waited outside the church while Verry frantically tried to apply the lipstick and mascara she kept in her training bra, using an oak table as a mirror. She recognized Sam by his height. Being older, he did not have to wear uniform on weekends. He had a leather jacket and black gloves. Verry felt much hampered by her heavy blue overcoat and laced shoes. He walked her through town to the orchard door at the back of her school. They did not touch. They did not speak much.

'You ski?' he asked. No.

Verry had memorized a number of interesting facts ('The longest a great horned toad has been kept in captivity is twenty-five years') in anticipation of just such awkward occasions but when she produced them, in a studiedly casual tone, Sam looked bemused.

Verry kept thinking about him going to the lavatory in various ways. A fierce wind was making her weak eyes water and she could feel the black mascara tears running down her face. He offered her a cigarette. She accepted although she had to take off a woolly mitten to hold it and thus expose her blotchy red and blue hand and bloody nails. His own hands shook dreadfully as he tried to light it. Match after match twisted, blackened and died.

(At one of her many primary schools Verry had a gang. Each prospect had to lick up a puddle before they could join. Then Verry devises something wicked and usually rude for them to do each day – shoplifting sherbets, putting dogpoo on a baby's head. Whatever. Verry finds exercising such control most stimulating, until she is expelled.)

When Verry gets in after her first date with Sam and is hanging up her coat her friends swoop down, squeaking like bats. What happened, what did he do, what did he say, is he Mr Right?

Wrong, wrong, wrong.

Jane's death has remained in Verry's mind like an erotic jewel which she takes out and polishes regularly. It is impossible for her to forget. Several times each term the younger girls have a medical examination. A local, Dr MacSomething, whose own practice was almost non-existent, was lavishly rewarded for tending to three hundred adolescent girls and keeping his mouth shut. He was a brutal, obese man, speckled all over with red spots and freckles, like a raw hamburger. He was never without a black, smoking cigar heavily dampened with saliva and looking much like a new-laid, glistening dog turd. He checked the older girls to see that they weren't secretly using Tampax. Being a doctor he could determine this whether or not they were menstruating. The little girls had to be examined more frequently to ensure that they were developing correctly. So, the girls remove their vests and lie on a leather couch. The doctor rolls up his grimy shirtsleeves and palpates their small, aching nubs with his hairy fingers. He blows smoke at them, making their eyes stream. His breath smells of rot and farts. Always, accidently-on-purpose, a flake of burning ash lands on their flesh. Sometimes, with girls he finds displeasing, he absently puts the cigar down on a thin chest. With his favourites he often uses their belly-buttons as an ashtray. This is very jovial – flicking the ash – just for laughs! Nurse stands too close behind him all the time, breathing audibly. When certain girls lie shaking there, she whispers mockingly into the whiskers that coat the doctor's ears. The small room is thick with lust. Implicit, complicit lust.

The following week Verry and Sam went for a walk on the Sunday afternoon. Girls were permitted to do so with the boys from their coeval school at the weekend. The word 'walk' was literal – staff patrolled the town by car and bicycle to ensure that no couple sat down and thus risked the famously inflammatory lust of the boys. Verry had reliably assured her class that once boys were aroused they were forced to carry through to completion or else their balls burst.

On this date Sam's black leather glove held her woolly mittened hand. When she got back she pasted the mitten into her scrapbook, leaving her with one glove for the rest of the winter.

When Verry was about five, a neighbour's teenage son took her into a garage. He makes her lie on a wooden box, scrunches up her yellow and white spotted dress, twisting her cardigan, pulls down her pants and tries to put his thing in her. It is too big, she fights and cries, he hits her and runs away, locking her in. She has splinters in the backs of her thighs, her dress is damp and oily and she gets in trouble. She says that Neil locked her in next-door's garage but mentions nothing else.

Sam and Verry move forward inexorably. The following Saturday they sign themselves out, together (there was a list), for the whole afternoon.

Snow was whirling around in circles when Sam arrived to pick her up. He was wearing a long black overcoat (vicuña, she thought) and the crystals in his cinammon hair made him look like a particularly pretty Christmas ornament. He put on his shades – 'against the glare,' he said, as though they were in the Arctic. Verry pushed her bare hands deep into her pockets. If not exactly relaxed they were now slightly more at ease with each other. Sam put his arm round her but he was so much taller that it was uncomfortable, so she unsheathed some flesh and they reverted to hand-in-glove. Sam didn't like books so he talked about the car he would get and the football results. Verry sang out loud to show she despised pretending to be interested. She decided that all men who were not writers must be born without a sense of humour.

They went to a large park by the river. It had a big white museum, closed, surrounded by *faux*-Grecian scrolled columns; some scrambled Roman ruins and an old church, also locked and shut. The snow had edged through sleet into icy rain but the wooden benches tucked into niches of church architecture provided some shelter.

They sat down.

Sam put his glasses in his pocket and took off his gloves. He had an intent look like someone about to perform surgery.

He put one long arm along the back of the bench and gathered Verry up close to him. She hung her head so that the black hair enclosed her face. Sam pushed it away, not very gently, and started bumping kisses on her cheek. She didn't know where to put her hands. She wished she had a book. Sam's mouth leeched closer to her own and suddenly they were exchanging spit. Verry wondered vaguely why it didn't taste of orange juice. This went on for a while until her lips burned and her cheeks were rubbed raw.

The park seemed deserted apart from the occasional wet, galloping dog and distant owner. The bare black trees were bent over by the force of the rain, as if in mourning for something they had forgotten. The wind was working up to a Gothic howl. Only the tumbling flashes of litter seemed joyful.

'Fuck, it's cold.' Sam stamped his boots. He put his big warm hands over Verry's pitiful paws. 'God, you're frozen.' He pulled her clumsily on to his knee and wrapped his black coat round her. Although very slight she felt like a ridiculously bulky baby kangaroo in her uniform coat, the buttons of which were being determinedly wrenched apart. Sam reached her jersey and began rubbing her tiny tits in a manner that insistently recalled Dr Mac. Sam clamped his mouth on hers again and began pushing up her jumper and Viyella blouse to expose her protuberant, childish ribs. I'll die of frostbite, she thought. She kept her eyes open during all this kissing. It was funny to see someone looking so vulnerable. Wriggling a little – she was bored – Verry thought she glimpsed someone shambling round the corner of the church towards them, head down against the driving rain. She felt something warm and very hard pressing against her thigh. Unsticking her face, she swung round to look at the intruder. The hard thing went on thrusting against her bottom. Dazedly, Sam followed her line of sight, his hands still clasping her torso as if she were a shop dummy.

'S'just a tramp,' he muttered and fastened his mouth on her neck. Verry put each foot down carefully so that she was sitting astride Sam's leg with her back to him. The thought of her opened cunt seemed to make Sam frantic and his hand scrabbled to reach it under her skirt.

The man in the rain was very close now, weaving a little as if drunk, muttering and mumbling to himself. He was quite old and his hair was white, long and sodden. Between all the hair and lips and cheekbones and Sam's struggles, Verry caught fragmented, jigsaw glimpses of him. He shook his fists weakly at the air. He was almost in front of them now, swaying to and fro, ranting and striking at invisible foes. He wore a plastic mackintosh – of that greyish skin colour common to cheap plastic. His legs were bare. His shoes, lacking laces, were boats of rainwater. Verry half turned back to Sam to stop him, for she felt exposed despite the man's unseeing glare, but Sam's hand had reached its almost hairless goal and he resisted furiously.

Suddenly, as if reaching a decision, the man slid off his plastic mac. The world rocked and splintered. He was completely naked. Verry saw jagged details – water streaming over bony shoulders; a dirty white thatch of pubic hair; a maroon worm shaking atop two droopy sacs scabbed with grey fur; bones, shanks, bruises.

Sam continued to thud into any part of her body, grinding towards climax while his fingers dipped in ecstasy between her thighs. Verry hardly noticed. The man stepped forwards. He had gathered rainwater in his cupped hands and seemed about to pour it over them in deranged baptismal zealotry when he stopped and tipped his streaming head sideways as if listening to voices far away. He slunk backwards. His milky eyes twitched wildly in their sockets; his face boiled with emotion. Picking it up, he started stuffing his mackintosh into his mouth, tearing off chunks of it with yellowed teeth and swallowing them. Was his dark-red penis really engorged and rising? His jaws churned in emetic exaltation as he devoured the plastic, gagging and swallowing, while his spindly limbs shook spasmodically in an involuntary parody of orgasm.

Verry tore herself from Sam's restraint and stepped forward, trying to bunch her clothes back into place. The rain hit her like a bomb. Blindly, she started down the path away from the church, smearing tears and water from her eyes with the back of her hand. A few yards along she stopped and looked back through the greyness. Sam was following her, casually zipping up his trousers. The old man had vanished.

Verry looked at Sam doubtfully. She had no idea what stage he might or might not have reached in his mysterious sexual sequence. He showed no indication of testicular combustion. He didn't seem bothered. He caught up with Verry, took her wet hand idly and swung it. There was no shelter anywhere. The rain drummed down, darkening his hair. They did not speak. At the park gates Sam kissed her on the forehead. 'See ya next week, babes,' he said and walked off into the fading light.

At first, as she dragged herself up the hill she thought over and over again, automatically, 'He didn't even walk me back.' Then she thought, 'How can someone so beautiful be so boring?' Then she thought nothing.

Underneath, all the time she was thinking, 'He ate his plastic mac. He ate his plastic mac.'

The next Sunday she got another boy to walk her back from church. She always ignored Sam and they never spoke again.

Every few years the city liked to seduce tourists with a celebration of its quaintnesses and architectural glories. This always included the staging of a medieval drama cycle against the backdrop of summer sunsets at the Roman ruins in the park. The main parts, those of the

Virgin Mary and the Devil, were traditionally played by a girl from Verry's school and some extremely famous actor. That summer a stately brunette senior with – from a distance – the requisite look of creamy spirituality, was to play Mary. At closer range Marianne was a large girl, dim and amiable, with hyperthyroid brown eyes, a dark moustache and vast buttery bosoms. The Devil was a saturnine super-celebrity, irresistible to any schoolgirl.

By chance, Marianne, the daughter of a brand-new sausage millionaire from Halifax, had the bed next to Verry's in the dormitory. Throughout the play's run she climbed back very late each night through the window from the fire escape. The Virgin Mary spent every spare moment fucking the Devil. Nightly she hissed the details to Verry in her coarse, ineradicable Yorkshire accent – 'We done it doggy-style again and again . . . He come inside me and then he licks me out, it were great . . . He had me right up the arse tonight, I thought I'd split, I've got his stuff all up me backside now. . . He's got a right big un, curves to the left, always dead 'ard . . .' When the Devil sprang back to London she was inconsolable and soon afterwards married a journalist on a northern daily.

And what became of Verry? The predictable circuit of lovers and husbands, career and childcare? Not really. I can disclose that she was never, ever sexually aroused by any of the ordinary things – not by pornography, erotica, scatology or exhibitionism. Not by violence, death, necrophilia, coprophilia, paraphilia. Bondage, micturition, sado-masochism, rape fantasies, romance, piercings, bodily fluids, fleshly modification, thongs, obesity, amputees and the donning of rubber or leather all left her cold. In fact, it was only matters so curious and bizarre as to defy description that, in adult life, were able to turn her on at all.

The Invisible Husband
John Burnside

When I came home, that first night, the radio was playing at full volume in the kitchen. I heard it as soon as I opened the door: a deep, authoritative man's voice announcing the sporting results to a house I instinctively knew was empty, and I went through quickly to turn it off. There was no sign of Laura. It was already dark outside; I could see the orange and pale green lights of the harbour, and the intermittent white of the lighthouse, flashing, then disappearing, across the firth. I went to the foot of the stairs and shrugged off my coat.

'Laura?'

I called loudly enough for her to hear me, even upstairs, at the top of the house, but there was no answer.

'Laura?'

The sound of my own voice worried me. It was too loud, too insistent. I suppose I already knew something was wrong; looking back, I see now that there had been signals I should have noticed, odd remarks and fleeting gestures that should have alerted me long before things came to a head, but I had tried to keep going, to pretend I hadn't understood, in the hope that the momentum of normal life would carry us through. I had been relying on that momentum for a long time; that was why I was so ill-prepared for Laura's illness. The secret of carrying on, the secret of that momentum, is to pay attention only to what suits you, and ignore everything else.

When I went back to the kitchen, I noticed the open door. I could have sworn it had been closed, only a moment before; now it stood wide open to the gathering night, and I stepped outside, into the cool clear air. Laura was standing in the middle of the lawn, in her white blouse and blue jeans, her head tilted, her eyes fixed on the sky.

'Laura?'

She moved only slightly, almost imperceptibly, but I was certain she had heard.

'What is it?' I asked.

She turned then, and I could see that she was smiling.

'Listen,' she said.

I stood quietly for a moment, listening, expecting to hear something out of the ordinary – a night bird, or music, or some atmospheric hum, but there was nothing.

'I don't hear anything,' I said.

She glanced at me, as if she had just noticed me for the first time, and was wondering who I was. That look scared me: it was as if she was deciding whether I was real or not, whether I was some illusion she had entertained for a moment, and was now dismissing. It was then that I noticed she was barefoot.

'You'll get cold,' I said. 'Come into the house.'

She turned away. Her shoulders and back looked thin; she had been dieting over the last several weeks and, for a moment, I thought she had overdone it, and made herself ill. It was one of the signs I should have noticed earlier, that obsession with her weight – she had never been fat, or even plump, but for some time she had complained about her body, standing in front of the mirror and worrying that her dress didn't fit, that she couldn't get into her jeans. For a moment, given this wisp of an explanation, the momentum of life resumed, and I was about to take hold of her, to bring her in and call the doctor, when she laughed softly and shifted away, lithe and quick as an animal, vanishing into the shadows by the hedge. I heard her laugh again, but I couldn't see her now, and it was a while before I realized that she had slipped through the gap in the wall and out into the cold, still night.

She came back about two hours later. The cuffs of her blouse were streaked with mud, and there was a long dark stain on her thigh; her feet were dirty and scratched at the ankles and heels, where she must have walked through brambles or thorns. Yet she had the same half-smile on her face as before, and when I asked her where she had been, she just laughed and stared at me, as if she still didn't quite believe I was real. I was at a loss. When I'd left her the previous morning, she had seemed fine; now she was acting like a mad woman. I ran her a bath and told her to get out of her dirty things and clean up, and she laughed again, but she did as she was told. In the meantime, I went downstairs to make myself a drink, thinking she would be a while, but after about ten minutes I heard her moving around upstairs and, by the time I reached her, she had gone to bed, still wet from the bath. I sat and watched over her for a while then: she seemed to be sleeping soundly, with her hands folded outside the covers, reminding me of a child, newly put to bed after a long hard day, and I didn't think it was a good idea to wake her. I was disturbed by her behaviour, of course, but I suppose, even then, that I blamed the whole incident on stress and told myself it would soon be forgotten, after we'd both had a good night's sleep.

I woke early next day. It was still almost dark, wet and windy, like a morning from childhood, when you wake too soon after a night of bad dreams and lie in bed, listening to the weather. I could hear Laura breathing softly beside me; I assumed she was still asleep, so I got up quietly and went downstairs. I had breakfast, then I called the office to tell Alicia I was sick. It was the first day's work I had missed for as long as I could remember and I couldn't think of an excuse at first – it felt odd to be lying, saying I had a cold coming on, and I was ashamed when Alicia was more sympathetic than I had expected, telling me to take it easy and not to come back till I was fully recovered. She would get Tom to keep an eye on the system build, she said, and Nicole could sort out the rest of the team. There was a moment – nothing much, just the slightest of pauses when she said Nicole's name – when I thought she knew what had been going on, and I was glad when she rang off. Just before she did, she told me again to take it easy and have lots of hot drinks, and I remembered that about her, that way she had of never getting through a conversation without offering a word of advice or encouragement. It was a trait that had annoyed me on occasion; now I found it endearing.

Nicole telephoned just before noon. I wasn't surprised, but it bothered me that she would take that risk and I suppose I sounded edgy when I answered. Laura was still asleep as far as I knew – I'd checked on her about twenty minutes before – but there was still the chance that she would wake and pick up the extension in the bedroom.

Nicole sounded uncertain of herself, but I couldn't tell if she was unsure of me, or just nervous because of the circumstances.

'Are you OK?' she asked.

'I'm fine,' I replied, and I noticed that my tone was just a little sharp. I paused a moment to listen for any movement overhead, before I continued. 'It's Laura,' I said. 'She's not well.'

'Oh.' She sounded put out, as if I had lied to her directly. 'I was worried.'

'Don't be. I'm fine, honestly.'

There was a longish silence. I felt paralysed, afraid I might say too much.

'Is it difficult to talk right now?' she finally asked.

'Yes.'

'Oh.' She still sounded upset, as if she thought I was putting her off for no good reason.

'We'll talk later,' I said.

'Fine.'

She hung up immediately, and I felt guilty, as if I'd dismissed her; nevertheless, I waited a moment longer, listening to hear if Laura had picked up.

The affair with Nicole was four months old, and already past its sell-by date. It had never been that serious – in fact, it had started almost as a game. She knew I was married, and at first it seemed nothing more than an elaborate flirtation, something we had been working towards for weeks after she joined the firm. I suppose I should have known the risks I was taking – perhaps I did. Looking back, I see how easily I managed to convince myself that our wager – that moment when things began to get complicated – was nothing more than innocent fun. It was simple: whoever got their system in first would be the other's guest at a local restaurant. As it happened, she won. That first night should have been enough to alert me to the dangers I was running, but maybe by then it was too late. Nicole was sharp, attractive, highly intelligent. We liked the same music, the same books. It was easy to enjoy her company, especially after a few drinks;

later, as we were getting into the taxi home, she turned around and kissed me, her face tilted, her mouth dark and wet. All the way back to her flat, we ignored the driver and behaved abominably, kissing and petting like a pair of adolescents. When we stopped, she invited me in, and I accepted without a second thought. Upstairs, she went through the motions of making coffee for about three minutes, then we forgot all about that and went to bed. It was all very beautiful and strange and a little intense, like being sixteen again, vividly alive, and innocent of anything outside of our own pure lust.

After that, we spent as much time as we could together. At home, I invented trips and late-night meetings so I could be with Nicole; in the office, we used every excuse we could think of to work on the same projects, so we could spend time away together. It was exciting, making plans, meeting in hotel rooms, sneaking back and forth in the night, but we were always discreet; Nicole didn't want anyone to know about us, not because I was married, but for her own reasons. For as long as the situation lasted, I don't think anyone really knew what was going on, even if Alicia had her suspicions. I felt guilty, of course; yet, in a way, it was Laura who had pushed me into the affair in the first place. I had always worked away from home, even before we were married; it was an essential part of the job. I was working in technical support then, so I had to be on client sites for days at a time, and if those sites were overseas, I might be absent for a fortnight or more, living in hotels and ringing home as often as I could. It was a hardship at first, but there was a pleasure, still, in calling her up and talking across time zones, having breakfast in Sunnyvale, in the clear Californian sunshine, and knowing she had just come in out of the wet and was standing in the kitchen, drinking tea, the raindrops still glistering on her face and hair. It felt right, somehow, to have to work at marriage – it allowed me a sense of gravity, of justness, when I came home after a job well done and we quietly resumed our normal life. In all that time, I don't think I once suspected her of infidelity – the thought wouldn't have crossed my mind. I felt assured, and I expected her to feel the same way – not to take things for granted, not that exactly, but to feel safe and sound. Before Nicole, I had never been unfaithful to Laura – though I'd had my chances. As the years passed, the sex became less exciting, and I suppose my frequent absences put a strain on the marriage from time to time, but the rewards were still pretty substantial, and whenever we talked about it, in the early days at least, we agreed it was all worthwhile. My job paid for a nice house, in a nice neighbourhood, and a few luxuries besides. We had a pretty good lifestyle, all in all. If I was a little less intense than I had been when we were first married, that was all to the good: intensity had been replaced by a quiet, steady flicker, an assurance. I thought we were happy enough, under the circumstances.

I don't even know when the problems started. All I can say for sure is that, for more than a year before I even met Nicole, Laura was on edge, telling me I didn't love her any more, constantly complaining about my trips, more or less accusing me of having an affair long before anything ever happened. When I had been abroad for a while, or if I came in late after a night out with people from the office, she would meet me in the hall, while I was still taking off my coat, and stand close beside me, sniffing delicately at my face and neck – my mouth, my hair, my shirt collar, even my hands sometimes, as if she thought I would come home with the scent of that imaginary woman on my fingertips. That upset me, to begin with, and I would try to think of something to say, something reassuring: I would tell her where I had gone, who else had been there, what we had talked about, even what I'd ordered. I would say I was sorry I was late, or offer to talk to Alicia so I could be away less often, but it was a waste of time. Eventually, I realized my mistake: the truth was that, no matter what I said, she already knew I was only saying it to cover my tracks, that I had probably rehearsed the whole story on the way home. Besides, I had only to mention one of the women in the office – Emma, or Christine, say – and she would know, just by the tone of my voice, or my furtive expression, that I was hiding something. Finally, I gave up: I would say nothing and just stand there, stock-still, while she checked me over for traces of a lover I didn't have. Ironically, it was about that time – about the time I gave up on her – that Nicole arrived. The attraction was instant: though I managed to hide it from myself for a while, Nicole told me later that she'd seen through my act right away – and maybe Laura had too. Maybe I had been giving out signals for a long time before anything happened: the affair was just the outward evidence, the explanation for a process of decay that we had been living with for years, without knowing it.

The strange thing was, we had started from a position of such strength. We had married just before my twenty-eighth birthday; Laura was just twenty-one. It had been a difficult time: my father had died the year before, and I suppose, looking back, I was trying to fill a gap, to resume something. I don't want to suggest that this was the only reason I fell in love – Laura was beautiful and intelligent, exciting to be with in those early days – but it was always there, half suspected and only half dismissed. Looking back, I can see that I wanted to be married – I had decided it, and everything I did was intended to reinforce that decision. Still, in those first few years, I delighted in everything about her: the way she dressed, the way she moved, her voice, the way she did her make-up or her hair. I woke in the night to watch her sleeping; I stole her perfume and dabbed it on my wrists so I could remember her when I was working away. Sometimes I drove all night and came home in the middle of the morning, after she had gone to work; I would come into the house and feel her recent presence there, her mixed scents, the dishes she had left, stacked neatly in the sink, the clothes she had discarded the night before. I would play the tape she had been listening to, taking up the music where she had left off. I would run a bath and lie there for hours, using her soap, her shampoo, her loofah. In the evening, when she came home and stood in the hall, hanging up her coat and scarf, I would ache with the desire to be her, just for a moment, just to know what it was like. I wanted to feel what she felt, see her dreams, think what she was thinking. In bed, I would lie beside her, my head touching hers, trying to listen in to her mind. When I asked her about it, she'd say she hadn't been thinking at all, and I would wonder what that was like, what it was to be absent, to be somewhere else. At times, I was jealous of that elsewhere – as jealous as I might have been of a rival. Yet even then, even as I succumbed to what I knew was folly, I also knew, somewhere at the back of my mind, that this was all theatre, a way to keep something alive, something I constantly suspected of being fragile and transient.

At the same time, I spent hours thinking about our future. I wanted to plan everything – not just pensions and insurance schemes and careers, but everything down to the last detail, to the holidays we would take when we had more time, to the places we might live when we retired, to how we would be together, the pleasures we would look forward to, the tests our marriage would survive. Once, when I had a minor eye complaint, waiting for my appointment at the Royal Victoria, I came across a man and a woman, walking in the courtyard garden that had just been planted next to the eye clinic. The nurse had told me I would have an hour or more to wait, so I'd gone for a stroll around the hospital corridors, stopping off at the Post Office and the bookshop, lingering in places where the sick gathered, for the tastes and scents of their alien life, somehow so reassuring, so comforting. After a while, I began making my way back to the clinic and found myself in the garden. It was a warm, bright day. Even before I stepped outside I could smell the plants: carnations and lavender, lilies, roses, all the strong, sweetly scented flowers you find in gardens for the blind. There was no one else in the courtyard, just this man and woman, an old married couple who must have been together for years, so that every gesture, every word was minimal, just enough to convey what was needed. The woman, I assumed, was blind: she wore dark glasses and she was holding her husband's arm; whether from necessity or habit, she seemed to depend on him entirely – so much so, in fact, that he guided every step she took. Perhaps she had only just lost her sight, perhaps the loss of vision was temporary, yet it could as easily have been a game they had developed over months or years, another way of sealing their marriage, of binding themselves to one another. As they walked, the man described what he could see in an even, matter-of-fact tone: a yellow and scarlet rosebud, a bed of petunias, a tall evergreen shrub with spikes of red flowers and fine silvery foliage whose name he didn't know. The woman listened; from time to time, she would ask a question, then wait; the faint smile playing about her lips suggested that she was more of a gardener than her husband; that, while she enjoyed this walk in an imaginary garden, she was also humouring him a little. I watched them for a while, as they moved on, completely unaware of my presence, and I felt an odd pleasure, almost delight, at the idea of such a life. I could imagine myself with Laura, at their age, walking in a garden and sharing it, as they did. I could imagine myself, blind, listening to her voice, and seeing the flowers and the foliage, and the watery sunlight playing on the flagstones.

Finally, as they reached the far corner of the courtyard, the man looked up and, seeing me, gave a soft, apologetic smile, as if he felt he was depriving me of the garden in some way. At the same time, I couldn't help noticing the sadness in his face, a sadness he wanted to conceal from his wife at any cost. At first, I thought this sadness was nothing more than the predictable sorrow of a man whose wife's sight has been taken, perhaps unexpectedly, and I felt a surge of almost pleasurable compassion – for her, for them both, but most of all, for him, because he was the one who had to keep his real feelings a secret – he was the one who had to pretend. That pretence seemed beautiful, an act of love and nobility. Only after I had turned aside and began making my way back towards reception did it occur to me that the man might have been sad for another reason – sad, of course, for his wife, because she was blind, and because she was also pretending, but sadder still, sad to his very soul, for himself, because he was bound to her, by pity and habit as much as by love. I thought of my mother then, on the day Dad died: how she came home and tidied the house, and finished ironing his clothes, not for something to occupy her, as a distraction, but something done for its own sake – and I remembered the realization I'd had at the time, that she wasn't really thinking of him, that she had already started the work of forgetting and moving on. The thought scared me, all of a sudden: I saw Laura, alone after my death, working to create an order I would never share, because it would give her a sense of herself as solitary and self-governing, not as a wife, but as a woman. When I went through to the examination room and sat, with my head in the frame, while the doctor applied drops and shone thin beams of blue light into my eyes, I thought of Laura, and I understood, for the first time, that I knew almost nothing about her, that, when I looked at her, what I saw was as much my own invention as anything else, a woman I had decided to love, for no good reason – as an act of faith, almost – a woman who could have been anyone, who could change at any moment, and might stop loving me on a whim, just as I might stop loving her, if chance intervened, or I no longer made the effort to continue.

Later that afternoon, Laura woke. I heard her moving about upstairs; when I went to see what was going on, I found her in the bathroom, still naked from the night before. She had brought down the potted plants from the top of the house and emptied them, soil and all, into the bath; now she was dragging a large fig tree across the landing.

'What are you doing?'

She looked up. She seemed surprised to see me, even a little frightened. She paused for a moment, then continued working, grabbing the fig by the trunk and pulling it towards her, eyes closed, as if she thought that I would disappear if she didn't look at me.

'Laura!'

I grabbed hold of the plant pot. As soon as she felt resistance, she let go and turned away; she was standing at the top of the stairs now and I suppose, in her bare feet, she slipped on the carpet. That was how she fell – I didn't touch her; I didn't even exert any force when I pulled away the plant pot. The fall was entirely accidental.

She wasn't hurt. She lay still for a moment, like an animal playing dead, then she scrambled back up and made for the front door. I caught her in the hallway; even though she was naked, I was certain she would have gone out if I hadn't held her back. I tried to hold on to her, then, to keep her from doing anything really crazy, but like Tam Lin in the old ballad, she seemed to change form, becoming an animal almost, as she struggled to escape. Eventually, we ended up on the floor. I was sitting astride her, pinning her down by her arms, desperate, almost exhausted, and for an hour or more, I didn't dare let go. The phone rang twice; Laura seemed not to hear, or if she did, she pretended she couldn't. I tried talking to her, keeping my voice as calm and reassuring as I could manage, but she paid no attention – she wouldn't even look at me, twisting and turning every which way so I couldn't see her face. It was absurd. I could hear people passing in the street outside; I could hear cars and voices, children walking home from school, the dog at the pub, barking at every noise.

Eventually, the tension in her body dissolved and she lay still, as if sleeping. I relaxed my grip a little and she made no effort to escape. After a while, I struggled to my feet and stood over her, on guard, watching. She was more than still – she was inert, almost lifeless and, for the first time, in that moment's calm, I fully understood what had happened. All of a sudden, I felt cold and decisive: I fetched a throw from the sitting room and spread it over her, then I went to the front door, locked it, and put the key in my pocket, so she couldn't get away while I was phoning the doctor. Four hours later, we were on our way to the Royal Victoria and, that same night, she was admitted to Brookfields.

I have only the most fragmented memories of her time there. Every day – at work, or going around the supermarket, or driving home – I thought about her, imprisoned on the ward while the outside world continued, while the sun shone and the roses flowered and died in the garden, while the postman came and went, with letters for her, which I left unopened on the mantelpiece. I thought about her all the time – yet when I drove out there, I felt as if I was visiting a stranger. Most days, I barely recognized her, though she hadn't changed that much. It was as if I lacked a sense of her, a focus that had been there before; I felt if I could just make some tiny, almost negligible adjustment, she would become real again, and I would see her as she had been when she was still my wife. I even thought I could bring her back from whatever limbo she inhabited, sitting there in the chair by the bed, or in the day room, her head tilted to one side like a bird's, as if listening for something far away. Most of the time, she didn't talk or move, but sat by the window, with an intent look on her face; once, when the nurse brought me in and said gently – 'Laura. Your husband is here' – she looked up with a start and fixed her eyes on us. There was a flicker of life in her face for a moment, a look of excitement, of hope almost, then she turned quickly away, and resumed her vigil.

'That's not my husband,' she murmured after a pause, and it was clear that she was talking to the nurse, not to me. That was hurtful, of course; more so, perhaps, because I'd met Nicole that very day to tell her we were finished. She had been marvellous about it, but I knew she was disappointed. We'd sat in the theatre café for over an hour, while I tried to think of something more to say, some explanation for what had happened. If things had been different, I said – but she interrupted me there, and we'd finished the meal in silence, while the waiters came and went, asking if everything was all right, or if there was anything more they could bring us.

One afternoon, I took Laura out for a walk in the grounds. She had seemed fine when I arrived – she hadn't acknowledged me as such, but she hadn't rejected me either – and I had the idea that a walk would be good for her. To be honest, I felt more at ease myself in the open air; I always found the wards oppressive. It was a warm day; we crossed the lawn and stood by the cedar tree, in silence, like an old married couple, beyond the need for words. I felt almost content for a while; I was managing to convince myself that this was the first stage of her full recovery, when she began talking. It didn't make a lot of sense, but I gathered from what she said that there was someone – a man – who was lost somewhere, possibly in some kind of spacecraft; she called him by my name, but when I asked her if it was me, she laughed and shook her head, then went on talking. The man was lost, but he had made contact with her; now, wherever she was and whatever she was doing, even when she was asleep, that man was talking to her, and she was listening. If she stopped, he would be lost for ever: he would drift away into infinite space, and never return. The one thing that kept him in place, his one salvation, was the fact of her attention. I think she was proud of that. She felt the burden of her responsibility – and there was no doubt in my mind that she believed what she was saying – but she was proud, too, proud and fiercely glad, utterly convinced of the importance of her task. It was obvious that she had decided to let me in on her secret so that I would stop worrying about her, because she pitied me, even while she failed to understand why I was there.

For my part, I couldn't see why *she* was there. Within the usual limits, I think I understood the other patients. There were some young people, but most were middle-aged; they sat in the day rooms, or walked up and down the corridors in stale, shapeless clothes, waiting for whatever it was they expected to happen: a visit, or a death; release, or some deeper madness. At times, I think, they suspected themselves of acting. Even as they sat in their institution chairs, watching daytime television and sipping at weak, milky tea, they wondered if they were suffering nothing more awful than the daily disappointment, or the vague loss of equilibrium that troubled others from time to time, and that suspicion would provoke them to action – some piece of theatre, some diversion that would serve to convince both themselves and their imagined audiences that they were enduring a form of living hell. What troubled them most, I think, was the idea that anything is bearable, yet the only reason it was bearable was that, for them, time had stopped. I remember on one visit, I glanced out of a window and saw a woman in a night-dress crossing the lawn, heading for the cedar tree, with another woman in pursuit, not calling out, or even in much of a hurry, confident she would catch up before any harm was done. It was odd, how people did that: being pursued in some open place, they always made for a tree, or a building, like animals going for cover, as if they thought they would somehow disappear into the mass of this solid object, or at least be less visible, out of the light and the air. Because time had stopped, I knew there was something pointless about that woman's flight, just as she knew, even as she continued to run. It was as if it were nothing more than a rehearsal, with no real purpose, no possible end. Watching her, as she stumbled towards the shadow of the tree, her nightdress flapping in the breeze, I knew this scene would be replayed again and again, in the days and weeks to come. Nothing would ever change: not the stillness of the day room, not the pale green of its walls, or the man at the recreation table, mumbling softly to himself as he assembled, for the thousandth time, the puzzle he had been given by his daughter, a month, or perhaps a year, ago.

But Laura was different. She should have been more resilient than those others; she should never have become the kind of person to allow herself the luxury of such descent; she should have known, as I did, that time continued because we willed it to continue. What shook me most was the idea that the woman I had married could even exist in such a place. I had always imagined people like us as strategists: while it was possible that we might be damaged by something unavoidable, something from outside, it had never occurred to me that the destruction could happen in our own house, while we ate and slept and went about our business. Every time I visited the hospital, I was shocked to realize that she had done this to herself, that she had let it happen and was letting it go on – that she had made it through the days, for weeks or even months, while I suspected nothing, giving no sign, but letting herself fall, slowly, to this point.

Nevertheless, she wasn't like the other patients. Even in the day room, she looked different from them: they were solid and dull, they appeared immutable, while she shimmered with light, no matter how lost or distant she seemed. That, I think, was what troubled me most:

it was as if another woman, one I had never seen, was hidden in some fold of her mind, waiting to emerge, for reasons that had nothing to do with me. Sometimes I even believed – for seconds at a time – that the other man, her other husband, was real. While she was in the hospital, I began to wonder if I'd ever really known her, if, somehow, he had been there all along. It made me think we must always have been strangers at some level, when I couldn't decide what to say or do to help, or even how to be with her. No one had told me what I could or could not say. I'd expected some kind of guidance, but the nurses were noncommittal, and in all the time Laura was at Brookfields, I only saw one doctor, for about ten minutes. That was the day after she was admitted, when I was still confused; the proper questions didn't arise till almost a week later. Did I pretend everything was all right, or did I acknowledge her condition? When she told me I wasn't her real husband, was I supposed to insist that I was? When she looked on me as a stranger, was I supposed to scream and shout, and refuse to be erased from her mind – or was I supposed to go along with the idea that I was a phantom, that the real man, the real husband, would show himself sooner or later, finally realized, and ready to take my place? Then, when they decided she was on the road to recovery and would make quicker progress at home, was I the only one who suspected her of a pretence? Did the doctors really think that, in a matter of days, she had discarded her imaginary husband? Perhaps they did – after all, they had never known her, they had never met my real wife. How could they see, as they released her into my care, that I was bringing home a stranger? How could they know that the woman I had married had disappeared?

For several months, before I finally left, I lived with the woman who had been delivered into my charge. She went about her business, she functioned normally, but she lived in another house, with another husband. People – our friends, my former colleagues, even some members of my own family – despise me because they think I abandoned my wife at a difficult time, when she most needed me, but the truth is, I left because she had already abandoned me. The man she lives with now is her surest possession: he exists, somewhere, because she has saved him, he is tethered to her mind, to keep him from drifting away altogether, into the chill of infinite darkness. I have no idea who this man might be – perhaps he is the memory of a real person, some former lover or friend, perhaps he is a figment of her imagination, or even some twisted version of myself, a creature she has invented to fill the gap I must have left in our marriage. I don't know and, in those last several days, just before I left, I didn't really care. All I knew was, I had to get away, because that man, that invisible husband of hers, was beginning to become a reality, for me almost as much as for her.

On the last day, the day before I drove away, I was in the garden. It was Sunday: I had gone out, I suppose, with the intention of working, but by the end of the afternoon, I found I hadn't done very much at all. I'd pottered around with a trowel for a while, but mostly I'd just enjoyed being out of doors, listening to the birds in the neighbouring gardens, the gulls drifting overhead, the occasional harbour sounds. It was warm, but autumnal; I could smell winter coming, that faint, watery taste on the air, that suggestion of ice and smuts on the windows. Maybe it was the atmosphere, maybe it was just my frame of mind, but there was a fleeting and elusive moment when I felt someone was there – or rather, when I felt someone had been there, a split second before I turned, watching me from the other side of the garden. I don't want to make too much of it – I didn't actually see him, and I'm certain I imagined the whole thing – yet it shook me, and I felt a sudden wave of fear; or not fear, so much as doubt: a dizzying sense of myself as imagined, as transient and insubstantial as any ghost, and I went indoors quickly, like someone fleeing a sudden rainstorm. The house was quiet and eerily still. Laura was asleep in the armchair by the fire; I saw that the book she had been reading had slipped from her lap, so I picked it up and put it face down on the arm of the sofa. Before the hospital, she'd read novels and the odd book of popular psychology; now, she was into physics, theories of time and space, semi-technical volumes on the new science, full of references to Schrödinger's Cat and black holes. It was as if she was moving outwards, away from herself, towards some universal uncertainty which, by its very universality, became a law in itself. Such law was, naturally, indecipherable, but it was still law and, because it was indecipherable, it could never be refuted.

That was the day I decided to leave. I had already started

learning how to be alone, so the fact that Laura was never there, that she was already living with her other husband, no longer mattered to me. In one sense, I was the invisible one: as soon as I understood that home consisted of the inexplicable and difficult as much as the comfortable and familiar, and that nothing I could do, no effort, no mind-game or self-deception could alter that fact, I began to disappear. That was the day I decided to leave, once and for all, but in truth, I had already been gone for some time. As I stood beside Laura, unsure, now, if she really was sleeping, I reached out my hand and brushed my fingers across the wall, an idle movement, almost involuntary. The wall was covered with that old-fashioned, dusty paper that flaked to the touch, coating my fingers with tiny scales, like the flakes of silvering you find on oranges or moths' wings and, for a moment, the impression formed in my mind that the house was a figment of my imagination, something insubstantial, no more real than that husband of Laura's, or the fairy palaces in my childhood story books. It was an illusion that had been held in place by our marriage, by the aims and wishes and hopes we had shared there. Now that this illusion had collapsed, I could see that everything was just as illusory – the street outside, the parked cars, the shrubs in the garden – the idea of a world that existed because of some involuntary collaborative effort, a vague sense of shared reality that we had managed to maintain with one another, with the people at work and the postman and the couple next door. That impression only lasted a moment but, for some reason, it was as much a factor as anything in my decision to go. I almost laughed out loud when I realized what I had seen: it was a liberation, somehow, to think that I was part of an illusion, that even my sense of it as illusion was illusory, and I realized that, when Laura woke and saw that her book had been moved, she would think it was the other man who had moved it. Perhaps she wouldn't even notice that I was gone.

There is no way to explain this, not to the people at work, or the postman, or the couple next door, not to Nicole or my former friends, not even to myself. I could say something else, I could tell a different story entirely. I could talk as if it were a private myth, something I had put together from newspaper articles and scraps of hearsay: a man wakes early and slips away before anyone else is up, leaving his job, his wife, the house he has lived in for years. He is an

ordinary man, cautious, and not in the least unconventional. He pulls
in at the first garage to check the oil and the tyres, the way he would
on any long journey, then he drives on, with no sense of urgency,
aware of the light on the water as he crosses the firth, stopping here
and there in the Borders to notice how the landscape softens the
further south he goes, the villages honey-gold in the morning
sunlight, the leaves turning red or butter-yellow in the deep woods.
He stays off the motorway as much as he can: there is something
about time, something about being slow and easy, written into this
journey – an escape, not only from the place that had held him for
so long, but also from the sheer mass of his life, the bearable pretences
of marriage and work and home. He is searching for something, for
a stillness in his own mind, a new way of being that doesn't involve
maintenance. It's something he has been ready to believe in all his
life. As a child, he would have prayed to die in a state of grace,
holding the image of some ice-clean purity of soul in his mind as he
waited at the altar rail to take communion, dizzy with the smell of
lilies and incense. I could say that grace is something he has
expected, the one thing he trusts in an otherwise suspect world, a still
from an old black-and-white film he once saw on television, a snow
scene with pitched roofs and pine trees implicit in the distance.
Naturally, I have always imagined this man as a character in a story;
he couldn't properly exist. It was a myth, this idea of departure, like
the tale of the vanishing hitchhiker, or the crocodile in the sewer.
Everybody wants to be someone else; we get so used to ourselves we
hardly notice we exist. Some people want to be footballers, or opera
singers, but all I wanted was to disappear. I never would have gone,
if Laura's invisible husband hadn't come to take my place; in a way, I
owe him a debt of gratitude. Even now, I think of him, moving
quietly from room to room, setting things to rights, or standing in
the garden, in the summer moonlight, speaking softly in my ex-wife's
dreams. I have no way of knowing what he looks like, or if she even
sees him, and I have never heard his voice, but I like to imagine, from
time to time, that he looks and sounds like me or, if not me, exactly,
then someone I might have become, once upon a time.

Contributors

John Burke
John Burke was born in Rye, Sussex in 1922, and brought up in Liverpool. He now lives with his wife in Dumfries and Galloway. In almost fifty years, he has published more than 120 books, including *An Illustrated History of England*, *A Traveller's History of Scotland*, three *Tales of Unease* anthologies and forty-five television and film novelizations. His first novel, *Swift Summer* (1949), won an Atlantic Award in Literature.

John Burnside
John Burnside was born in 1955 and now lives in Fife. He is the author of several collections of poetry, including *Swimming in the Flood* (1995) and *A Normal Skin* (1997), and one novel, *The Dumb House* (1997). He has won a number of awards, including the Geoffrey Faber Memorial Prize, and was selected as one of the twenty Best of Young British Poets in 1994.

Pat Cadigan
The author of *Mindplayers*, *Synners* and *Fools*, Pat Cadigan has a new novel, *Tea from an Empty Cup*, forthcoming in autumn 1998. Having resided in Kansas for twenty-three years, she now lives with her husband in Harringay, north London. Twice a winner of the Arthur C. Clarke Award for her novels, her short stories have been published widely, most recently in *New Worlds*, *Dark Terrors 3* and *Disco 2000*

Madeleine Cary
Madeleine Cary was born in Blackburn, has lived in Canada and Denmark, and now resides in Brighton. She has had essays published

in *Soul Providers* (Virago) and *More Women Travel* (Rough Guides); her short stories have been published in *Acclaim* and *Metropolitan* magazines, and broadcast on BBC Radio 4. In 1996 she was awarded a writer's bursary by South East Arts. She used the funding to help her write her first novel, *Northern Lights*, which she has just completed.

James Casson
James Casson is an Australian author who writes in London and Melbourne. His stage plays, written as Ted Neilsen, have been published by Currency and Yackandandah Presses. He has been fascinated by John 'Longitude' Harrison since 1983 and is hopeful that a production will be mounted of his definitive 1992 play, *Mr Harrison Wishes to be Remembered*. He is currently finishing a novel which tells the story from the perspective of an inglorious member of the family who has until now remained seriously unknown.

Geoff Dyer
Geoff Dyer's published works include the novels *The Colour of Memory*, *The Search* and *Paris Trance*; *Ways of Telling*, a critical study of the work of John Berger; *But Beautiful: A Book About Jazz* (recently reissued by Abacus); and two other non-fiction books, *The Missing of the Somme* and *Out of Sheer Rage: In the Shadow of D.H. Lawrence*. He writes for the *Guardian* and is a contributing editor of *Esquire*.

Bernie Evans
Born in Warrington in 1952, Bernie Evans lives in London with his wife and two children. He has published one short story in *ABeSea* magazine, and recently completed a collection, *Passing Fancies*, for which he is currently seeking a publisher. He has two novels in progress, *Donkey Dick* and *Eating Hope*.

Edward Fox
Edward Fox was born in New York in 1958 and now lives in London, where he works as a freelance journalist. His short stories have been published in magazines and in *The Time Out Book of New York Short Stories*. He is the author of one non-fiction book, *Obscure Kingdoms: Journeys to Distant Royal Courts*.

Laurie Graham

Born in Leicester and now living in Cambridge, Laurie Graham is the author of the novels *The Man for the Job*, *The Ten o'Clock Horses* and *Perfect Meringues*, as well as the best-selling *Survival Guides*. She is a regular contributor to national newspapers and magazines.

M. John Harrison

M. John Harrison was born in 1945. He has published three collections of short stories and eight novels, of which *In Viriconium* was nominated for the Guardian Fiction Prize in 1982, and *Climbers* won the Boardman Tasker Memorial Award in 1989. His latest novel is *Signs of Life* (Flamingo). His short stories have appeared in a range of magazines and anthologies from *Omni* to *Woman's Journal*, and *New Worlds* to *A Book of Two Halves*. He lives in London.

Hilaire

Hilaire moved to London in 1986 from Melbourne. In 1990 she was runner-up in the *Elle* writing competition. Since then she has had fiction published in *Passport*, *Metropolitan*, *Underground*, *ABeSea*, *Technopagan* and *5 Uneasy Pieces* (Pulp Faction). She has recently been awarded a grant by the Australia Council to write her next novel.

Liz Jensen

Born in Oxfordshire, Liz Jensen lives in south London. She is the author of two novels – *Egg Dancing* and *Ark Baby* (Bloomsbury) – and a number of short stories. She has lived and worked in Hong Kong, Taiwan and France.

Russell Celyn Jones

Russell Celyn Jones grew up in Swansea and now lives in north London. A regular book reviewer for *The Times*, he is the author of four novels – *Soldiers and Innocents* (1990), *Small Times* (1992), *An Interference of Light* (1995) and *The Eros Hunter* (1998). He has taught at the universities of Iowa, East Anglia and the Western Cape.

Christopher Kenworthy

Born in Preston in 1968, Christopher Kenworthy has lived in Garstang, Ludlow, Bath, London and Western Australia. He ran the influential independent press Barrington Books and edited three anthologies of original short fiction, *The Sun Rises Red*, *Sugar Sleep* and *The Science of Sadness*. His own first collection, *Will You Hold Me?*, is published by the Do-Not Press.

Joel Lane

Born in Exeter in 1963, Joel Lane lives in Birmingham. His first book, *The Earth Wire and Other Stories*, was published in 1994 by Egerton Press and won the British Fantasy Award for Best Collection. In 1993 he won an Eric Gregory Award for his poetry. He is currently writing a novel, *From Blue to Black*, set in the world of post-punk rock music.

D. F. Lewis

D. F. Lewis has sold around one thousand short stories to a wide range of anthologies, magazines and fanzines. Two collections of his work have been published in the US. He lives by the sea in Essex.

Nicholas Lezard

Nicholas Lezard writes book reviews and other journalism mainly for the *Guardian*. His short stories have appeared in *A Book of Two Halves* (Indigo) and *Interzone*. He was born in west London in 1963 and is currently writing a book about fun for Faber.

James Miller

James Miller was born in London in 1976. His short stories have been published in *The Third Alternative*, *Violent Spectres*, *Time Out Net Books*, *Dreams from the Strangers' Café*, *Last Rites and Resurrections* (TTA Press), *A Book of Two Halves* (Indigo), *Dark Terrors 2* (Vista) and elsewhere. Having studied English at Oxford, he is currently travelling in India before returning to London to take an M.A. and start work on a novel.

Tim Nickels

Born in Torquay, Devon in 1960, Tim Nickels has had stories published in magazines and anthologies, including *Auguries*, *BBR*, *Scheherezade*, *The Third Alternative* and *The Science of Sadness* (Barrington Books). He runs a hotel in Salcombe, Devon.

Contributors 273

Elisa Segrave

Elisa Segrave is the author of a non-fiction book, *The Diary of a Breast*, and a novel, *Ten Men* (both published by Faber). She edited an anthology for Serpent's Tail entitled *The Junky's Christmas*. Her short stories have appeared in several anthologies and she has written for a variety of newspapers and magazines. She lives in London.

Nicholas Shakespeare

Nicholas Shakespeare grew up in the Far East and South America. Voted one of the *Granta* Best of Young British Novelists in 1993, he has published three novels – *The High Flyer*, *The Vision of Elena Silves* and *The Dancer Upstairs*. He lives in London, where he is currently writing the authorized biography of Bruce Chatwin.

Michael Marshall Smith

Born in Cheshire in 1965 and brought up in the USA, South Africa and Australia, Michael Marshall Smith is the author of three novels – *Only Forward*, *Spares* and *One of Us* (HarperCollins) – and a forthcoming collection of short stories. Formerly a comedy writer and performer for BBC Radio, he has also written several screenplays. His second novel, *Spares*, has been optioned for filming by Steven Spielberg's DreamWorks SKG. He is recently married and lives in London.

Erica Wagner

Erica Wagner was born in New York in 1967. Since 1986 she has lived in the UK and is now literary editor of *The Times*. Her début collection of short stories, *Gravity*, was published by Granta Books in 1997.

Conrad Williams

Conrad Williams' short stories have appeared in a wide variety of magazines and anthologies, including *Sunk Island Review*, *Panurge*, *A Book of Two Halves*, *Dark Terrors 2* and *3*, *Northern Stories 4*, *Darklands 2*, *Blue Motel* and *ABeSea*. His first novel, *Head Injuries*, was published in 1998 by the Do-Not Press in their new cutting-edge fiction imprint, Frontlines. Born in Warrington in 1969, he now lives in north London.

Elizabeth Young
Born in Lagos, Elizabeth Young lives in London. The co-author of
Shopping in Space: Essays on American 'Blank Generation' Fiction, she is
widely published as a literary journalist and her short stories have
appeared in a variety of anthologies and magazines. Her collected
criticism and essays are due to be published as *Pandora's Handbag*.